MW01285838

THE V
FROM LAK

ALSO BY ADRIANA TRIGIANI

FICTION

The Good Left Undone
The House of Love
Tony's Wife
Kiss Carlo
All the Stars in the Heavens
The Supreme Macaroni Company
The Shoemaker's Wife
Viola in the Spotlight
Brava, Valentine
Viola in Reel Life
Very Valentine
Home to Big Stone Gap
Rococo
The Queen of the Big Time
Lucia, Lucia
Milk Glass Moon
Big Cherry Holler
Big Stone Gap

NONFICTION

Don't Sing at the Table: Life Lessons from My Grandmothers
Cooking with My Sisters (coauthor)

SCREENPLAYS

Our Lady Goes Bananas
Very Valentine
Big Stone Gap

The VIEW *from* LAKE COMO

A NOVEL

Adriana Trigiani

DUTTON

DUTTON

An imprint of Penguin Random House LLC
1745 Broadway, New York, NY 10019
penguinrandomhouse.com

Interior artwork illustrated by Bob Eckstein.

BOOK DESIGN BY KATY RIEGEL

LIBRARY OF CONGRESS CATALOGING-IN-PUBLICATION DATA

Names: Trigiani, Adriana, author.
Title: The view from Lake Como : a novel / Adriana Trigiani.
Description: New York : Dutton, 2025.
Identifiers: LCCN 2024040007 | ISBN 9780593183359 (hardcover) | ISBN 9780593183366 (ebook)
Subjects: LCGFT: Novels.
Classification: LCC PS3570.R459 V54 2025 | DDC 813/.54—dc23/eng/20240830
LC record available at https://lccn.loc.gov/2024040007

Printed in the United States of America
1st Printing

The View from Lake Como is a work of fiction. The characters are entirely imaginary. However, the citizens of South Belmar, New Jersey, elected to change the name of their borough to Lake Como, New Jersey, on November 2, 2004. The borough officially became Lake Como on January 4, 2005. The author was inspired by the local chutzpah, but in no way intended to besmirch the democratic process of local government in the state of New Jersey in the United States of America.

The authorized representative in the EU for product safety and compliance is Penguin Random House Ireland, Morrison Chambers, 32 Nassau Street, Dublin D02 YH68, Ireland, https://eu-contact.penguin.ie.

In memory of my uncles

The Four Heavenly Horsemen

Orlando A. Bonicelli, Michael F. Ronca,

The Honorable Michael F. Godfrey

and

Michael R. Trigiani

One day Elsie de Wolfe said to Ludwig Bemelmans,

"Italians are fortunate.

They can always cry it away or sing it away or love it away."

PART ONE

Cry It Away

1

Thera-Me

Exercise 1

I shove the pencil behind my ear. I hold the sketch pad next to my face and lean into the mirror. I take inventory of my features in the self-portrait. Let's see. I have rendered the oval shape of my face, neatly arched black eyebrows *alla* Puglia, and a satisfactory Tuscan nose, prominent yet not too large. The lips are full in the center with commas in the corners. And finally. The eyes. Two round, dark planets of pain.

I prop up the pad on the table and stand to observe the drawing from a different perspective. I've been looking at this mug for thirty-three years, so you'd think there'd be no surprises. I lean over my work and squint. The hair is not right. I hold the tip of the soft HB graphite pencil flat, whisking it above the forehead in quick, successive strokes, smudging the hairline with my thumb, softening the fine strands at the temples. I've used every technique to lighten the overall effect and lift the mood of this *faccia*, but no matter how I tinker, I'm looking at the portrait of an unhappy woman.

I snap a photo of the sketch.

Dear Dr. Sharon,

The self-portrait you requested is attached. I make my living drawing marble installations to scale. I'm a draftsman who also provides designs for customers. Forgive the lack of nuance in the sketch, but it is a truthful rendering of how I see myself.

They say the journey of a thousand miles begins with a single step, but it would appear my sojourn began with a litany of missteps that led to a face-plant. This is why I am here. I need your help to get up and move forward. Emotionally.

I read your Keys to Contentment online. **Make your own happiness.** I will be happy to when I am able to define it. **Follow your heart.** Easy for others to say, sure, follow your heart but only if you have a good sense of direction. **Listen to your inner voice.** Trying. When I follow the daily Instagram posts that feature a cup of coffee, a cookie, and the advice of general philosophers, it seems my life gets worse. I'm trying to change, but reinvention is impossibly hard work for someone who isn't sure where to begin. Or how.

You see, I'm the people pleaser in my family, the unsung cook, maid, babysitter, and driver. Looking down the road, I will become the nurse, responsible for our soon-to-be-elderly parents, because my brother and sister have families of their own. I am newly single and childless, which means I'm available to serve—more. My role has been carved as if it were etched in marble. And I know marble.

I created a dream board, with pictures and images of all I long for: it's in the shape of the country of Italy, which should tell you something about my heart's desire. There are the rolling hills of Tuscany, the marble quarries of Carrara, and the speedboats of Lake Como. I want to celebrate life, not dread it.

I moved into my parents' basement apartment when I decided to leave my husband. My family prays that I reconsider and return to my ex. They are not alone. The general population of my hometown concurs. In fact, at our church, the Sodality, the women's service organization equal to the Knights of Columbus for the men, even offered a (humiliating) mass for reconciliation. They were fervently praying one way, while I prayed the other. I said the rosary so many times during my divorce proceedings, I rubbed the face of Jesus off the crucifix.

I've held a passport since I was eighteen years old but have yet to use it. It is just one empty page after another of pristine navy jacquard without a single stamp to anywhere or the slightest scuff on the leather cover. When I went to renew it last year, the man at the passport office said, "Why bother?"

I want to bother! I want to know what it's like to see the places that have lived in my imagination since I first read about them in books. Is there something out there for me, Dr. Sharon? Is there such a thing as bliss? If so, can you help me find it? With or without the cookie.

G.C.B., Lake Como, New Jersey

2

The Family Business

THE RED TAILLIGHTS on Uncle Louie's chartreuse Impala blink as he backs the car out of his garage on his way to pick me up for work. He and Aunt Lil live in the last house on the corner lot before the intersection of Surf Avenue, which leads to the beach. Their Cape Cod, the most landscaped home in all of New Jersey, stands out among the mix of white split-level and soft blue saltbox houses that hug the curve of the shore of Lake Como like a rope of shimmering opals.

Through the years, Aunt Lil and Uncle Louie have installed every manner of ornamentation and architectural interest on their half-acre lot. There's a koi pond, a three-tier marble fountain, and a walkway of gold-streaked pavers that swirls up to the front door like a yellow brick road. The backyard has a replica of the Parthenon built out of Carrara marble where they host the Knights of Columbus Weenie Roast every July Fourth. "My home is an advertisement for my business," Uncle Louie says. "Italian craftsmanship and American elegance?" he asks, before he answers, "I'm your man."

If he's your man, then I'm your wingman. Uncle Louie is my

boss at Capodimonte Marble and Stone, our family business since 1924.

My uncle pulls up to the curb. I inhale the chill of the morning air. It tickles my nose and fills my lungs, which causes me to sneeze with my whole body. I fish through my purse for a tissue.

"Jess. Are you serious?" Uncle Louie says through his open window as I wipe my nose.

I climb inside and snap the seat belt. He rolls his fist. "Leave your window down so any germs blow out."

"I'm not sick. It's the temperature."

"Now you're a scientist? If you don't catch a cold, it won't catch you. Words of wisdom from my mother."

"Your hypochondria flares up whenever the seasons change."

"You noticed, huh?" Uncle Louie's mouth curves into a smile.

I see everything, but there's no point in bragging about it. A worldview doesn't do you much good when you live in a small town, unless your passport is current. When it comes to Lake Como, New Jersey, the Capodimonte and Baratta families own North Boulevard. My Cap grandparents lived two houses down while the Baratta grandparents lived three houses down in the other direction. They're all gone now; the Baratta homestead went to our cousin Carmine in 2019, while the Cap house has not been touched since Grandma died in 2022. We call it the Lake Como Museum because it remains intact; not a single teaspoon has left the premises since her death. Around the loop of the lake, the rest of the houses are filled with relatives.

Whenever we had a block party, we closed down the street and became a version of the Villa Capri in Paterson on their All You Can Eat Family Night. We were an Italian American a-go-go minus the floor show, free hors d'oeuvres, and two-drink minimum. Beyond our social lives, our family shares the street, a canoe, and our devotion to the Blessed Mother. A statue of Mary can be found in every yard on the lake. It may appear the patriarchy is thriving, but Italian Americans know it's the mother who has the power. Philomena Capodimonte Baratta, my own *mamma mia Madonne*, is proof of that.

"What's with the jacket?" Uncle Louie gives my outfit a once-over.

"Connie gave it to me."

"You're still in your sister's hand-me-downs?"

"Does it look bad?" I smooth the navy linen with my hands.

I am not up to Uncle Louie's sartorial code. Never have been. Louie Cap is the last of a group of Italian American men who came up on the Beatles but never forgot Louis Prima. He's a sharp dresser, Rat Pack debonair. He wears size 8 suede loafers like Frank Sinatra and three-piece suits like Jerry Vale, altered for a streamlined fit on his trim frame. He is never without a fitted vest under his suit jacket because he likes the feeling of being cinched in.

"Clothes make the woman," Uncle Louie reminds me. "What the hell happened over here? You're Depression Central."

"I'm working on it. I signed up for Thera-Me. It's an online therapy program. I got so many Instagram ads for it I must be in their target market."

"Whatever that means," Louie groans. "My goal is to make it into the arms of my Savior without having to install another app."

"I was assigned to Dr. Sharon over Zoom."

"Is she a real doctor?" Uncle Louie asks.

"Board-certified. She had me draw a self-portrait. And she asked me to journal. Wants me to write down my memories, the happy ones and the painful times. She said past experience is the foundation of future mental health." I show Uncle Louie my self-portrait.

Uncle Louie glances over as he drives. "That don't look like you."

"What do you mean?"

"I'd take another run at it." Uncle Louie makes a face.

"Too late. I already turned it in."

"Is this therapy operation expensive?"

"Around the cost of a gym membership."

"Hmm. What a racket. Why do you need a therapist when you have me? I'm like a priest. At my age, there isn't anything you could tell me that would even slightly shock me."

"There are things I can't talk to even you about."

"Even though I have a very sensitive female side?"

"Not funny, Uncle Louie."

Uncle Louie's phone rings. He taps speaker. "Yo, Googs."

"I got a couple sleeves of black granite. You got a need?" Googs sounds far away, like he's calling from the moon.

"Putting a floor in over in Basking Ridge. How much you got?"

"Ten by six. Looks like I have six sheets total. Foyer? Small?"

Uncle Louie looks at me. I confirm that we could use the stock.

"For a price," Uncle Louie says into the phone. "Don't soak me, Googs. I'm not in the mood."

"Text the address and I'll deliver." Rolando "Googs" Gugliotti hangs up. He is one of Uncle Louie's oldest work colleagues. He would be the Joey Bishop in Uncle Louie's Rat Pack. He shows up, does his business, and disappears like a vapor until you need him again, or he needs you.

I look down at my phone. "How does he know exactly when to call? It's creepy."

"Not in the least. He's an intuitive salesman. Make a note."

I scroll to the notes app on my phone and await instructions.

"Aldo and Rena Lovisone's reno. Granite drop. Arrange with client." Uncle Louie dictates as he takes a right turn off Sixteenth Avenue and onto Main Street into the business district.

He slows down, surveying the buildings from one side of the street to the other.

"The Italian American Riviera is on the comeback." Louie gives a low whistle of approval as he observes the new apartment building next to the renovated mixed-use warehouse, set among the restaurants, liquor store, radio station, and condos on the main drag. He stops the car in front of the vacant firehouse and leans out the window and squints. "They're putting in a barbecue joint, Five Alarm, they're calling it. It suits. Names matter."

Yes, they do. I was thirteen years old in 2004 when South Belmar, New Jersey, had become a sorry suburban pit stop between Belmar and Spring Lake. Our pretty, working-class town had turned into a zoo for party animals. Property values had plummeted. It was decided that the best way to save our town was to start over. We needed a new name.

The residents agreed the sooner South Belmar was in the rearview, the better. Our town was settled on the lake close to the ocean one hundred years ago by Irish, Dutch/German, and Italian immigrants, and here, three generations on, they remain. The local Italians ran a campaign to change the name from South Belmar to Lake Como. The Irish and Dutch/Germans initially balked at naming the town for the lake, but the Italians argued that *Como* was easy to spell. Good point. It was also true that nobody was elated about the alternatives: Fuerstenfeldbruck or Lake Nobber.

Uncle Louie led the charge, and under his leadership, Lake Como won in a landslide, by 167 votes! We were South Belmar, New Jersey, no more. The new name proved to be lucky. A lyrical name creates a space to fill with beauty, like a contralto as she steps into a circle of golden light on the stage of an opera house.

No one knows that names matter more than me, as I have been tortured over mine. When I was born, my parents, determined to swaddle me in family history and my mom's version of Tuscan style, named me Giuseppina Capodimonte Baratta. When my brother couldn't pronounce it, he called me Jess for short. It stuck. Everyone calls me Jess except my mother, the purist.

Uncle Louie and I coast to a stop, joining the line of stalled traffic on East Street.

"Poor timing," Uncle Louie grunts.

"Drop-off." I watch a gaggle of girls in navy jumpers walk up the front steps. How is it possible that the girls of Saint Rose School are wearing the same uniform I wore twenty-five years ago? While we wait in the traffic, I open the notes app on my phone. I follow the prompt from Dr. Sharon. I connect the feeling to the words as I remember waiting for my mother. I write.

It was one of those warm October afternoons that felt as hot as the soupiest, most humid days in August. I dripped sweat as I wove through the line of cars throwing heat. The moms waited in air-conditioned comfort with their engines idling, ripping a permanent hole in the ozone layer over New Jersey. There was a reason we said a schoolwide rosary on Earth Day. We wanted to live.

I climbed into my mom's Plymouth minivan with plastic seat covers that stuck to my legs when I sat down. It was the year 2000; I was nine years old. I wore a hand-me-down school jumper and Lands' End loafers. My sister, Connie, was eleven years old. She wore an identical uniform one size up. She was strapped into the back seat behind Mom. I sat in the back seat my entire life until Connie learned that whoever sits in the front passenger seat is most likely to die first in a car wreck; ever since then, it's had my name on it.

My classmates looked like a flock of bluebirds in their jumpers with their regulation cardigans tied around their waists like aprons. It was so hot, the girls rolled their white knee socks down into small inner tubes around their ankles. This was the kind of fashion trend that caught on at Saint Rose, and everyone had to follow the fad or die a slow social death. I refused to roll my knee socks until I was allowed to shave my legs.

"Mom, when can I shave my legs?"

"You have to wait," Connie piped up. "I just got permission."

"I didn't ask you. I asked Mom." If the hair on my legs grew for three more years, I'd need to shave twice a day like Cousin Bear Baratta, who grew a full beard between breakfast and dinner.

"Let me think about it, Giuseppina."

"Hey, Jess!" Lisa Natalizio called out from the sidewalk. Lisa's blond braids were as thick as hay and had expanded in the humidity. Her smile was as wide as her round head. She held her Butterfinger candy bar in the air like Sister Jean's pointer in music class and shouted, "Don't forget the milk carton!"

"Ma, I need a milk carton for school tomorrow. Lisa and I are going to make a mailbox. We're going to send get-well cards to the pope."

"Those nuns. Always with the projects. All right. I can air one out tonight. Good thing your brother is going through a growth spurt. He's a milk lush. Put on your seat belt." Mom wore a pink spandex jumpsuit with a ruffle around the waist that made her look like a piece of saltwater taffy. She'd just come from Zumba class. Her chest was freckled, a gold cross on a delicate chain nestled in her cleavage. She gave me a quick kiss on the cheek and flipped open the lunch box on my lap. "You ate your lunch! Good girl."

"Bobby Bilancia stole it."

Mom frowned. "Did you tell Sister Theresa?"

"Nobody likes a snitch," I reminded her. "Bobby steals from Lisa's lunch too, and she gave up. Now her mom includes an extra pack of Tastykakes, just in case he comes prowling."

"I refuse to feed the entire fourth-grade class at Saint Rose." My mother lit a Virginia Slims cigarette on the third try and held it as far out the window as she could so we wouldn't get secondhand cancer. "I am calling the school when we get home." She sighed. "Giuseppina, you have to stand up to him."

"I can't, Ma."

"Why not?"

Connie answered for me. "Because every girl in her class and every nun in our school is in love with Bobby Bilancia. And Jess likes him too, don't you, Jess?"

"Can we stop for ice cream?" Why did the name Bobby Bilancia make me hungry?

"I made lasagna for dinner."

"I can't wait until then. I might faint." I leaned against the door and put my face in my hand.

My brother, Joe, fourteen years old, climbed into the minivan and closed the door. He wore a pressed baseball uniform; his black hair was neatly parted on the side. He placed his backpack on the seat. It didn't have a scuff on it; it looked as new as the day Mom bought it at Target.

"How was your day, Joe?" Mom said pleasantly.

"Okay. Ma, can you drop me at the practice field?"

"I live to serve." She smiled. "How was your day, Connie?"

"Annoying. They were making fun of Jess's name."

My mother's dark eyes darted between Connie's in the rearview mirror and mine in the front seat. "What do you mean 'making fun'?"

"Some of the girls tease her," Connie said.

"They call me Giuseppina-colada."

"After the cocktail?" Mom frowns.

"Sometimes worse, Ma," Connie said. "They call her Jooz-uh-*penis.*"

"Idiots," Joe muttered. Joe was already above the antics of grade school even though he was still technically in it. He was more like a father to me than a brother.

"Who teased you?" Mom wanted to know. She glared at my sister in the rearview mirror. "Connie, what did you do to defend your sister?"

"I can't be creeping around the halls of Saint Rose taking on the mean girls who pick on Jess."

"And why not?" my mother yelled. "You only have one sister!" She turned to me. "Giuseppina, you have to get tough!"

I felt my throat constrict. I put my hands on my neck and tried to inhale air, but I couldn't get enough in. The panic attacks were usually triggered by a series of challenges I couldn't meet. That day had been particularly brutal; I couldn't do anything right, and then there was the teasing. It was too much.

"Connie! The paper bag!" my mother shrieked. Connie handed a bag to Mom calmly from the back seat. My sister knew the routine. Mom snapped the bag open and gave it to me. "Breathe into the bag, Giuseppina! Into the bag!"

My panic attacks began in kindergarten. Our pediatrician taught me the paper bag trick. Whenever I couldn't breathe, I would place a paper bag over my mouth, force air into it, then suck the same air back into my lungs. As the bag shrank, I refilled it with my breath. I learned to like the crinkle sound the bag made when I filled it with air. Soon, the thoughts in my head matched the rhythm of my breathing. I repeated *Bobby Bilancia Breathe, Bobby Bilancia Breathe* in my mind, until my heart stopped racing and my lungs opened up.

"When am I gonna grow out of this?" I looked at my mother and wiped away a tear on my sleeve.

"The doctor said it could happen anytime. You have to be patient."

Mom pulled off the road to drop Joe at the field. He reached forward and squeezed my hand before jumping out of the car. He slammed the door and ran to join the team. Soon, he was engulfed in a sea of red-and-white-striped uniforms as though he had dived into Grandma Cap's candy dish filled with peppermint wheels.

Mom pulled out into traffic and looked for the Mr. Twisty ice cream truck. I felt better after I took the first bite of the cone, through the hard shell of the chocolate dip to the cool vanilla custard underneath.

STUCK IN A traffic jam, Uncle Louie observes the school bus as it empties into the courtyard. The students split into two lines, forming a river of blue that flows past the statue of Saint Rose of Lima and into the school foyer. "Can you believe you were ever that small?"

"I was the shortest girl with the longest name." I close out of the notes app.

"I told my sister to name you something normal. She had to name you after that maiden aunt of ours because no one else would saddle their kids with that honker. Zia Giuseppina was a bruiser." Uncle Louie holds up his index finger to prove his point. "At five foot eleven she was the tallest person in the Capodimonte family, man or woman."

I never met my great-aunt—she died before I was born—but by all accounts, Zia Giuseppina was a force on North Boulevard.

"She was built like an ice truck," Uncle Louie explains. "She had a voice so loud it echoed across the lake when it wasn't peeling paint. She did not so much move as reverberate."

I have neither the stature nor the gravitas to carry a big name; from the start, it was too much. It was like asking an eight-year-old girl to wear her father's shoes to school or operate a cement mixer. "Why was she the maiden aunt?"

"She took a shot at romance, but they sandbagged her."

"Who?"

"My grandfather and his brothers, the Caps from Italy. The story goes that on a snowy night in 1949, Nonno Cap and the boys staged an intervention, which, in hindsight, these days would be called a kidnapping."

"Where was she?"

"At the Motel 6 off the Garden State Parkway. Let's just say that ever since, I refer to room 7 in any motel as the Boom-Boom Room."

"Zia was there for fun?"

"For all practical purposes. Yes. But Nonno and the boys arrived in the nick. He pulled his daughter out of the arms of her lover, Petey Palma, a real bargain out of Manasquan. Let's just say whatever went down or didn't, Petey went back to Manasquan alone."

"I never heard this." I'm not surprised. Any stories involving sex are buried deep in the backyard like the statue of Saint Joseph whenever we go to sell a house.

"Zia gave up on romance entirely, such was the impact of the situation. That was the night she became the maiden aunt, and she chewed on that shame like bitter dandelion until the day she died. But she was also a devout Catholic, so she turned her sin into service. Zia dedicated her life to the poor, and when she wasn't busy with them, she took care of her elderly parents and babysat us. She made Sunday dinner every week."

"What a life."

"Did I say she was happy?"

"No wonder she was angry." I sit back in the seat. "Her life was not her own."

"Nobody says you have to *be* like her," Louie assures me. "You're not the maiden aunt."

Not yet, anyhow, I'm thinking as Uncle Louie drives past the sports fields and out of town. I didn't know Zia Giuseppina, and yet, I carry the name of someone I never knew into a life I don't want to lead. Another issue to bring up in therapy.

As we approach Spring Lake, the street narrows into a corridor of green-and-white-dappled willow hedges. We leave the casual ranch homes and plastic jungle gyms of Lake Como behind and enter Spring Lake, where rows of stately mansions have manicured lawns studded with bronze statues. I lean out the window to inhale the fresh scents of the tall cedar and fir trees as Uncle Louie speeds toward our appointment.

We pull into the church parking lot. If you could fly a duomo, a beaux arts cathedral, and a meditation garden worthy of the Medici family from Florence to New Jersey, Saint Catharine Church would be it. The sleek white granite, carved spires, and bell tower, positioned at a stately angle on the banks of the lake, are a sample of the architecture of the Italian Renaissance at its most divine. The Caps and Barattas are baptized, married, and buried from this church, and have been for a decades.

Uncle Louie pulls into the parking lot. I get out and stretch. Uncle Louie joins me in a shoulder roll.

"Ouch."

"If it hurts, stop doing it," I tell him.

"What doesn't hurt yet is about to. I'm seventy-three years old."

"You remind me every morning."

"Because I can't believe it. Look at me. Just yesterday I was young and vibrant. I didn't have to wear a shirt anywhere. I could've walked around in nothing but a diaper and strangers would've applauded my physique."

"Lucky man."

"I'm serious here. I was built like the statue of David except not as tall. Look at me now. I'm wizening."

"You are not old."

"Face it. What's in front of me you could clock on an egg timer, and I'd still be late to the party. I have limited potential. And with that comes one of two things: either crippling despair or a propulsion to get things done. So, I was thinking. What becomes of this family business that's a hundred years old? What happens to Cap Marble and Stone?"

My heart sinks. Here we go. The only thing in my life I look forward to is my job. If this goes, I don't know what I'll do. "Are you selling the business?"

"The business has to go to someone who has a passion for it. I'm not looking to sell it; I'm hoping to ensure its future. To that end, it's time that you take the reins when I can no longer hold them."

"Me?"

Uncle Louie looks around. "Is there anybody else standing here? Yeah, you. Of course, *you*. But first, you need an overview. You need to see the quarries in Italy. I don't think anyone can run this company who does not understand the mining in Carrara. So, let's go. You up for it?" Uncle Louie invites me to Italy casually, as if we're making a plan to pick up a sink in Passaic.

I can't speak. I didn't see this conversation coming when Uncle Louie picked me up this morning. If I had, I would have dressed better.

Suddenly, *illuminata!* The autumn sun soaks the church steps in coral light. Am I a witness at the site of an actual miracle? I must be! I have tried to get to Italy all my life, but something always derailed my plans. I couldn't afford the study-abroad program in college, even though I was an Italian culture major and had the grades to qualify. I wanted to go to the Amalfi Coast on our honeymoon, but Bobby said Las Vegas would be more fun. I thought about going to Italy with a group, but I wasn't interested in the tourist stops. I wanted to see the villages of my ancestors. Truthfully, I was afraid to go alone. Look what happened to Katharine Hepburn in *Summertime* or Daniel Craig in *Casino Royale*. Uncle Louie reads the fear on my face.

"Think about it, Jess. You don't have to give me an answer now."

The only concern I have about Italy is that something will ruin this opportunity. "It's a big yes, Uncle Louie! Yes! Yes! Yes!"

"All right already. Good. So, we plan a trip, you get your feet wet, work with the guys over there, and then decide how you want to proceed with the company. Perhaps we pray on the matter?" Uncle Louie is only half joking as he holds open the bronze entry door to the church.

3

Prosciutto, Figs, and Digs

We enter Saint Catharine's not as parishioners but on official business. Our company maintains one of the only churches in America constructed completely of Carrara marble. This church may be more Italian than I am.

I walk through the shaft of light that extends down the aisle to the altar. On my wedding day, December 28, 2019, there was no aisle runner of heavenly light; it poured rain, then iced over, followed by a blizzard that had us detained at Newark for the first eleven hours of our honeymoon. I didn't perceive the delay as bad luck. At the time, I chalked it up to inclement weather due to climate change.

The artistry of this church is celebrated in the frescoes painted by Gonippo Raggi of Rome and Thomas O'Shaughnessy of Chicago. Whoever says the Irish and Italians are *simpatico* is correct. The church is a feast of classicism, inlaid panels of gilt and plaster, a circumference of saints floating inside the duomo tower, splendid arches that fan out from the vaulted ceiling, and windows so high there are times when all you can see through them are stripes of gold through the clouds.

Uncle Louie and I kneel in the front row of the empty church and make the sign of the cross. In my family, we pray because we're terrified. We have an unshakable faith rooted in the paralyzing fear of burning in hell for all eternity. We pray as much as we argue, or laugh for that matter, which is a lot.

"Are you crying?" Uncle Louie asks. "*Not again.*" He frowns.

I quickly wipe away my tears. "I can't believe we're going to Italy."

Uncle Louie hands me his handkerchief. "I thought you said you were getting over your blues."

"I am," I promise him. "I'm happy at the news, that's all."

"Italy is the great healer." Louie checks his watch. "Father Belaynesh said he'd meet us here. Priests and doctors, never on time."

"Dad is meeting us too." I turn around and crane my neck to the back of the church, when I hear the confessional door on the side aisle creak open. My six-foot-two dad emerges, white hair first, ducking as he exits the confessional as though he's crawling out of a dollhouse. My father is built like a linebacker but never played football because Grammy B was afraid he'd get hit in the head and turn *stunod*.

Dad genuflects and joins us in the pew. "Got here early," Dad whispers as he sits with us. "Went to confession."

"Interesting." Uncle Louie keeps his eyes on the gold tabernacle behind the altar. "How'd you do in there?"

"It felt good." My father folds his hands.

"Do you think I should go in?" Louie keeps his eyes on the tabernacle.

"Wouldn't hurt."

"The poor bastard wouldn't know what to make of my sins. I

haven't been to confession since Father Fuzigamo took off with the second collection and the church secretary in 1986. Left a sour taste in my mouth. I had confessed the worst to that guy and felt like he stole my sins along with the plate. So much for *simpatico.* Fuze was the last priest of Italian American descent we had," Louie says wistfully. "And they ain't makin' new models."

"Father Belaynesh is as close to Italian as you can get," my father says cheerfully. "He understands the nature of our people. You can tell him anything in there and he won't hold it against you. In my opinion, he's a gift from Bali."

Father Belaynesh emerges from the confessional and genuflects to the altar. He turns to us. He is slim, young, and fresh scrubbed, like a Catholic Olympian on the cover of the Maryknoll missionaries pamphlets left at the ends of the pews during Vocations Week. American priests have dwindled in number, so the church opts to bring in mail-order priests from other parts of the world, a bit like mail-order brides during the gold rush, without the marriage element of course.

Uncle Louie stands. "What's the issue, Padre?"

Father's bright white smile turns into a slim black line. "The baptismal font leaks."

I pull my sketchbook out of my purse. We follow the priest to the side altar. Uncle Louie gets down on his knees to examine the base as I sketch the shape of the font. I measure the dimensions as Uncle Louie pulls a small flashlight out of his pocket and turns it on. "There's a hairline fracture. Did you get this, Jess? We can apply a sealant for now and order a new base out of Italy."

"Just like this one?" The priest is concerned. The last thing he wants to be is the priest who changed a single detail in Saint Catharine's.

"Can do, Padre. What do you think, Joe?"

Uncle Louie looks at my dad.

My dad is an insurance adjuster; he handles all of Cap Marble and Stone's claims on the company side. My dad gets down on his knees and takes a look at the break with the flashlight. "Looks like trauma. I'll put in for it, Father."

"And whatever insurance doesn't cover, I will," Uncle Louie promises the priest.

Father Belaynesh beams in gratitude. "The bishop will be happy."

"That's what we want, an ecstatic bishop," Uncle Louie says.

The doors in the back of the church burst open; the afternoon sun in mid-sky blazes up the main aisle like a fireball, illuminating the altar and the tabernacle wall behind it. I squint and look into the light. Four men. They move through the light in lockstep like a boy band. When my vision adjusts, I realize it's my ex-husband, Bobby, followed by three of his workers wearing Bilancia Meat aprons. Instead of guitars and microphones, they haul cases of wine, glasses, and plates, I'm guessing for a catered affair, because the last guy, Peachy, a jokester who has worked for their family for years, brings up the rear carrying a large tray.

"Excuse me," Father says. "We have a Knights of Columbus meeting tonight."

"Cheeses of Nazareth," Uncle Louie jokes. "Gonna drink the wine like water."

The priest offers Uncle Louie a weak smile. My dad makes eye contact with Bobby, who looks at Uncle Louie, and then all eyes turn to me. Oh, this is suddenly one of those awkward small-town situations, where they gauge my reaction before being nice to my ex-husband.

Bobby Bilancia has a sculpted physique with a shoulder span that comes from lifting sides of beef off hooks and cutting them into lucrative puzzle pieces to sell at a tidy profit. Muscular and tall, like the robust statue of Saint Michael in the alcove of the side altar,

Bobby hasn't let himself go since we divorced; quite the opposite. His rippled biceps strain through the short sleeves of his T-shirt as though he's inflated them with a bike pump. His face is as superb as his physique. Bobby has bright blue eyes and black hair, a straight Irish nose, and sultry Italian lips.

"Hey, Jess." Bobby does this thing where he stretches tall and expands his chest when he is anxious, like the top half of a balloon poodle when twisted at the waist.

"Hi, Bobby. That's some tray."

"Two of them. Charcuterie. Still at your parents'?"

"Yeah."

"I got a house." His voice drops as if he's in the confessional. "The apartment had too many memories."

I find it fascinating that my ex-husband moved out of our large one-bedroom apartment and into a house alone. When we married, he wanted to rent. He said, *Let's squirrel away some dough and save for a house.* Whatever he squirreled away then was enough for a down payment now.

"Prosciutto rosettes with figs and capicola." Peachy shoots me a smile. "Your favorites." He turns to the priest. "Where do you want the meat platters, Padre?"

"Follow me," Father says.

I give Bobby a weak wave goodbye as he trails the priest, and the rest of the men fall in behind him in single file through the sacristy to the church hall.

Uncle Louie spins on his heels to face me. "That was not planned."

"I was bound to run into him sometime."

"But at the scene of the crime?" Uncle Louie checks his phone. "I have a wake in Cape May. Sorry, kid. Take the rest of the day to catch up on whatever's on your plate. Joe, can you give Jess a lift?"

"Sure. But don't you have to go home and change?" Dad asks.

"Nah, I keep the K of C tux and sword in the trunk. At my age, we're circling the drain like day-old suds. Soon enough, only one Knight of Columbus in shining armor shall remain. Fingers crossed, it's me." Louie chuckles and goes.

"YOU OKAY, JESS?" Dad starts the car as I climb in.

"Yep." Running into Bobby Bilancia was unexpected, but growing up in a small town has prepared me. "Thanks for the lift, Dad."

"We're going to the same place." Dad shrugs.

My father is a practical man, but what he loves, he adores. He is the parent we go to in a crisis. When I decided to leave Bobby, I went to my father first, to seek his counsel about how to handle my mother.

"You ever going to fix your car?" Dad asks.

"I like riding with Uncle Louie. We get all our work done going to and from the jobs. And then there's lunch."

"Louie lives to eat." Dad smiles. "He once drove me all the way to Pennsylvania for a pair of hot dogs at Potts' in Nazareth. I had no idea it was a two-hour drive one way. Could've gone to Chicago in less time. Your mother is still giving me grief about it."

Throughout my lifetime, Dad and I have had our deepest conversations in the car. Now that I'm in therapy, it's time to ask my dad some tough questions. "Are you and Mom happy?"

"I have a philosophy when it comes to your mother, which is why we've lasted. My job is not to make things worse."

"You go along with her program."

"Yes. And sometimes you're holding on so tight to the rope, you get a callus. Or you bleed. Every marriage can't be perfect like

Chuck and June Piola; those two are like a couple of saints. They haven't had an argument in thirty-six years. I used to think it was odd and now I'd give my right leg to live in that kind of peace."

My phone buzzes. I check the texts.

BOBBY: Sorry Jess. That was weird.

JESS: No problem. The trays looked amazing.

Then nothing. I stuff the phone into my pocket.

"You're a lot like my mother, Jess. You're a thinker. That's why she chose you to be with her when she died. You two had an understanding."

I sit back in the seat and remember when Bobby Bilancia proposed to me. I may have ignored certain signs at that time. I went to Grandma Cap's first to show her the ring because the Caps are flashier than the Barattas and carat size mattered to her. Once she approved, I walked down the block to show Grammy B the ring.

"Grammy B, I got news!" I practically sang when I entered her kitchen. The orange and avocado-green cabinets glistened. Her floor had just been scrubbed; the scent of lemon oil on the wood filled the air. Grammy B was asleep in her chair. She had brought Grandpa B's rocking chair into the kitchen after he died. She got a smaller kitchen table and turned the place into a baking haven. She kept busy while she grieved. When she wasn't making pies or cakes or cookies, she was rolling gnocchi or kneading the dough to make *homemades.* She used to make pasta in the basement, but when her knees started giving her trouble, she made everything in the upstairs kitchen. I couldn't wait to share my news. I sat down across the table from her and waited, until I realized she was not asleep. I panicked; that's when my memory lost focus. I remembered I couldn't breathe.

Dad's voice interrupts my thoughts. "You came and got me in the garage," Dad says. "You didn't have to say a word. I *knew*."

"She was so wise."

"She didn't like the Bilancias."

"*Now* you tell me?"

"What good would it have done? You were set on him."

"Did you like him?"

"Nice guy."

"He is. But did you like him for *me*?"

"You're a girl of simple tastes. You don't aspire to things; you like books and museums. What can I tell you? Here's the problem with the Bilancias. They wouldn't know art if you broke the *Mona Lisa* over their heads. They value the purse. They have the first buck they made in the butcher shop."

"The goal of a business is profit," I remind my father.

"And there's plenty of that at Bilancia Meats, believe me. My problem with them is their attitude. It was implied to me several times that perhaps we couldn't handle the expense of your big wedding and they wanted to help. I didn't take any money from them. I wanted them to know they were getting a priceless jewel in you and that we couldn't be bought."

"I guess it wasn't to be, Dad."

"That was your choice." Dad pulls into our driveway.

Through the window, I see Mom standing at the stove. We enter the kitchen, which is filled with the scents of butter, lemon, and garlic. Mom dredges a chicken cutlet in breadcrumbs and places the cutlet in the pan. It sizzles in the olive oil. "Bobby Bilancia got a house," Mom says without looking up.

"We heard," Dad says. "We ran into him at church." My father kisses Mom on the cheek.

"Should've invited him to dinner. I'm making his favorite." She waves the spatula in the air like it's a magic wand. "Those were the days. Bobby loved my cutlets so much he shook our daughter down for her lunch. Remember?"

"Philly," Dad warns her.

"Too soon for humor? We need to laugh around here to keep from roiling in regret. How do you feel about Bobby's house, Giuseppina?"

"I'm happy for him." Am I? I think I am.

"Why did he wait to buy a house until after the divorce? I don't understand. His own mother is mystified." Mom shakes her head. "A split-level on Ocean Avenue in Bilancia Land isn't cheap. Go figure."

"The boulevard side is nicer." Dad winks at me. "We have the lake."

"Yeah, but we have bugs in the summer," Mom says. "Bilancia Land is mostly concrete."

Daddy looks at me; he puts his finger to his lips, reminding me not to bite. He hates arguing as much as I do.

Oblivious, Mom says, "Bobby told Babe he wanted to buy Giuseppina a house all along." She says this as though I'm not in the room. "Now he'll be in a house all alone with the complete set of Haddon Hall china we gave you for your wedding. What's Bobby gonna do with service for twelve?"

"Philly, knock it off." My father mixes himself a bourbon and iced tea cocktail. "They're just dishes."

"In the history of the institution of marriage, no woman ever walked out with just a suitcase and her cell phone." She turns away from the fry pan and looks at me. "Your wedding gifts were abandoned like war orphans. Michael Aram picture frames. A Shark vacuum cleaner. I don't even have the deluxe model! The KitchenAid mixer. Top of the line!"

"Let it go, Phil," my father says quietly. "We've been through all of this."

I choose to leave the kitchen before this situation snowballs into an avalanche and buries me. In my mother's version, I am not buried in Alpine snow; death comes after I'm dredged in seasoned breadcrumbs and fried like a chicken cutlet.

I slip down the cellar stairs to my apartment underneath the kitchen. The temperature plunges with every step I take on the narrow stairwell. It's so cold down here, someday they'll find me curled up in my sleep like a ring bologna. This apartment was built for Grandma Cap, who died two weeks before she was scheduled to move in. She told me privately that she would rather die than live in our cellar, and so she did.

I skitter around the damp basement, throwing switches to produce heat. I turn on every lamp to brighten the place, including the overhead fixture, which was repurposed from the garage. Never mind it's meant for exterior use and is so bright I could perform my own appendectomy beneath its beam. It throws cold blue LED light, the kind you find in the parking silo at the mall. When I catch my reflection in the mirror, my skin tone glows an odd blue-green similar to the hue of a varicose vein.

Our basements have two purposes. When we're not housing someone old or newly divorced, we use them as bonus kitchens and storage units. It is impossible to find an Italian American who ever pays rent at a storage facility. We consider it a waste because we can always store underground. Our family saves everything and discards nothing, because someday, the item you kept will save the day, be it wax paper from cereal boxes (the perfect size to cool manicotti crepes) or plastic bags (there's a sack of plastic bags under the sink that rivals the size of the globe of the 1964 World's Fair) or squares of tinfoil (we haven't purchased a new roll since 2009). Italian Americans don't believe in recycling because we never throw anything away. This is why my mother cannot give up hope that I will go back with Bobby. Evidently, we don't throw people away either.

I sit down on the bed and prop my laptop on a pillow. I open it and log into my Thera-Me account. I can't wait to tell Dr. Sharon all about my day. Before I type in my password, I stop to think. I'm about to share, with a total stranger at an undetermined location, that I'm going to Italy, and I didn't tell my parents. Why?

That's a question for the doctor even though I already know the answer. I fear my parents would convince me not to go. They would be afraid for me in a foreign country. The truth is, they'd be afraid for me in the next county. My parents would have me dead before I got to the airport. Yet I'm dying inside a day at a time in their cellar. I have to tell someone in order to make Italy real because I haven't been this happy in a very long time. So I type in my password. A stranger with a medical degree is a better confidante than none at all.

I hit enter.

A return message, typed inside a cartoon of the human brain, says: *Dr. Sharon is unavailable. Click here to schedule an appointment with Dr. Raymond. Please fill out Exercise 2.*

I snap the laptop shut. Dr. Sharon didn't mention I would be fobbed off to Dr. Raymond! Feeling betrayed, I reach for my phone to make myself feel worse. I look Bobby up on Instagram. I muted his account when our divorce became final. Our wedding photos remain on his profile. I go into Messages and send him a text.

It was good to see you, Bobby.

I examine the text as though it is a diamond and I'm trying to predict carat weight. I text,

Miss you.

4

Sunday Dinner

The perfume of Sunday dinner *alla* Puglia fills the Baratta family kitchen. After hours on the stove, the gravy creates a symphony of scent, sweet butter, tender basil, and fresh garlic, with a base of our own robust marinara crushed from tomatoes gathered from our gardens. The canning of the tomatoes is a family affair. Our cousins show up every August, their yields in tow, along with their Mason jars, to can the tomatoes on the stove in the cellar. Every family on the lake has their own recipe, with their own particular spin. You know your people by their gravy.

The hearty pot simmers, filled with delicate hand-rolled meatballs, braised pork ribs, crispy chicken thighs, and spicy Italian sausage that poach and thicken the sauce. The rib meat is so tender it falls off the bone as I stir. *Perfetto!* Grammy B used to eat the bones, leaving the meat for others; this afternoon, in her honor, I may too. Behind the gravy, a high-hat pot roils with salted water awaiting the ravioli. In a covered skillet, broccoli rabe softens in olive oil on a low heat. A tray of stuffed artichokes, steamed this morning, bakes in the oven, blanketed in a mixture of buttery breadcrumbs, fresh herbs, and Parmigiano-Reggiano, carved off the wheel from Parma that takes up half a shelf in the refrigerator. I snap a photo of the operation and post it: *#marinara to share-a*. Maybe Zia Giuseppina wouldn't have been so angry if her Sunday dinner could've been posted on Insta.

"How many we got for dinner, Ma?" I call out to my mother, who irons her mother's lace tablecloth from Italy on the dining room table in the next room. It was a revelation to watch the servants on *Downton Abbey* press the cloth directly on the tabletop with a hot iron. Ever since, we do the same, skipping the ironing board.

"What's the ravioli count?" my mother hollers back.

"You first."

"I'm setting the table for fourteen." Mom places the hot iron on the sideboard to cool. She picks up a stack of her good china (pink-and-gold-rimmed Lady Carlyle) and places the dishes around the table. Mom cranks up Jim Croce's greatest hits, shaking her hips as she tinkers with the cloth napkins and silverware, placing them just so. I wonder if she senses this is my last Sunday dinner. While the broccoli rabe sautés, I sit down at the counter, pick up my phone, and journal about the moment I decided to change my life for good.

The trees along the walkway on the Hudson River in Hoboken were tall and lush with green foliage. Their leaves fluttered like feathers against the backdrop of the silver skyscrapers of Manhattan across the water. The slate-blue sky overhead swirled with tufts of white clouds that matched the foam on the waves of the river as it rolled out to sea.

"Never gets old." Uncle Louie leaned against the railing and gazed at the skyline of Manhattan like it was a long-lost lover that hadn't aged and still desired him. "She gets prettier and prettier over time. Every city is a woman. If New York City were a woman, in fall, she'd be Sophia Loren. In summer, Claudia Cardinale. Spring? Giulietta Masina. Winter, she's Kaye Ballard in a babushka."

"I'll meet you after lunch."

"Where you going?"

"I thought I'd walk around. Get some air," I lied. It was the first lie I ever told Uncle Louie.

"I'm gonna grab a calzone at Rocco's. You want one?"

"Yeah, that'll be nice."

"Good work on the installation. I'll pick you up in an hour."

Uncle Louie and I had done a final walk-through for our marble wall fountain installation in the courtyard of the Riverview apartment complex. I was sad when the work was complete because I couldn't help but feel a personal connection to the neighborhood.

Hoboken was the first stop the immigrant Capodimonte men made in 1920 before moving down the shore to start our marble company. The women, my great-grandmother and grandmother (who was a little girl at the time), followed them to the United States in 1936, after my great-grandfather sent them the passage. They moved quickly to emigrate with the war brewing, leaving everything behind in Carrara. Maybe the idea of Hoboken as a refuge is in my bones. Hoboken carried our dreams while Manhattan was the glittering backdrop for them.

The doorman spun the revolving door like a lucky wheel of fortune.

"Miss Baratta?" The building Realtor, Margarita Cartegna, wore a black pantsuit and reading glasses around her neck on a gold chain. "I've got two studio units to show you. Do you prefer courtyard or riverside?"

"The Hudson River side, please."

Mrs. Cartegna was surprised. "I thought you might like to overlook the fountain you installed."

Once I have drawn the project; chosen the appropriate materials; worked with the stonemason, plumber, and electrician; and overseen the construction of a marble installation, I move on. The fountain in the courtyard is spectacular, but there was no need to look at it every day.

We got off the elevator on the seventeenth floor. Mrs. Cartegna opened the door of 17C and allowed me to enter the empty apartment first. There was nothing but windows and light in the L-shaped space. We were so high in the sky, I could reach out and touch the clouds as they floated by.

"I don't have any one-bedrooms right now, but I personally believe that the studios feel more spacious. And truthfully, the wall closet is bigger in the studios than in the one-bedrooms . . ." She kept talking, but her voice faded away as I walked through the empty apartment, my heels clicking against the hardwood floor. Mrs. Cartegna did a hard sell on the new kitchenette and the bathroom, but I was not listening. I pushed the doors to the balcony open and stepped outside. Air! Light! Sky! The cold autumn air sent a chill through me. I was transfixed as a white cargo ship slowly sailed down the green river and out to sea.

Mrs. Cartegna joined me on the small balcony. "Wait until the leaves change. From here, they look like they're made of gold velvet." She leaned on the railing and looked down at the Hudson River and sighed. "Get the apartment of your dreams now, because when you have kids, a balcony is the first thing to go. Only singletons rent the balcony apartments."

At least Mrs. Cartegna could see that I was a *singleton.* I liked that I didn't have to explain myself to her. Maybe it was obvious because I had a gray pallor, a sign of cellar dwelling. I had been living in the dark for so long, she could actually see me blossom in the light. I wondered how I thought I could make a reasonable decision about *anything* when it was so easy to hide myself in the basement like a broken machine that had lost its purpose. I reminded myself that I moved home out of necessity because Mom and Dad needed me. During my separation, when I was falling apart, my parents were too. Mom had a knee replaced, and Dad had his shoulder done. I had to hold them together. They even believed moving home and tending to their needs would take my mind off my "troubles." If only that had been true.

I leaned against the railing next to the Realtor and looked out. "I made a dream board," I told her. "I saw all of this. I made a collage of pictures from *World of Interiors, Traditional Home,* and *Elle Decor.* I saw myself high in the air, above the treetops. Like this. Only thing, there was an elegant bathtub on my board. And there's no tub in this bathroom."

"Ah-ha-ha." She smiled and shook her finger. "There's a hot tub and a pool on the roof." She pointed. "I'll show you. Full amenities. Parking. Do you have a car?"

"It's a wreck."

"You don't need it. PATH is down the block. The train can take you anywhere."

"Anywhere is exactly where I want to go."

We went back inside the apartment. It was quiet inside, not a sound from the world below. I imagined sleeping without the whoosh of the sump pump, the constant whirl of the dehumidifier, and the clunky sound of my parents' footfalls over my head. I could fill this apartment with books, a sofa upholstered in a paisley of coral, peacock green, and midnight blue. The walls? Eggshell, with a few drops of cobalt blue stirred into the paint for that hint of Italian sky.

"The super can paint the place any color you like," she said, reading my mind.

That would be a first. My sister, Connie, chose gumdrop lavender for our bedroom walls when we were girls. Dad painted the cellar apartment egg-yolk yellow, consulting no one. I think he had paint left over from a summer in the eighties when he painted the curb to prevent beach bums from parking in front of our house. I even relinquished my color rights when I was married. I acquiesced to Bobby's favorite neutrals, silvers, and black. I pretended to like his masculine palette, but it was like living inside a box of razor blades.

"*Any* color?" I asked Mrs. Cartegna. "Do you mean it?"

"WE SHOULD HAVE enough ravs," Mom says from the kitchen doorway.

I jump.

"Sorry," Mom says. "You were someplace else."

"Nope." I put down my phone and go back to the stove. "Right here, manning the gravy," I lie. I *was* in Hoboken, New Jersey, in my imagination, in a new high-rise, slowly stirring a martini for one. All I have to do is drop off the deposit to Mrs. Cartegna, and I'm out of here.

"Turn the gas down. You know what they say—if you burn the

gravy, there's no saving it. You have to throw it out and start over." Mom smiles.

That may be the most profound wisdom my mom has ever shared with me. It's true. When you burn it down, whether it's marinara or your life, you must rebuild from scratch.

"If you don't think we have enough ravs, I have an emergency stash. From Petrini's," she says.

I toss delicate garlic buds into a small skillet; they turn glassy in the butter.

"Watch it," my mother says over my shoulder as she takes a crystal vase of sunflowers off the kitchen table and carries it into the dining room. "Nothing worse than burned garlic."

"I can think of a few things," I say under my breath. I turn off the burner and set the pan of garlic aside before making my way out to the garage. A white cloud of cold air blasts my face as I open the top of the industrial freezer. When the haze dissipates, the first thing I see is my married name, *Bilancia*, on the packages of frozen beef. I find it fascinating (weird?) that my family remains loyal customers of my ex-husband's butcher shop since the divorce. It's not like I expected my family to become vegetarians in my defense, but shouldn't they get their meat at Costco?

I find the boxes of ravioli easily in the emergency freezer, where my mother keeps a medical gel strap from the Hospital for Special Surgery on top of a sleeve of twenty-four industrial count chicken breasts, so we might have enough protein to survive a Canadian invasion. Hopefully when it happens, they'll pour in from Toronto and bring their own marinara. After all, Dad has cousins from Puglia up north.

"Need you to bartend," Mom whispers as I pass through the dining room with the extra box of ravioli. "Daddy's in the shower. Your aunt and uncle are *early*." She makes a face.

"Roll with it," I whisper back.

One of the jobs in my family is to pull my mother back from the brink before she spirals out of control when things don't go exactly according to her plan. Her anxiety percolates to panic level whenever she has to feed a large group of people, and yet, she invites them. This is one of the many mysteries that is my mother. Her dreams of what might be exceed her ability, which frustrates her. Instead of knowing her limitations, she pretends she has none. Our family has learned to work around her impossible expectations. You want to nip the crazy before she pulls her own pin and explodes like a grenade and we are forced to serve my mother's rage on crackers during the appetizer course.

"Ma. Don't get worked up. Go put on your lipstick. I will take care of it."

"I don't know what I'd do without my Giuseppina." She slips up the stairs.

"Long time no see," Uncle Louie jokes from the booth at the kitchen table.

"How's the boss?" I ask.

Louie turns to his wife. "How *are* you, Lil? Please advise."

Aunt Lil is tucked into the booth next to Louie. I kiss her on the cheek. She doesn't have a line on her seventy-six-year-old face. ("Sign of a woman without children," my mother says, "or a woman a few years older than her husband who doesn't want to look it.") I see my aunt differently. Aunt Lil is strong. She knows her own limitations and doesn't drive herself nuts trying to please people. She's an in-law with functioning self-esteem.

"You always smell good, Auntie."

"It's a cologne called Expensive," Uncle Louie jokes.

"White Diamonds by Elizabeth Taylor," Aunt Lil corrects him. Auntie's short haircut has fresh blond highlights, even though she wears a casual navy velour jogging suit and platform sneakers (which raise her height to five feet). Like Beyoncé, her hands, neck, and ears are encrusted in diamonds. Real ones. And Auntie didn't have to jump into a mosh pit while wearing a crystal-studded unitard and a cowboy hat to earn them; she didn't even have to leave her house.

"How about a Baratta highball, kids?" I offer.

I mix gin, ginger ale, and a splash of Dubonnet in two tall glasses with lots of ice. I anchor each glass with a lemon peel.

"So glad you're early," my mother fibs as she greets her brother and sister-in-law. "I was hoping we could sit in the living room for cocktails. You know, civilized."

"Another time, sis. The kitchen is where the action is." Uncle Louie toasts her and sips.

Mom shrugs and serves the appetizers: hunks of Parmesan cheese, thin slices of salami, and crispy tarelles. She peels off a cocktail napkin from the stack, one for each of the guests, embossed with the message *One sip away from being a chooch.*

"Sit down, Phil. Make yourself at home. Who made these?" Uncle Louie holds up a tarelle.

"I did." Mom hand-irons the red-checkered tablecloth. "How are they?"

Uncle Louie doesn't answer; instead he greets my dad. "There he is!"

Dad enters the kitchen in a sweet cloud of Aqua Velva cologne, his hair combed back wet off his face like it's the first day of school. "How are you, Lil?"

"I'm all right, Joe."

"You want a highball, Dad?"

"Why not?" Dad sits in his chair at the head of the table. It's the only chair with arms and a cushion on the seat because Dad doesn't fit in the booth and the pitch of the straight-backed chairs gives him sciatica. "What's new?"

Uncle Louie looks at me. Before I can stop him, he announces, "I'm taking Jess to Italy. On business. Lil doesn't want to go. She can't do without her stories, and I don't know if the satellite picks them up in Italy."

"I could tape them," Lil offers. "I just don't feel like traipsing. Autumn is for hunkering." Lil folds her arms as though she's cold; by contrast, I'm sweating like I'm fighting typhoid fever in the hot kitchen.

Mom claps her hands together. "Your dad and I will join you on the trip. We never hunker."

"It's a business trip, and we—" Uncle Louie begins.

Mom cuts him off. "We'll ask Joe and Connie. They'll bring the kids. They're still small enough to pull out of school without repercussions. We'll stay in B and Bs. Or we can do one of those Mediterranean cruises. They have family plans! You want to stay on the boat? Stay! You want to get off and explore? Get off! Our Return to Our Italian Roots trip! This is my dream! Even movie stars are flocking. Lorraine Bracco bought a house in Sicily. And Stanley Tucci ate his way through the mainland. Italy is a hot destination! What is Social Security for anyway? Nobody lives forever."

"You are not invited."

Mom, Dad, Aunt Lil, and Uncle Louie look at me oddly. Maybe they think I'm drunk. (I wouldn't be the first Cap or Baratta woman who drank while she prepped Sunday dinner.) I don't care! I will not let this trip turn into someone else's idea of an Italian adventure before I have one of my own. It's just too important. The most horrible phrase in the English language is not *unexpected turbulence* or *freak accident* or *loose skin*. It is *family vacation*.

"Well." My mother puts her hands in her lap.

"I mean it." A hush falls over the kitchen table. The only sound is the gravy as it simmers in the pot. "You can't come." I clutch a slotted spoon in one hand and a serving fork in the other like weapons. "This is my first trip to Italy. I'm not sharing her."

"It's a *country*, for God's sake." My mother looks hurt. "It's for everyone."

"Not this time. It's a *business* trip. There won't be time for sightseeing and shopping. Right, Uncle Louie?" My voice cracks. I look to him for reinforcement.

"We may do some bartering, and that can get ugly." Louie plays along. "Just me and Jess this time." Uncle Louie motions for me to put down my weapons. "This is strictly business and we have a lot of ground to cover."

Mom throws up her hands. "All right. We won't go. I've never felt so dismissed in my life. I thought we were fun."

My mother is a black arrow; her straight nose and full lips are offset by her thick eyebrows. She didn't overpluck in the 1970s, and now that she's almost seventy, resisting the urge has paid off. She looks youthful even though her hair resembles Nero Marquina marble, ebony with white strands, but only because she's due for a dye job.

"Philly, look at this like a scout for the next trip, where everyone can come. Jess and I will go and scope out the situation. I promise I'll get you over there. But for now? Two-man operation."

Thankfully, my sister, Connie, her husband, and their three daughters push through the front door, making a commotion.

"The Dominguez family has landed. Shoes off, everybody!" Mom hollers from the kitchen. She lowers her voice and turns to me. "I'd like to see how you're going to tell your sister that you're going to Italy without her and her husband and children. Not going to go well."

I shoot Uncle Louie a look of desperation. He pats imaginary dough on the kitchen table. *Don't react. Don't bite, Jess.*

"I can't tell you how hard it is to get three girls ready for Sunday dinner," Connie announces as she comes into the kitchen, looking effortlessly chic in beige slacks and a silk blouse. Despite three births, her stomach is concave, like the flour well we dig on the marble cutting board when we knead the dough to make fresh macaroni. "Ma, you're a saint. I don't know how you did it."

"It wasn't easy. Believe me." Mom sips her highball.

Connie makes the rounds kissing everyone. She's slender; her dark blond hair, blown straight, cascades over her shoulders without frizz.

"Thanks for having us." Diego shakes Dad's hand and gives Mom a kiss. He's tall and slim, with a small nose and thick eyebrows. He wears glasses, which give him the look of a very smart professor, even though he's in finance. "Girls, say hello to Nonna and Nonno, Zio Louie and Zia Lil."

Alexa, Alicia, and Abby are ten, nine, and eight and could be triplets. They have brown eyes and wild dark curls, which they inherited from me.

"And don't forget Aunt Jess," Diego tells his daughters.

"Don't come near the stove. I'll come to you," I tell them.

"You girls have Aunt Jess's hair," Diego says.

"I'm sorry." I kneel and deliver a group hug to the girls.

"No, we love curls, don't we?" Connie glares at me. "When God sent the girls down from heaven, he wanted them to have curls in their hair, like the kind you find on top of a present. Curling ribbon, right, girls?"

"Sorry." I hug my nieces. "You are curliewhirlies and I love you."

"Who wants a tarelle?" Dad holds the platter.

"They need more salt," Diego says thoughtfully as he chews. "Texture? Perfect."

"Diego, you're practically Italian," Mom observes.

"Why can't the Italians be practically Colombian? Italians think they're the best," Diego jokes.

"Because we are." Uncle Louie smiles.

I hand Diego a cocktail before he attempts to take on Uncle Louie. The highball will take the edge off, and there are plenty of edges around here in need of filing and polishing, like a slab of marble, starting with in-law relations. Connie and Diego have been married for twelve years, yet he remains on probation. This is how it goes with in-laws in my family; there's an assimilation period for everyone who marries in, except, of course, for Bobby Bilancia, who was revered because he was the catch of Lake Como.

Diego raises his glass. "To the Italians!" Diego runs a small hedge fund; he's not rich yet, but he will be someday, and then everything he says in this house will have clout.

My brother Joe calls out, "Ma, we're here," as he comes through the front door. The King of Clout has entered the building. Katie—his wife, the interior designer—and their children remove their shoes in an orderly fashion and line them up neatly under the upholstered bench. My brother, however, defies the house rule and remains in his polished Tod's loafers because he can.

"Put the ravs in," my mother orders. "Your brother is here." Joseph Baratta Jr.'s arrival is announced as though NASA has found a star in the heavens that burns hotter and brighter than the sun.

Joe wears a jacket and tie and always has, except for the times he played on the Saint Rose baseball team and wore the uniform. He favors the Cap side, with the large, straight nose, full lips, and flinty brown eyes. His wife, Katie, is a petite redhead, with a smattering of freckles on her nose, electric-blue eyes, and a slim, athletic build.

Their son and daughter are blue-eyed redheads, a coordinated set of lit matches. They look nothing like my brother or our side of the family.

"Which one are you?" Uncle Louie asks my brother's son, who climbs into the booth next to him. "Rattigan?"

"Rafferty." My seven-year-old nephew giggles.

"And who are you?" Uncle Louie points to Joe and Katie's six-year-old daughter, who hides behind her mother.

"That's my sister," Rafferty shouts. "She's scared."

"What's her name? MacDougal?" Uncle Louie asks, genuinely forgetful.

"Mackenzie!" Rafferty and Mackenzie say in unison.

"Mackenzie is a family name on Katie's side, Uncle Louie," Joe says impatiently.

"Come on, Joey. I tease. You know me, just looking for the Italian. Evidently, I gotta dig deep in the dirt with a fork with your crew until I hit an Etruscan tomb."

Katie jumps in. "No need to dig, Uncle Louie. They're Barattas; the Italian side is represented in the surname."

"True enough," Uncle Louie says pleasantly. "Forgive me. The Italians of my generation are named for dead people we never met. Such was the custom. You name your kids for Irish pubs. That's progress."

I place a tray of crostini on the kitchen table. The hands go toward the platter like it's betting time on a blackjack table in Vegas. Soon, all the kids stampede through, throw open the basement door, and go down to the cellar.

"Don't touch anything down there!" Mom calls after them. "There's all kinds of equipment down there with wires."

"It's fine, Ma," I assure her. Later, I'll think about why it's okay for me to live in a potential electrocution situation with all those wires, but not safe for the kids to play down there.

"In all sincerity, Katie, Joe. They're beautiful kids. After dinner, we'll have some fun," Uncle Louie says. "I brought a roll of quarters."

"Kids don't want quarters anymore, Lou," Aunt Lil scolds. "They have video games and iPhones."

"Can a phone do magic tricks?" Uncle Louie pulls a shiny quarter out of Aunt Lil's ear.

The kids come up from the basement apartment. Alexa holds my therapy exercise high over her head. "What's this, Aunt Jess?"

My family turns to look at a collage I created on a flat board with inspiring words and images from magazines.

"What is that?" Ma squints. "It looks like a knee-length boot."

"It's Italy, sis," Uncle Louie corrects her.

"That's my dream board." My voice breaks. For someone who draws for a living, the collage is an amateur attempt at self-realization. I feel naked. Exposed.

"Alexa, you are not to go into Auntie's personal things. Take it back downstairs," Connie reprimands her daughter. My niece looks as though she may cry.

"It's okay. I'll show you how to make one later, Alexa." I ladle the ravs out of the boiling salted water and onto a serving platter.

"What's that board all about?" my mother asks.

Now that the dream board has been revealed without my consent, I might as well share that I'm seeking enlightenment, not that it's any of their business. "It was an exercise in visualization. I'm in therapy."

"What?" my mother shrieks.

"Therapy is a good thing, Ma," Katie says.

"Depends on the doctor." Diego nods. "But if he has you making collages, that sounds creative."

"*She.* A lady doctor." I ladle the marinara onto the ravioli. "Online."

My mother dabs her brow with a cocktail napkin. "You're going online and talking to strangers about your problems? What about Father Belaynesh?" Mom asks. "He's local. Can't you talk to him?"

"I'm not going to a priest."

"There isn't any problem they haven't heard in a confessional," Dad says.

"They haven't heard mine," I assure him.

"Well, a priest won't charge you," Mom says.

"I don't think it's about the money. Is everything okay, Jess?" my brother asks.

My sister jumps in. "I think it's good. Jess has been through a lot. Sometimes you need an outside perspective from a total stranger who couldn't pick you out of a lineup at the police station."

"Thank you, Connie." I can always count on my sister to support any mental health remedies. She went into a saltwater floatation tank after she had Alexa. There aren't enough soaking tanks on earth to heal my issues. My family doesn't have a clue about me.

"Board or no board, your sister is going to Italy with Louie and she's not taking any of us with her," Mom announces.

"Another time," I remind Mom. "Italy isn't going anywhere."

"I don't understand what we did wrong."

I look at my sister and implore her to help shut Mom down before I lose it.

"I think it's wonderful. Jess has never been to Italy," Connie jumps in. "She's wanted to go all of her life. When we were growing up, she had a map of Italy over her bed and a poster of an Italian soccer team on our closet door. Did you ever watch a soccer game in your life?"

I nod that I haven't. "I just thought the guys on the team were cute."

"That's as good a reason as any to hang a poster," Uncle Louie says diplomatically. "I had a Loni Anderson in my office."

"I made him take it down." Aunt Lil winks at me.

Connie goes on. "Jess majored in Italian culture. She didn't get to study abroad. It's time. Let her go."

"Dinner is ready. Please call everybody to the table." I grate Parmigiano-Reggiano with a vengeance onto the ravioli.

We move into the dining room, taking our seats. Everyone but me, of course, as I am not only the cook but the waitress as well. My father takes his seat at the head of the table. I place the ravioli in the center of the table and set the serving spoon near Connie. From the sideboard, I lift the serving dish of broccoli rabe, placing it on the table. Mom rises from her chair at the table. "What can I do?"

"Nothing. I got it."

The children climb into their seats at the far end of the table.

"Isn't it nice that the kids are old enough to seat themselves?" Mom marvels. "I love a baby, but those high chairs." She makes a face. "I was so happy to put ours in the Saint Rose tag sale."

"You may have sold them too soon," Diego says.

"Do you have news, Connie?" Mom says hopefully.

"No. And there will be no news."

Katie waves across the table. "No news here either. Ever again."

"But Jess may have a baby someday," Diego offers. "Hold on to all that plastic crap. You may need it."

Aunt Lil pipes up, rescuing me. "Do you need any help in the kitchen, Jess?"

"Absolutely not, Lil. You sit." My mother smiles at her. "This is Giuseppina's show."

"Happy to create Sunday dinner like Zia Giuseppina." I force a smile.

Uncle Louie slices a delicate pillow of ravioli in half. He closes his eyes and tastes. "Jess, you resemble your great-aunt in one way and one way only. You make a good gravy."

"Cooking is one thing," my mother begins. "But there are more important things. I hope all my children and their children have a teaspoon of Zia's deep faith. She had very high moral standards." My mother sits up straight like those acrobats from Slovenia who form a pyramid as they balance their entire family overhead on chairs.

"I'm honored to carry her name and make her recipes." I serve the children. "Nothing is as important as family."

"I didn't see us on your dream board," Mom says under her breath.

"The artichokes are perfection. Just the right amount of breadcrumbs," Dad says, diverting attention away from my mother's criticism.

"You're welcome, Dad."

"These are work intensive. You have a job, you're busy, and I appreciate it."

"Least I can do, Dad. You don't charge me rent."

"You're our child," Mom pipes up.

"Not to worry. You'll be able to rent out the cellar soon. I'm looking at apartments."

Mom puts down her fork. "Apartments? Where?"

"Hoboken."

"Hoboken! The Caps fled that dump as soon as they made a couple of bucks! Why would you ever move back?"

"Philly, it's an hour in the car," Dad says.

"Jess can live anywhere she wants," Connie says. "She's over thirty."

"Let's not advertise. Shall we?" Mom warns her. "We're all fighting the big clock."

"I like Hoboken." Uncle Louie winks at me.

"Hoboken is a *nowhere*! It's not even an *anywhere*!" Mom says.

Uncle Louie, Aunt Lil, and my father exchange looks. Despite my earnest efforts, my mother has pulled her own pin. The secrets I wanted to keep are out. Well, three of them anyway. Italy, Hoboken, and therapy are now on the table, served hot like the meat platter. My life choices will be analyzed, stabbed, and consumed like meatballs, chicken thighs, and beef ribs.

"You're leaving us, kid," Dad says sadly.

I DON'T SHARE major decisions I've made in advance with my family because in their eyes, I usually make the wrong ones. But Dr. Sharon, in a single session, taught me one thing: Out with it. Do not hold back. Release your secrets like a bunch of red balloons on a sunny day and let them fly away as they will, because where the truth goes is not your problem; it's just important that you say it. The first of November cannot come fast enough.

"You're serious. When are you moving out?" My mother's voice breaks.

"I plan to move as soon as I can," I tell her.

"You haven't thought this through. The traffic is terrible in North Jersey," Mom grumbles.

I take a firm tone and look at my mother. "Hoboken has changed. It's beautiful."

"I've heard they have a good Target," my sister says supportively. "It's actually very chic now."

"Thanks, Connie. It's time for me to leave the nest. Though I don't know of any birds who live in cellars."

I go into the kitchen and return, carrying a silver tray with coffee cups and saucers, a pot of espresso and one of hot coffee, and the creamer and sugar bowl into the dining room. We are in the last lap of Sunday dinner. The tiramisu, in a rectangular spring pan, looks like a small football field dusted in chocolate powder. I place it in the center of the table to a chorus of compliments. Katie takes the tray from me and serves the coffee. I place two large wooden bowls of mixed nuts in their shells on either end of the table. I fan the silver nutcrackers and picks on the tabletop.

"Call the kids, hon," Mom says to me.

"I gave them each an ice cream sandwich. They're going to town in the backyard," I tell her.

"Tell us about your trip to Italy," Katie says as she cracks a walnut. "What's on the docket, Uncle Louie?"

"For starters, we're going to the quarry in Carrara. Where I worked. What year was that, Lil?"

"I don't know. It was before you met me."

"So it had to be '71 or '72."

"That's right. We met in '73."

"How could I forget? You blew the roof off my life that summer when you wore that little sundress. We were at the Feast."

"You're obsessed, Uncle Louie." Connie passes the cream to Diego. "See how they are? Married forever and still in love."

"It's a beautiful thing." Diego rolls his eyes. "Maybe because they didn't have kids."

The dining room is silent except for the sound of my father cracking a tough walnut.

"We would have loved to have a baby," Aunt Lil says quietly, "but we weren't blessed in that way."

"I'm sorry, Aunt Lil." Diego is truly contrite.

"Anyhow," Uncle Louie continues, "when I lived over in Italy, they had me do all the jobs in the mine. I started out as a runner. Then those guys taught me to cut stone. Once you cut stone, you fear nothing. I was on the mountain. Literally. Dangling in midair on ropes like a trapeze artist."

"When you weren't busy being a skirt chaser." Aunt Lil rolls her eyes. "He reeled in the girls with his bad Italian."

"That's not all he did, Lil. You almost died on that mountain, didn't you, Lou?" Mom asks.

"Yeah, but I made it. I take all the danger in the world, if you give me Italy." Uncle Louie winks at me.

"Katie and I will do the dishes for you." Connie smiles before draining the last of her wine.

"Thanks, Con." They're technically *all* of our dishes, because we all ate the meal I prepared on them, but okay. I cut a hefty slab of tiramisu out of the pan and place it on a plate. I wonder how they'll manage next week when they have to do all the cooking, serving, and cleaning up. Not my problem. I move seats, sitting down next to Aunt Lil and Uncle Louie.

"You made this?" Uncle Louie takes a bite. "Just right on the Amaretto, doused but not soaked to the point the cake is mush." Uncle Louie puts down his fork. "Tell the kids to come see me," he says to Connie. "It's magic time."

"You promise not to teach them any curse words in Italian?" Connie says on her way to the backyard.

"You know what, Connie? You're my niece and I love you, but you take the starch right out of life with your rules. Loosen up. One of the happiest moments of my life was the day my uncle Mike taught me to say *fongool*. I have used it in his honor ever since."

"How sad is that?" my mother barks. "Instead of the f-word, honor Uncle Mike by taking apart an engine and putting it back together."

"Do as Connie asks, Lou," Lil says. "They're *her* children."

The kids gather around Uncle Louie, who has pushed his chair away from the table. He sits.

"Who wants a quarter?" Uncle Louie asks the kids. They squeal as Uncle Louie pulls a shiny new quarter out of Alexa's ear and hands it to her.

"Me too, Uncle Louie!" Rafferty jumps up and down.

One by one, Uncle Louie tickles their ears and produces a quarter like magic. I've turned to take the coffeepot into the kitchen to refill it when Mackenzie says, "What's wrong with Uncle Louie?"

I turn back around. Uncle Louie has slumped forward in the chair. The quarters fall out of his hand and scatter across the floor.

My dad gets up and shoves his chair out of the way.

"Louie, what's the matter?" Aunt Lil shrieks. "Louie!"

"Ma, take Aunt Lil to the living room," Joe says calmly. "Everybody out. To the living room. Now." Diego takes Connie and Katie and the kids to the living room. For the first time since they arrived, the kids are quiet. Aunt Lil, however, is crying out in desperation. She calls her husband's name while Mom ushers her out to the living room.

"I'm calling 911." Joe taps his phone.

"Lou, you all right?" My dad tries to lift Uncle Louie upright on the chair.

Uncle Louie doesn't answer; his eyes are glassy and unfocused.

Soon enough, two medics burst through the front door. Connie shows them into the dining room. They're young, in their early twenties. They kneel and take Uncle Louie's vitals. There's equipment and a stretcher, two more medics lift him off the dining room floor, and within seconds, my uncle is loaded onto the gurney. One of the medics speaks to him in a low voice, explaining exactly what they're doing, but I doubt Uncle Louie hears him. He is the same shade as the ash-speckled terrazzo floor he installed in our dining room in 1992.

As they carry Uncle Louie out on the stretcher, my mother, in a panic, pushes me toward the door.

"Go with him in the ambulance," she says. "I'll follow with Lil. She's hysterical."

5

Louie, Louie

Uncle Louie sleeps supine in his hospital bed underneath a thin blanket the color of lime sherbet. I welcome the snorts between his breaths; they are as rhythmic as the faint dings from the screen on the monitor over his bed. The doctor assured me they would have the results from his tests in the morning. The sun can't rise fast enough.

I don't know what my mother was thinking when she dropped off food for us. Her brother had a major cardiac event. Meatballs, sausage, pork, and gravy are not ideal food choices for a man with clogged arteries. I rearrange the square plastic containers filled with the leftovers from Sunday dinner perched on the windowsill as though I'm ten years old and they're Legos. I remember the hoists and the crane on the pier the last time the marble arrived from Italy. I can't sleep, so I open the notes app and write. I feel an urgency not to forget a single detail about my life with Louie Cap.

Perth Amboy is a small city situated on a wide inlet off the Atlantic Ocean, the host of the busiest industrial pier on the New Jersey coastline. Twice a year, a cargo ship arrived from Italy and delivered a load of Carrara marble and Tuscan granite. The Perth Amboy drop is a Capodimonte family tradition that began with my great-grandfather. Uncle Louie figured that as of the spring of 2024, this was his ninety-sixth drop.

Uncle Louie stood back as a slab of Carrara Borghini, secured with ropes and hooks, was hoisted off the deck of the freighter and up into the sky. The marble slowly sailed through the air on a pulley operated by the men on the dock. The expanse of glistening white stone, veined in streaks of pale blue and gold, twenty feet high and almost as wide, blocked the sun as it was lowered onto the dock.

The gloved workmen rushed to surround the slab. They unhooked the ropes and glided it upright into a storage sleeve, where it would stand until the marble was transported by truck to destinations all over the state of New Jersey. One by one, the slabs flew through the air, and soon the wooden slats of the pier groaned beneath our feet from the weight of the stone. The process was like watching the skyscraper construction scene in *The Fountainhead*, Grandma Cap's favorite old movie to watch on TCM. Perth Amboy had everything but Gary Cooper and his drill.

Uncle Louie was a bag of nerves during the transport. Marble is delicate, even though it's a workhorse. Hit the stone in a vulnerable spot, it shatters, and you end up with slag. In this way, marble is a lot like a human being.

A black Cadillac SUV pulled up at the end of the pier, gliding into a spot next to Uncle Louie's Impala.

"Hey, Googs." I waved to him as he got out of the truck. "Over here."

Uncle Louie's occasional business partner walked toward us. He wore a navy pinstripe suit with a white shirt and a hot-pink tie. His white hair was brushed back neatly with gel. His jowly face gave him the look of an Italian bulldog.

"How we doin'?" Googs squinted at the final slab of marble as it floated through the air on its way to the dock.

"Looks good," I told him. "No problems."

Googs grunted. "Not yet."

I followed him onto the pier to join Uncle Louie.

"Where the hell were you?" Uncle Louie asked him.

"Paperwork, Lou," Googs explained. "I'm swimming in it."

"Like a shark." Louie kept his eyes on the marble slab in midair. "You got a gold vein in that Nero Azzurro that's to die for. The cut is as smooth as fondant. It's half the shipment I was expecting, but that's the Italians for you. They send what they want to send, no matter what you ordered."

"I will rectify the situation, believe me," Googs assured him. "The Kerrigan kid is a good egg. He'll make it right on the other side if there's a shortfall."

Uncle Louie made a popping sound with his lips, a sign he was thinking and not liking where his thoughts were taking him. He placed his hands in his vest pockets and walked to the end of the pier, where he joined the cargo manager dressed in coveralls. The pulleys squeaked as the stone was lowered.

Uncle Louie went up on his toes and down on his heels as he observed the end of the transfer. Googs shadowed Uncle Louie and stood close by, with one ear cocked toward the conversation between Uncle Louie and the boss on the pier.

Uncle Louie loved an exclusive. He assured customers they couldn't find Carrara marble like his anywhere else in the marketplace. Sometimes we ended up with more freight than we needed. The goal was to try to estimate the amount of stone needed and not end up with a surplus, but we usually did, no matter how many calculations we made. Every sink in every half bath in every home on the lake had been installed with Arabescato, a pink marble with swirls of eggnog yellow, from Louie's surplus, which he refused to unload on the open market.

Uncle Louie agreed to take the entire inventory with Googs, who nodded in agreement.

Once Uncle Louie wrapped up with the manager, he and Googs crossed the pier to where the workmen were lined up in front of the sleeves of marble. Uncle Louie shook the foreman's hand with his right hand, and with his left he pulled a white envelope from the breast pocket of his suit jacket. The foreman took the envelope and slipped it into his back pocket for distribution later. The Amazing Kreskin could not have moved a sealed envelope so easily.

Cash tips were stacked inside that envelope, bills as crisp as the day they came off the presses at the United States Mint, and I would know. I counted the money and sealed the envelope. I observed as my uncle shook the hand of every workman on the dock, personally thanked them for their service. Googs stood behind my uncle and nodded as he moved down the line. In these moments, Uncle Louie possessed the gentility of another time, when taking care of people was important and gratitude was expressed in ways that made a difference to the person doing the work.

"How about lunch?" I offered upon their return.

"How about it?" Uncle Louie clapped his hands together and washed them with invisible Purell. "I'm famished."

"Mom made it."

"That's a ringing endorsement. My sister can cook." Louie cocked his head toward the picnic area by the pier. "Shall we dine alfresco? Googs? Would you care to join?"

"I appreciate the invitation, but I got business in Brielle."

"Animal, vegetable, or woman?" Louie prodded.

"Gravel." Googs grinned and gave my uncle a military salute before returning to his car.

"Googs never eats with us," I said as I took the thermal bag out of the back seat of the Impala. "How come?"

"Gravel, my ass. The only hunger he has is for women."

"Doesn't seem to hurt his bottom line," I offered.

"He's a good salesman," Uncle Louie admitted.

When it came to salesmen, Uncle Louie taught me, *If someone has to tell you they're a good person, they're usually not.* At Cap Marble and Stone, I handled the designs, the customers, and occasionally lunch. Louie Cap made the deals.

Uncle Louie took a seat at an old picnic table that had turned, over time, to mottled driftwood. "It's rickety, but it'll hold you," my uncle said as his phone rang. "I gotta take this. Italy."

Uncle Louie FaceTimed with our shipping partner, Conor Kerrigan, in Italy.

"Yeah, Conor. Yeah . . . it's all good. A little light on the Borghini . . . See what you can do about that. I could move four tons of it if I had it on hand. . . . Uh-huh. . . . *Va bene.* Say hello to my niece." Louie aimed his phone at me.

"Ciao, Giuseppina." Conor Kerrigan was thirty-five, and a looker. Conor's father began working with Cap Marble around the time Uncle Louie took over from my grandfather. Conor took over the importing side when his dad passed away a couple years ago. The marble business is a family affair, and not just for Italians.

"Are we ever going to meet in person?" I asked Conor.

"I'll let you know when I come to Jersey. We'll get together," he replied pleasantly.

Uncle Louie and Conor went over a few final details on the shipment as I unpacked the feast: spicy capicola ham, sliced paper thin, on buttered fresh knotted rolls, all neatly wrapped in wax paper; a small container of sweet peppers; a thermos of lemonade; and a sugar cookie, one for each of us, for dessert. Uncle Louie ended the call. He carefully unwrapped the sandwich and studied it. He took a bite and chewed. "This is my favorite sandwich." His eyes narrowed. "What's my sister after? She's up to something."

"I think she's just being nice to her brother. Do you think she has an agenda?"

"Always." Uncle Louie sipped the lemonade. "This is delish, but you hit a point in life when nothing tastes like it used to."

"That's sad."

"Can be. But let's not be grim, shall we?" Uncle Louie fished a red pepper out of the jar with a plastic fork, popped it into his mouth, and chewed. "Philly canned these?" Louie nodded his approval. "My sister should've opened a restaurant. I offered to put her in business, but she couldn't get past that I didn't want her in marble."

"What was the problem?"

"An Italian family in business cannot endure."

"You're joking, right? Ferragamo? Prada? The House of Gucci is one hundred years old."

"You think those people cut the leather and make the shoes? *Mannaggia.* You think they work like you and me? No way! They farm the jobs out to manufacturers and put their name on it while they sit under a loggia on the Isle of Capri, drink wine, and fan themselves all summer as they watch the oligarchs sail by on their yachts. They work all right. They count the money; that's about the extent of the manual labor they do. That's why I like the Kerrigan kid. I got an honest set of eyes and ears in Italy; he's true-blue like his father before him. You never do better in business than a partnership with a good Irishman."

"What happened with you and Mom?"

"Your mother is not good with the public." Uncle Louie chose his words carefully, as though he was allowing himself to choose just one sweet off a cookie tray. "Philly does not possess what we call a human touch. She'd talk customers out of projects when her job was to talk them *into* an installation. If your mother were left to run Cap Marble and Stone, there'd be nothing left but slag by the time she was done with it. She just didn't have the knack."

"We asked her why she left the company. She always gave us a different answer."

"I fired her."

"We thought she quit. When she left the company, all she said was, 'I will never speak to my brother again.'"

"And that's another thing. Philly was conflict averse. Or should I say she was solution averse? She could fight all right, but she never knew what *for.* She read every situation as personal and took offense. Communication in business is everything. Did you hear me on the phone with Conor? We discuss, we plan, and I finesse. But my sister? Incapable. Philly would blow up, put me on ice, stonewall, and send me packing with a one-way ticket to the Island anytime she disagreed with me."

The Island was an imaginary place the Caps sent you when they weren't speaking to you. In other families, it's called the deep freeze or the silent treatment. Sometimes you didn't know why you had been banished to the Island. When circumstances changed and they decided to speak to you again, you had no idea how you got off the Island, and you didn't ask because you didn't want to go back on the Island.

I chewed a bite of the sandwich thoughtfully. My mother had sent so many people to the Island she had a timeshare on it. "Mom said that her failure in the company was preordained. She told us that your father favored you over her."

"That's a fair assessment. Look, my father was a good guy, but he was a typical immigrant. He didn't just move out of Italy; he packed it up and brought it with him. In that culture, a firstborn son can do no wrong. Ergo, your mother couldn't do anything right. That's just the way it was. Pop used to say when you have a son, you worry about one dick in town. When you have a daughter, you worry about every dick in town." Uncle Louie chuckled. "He had one of each, so he knew." He unwrapped his cookie from the wax paper and broke it in half. "Did Philly bake these?"

"Caroline Giovannini."

"Best baker in Lake Como." He dusted the crumbs off his hands with a paper napkin. "Enough with the biscotti. It's time, Jess, and I mean this sincerely. You gotta get back in the game. An overhaul is in order. I'm going to put a little extra in your paycheck this week. Buy yourself some clothes that aren't black. You're not in mourning; you got divorced. There's a difference."

"This is my professional look."

"If you're a Jesuit. You must up your game. Lil and I always say you are the prettiest Baratta girl. That face. You need a wardrobe to go with that face."

I looked down at my schlumpy black pants with the loose elastic waistband, shot from wear. I wore practical shoes because I didn't want to ruin my good ones on job sites. My uncle was right. I dressed like the aide who hands out the ice cream cups in a mental institution.

I cleaned up the picnic table and put the thermos back into the lunch bag. "I'm getting my hair done this weekend," I offered. "I may get bangs." I sounded pathetic.

"Get it out of that Heidi braid. The Alpine look is for saps unless you're wearing skis."

Slightly offended, I patted the long brown braid that rested on my shoulder like a pet snake. "This is a cascading braid," I clarify. "I'm in a rut."

"Climb out! You're squandering the juicy years. The time will come when you won't desire a new purse or good shoes. You'll give up entirely and keep your cash in your bra and wear foam sandals that seal with Velcro."

"I'm not there just yet."

He drew the letter *O* in the air with his finger. "You're circling."

I'M BEGINNING TO understand the importance of journaling. Writing helps me recall Uncle Louie's particular turns of phrase and his way of speaking and, in it, his intent.

Uncle Louie snores so loudly in the hospital bed, he'll eventually wake himself up. His long nostrils expand and contract as he breathes. He looks frail. Maybe it's the gray overhead light in the yellow room. My thoughts go to the worst outcome. I cannot imagine the world without him. I want a warning so I might prepare myself, but in my family, people don't linger; they sigh and die.

My phone buzzes on top of the plastic food storage tower on the hospital windowsill. I check my texts.

BOBBY: How is Louie? Ma called me.

JESS: Sleeping. They are running tests.

BOBBY: 🙏

JESS: Thanks. ❤️

BOBBY: ❤️ Hey. I didn't text back because I didn't know what to say. I was surprised to hear that you missed me. Let's talk later.

JESS: K

I have nothing to do in this hospital but agonize. Sometimes I wish things had worked out with Bobby, because there is nothing worse than being alone when you're afraid. So I open the notes app again and remember the moment I knew I loved Bobby Bilancia in the first place.

I stood stage right on a riser with a cluster of girls, all of whom, like me, had pleasant singing voices. We were the chorus for the 2004 annual musical, *Beauty and the Beast*. None of the girls in the chorus had auditioned for speaking roles because we were too terrified to compete. But we were also thirteen years old and seized the opportunity to defy our mothers and wear as much makeup as we wanted in public with the excuse that it was for theatrical purposes. I had troweled on so much mascara I could barely keep my eyes open. I wore pink blush and cranberry lip gloss, which up close made me look like a candy apple with eyes, but my intention was that the makeup would make me recognizable from the back row of the auditorium.

My fellow chorus girls were dressed as townspeople, in bridesmaid gowns borrowed from our mothers' closets. Grandma Cap provided aprons from her collection, which gave us the look of old-timey scullery workers. I wore a full-skirted mint-green taffeta gown with poofy cap sleeves with a deep V in the back. No fool, I'm wearing a T-shirt under the dress, to cover the backless triangle, so I'm not exposed in the rear. My apron has the country of Italy outlined in red rickrack, with a lone red felt star marking Carrara on the map.

Sister Theresa motioned to me. "Jess, will you please run lines with Bobby Bilancia?" she asked.

The girls looked at me with awe.

"*You* get to run lines with *Bobby*?" Hannah Malpiedo swooned.

"I help him with his math homework," I explained. Bobby lived two streets over, and around the time he stopped stealing my lunch, he began his struggles with math and I became his peer tutor. Sometimes we worked at his kitchen table, and sometimes we worked at mine. Both moms provided snacks, our choice of meatball heroes or *pastina in brodo* or chicken cutlet strips with marinara dipping sauce.

"I suck at math." Piera Casciano sighed as I followed Sister

Theresa off the stage and into the auditorium. "I can help Bobby with English!" she called after me.

Bobby sat alone in his Gaston costume on the floor of the hallway outside the auditorium. His mom had shredded one of his dad's old white dress shirts at the arms and waist. He'd belted his jeans with a rope and rolled them up to his knees. His black hair was combed into a pompadour. It was so high, it looked like he was wearing a black hat. He had a number 2 pencil tucked behind his ear.

Sister gave me her script because it had all the lines in it, and my script only had the pages with the scenes that involved the chorus.

"Bobby, Jess is going to run lines with you. You have to be off book by Saturday."

"Yes, Sister."

Sister shot me a look and went back inside the auditorium. The heft of the script with all of Sister's markings was impressive. I was empowered. After all, she put me in charge of the lead actor. I could not help but feel confident. I sat down next to Bobby.

"I don't remember the lines," he said sadly.

"You can do this," I told him. "Come on. I'll help you."

He smiled. "You always make me feel better, Jess." Bobby's eyes matched the high-gloss sky-blue industrial paint on the school walls. The chorus girls were right. Bobby Bilancia was definitely the best-looking boy in all of Saint Rose School. He drummed the pencil against his script. He turned to me, reached up with the pencil, and twirled the lead tip through a curl that stuck out of my kerchief.

"My hair is too curly."

"I like it." He smiled. "Does this costume look stupid?"

"Your mom needs to soak the shirt in tea, so it looks old."

"I'll ask her." Bobby looked into my eyes, which freaked me out a little. "You wouldn't tell me if it looked stupid. You never say a bad word about anyone."

"Would you tell me if I looked stupid in this dress?"

"You don't."

I blushed. "My mother wore this in 1986 when she was in a wedding. There's so much padding, it's like having boobs on my shoulders."

Bobby laughed. "You're hilarious."

I opened the script. "Let's start with the first scene." I cued his line.

BELLE
Get out of my way, Gaston.

Bobby Bilancia looked into my eyes. I couldn't tell if he was acting or if he liked me, but I was definitely into this pretend game.

Bobby delivered the line.

GASTON
You belong to me, Belle.

"Go ahead," I coached.

GASTON
You must never go into the forest alone, Belle.
It isn't safe . . .

"*You need . . .*" I prompted him.

"*You need a strong man to take care of you,*" Bobby read.

"Let's go over this again." I cued him. Sister Theresa had written her own adaptation of the story, and it sucked. I wanted to tell Bobby the truth, but I didn't want to undermine his confidence. I turned the page back to the top of the scene to run the lines.

"You have pretty eyes, Jess."

I looked down at the script, but before I could cue the next line, Bobby Bilancia kissed me. It was a quick kiss on my lips, but it was so exciting it felt as though it lasted about an hour and a half. My first kiss! I wanted to get up, run into the auditorium, and shout the news to the chorus. Instead, I looked down at the script.

"Sorry." He smiled. "I couldn't resist."

I pushed away from the wall and sat across from him on the floor instead of next to him. "We have to focus," I told him, but I didn't care about the musical, not really, because I'd just kissed Bobby Bilancia.

"YOU'RE ALWAYS ON that phone." Uncle Louie wakes and tries to sit up. "I miss a phone with a cord. We were tethered yet free."

"Rest." I put down the phone. "I'm journaling."

"That therapy thing is turning out to be a side hustle."

"No freakin' kidding." I laugh.

"Glad you think this is funny," Uncle Louie jokes.

I adjust the hospital blanket to cover Uncle Louie evenly from neck to toes.

"Where's Lil?"

"Sent her home with Ma to get some rest."

"How long have I been in here?"

"I'm not sure."

"There are only two places on earth where you lose track of time: the corner bar and hospitals. I'd place a long marriage in third place." Louie lies back on the pillow.

I check the clock on the wall. "You were admitted yesterday afternoon. It's two o'clock in the morning. Monday morning."

He sighs.

I grip the bed frame. "How do you feel?"

"Like I was hit over the head with a refrigerator."

"They're going to make you better." My voice breaks; the events of the last twelve hours catch up with me.

He looks around. "Is this a good hospital?"

"Who knows?"

"I appreciate your honesty. This is the first time I was ever in a hospital. When I was eleven years old, I broke my arm. Set it myself with duct tape. Ask your mother."

"She scared us with that story when we were kids. A cautionary tale."

"My elbow was never in the right place after that. Still isn't. The left one. Thank God elbows don't face front. Philly is still mad that I didn't go to the hospital. My sister believes there's always somebody in the world who knows more about you than you. That includes doctors."

"I googled your doctor. He has four stars on Star Doctor."

"Thanks, but the facts are the facts. Genetics matter. My father died after his third heart attack. Had two at home. The third one, on the way to the hospital, took him out."

"You've only had one incident," I remind him.

"Do you remember my father?"

"A little. He looked like the Monopoly man."

"That's him. Louie Cap Senior. Had white hair and a mustache. Compact in height yet sturdily built, like an anvil. He hated hospitals too. That's probably why he died en route in the ambulance. The thought of dying in a hospital killed him." Uncle Louie frowns. "If this is my last hurrah before the dirt nap, what a shame. Look at this place. I'm lying in a shitty Florsheim box when I've worn nothing but Guccis all my life."

"Because you have a narrow foot."

"I'm pleased you pay attention to the details." He smiles.

"You'll make it out of here."

"One way or the other. If it's the other, there are a few things you need to know. Lil is taken care of. When she dies, you will inherit whatever is left from Lil. You are our sole heir."

"Me?" The thoughts in my brain tumble over one another like confetti.

"You're also the executrix of my last will and testament. In the event of my demise, you get the business. I kept meaning to talk to you about it, but we were so busy with installations, I never got around to it. By the way, Guido and Rita Battaglini's pump went on the fritz. Order a new one. They're in Spring Lake."

"I'll take care of it."

"You'll take care of everything. When I get off this hayride, somebody has to drive the buggy."

"I'm not ready, Uncle Louie."

"I'm leaving you everything because I trust you."

"I don't want to talk about this. You'll be fine," I assure him.

"Wishful thinking is *stunod* thinking. Let's look at this like a fire drill. A precautionary conversation for an inevitable blaze."

"I can handle that." I pull up a chair next to his bed.

"I no longer own the clock. Time is slipping through my hands like a satin nightie on a gal named Slim in a whorehouse on my eighteenth birthday."

"You're going to get better."

"I don't think so," he says. "I'm not feeling it."

I stand up. My uncle is not horsing around. He believes he is dying, and he has never lied to me. "Are you scared?"

"No. And I don't want you to be scared either. This is the cycle of life. I went through it with my parents; you'll go through it with yours. We get sick, we get old, and we die, and if we're lucky, there's family around to transition us from this side to the other. I pity the people that got nobody. I'm grateful I got you."

"Do you believe in the afterlife?"

"I think it's a requirement of membership in the Knights of Columbus. So, yes. I do."

"Do you want to see a priest?" My voice breaks.

"When he makes his rounds. And not sooner. I have a rule regarding priests. Never call the rectory in the middle of the night unless you're delivering a pizza. I don't need a disgruntled cleric in here with an attitude. I want to go like I came in, unfettered by bullshit."

"I won't call the priest." I begin to sweat like I'm manning the deep fryers at the zeppole tent at the Feast in the hottest week of July.

"One thing about the estate. Lil's jewelry. When the time comes, that will go to her side. She has that whack-a-doodle sister, Carmel, and that strange niece. You know, Marina, the one that says she's allergic to the sun, so she goes nowhere—that one. Like she needs a brooch. Where's she goin'?"

"I'll take care of it."

"You're like a daughter to me and I want the company to stay in the family. You've been with me since high school."

"*College*," I correct him. "And only because I was a commuter and stayed local."

"Yeah, yeah. That's right. You were scared to go away to college, and I was the beneficiary."

"My college fund was lost in the 2008 market crash. Remember?" No one ever gets the details of my life right, not even Uncle Louie. "That's right, you wouldn't remember the date because Mom had sent you to the Island."

"Regardless. You could've come to me. If you wanted to go away to school, I would've sent you. No questions asked."

"I couldn't ask you for help. Mom would've disowned me."

"Right. Right." Uncle Louie nods. "Philly and her grudges. Epic."

I felt tremendous guilt whenever my mother and uncle had a falling-out, which, if I'm being honest, seemed to happen frequently through the years. I had to remain loyal to my mother, but I was torn. Aunt Lil and Uncle Louie are my godparents. I was in their house every chance I got. Their home was quiet, warm in the winter and cool in the summer. Nothing was broken. They had plush carpeting in every room. They never ran out of cold soda and potato chips. Aunt Lil and I would watch *General Hospital* together every day at three p.m. if I was around. Luke and Laura and Sonny and Carly were like family, even though they had better hair.

It was Uncle Louie who took me to see the Jonas Brothers in the city when I was fifteen. It was Uncle Louie who took me to my first ice show in Atlantic City, *Holiday on Ice* with Brian Boitano. I wanted to marry that ice skater someday. It was Uncle Louie who broke it to me that Brian would probably not want to marry me.

It was Uncle Louie who gave me my first diamond ring. It had a chip so small you had to rotate it in the noonday sun to see a glint of sparkle, but still, it was real. When it no longer fit, I wore it on a gold chain around my neck. Still do. It was Uncle Louie who cried throughout my wedding and danced with every woman in the room at my reception before he formed the conga line that included our ninety-seven-year-old cousin Schemer Romano in his wheelchair.

My uncle has feted, celebrated, and done right by me all my life. No wonder it seems like I've been working for him for sixteen minutes instead of sixteen years. He roots for me, and he doesn't have to; he could've been the typical Italian American godfather and given me a check for my birthday, a crisp fifty-dollar bill in a white, pearl-handled girl purse for my First Holy Communion, a novena card and an add-a-pearl gold necklace for confirmation, and a savings bond and extra cash to cover the plate when I got married. He's done so much more for me than the obligatory gifting; he believed in me when I didn't believe in myself.

My uncle taught me a trade and sent me to apprentice with a draftsman to learn how to draw. He schooled me in marble: how to import it, work with it, and install it. I know how to deal with people because of him. He pushed me through my anxiety and past my fears. When I mastered my nerves, he noticed I could talk to people and was a good listener. I dab my eyes.

"Don't cry. Doesn't matter now, Jess. So what? What is college anyhow? You missed out on tailgates, group gropes, and beer pong."

"They didn't have tailgates for day students at Montclair State." Doesn't Uncle Louie realize I couldn't care less about all I lost, because I could lose him?

"So you missed even less. Who needs a Philly cheesesteak on a soggy bun from the back of a station wagon anyhow? Forget it. That's not us. We may not be kings, but we eat like them. You got a better education on the road with me than you ever would have gotten at sleepaway college. And I know for sure you ate better lunches. Now. There are a few things you need to know. Specifically, the financial end."

"Sal Martino is your accountant, right?"

"He has a set of books, yes. But there's a second set."

"What do you mean?"

"There's Capodimonte's Marble and Stone. And then there's the Elegant Gangster."

"Who is he?"

"*It*," he corrects me. "That's my corporation in a secondary fiduciary position to the primary company."

My mind reels, alarm bells going off. "Why do you have two companies? And why is this the first I am hearing about it?"

Uncle Louie checks for nurses or eavesdroppers before he says, "*Uno per me, uno per Cesare.* One for me, one for Caesar. You know, Uncle Sam. I kept the ship afloat with this dual business model for many, many years. Served many masters, including my country. Nothing wrong with the model."

"Unless the IRS comes after us." I look around the hospital room for a paper bag. I choke on the imaginary smoke of my job as it goes up in flames.

"Take it easy." Uncle Louie hands me the Styrofoam cup with ice water. "Sip this slowly."

I drink the water. It goes down ice-cold like the truth. "I wish it were a highball."

"Me too." Uncle Louie goes on. "The Elegant Gangster is a company I use to resell whatever marble I don't use on the jobs. Call them remnants. What were we gonna do? Return them?"

"Who is we?"

"Googs and me. He distributes what we don't use."

"Uncle Louie, it's called double-dipping." I wipe my damp forehead on my sleeve. Uncle Louie makes money on product that he has already sold that does not belong to him. It belongs to the customer. Now I understand why he buys double and sometimes triple what he needs for an installation. I thought he overbought because he was afraid there wouldn't be enough stone to finish a job, but he knew what he was doing. So I clarify, "The marble is paid for twice."

"I bill separately. What are you worried about? I'm a typical small business. You call it double-dipping. I call it refusing to waste precious natural resources."

"How do you report the additional sales?"

"I do not. The sales were made on international waters. Free and clear of all tax liability."

"But the ship docks in New Jersey! Where does the money go when you collect it?"

"There are a couple of accounts offshore in the Cayman Islands."

"Oh God." I feel faint.

"Hey, I have overhead. Taxes are a yoke. I pay them handsomely on round one; why would I be compelled to pay them twice? Caesar wasn't stupid and neither is Louie Cap. I got a big nut. You think my home with all manner of accoutrements is cheap? Me and my wife have all the luxuries. You see your aunt. They call her Diamond Lil for good reason. And steam rooms aren't cheap."

"You could've joined a gym! You didn't have to build one! Does Aunt Lil know about the Incomparable Gangster?"

"Elegant," Uncle Louie corrects me. "No. I never troubled her. Not that she took an interest. I wanted her to have a cushy life with no worries. It was the least I could do. She had enough of a burden. We weren't blessed with children, so we had fun. I couldn't do enough for her. I filled her life with jewelry, chandeliers, cars, and her own walk-in closet. And trips."

"You didn't splurge, really. You went to Florida once a year." I rationalize my uncle's behavior, rehearsing a rap for future depositions. "You didn't even rent a car. You put the Impala on the Auto Train."

"Because Florida was the only place Lil would go. She's a rut person. Down south, on Miami Beach, we're known as the Predictables for good reason. We booked the same room at the Fontainebleau Hotel, number 317 with an ocean view, every year since 1979. The routine was such: Lil sunned from eleven to three. At three, she went into the room to watch her story, after which she showered and dressed for dinner. I can tell you what she ordered for dinner at Mirabella, their in-house restaurant, because it never varied. A whiskey highball with three cherries. Lamb chops crisp. Creamed spinach on the side. Chocolate flambé for dessert. Every time they torched the pudding her eyes lit up like it was Christmas morning and Santa Baby delivered another diamond ring. I wanted to show Lil the world, and we got as far as Miami Beach." Uncle Louie lays his head back on his pillow. "I wanted to show you Italy, kid. Ah well."

"We are going to Italy." I go to the window for fresh air. I inhale the air in sips.

"I had a love in Italy."

"A few, I bet."

"Nope. Only one. A tomato called Claudia."

I have tried to enlighten my uncle on the fringe elements of sexism, but he is incapable of change. He calls pretty women *tomatoes*, idiots are *artichokes*, and a *scungilli* is a creep. He calls a difficult person a *schiaccianoci*, a nutcracker, and anyone who bores him with a story and can't get to the pith is a *patata*, a potato, but I've also heard him call anyone with homely features a *patata*.

"Claudia was a beauty?"

"At the time, she was *it* for me. I saw her in the Piazza Alberica in Carrara. I made her tell me the story of the statue. Some lady with a bird. That's how I got to her. Pretended I was interested in local history. I'd like to see her again."

"You're a married man."

"I wasn't then. It doesn't count if you loved someone before the one you love. It's like a free space in bingo. Look, Lil is my wife, but that doesn't mean she was the only nugget in the mine."

"Ugh."

"What *ugh*? I wasn't her only love either. I just ended up being better."

"What was it about Claudia, the Italian girl?"

"I don't know. When you're young, you can't define love, or maybe you don't want to. Love is the divine mystery of life when it works out."

"But it didn't."

"In Italy, it isn't what the girl wants; it's what her father will allow. That guy hated me and sent me packing. No daughter of his was going to marry a stonecutter. An *Amerigan*. I wasn't worthy of her."

"But your roots are in Carrara. You're as Italian as they are!"

"Didn't matter to him. All he saw was Yankee Doodle Louie. I never said goodbye to Claudia, and I didn't go back because I met Lil and that was that." Uncle Louie squints at me without lifting his head off the pillow. "You all right over there?"

"It's a lot, Uncle Louie. A lot to take in." I have wrapped the cord from the window shade around my index finger so tightly the digit is turning blue. I unwind it.

"Who knows what I would have become if I had stayed in Italy?"

"You did all right. You did great. But the first thing we'll do when you're out of here is close down the Elegant Gangster. From now on, everything on the books. I mean it, Uncle Louie."

"Whatever you want."

I breathe deeply. "It's not a matter of choice; it's what's right. And let's get this straight. You're going to do what the doctors say and get well and get the hell out of here."

"Here," he says. "Take my phone. If you have any further questions about the business, call Googs. He can be elusive, so be persistent."

"Which business?" I jab, and immediately feel guilty.

Uncle Louie is pale. I squeeze his hand. "I want you to listen while I still retain my facilities."

"*Faculties.*"

"Them too. There's a laptop, you'll find it in my suit closet upstairs off the bedroom. There's a hard drive. It's in the medicine chest—in the powder room nobody uses off the kitchen."

"The one with the kooky wallpaper."

"That one. Scalamandre number 412. A hundred and seventy-five bucks a roll with no repeat. Worth every penny. Open the medicine chest. The hard drive is stored in a perfume box about yea big." He pinches his thumb and forefinger to measure. "It's either in Moonwind or To a Wild Rose. The whole freakin' medicine chest is filled with overstock Lil saved from back when she was an Avon lady."

Evidently Uncle Louie wasn't the only one double-dipping.

He continued. "The hard drive is in there. Find it. Put the drive in my laptop. If you put it in yours, they could come after you."

"Who?"

"The feds. They may not understand my business model."

"Neither do I!" I feel my throat close.

"Breathe, Jess. It's not that complicated. Everything is on the hard drive. There are lists. My contacts. The billing. The shipping. All of it. You will figure it out."

I inhale and exhale as I straighten the blanket on one side of the bed and walk around to smooth it on the other. "We'll deal with all of this tomorrow," I tell my uncle as he sleeps. I have leaned down to fluff the pillow when the square silver machine over the bed begins to beep. Soon the beeps accelerate and get louder until they blast like a smoke alarm. I panic and try to follow the wires to the electrodes on his chest and the IV in his arm when the nurses burst through the door.

"Out!" a nurse shouts at me as she crosses to my uncle. The rest of the nurses surround the bed; one carries paddles.

"What? Why?" I ask, but my plea is lost in the chaos as I'm pushed against the wall.

The nurse climbs on the bed and straddles Uncle Louie. She places the paddles on Uncle Louie's chest. The paddles seem huge and Uncle Louie small. She presses. His body lurches off the mattress to no avail. The machines go silent. The nurse climbs off the bed.

"We're sorry," is the next thing I hear. "Are you his daughter?"

"His niece."

Another nurse checks her watch. "Three thirteen a.m."

I look at Uncle Louie. The color drains from his face. He grows as pale as the pink paisley hospital gown he's wearing. "He's gone?"

"We tried. I am sorry," she says with great kindness. "We'll give you time with him. Take as long as you need."

"I have to call my aunt. My mom. The family. They were just here. They wanted to be with him." I panic.

She places her hand on my arm. "It's my experience that the patient chooses the person to witness his passing. That's you, hon. I'm sorry."

This can't be true. I look up as though I'll locate Uncle Louie's soul floating overhead and yank it out of thin air and put it back in his body. He'd give me a wink, like a secret signal, one only I would understand. But there's nothing but white pressboard over my head. I feel a strange chill and shudder. "Where did you go, Uncle Louie?" I look down at him. There's a little smile on his face, not smug, but a warm one that seems to say, *I told you I had a lousy ticker.*

My hand shakes as I call my mom. She doesn't pick up. I text my father to wake up my mother and tell her so she can go and get Aunt Lil and bring her to the hospital. I text my sister to go and be with my mother. I text my brother to go and be with my sister. I text my father again to make sure that my mother, sister, and brother are okay when I think: *Just group text.*

Uncle Louie is gone. He went peacefully at 3:13 a.m.

The nurses return to prepare my uncle for his trip to the Frank R. Cortese Funeral Home. I know for sure that's where he's going because I wrote it down on his admission form yesterday as Uncle Louie instructed. I thank the nurses and excuse myself to step outside into the hallway. I'm numb. I lean against the wall and slide down until I'm seated on the spotless, polished linoleum floor.

Uncle Louie used to say that the floors of the great institutions are always made of marble because it is the only stone that stands the test of wear over time. "Ain't the Colosseum still standing? The Vatican? Grand Central Station? Your mother's half bath?"

In honor of Uncle Louie, I look for the marble. I find it in the white baseboards along the corridor, which form a trim on the wall with rounded edges. A sign. Uncle Louie also said if you saw marble anywhere in New Jersey, he was the jackass who hauled it over from Italy. Louie Capodimonte was no jackass; what he knew, he knew. And he knew marble.

6

Birds of Passage

Some Italians who immigrated to America at the turn of the twentieth century eventually moved back to Italy. They worked and saved while they were here and returned home in better shape than when they left. These birds of passage had a love for Italy that was bigger than their American dream. The Caps and Barattas stayed, living and dying in their new country. We believe we take flight when we die, on a journey back to the source. In that sense, we are all birds of passage, even Uncle Louie. I wonder if he knew that he changed the lives of every person who had the privilege of knowing him. He was a man you were happy to see, regardless of the circumstance.

Every person in my family who was present with my uncle when he collapsed would remember what they needed to take away from the experience. The children would remember the magic quarters. Connie would recall that Uncle Louie said he loved her, while Joe would remember that he prevented further trauma by helping our uncle to the floor before he hit his head. Diego would regret that he mentioned Aunt Lil and Uncle Louie were childless. My father would lament that he didn't do enough to save his brother-in-law. My mother would remember that her brother disinvited her to Italy and keeled over before he could make it right and reverse his decision to include her. Aunt Lil would remember it as the night she lost her husband and became a widow. I would look back on that Sunday dinner as our Last Supper, the end of life as the Caps and Barattas knew it on Lake Como. I would recall that night as the death of my Italian dream, which also marked the moment when I lost the only person in my life who had my back.

THE MONA LISA BEAUTY SALON

"What are we going for?" Lisa Natalizio puts her face next to mine in the well-lit mirror. She sparkles with strategically placed blond highlights and shiny blue-green eyes, while I am pale and washed out, like a dirty *mopeen* at the bottom of the bucket after the car has been washed.

"Thanks for keeping the shop open for me." I avoid my face in the mirror because I haven't slept. "I want to look good for Uncle Louie. It was his dying wish."

"My pleasure," she says as she pumps the chair until my head is at eye level with her scissors. An appointment at the Mona Lisa Beauty Salon in the Belmar Mall is coveted: CLASSIC LOOKS FOR MODERN WOMEN, the sign over the door says. Lisa is all about her family and friends. (The shop is named for her mother, Mona, and the proprietor, of course. Bobby and I aren't the only graduates of Saint Rose who went into a family business.)

The shop is closed but Lisa stayed late for me. The final plans for Uncle Louie's viewing and funeral are overwhelming. The great hair stylists know their skills are needed most when looking presentable is the last thing on a woman's mind. Lisa and I have been friends since kindergarten; she's been styling my hair since she got her beautician's license at twenty-one. Even Lisa went away for school; she studied at the Bumble and Bumble salon in New York City.

"I can give you any look you want. You're in mourning, so nothing drastic," Lisa says. "What are you wearing?"

"I haven't thought about it."

"I got an LBD. It's C-U-T-E. I'll drop it off at your mother's."

"Y-E-S. Can we stop with the spelling?"

She ignores my request and goes on. "It's my go-to for wakes, funerals, and my annual visit to the accountant. It would be my honor to loan it to you. Your uncle was a good guy. Always with a joke." She squints at me in the mirror. "You realize I knew Uncle Louie as long as I've known you. So, let's lighten up in his honor. We're gonna do some highlights around your face. I can paint them at the sink."

"Paint me however you see me. Just don't give me the Saint Rose Primary School special."

"I had lousy equipment," Lisa says defensively. "Who can cut anything but pipe cleaners with those blunt scissors?"

"You did. You cut off all of my hair. You gave me the Scout cut from *To Kill a Mockingbird*."

"Will you ever forgive me?"

"I did. But my mother? Never."

"It grew out, didn't it?"

"Like weeds." I smile for the first time since Uncle Louie died. "Are you still seeing the electrician?"

Lisa makes a face. "Lights out."

"You'll meet somebody new."

"I'm two dates in with the guy that owns the Kiffle Kitchen. But there hasn't been a Norman invasion of this Italian girl since my sophomore year at Marywood," she says as glops of my brown hair hit the floor. I tense up in the chair.

"I'm cutting to the shoulder. It will give you movement," Lisa says soothingly as she snips. "So. Bobby Bilancia moved back to Ocean Avenue."

"I heard."

"Got a house."

"I know."

"When you guys got divorced, all hope was lost. If you two couldn't make it, what does that say about the rest of us?"

"It says don't look at anyone else to define your relationship."

"Good point. I mean, I'm trying. I'm out there. I persist. I'm on those crap apps. I've had more cups of cold coffee with un-hot men than I can count. Have you signed up yet?"

"Nope." I'm not ready to date. I'm not ready to think about dating, but I don't want to depress the only other single woman my age in Monmouth County, so I keep my thoughts to myself.

"Maybe you could put aside whatever issues you and Bobby have and take a run at it again?"

"I guess anything is possible." I can't kill Lisa's dream, not when she holds the scissors.

THE FRANK R. CORTESE Funeral Home of Belmar, a stately white brick Georgian with black shutters, is lit with powerful floodlights that mimic the kliegs at a movie premiere in Hollywood's Golden Age. The entrance is flanked by two large terra-cotta planters fanned with stalks of pink gladiolas and festooned with white ribbons. The Corteses have served as the undertakers for the dearly departed of our family for generations. The first investment the

Caps and Barattas make before buying a new car or putting the down payment on a house is to pay in advance for our funerals: *Lay away before you're laid away.*

Inside the marble foyer (Uncle Louie installed it in 1984), a junior version of the black-and-white diamond-checker-patterned floor of Westminster Abbey, there are jardinieres stuffed with day lilies and more gladiolas in brushed-gold urns.

The sign for Uncle Louie's viewing outside the funeral home is propped in a frame on an easel in white letters punched into a black velvet board. The table bearing the sign-in book also holds a crystal bowl of breath mints and a spread of Uncle Louie's Mass cards, with his dates of birth and death and words of wisdom from Saint Jude. The Mass card tree will soon be filled with envelopes as mourners line up to pay their respects. Cash donations in sympathy cards are a tradition in the same vein as *la busta*, where money is collected for the happy couple at a wedding. Family and friends donate to cover the expenses of the funeral, with extra for a Mass said in Louie's name at our church. There will be so many people praying Uncle Louie's immortal soul to higher ground in heaven, he will breeze through purgatory like it's the HOV lane on the Jersey Turnpike during rush hour on Friday afternoon.

The viewing rooms are painted a delicate seashell pink, from ceiling to floor. The walls match the carpeting. Uncle Louie is laid out in a mahogany casket under the same pink lights they use to keep the prime rib warm at the Sons of Italy Easter dinner.

Lisa Natalizio's LBD is JTT (just the thing). Honestly, it's a little tight, but who's going to be looking at me? I yank it down from the hem as I bend over to read the tribute cards on the flowers. There's a marble arch made out of white carnations from Louie's trade union. Next to it, a large round floral replica of the face of a clock made of red carnations with Louie's time of death, in clock hands made with yellow carnations, with a card signed by Googs, *Remember the Good Times.* Uncle Louie isn't here to remember. But I am. No more slices of pizza when he's feeling peckish at four o'clock. No jelly doughnuts from the Dunkin' drive-through when his sugar drops. I never minded his dietary quirks or hearing his stories on a loop. There's no one to tell the story of meeting Steve and Eydie in an elevator in Vegas in 1982, no one left to identify family members in old photographs, no one in the family who knows every lyric to "American Pie," and no one to perform magic tricks. Louie Cap is gone.

Joe has his arm around Aunt Lil's waist; she looks tiny in her black bouclé suit. Connie takes her hand as they stand before the open casket. My mother and father stand behind them. Mom has a bottle of smelling salts in her black patent leather dress purse, just in case Aunt Lil faints. After Aunt Lil pays her respects, my sister and brother help her to her seat in the front row to receive the mourners.

Connie, Joe, and I have taken our seats in the row behind Aunt Lil when Mom turns and jams her finger into my rib cage. "Stand and greet the mourners." I look to Connie and Joe—hardly kids, we're in our thirties, but suddenly we're nine, eleven, and fourteen again.

"I want this affair to roll out like Princess Grace's funeral. Class all the way," Mom whispers. We stand erect like we're the royal family of Monaco lining up on the balcony to witness cannon fire on a holiday. Mom and Dad move up to our row, taking the aisle seats.

Lisa Natalizio is first in line to pay her respects.

"That dress looks better on you than it ever did on me." Lisa tucks the Mass card in her purse and I accompany her to the kneeler in front of the open casket.

"Louie looks good," she whispers.

It means a lot coming from someone who has a certificate in cosmetology.

"Is it too soon to pray to him? I have a third date with Blaine Gundersen of the Kiffle Kitchen."

"Uncle Louie will help you from the other side," I promise her. "You have to make a space to fill it." So, this is how the process of grief is going to unspool. I'm going to quote Uncle Louie and sound like wisdom you find on a refrigerator magnet.

"All cried out?" Lisa looks closely at me.

"I haven't cried yet," I tell her.

"Open the floodgates. Trust me. You'll feel better." She squeezes my hand. "I'm gonna sign the book." Lisa makes a quick sign of the cross and returns to the foyer.

The Color Corps of the Knights of Columbus, some around Uncle Louie's age, a few older, march into the room wearing black tuxedos, capes, patent leather dress shoes, red-and-white silk sashes, and Napoléon-era chapeaus with white ostrich plumes. The somber fourth-degree knights move into formation, creating a semicircle behind the casket. Once in place, the men raise their swords like a flank of Roman centurions in the fourth century awaiting the command to attack Avellino.

I'm thinking I might finally weep when my sister elbows me and whispers, "Bobby's here."

Bobby towers over the mourners—not a stretch, because most of them are over eighty years old and under five foot three. In this light, Bobby Bilancia holds on to the golden hue of his summer tan. He is crisp and pressed, in a dark blue suit, white shirt, and navy-and-white-striped tie. He respectfully maintains his gaze on the casket while every woman in the room rests her eyes on him.

There was no need for Connie to announce that my ex-husband

was in the room because his delicious scent did the job for her. This is a man whose natural fragrance is a combination of peppermint and the Como woods after the rain, and while I am certain I made the right decision in leaving him, my single regret is that I had to leave the musk of Bobby Bilancia behind. But I couldn't take it with me and leave our issues behind; it was an all-or-nothing deal.

I'm glad I wore the three-inch black suede stilettos instead of flats. I'll think about why it's important that I look attractive for my ex-husband in a state of grief later. Bobby works his way from Aunt Lil through the line to me, expressing his condolences for our loss. From the looks on the faces of the mourners as their eyes travel from me to Bobby and back again, it's clear that the stench of my divorce lingers far and wide across the state of New Jersey like the emissions from the glue factory in Newark. They believe I was an idiot to leave him.

"You holding up okay, hon?" Bobby says in my ear as he embraces me, covering my body like a warm blanket.

"Thank you for being here."

"I wouldn't be anywhere else."

"I know," I whisper. Bobby may not be the best texter, or an avid reader, but he is a huge part of the first third of my life should I live to be ninety. This was the man I promised to love forever, and this is why, in some way, I always will. Bobby Bilancia is incapable of holding a grudge.

"Louie Cap was a good soul," Bobby says. "He loved you, Jess."

Bobby lets go of me and gently touches my cheek before kneeling before Uncle Louie's casket. Bobby's shoulders are so broad you could serve dinner for eight on his back. He begins to make the sign of the cross with his right hand. He taps his forehead, then his chest. He extends his hand to his far shoulder (it's a reach), then his near one. He presses his hand to his lips. Bobby's sign of the cross is technically smooth, like a secret signal detonated by the Giants quarterback as he alerts the offensive line before a play.

My mother narrows her eyes at me and cocks her head toward Bobby, with a look that says her physically proportioned ex-son-in-law is a loss she feels daily. Without saying a word, she makes the point that cutting this good man loose in a world where there are precious few of them was the biggest mistake of my life. I flash to a memory of her dancing with Bobby at our wedding, and it makes me sad, but not sad enough to cry. I'm going to return this handkerchief to my mother in pristine condition.

The Sodality of Saint Rose enters the funeral home single file. They walk slowly up the main aisle, forming a line on either side of the casket. Mom stands and joins them. The sound of purses snapping open and rosary beads rattling is soon replaced by the drone of Hail Marys as we enter the glorious mysteries with Babe Bilancia as prayer leader.

My former mother-in-law is a beauty. Babe is round and well powdered, like a zeppole. In her youth, she was small and curvy like a violin; now her shape is similar to a bass fiddle. She has kept the shoulder-length jet-black hair blown straight in a chin-length bob since I've known her. There's a furtive look in her bright blue eyes, but there always has been, all the way back to Saint Rose School, when she was the homeroom mother and brought thirty-six cupcakes to school with Bobby's face on them and it wasn't even his birthday.

At the conclusion of the rosary, Mom, Dad, and Aunt Lil stand. My parents flank Aunt Lil as they follow the Sodality and the Knights of Columbus out of the viewing room, through the foyer, and outside into the parking lot. Soon, I am alone with Uncle Louie.

The scent of roses fills the air, a sign that Saint Padre Pio is hovering over us, or it's possible that Mr. Cortese replaced the scent plug in the hallway outlet. (I'm going with the saint.) Uncle Louie and I talked about his devotion to Padre Pio on our long drives between jobs. He said, *Padre Pio cured everybody that touched him, but he couldn't save himself. Poor bastard. Suffered terribly. Got the stigmata, you know. He'd be eating a plate of macaroni and spring a leak.* We had hoped to visit Padre Pio's cell in the rectory in Puglia, sit on his cot, and try on his glove. Now I will never do any of those things, because a pilgrimage without Uncle Louie would not be the same; in fact, it wouldn't even matter.

I kneel before the casket. Uncle Louie is laid out in his best suit and tie, a forest-green pinstripe in silk wool, with a crisp white shirt and purple tie. I straighten the K of C sash and pat his cold hand. I'm glad they put the vest on him. He would not have wanted to go through eternity without the cinch. His hands are folded, a rosary of black beads woven through his fingers. Luckily, Uncle Louie and I had manicures over our lunch hour a couple of days before he went into the hospital, so his nails are short, neat, and buffed. He would be happy about the timing.

"You would be pleased with your wake," I say quietly. "Big turnout. The guest book is full."

Memories are the art of emotion, Uncle Louie said when we replaced a floor in Christy Ronca's home, exactly as it had been installed years earlier by Grandpop Cap. I had attempted to talk her into a modern, fresh design, but she wanted the same floor she always had. Uncle Louie told me not to push. *We remember in order to hold on.*

"Please help me hold on," I ask Uncle Louie. I make the sign of the cross and rise from the kneeler.

I grab my purse in the coat room. I'm starving. I'm looking forward to the array of bereavement desserts that await me at home in Mom's kitchen. When Grammy B died, it took me one week to eat an entire Texas sheet cake by myself, but I did it. After the first slice or two, I didn't bother to use a plate and fork; I just left the knife in the pan and sliced off a piece here and there until there was nothing left but crumbs and my low self-esteem.

When I arrive home, my parents are already upstairs in bed. Every surface of the kitchen is covered with pans, tins, and Tupperware containers full of desserts. There are trays heaped with lemon bars, seven-layer cookies, and cannoli. There are enough cakes on pedestals to pull an all-night cake walk at the Feast. There are two Bundt cakes soaked in rum that give the kitchen the scent of a dive bar in Freehold.

I search through the bounty until I find Genevieve Belcastro's Texas sheet cake. I grab a steak knife and cut a hefty square of the chocolate-and-coconut confection. I open the refrigerator and pour myself a glass of milk. The refrigerator is packed with charcuterie platters of capicola, sliced turkey, and roast beef. There are layers of casserole dishes and a gigantic plastic bowl with macaroni salad. Mom is all set for the funeral luncheon after the graveside service. Usually, the sight of all of this would make me cry, but I don't.

I make my way down to the cellar with the milk and cake. I place the cake on the table, wriggle out of Lisa's dress, and put on my pajamas. I check my face in the mirror as I brush my teeth. I look awful for someone who has yet to shed a tear.

I climb into bed and balance the laptop on my thighs. I log in to Thera-Me, where I find a response to my plea to stay with Dr. Sharon.

Dear Patient Jess,

We believe the patient is best served by rotation care. Team mental health care is effective and we provide the best online therapy anywhere. Please complete the form for Exercise 2 with Dr. Raymond at your earliest convenience.

Your Thera-Me Team

Ugh.

Dear Dr. Raymond,

Exercise 2 is attached. I have a pressing issue, however, for which I need your advice immediately. I just lost the most important person in my adult life and I cannot cry. Is something wrong with me? I'm frozen. Please advise.

G.C.B.

I look over at the cake and decide to save it for breakfast. I pull the duvet and quilt up to my chin before turning out the light. Mrs. Cartegna promised to hold the apartment in Hoboken if I could drop off the deposit sometime next week.

I'm trying to pray in the dark when a ferocious wind kicks up outside; the gusts are so loud they rattle the cellar windows that overlook the lawn. I sit up in bed as the screen door to the outside blows open and swirls of fallen leaves blow into the cellar. Soon, I make out a figure in the doorway. The shape of the head and line of the shoulders, the musculature, all familiar. Bobby Bilancia doesn't speak. He comes to my bed. In an instant, I look spectacular. My hair is shiny and smooth like I've been rolled over by a Zamboni. I've got smoky eyes, dewy skin, and moist lips. When I shudder, Bobby comes into my bed and holds me tightly until my temperature rises high enough to stop the shivers. I begin to sweat as though I'm hacking through brush in a sweltering jungle. The garden thermometer on the wall has a red line that rises to the top. The walls rattle and the bed shakes like the entire house is inside a blender on pulse. I can hear the swell of the ocean even though we are half a mile from the beach. The light of the full moon fills the cellar, which turns us pale blue, like Carrara marble.

Bobby scoops me up until we are standing next to the bed. There's wind; the lights blast; the moon shimmers overhead. Now we're on a dance floor under a tent, the last two guests at the party, except for the DJ, who plays music. The world has fallen away, and we don't care; we don't miss it.

Bobby's hands rest on my hips as he kisses my neck on the way to my mouth. I close my eyes as his lips gently touch mine. I melt into him with a feeling of belonging, the best part of being married to him. He pushes my new, frizz-free, perfect-length bangs off my forehead. He likes the new haircut! I don't hear the snap of the buttons as the top of my pajamas falls away, because they aren't pajamas; I wear a pink chemise I wore to see Cirque du Soleil on our honeymoon in Las Vegas. Bobby kneels down and slips my feet out of the feathered mule slippers, tossing them over his shoulder. I'm wearing pajamas again! These pajamas are embroidered in a palm-leaf design, like the exotic wallpaper in Aunt Lil's downstairs powder room. Bobby's hands travel all over me as he undresses me. The heat from his touch creates an urgency as we make love. Why is the cellar screen door off its hinges? Why is the world shaking? Why the thunder and lightning but no rain?

I remove his tie and unbutton his shirt. I kiss his chest and undo his belt. He cradles me tightly before he places me on his bed. He trips and covers me with his body. We laugh but do not speak. I can't speak. I cannot form words.

The light in the room dims. The moon must have gone behind the clouds, but inside, it's just bright enough to see his eyes as he drinks me in. He kisses me with urgency before he pulls the coverlet down; I climb under it. The sheets are cool as he pulls me toward him. I wrap around him with ease. He knows my body as his own; he knows how to please me. If only we could talk to each other! All the things I would say!

Bobby gently slides me on top of him, kisses me as though he has to make up for the time we've been apart. The bed begins to lift off the floor, like cake batter spilling over as it rises in the oven. I peer over the side as the mattress ascends. As Bobby kisses me, the bed lurches higher and higher toward the ceiling. Before we hit the ceiling, the bed stops. I slide off Bobby onto the mattress and cling to him. The cellar floor is miles away. I can't breathe. He wraps around me like a silk rope. His body is pressed against mine. The bed bounces up and down. I pull the coverlet over Bobby and hold him close.

"Giuseppina!"

I wake up and open my eyes. "Ma?" I'm groggy and feel lost.

"You were having some dream." My mother is fully made up while wearing her bathrobe. "Thrashing all around." She picks up the uneaten cake and glass of milk from the table from the night before. "I'll take this upstairs. We don't want to get mice."

I look down, relieved to see I am still wearing pajamas. I wrap the coverlet around me.

"We have the final viewing before the Mass at the church," Connie says brightly as she descends the stairs wearing a black wool suit and Pappagallo flats.

"What are you doing here?" I get out of the bed.

"I told Ma to let you sleep, and then we almost forgot about you. What are you wearing to the funeral?"

"I'll meet you upstairs," Mom says, and goes.

Connie looks through my closet. "This is easy. Everything is black."

"My hair." I look in the mirror. It is sticking up like the rays on a monstrance. Or maybe that's just the sun-kissed streaks seeking a light source. I pat down my new bangs and spray some curl enhancer, then realize it's a bottle of bug spray.

"Ponytail," Connie says. "When did you get bangs?"

Does anyone in my family ever look at me? I had the bangs at the viewing last night.

Connie holds up two clothing options for the funeral, a suit and the dress Lisa loaned me. "Which one? The dress?"

"I wore it last night." More proof that no one looks at me. "I can't breathe in it. I'll wear the suit."

"Mom won't like that you're in pants."

"Really? I lost my best friend in the world, and I can't mourn his passing in pants?"

Connie sits down on the edge of the bed. "Was Uncle Louie your best friend?" she asks sadly.

I nod.

"I'll be your best friend," Connie promises.

"You're my sister. That's enough of a load."

"Move it along, girls!" my father bellows from the top of the stairs. "Aunt Lil can't be late."

Connie helps me dress quickly. We run up the stairs and out to the porch. The family cars are lined up in front of our house, a pre-funeral cortege. Dad is helping Aunt Lil into Uncle Louie's Impala. Diego takes the driver's seat while Connie helps their girls into Joe and Katie's minivan, where the children squeeze in and sit on top of one another like a stack of sippy cups.

My mother rolls down the driver's-side window of her cabriolet and leans out the window. "Giuseppina. Come with me."

My new best friend, Connie, shoots me a look of support before tucking into the Impala. I get into the passenger seat as my mother starts the car.

My mother wears head-to-toe black: square-framed sunglasses, a black linen coat dress, suede knee boots, and matching gloves. If she wanted to kill someone, she wouldn't leave a trace in this getup. She frowns as she pulls out into the street behind my dad, who follows Joe. "I don't like pants at a funeral."

"I don't like that Uncle Louie died."

"Do you have anything to tell me?" She doesn't bother to wait for an answer. "Babe Bilancia called this morning and said you and Bobby were texting when Louie was in the hospital. I mean, something is going on. He put on a suit for Louie's wake. Is there something I need to know?"

"It's none of Babe's business. I don't think about Bobby anymore," I fib. At least not thoughts I can control.

"Aunt Lil wants you to make a few remarks at the funeral Mass."

"I can't."

I'm more concerned I might make it through *without* weeping, which would be worse than if I stood up at the lectern and collapsed in a tsunami of tears in front of the congregation. My mother hasn't noticed I have barely registered an emotional reaction to Uncle Louie's death. This is the reality of the forgotten, put-upon daughter; the only thing that matters is that I'm not wearing a skirt. As if appearances matter on this dark day.

"Are you sure you can't get up and say a few words? How about a reading? Or you could do something wordless like bring up the gifts. I really wish you had worn a dress."

"Well, I didn't. And you have me confused with someone else, Ma. I can't do any of it. No readings. No eulogies. No thoughts and no prayers." My thoughts are a jumble, and my prayers weren't answered, so I suggest, "Let Joe give the eulogy."

"All right," Mom agrees, fanning her fingers in black suede before gripping the steering wheel. "You were never one to take the stage." Mom nods with understanding. "When you did take it, you were in the chorus. Nothing wrong with that. The glare of the spotlight is not for everyone."

"I would have done anything for Uncle Louie—wherever he is, he knows."

When we enter the church, I feel eyes on me; the mourners are looking for my tears, as though I owe them a breakdown. But I can't cry. I'm angry.

7

The Grief Buffet

THE DINING ROOM table was loaded with food, prepared and dropped off by the ladies of the church Sodality. We're down to a few platters, some lingering friends, and our family. The topics of conversation were repeated on a loop: the funeral Mass was lovely, the burial windy, and the mini prime rib tea sandwiches from Bilancia Meats were scrumptious.

I clear dishes and carry them to the kitchen. My hands are deep in suds when I hear, "Lemme help you, Jess." I turn to face Bobby, who smiles at me.

"I'll take over," he says.

"You were always great about doing the dishes." I lift my hands out of the water. Bobby hands me a dish towel.

He bumps me with his hip. "You dry. I'm a better washer."

"Just like old times!" Babe Bilancia announces from the doorway. "You don't see me! I'm here for my Tupperware." She scans the kitchen and finds the square plastic container with a handle. "I'm outta here." Babe waves goodbye and goes out the kitchen door.

Bobby and I laugh.

"Let's get out of here," he says. "You up for a walk?"

BOBBY GUIDES ME across the street to the walking path along Lake Como. The setting sun glints like a brass button on a bolt of lilac flannel as the lights inside the houses on the lake turn on at dusk. The only sound is the trill of a Bonaparte gull as it swoops through the sky and skims onto the surface of the water. The bird is a sleek missile of Calacatta marble in her black-and-white plumage. I take Bobby's arm as we walk along the water's edge.

The newly fallen leaves crunch under our feet. When the path along the lake narrows, Bobby guides me to walk in front of him. He is a good communicator when we aren't looking at each other.

"We came up the same way, Jess. Those are the things in life you can count on. The only difference? You had the view of Lake Como, which made you just a little better off than my tribe over on Ocean Avenue." He smiles.

"Yeah, but you had an in-ground pool," I remind him.

"Would the swimming pool have kept us together?"

"It wasn't our pool; it belonged to your parents."

"You know the Bilancias. Someday, all of it would have been yours. But you never acted like you wanted anything," he says, "or that you needed anything."

"When you don't ask for what you want, you deserve whatever you get," I tell him.

"What are you going to do about Cap Marble and Stone?"

"Well, I have a mountain to climb there."

"You could get a job with any of the big commercial installation groups."

"I'll think about it."

"It'll work out no matter what you decide," Bobby assures me. "I'll always be here."

"Even though you don't answer my texts?"

"I just didn't know what to say." Bobby puts his hands in his pockets and walks ahead of me on the path.

When I left Bobby, I assumed he would always be a part of my life. Lake Como is a small town, and we were bound to run into each other. I hoped we could get to a place where we could be friendly because we have a history. But the vow that matters the most is the one we make when we decide it's over, because it's the one that sticks. The vow of goodbye doesn't involve a priest, lawyers, and in-laws, just two people who have to figure out a way forward without each other. It is the hardest work of all.

Darkness falls around us. The surface of the lake is a mottled green and brown, like an antique mirror. "We should head back," I tell him.

He turns to me. "We good?"

I embrace him and hold him close. He kisses me on the cheek. He takes my hand and leads me back to the house. We don't say anything, and we walk slowly. Bobby gets into his car, and I wave goodbye to him from the porch. I remember a time when I didn't want our walks to end, and when they did, I lived in a state of suspended joy until he returned to the house to pick me up for another one.

I sit down on the porch steps and watch his car take the turn back to Bilancia Land on Ocean Avenue. I go into my notes app. The walk with Bobby brings me back to the day I left him. I write.

I took one last look around our apartment on March 18, 2023. I'd tried to make it a home for Bobby and me. Bobby's bicycle and surfboard never found their way to the storage unit in the basement, despite my nagging, so whenever we entered, we dodged his claptrap in the small entryway. Once in the living room, inside the black and silver palette, there was modern, low furniture. Our wedding gifts were unpacked but remained unused, stuffed into the large mirrored armoire. Bobby's schedule at the shop, and mine at Cap Marble, prevented us from taking the time to put our gifts in places where we could use them. After a while, I decided to keep them in boxes, to make an eventual move to a house an easier transition.

A black-and-white photograph of Bobby and me in a floating frame from our wedding day hung over the sofa. I looked pretty in my Calvin Klein sheath, a knock-off, of course, made by Betty Cline in Parsippany. My upsweep was dotted with small silver stars on bobby pins, which matched the ones in my eyes whenever I looked at Bobby.

My suitcase was packed and by the door. Bobby left for work before the sun rose, kissed me on the cheek, as he always had. I pretended to be asleep, but I hadn't slept all night because this was the morning I chose to leave him for good. I chose a date that would work across the family, both our families. His mother's birthday was a few weeks away, and my dad's had just passed. I couldn't leave on just any day; it had to be a day free of any family anniversary or celebration. I got up, had a cup of coffee, and called Uncle Louie to take a sick day.

As I was about to go, I heard a key in the lock. Panic roiled through me. I couldn't imagine why Bobby would come home from work in the middle of the morning.

My mother-in-law was surprised to see me. My house keys jingled on her wrist on a plastic coil like charms. She carried the keys to all of her kids' homes. Babe was like a super without the plumbing skills.

"Dropping off a few goodies. You don't even see me. In and out! I hear nothing! I see nothing!" Babe walked through the living room to the kitchen, ignoring me. She carried a stack of portable food containers. "The platters are labeled. The homemades? They're fresh. Eat no later than Thursday. There's a port wine cheddar cheese ball. Bobby said he invited the boys over to watch basketball this weekend, but that will keep. The crackers are in the bag. And the struffoli. I wasn't going to get out the fryer, but then I said to myself, I only have one son and one daughter-in-law, so suck it up and do the work, Babe. My daughters have their own fryers."

Babe continued to talk as she passed me in the living room on her way out the door. She stopped talking when she saw my suitcase. She looked at me in my coat, buttoned to the collar. I wore a scarf because it was still winter and chilly outside. She saw the car keys in my hand.

She cocked her head. "An overnight trip?"

"Yes," I answered in a tone that said no further inquisition was welcome.

"Oh." She looked hurt, as though there was news and no one had told her. "Well, that's nice. Where are you going?"

"To my mother's."

Her smile fell away. "I thought Bobby and you had worked things out. He told me you were doing well."

"Mom"—this was the last time I addressed her as my mother-in-law—"we tried."

Babe inhaled slowly before she took a step toward me. She dropped her voice to a low growl. "Look, I've been married a long time. Has it all been rose petals and Prosecco? No. It has not. Too much of either is no good—one gives you hives and the other gives you gas. You have to look at the long haul when you're married, the big picture. Marriage is not about moments. It's about *years* invested. I don't understand. How could you be unhappy? We don't pretend that there aren't problems in life, but you two are well suited to one another."

"Mom."

"It's true. You share a common background! The same religion! You both have beautiful teeth. Our grandchildren would have perfect bites without braces. You would've saved *thousands* on orthodontist bills." She looked around the apartment and put her hand over her mouth. "He doesn't know that you're leaving him? Does he?"

"I'm meeting him on his lunch break to tell him."

"I'll put on a pot of coffee, we'll have a cookie and a chat, and by the time Bobby gets home from work, you'll feel like you can start all over again!"

"I'm sorry. I can't." I could barely get the words out because I was afraid I would cry and she would misinterpret my tears.

I don't remember what Babe Bilancia said after I told her I couldn't stay. I stopped listening. At the time, I felt strong. I stood up for myself and held my ground. I didn't buckle, take off my coat, drop my keys, and put on a pot of coffee to please my mother-in-law and assuage her fears. I was terrified, but instead of turning on myself and making her happy, I used my fear as jet fuel to leave. But I learned something as I stood and fought for myself and my decision. I learned I couldn't make my husband happy if I hadn't found happiness on my own first. I was determined to start a new life, but first, as these things go, I would slip back into my old one to find a way forward.

I TUCK MY phone in my pocket and go back inside the house.

I slip out of my shoes at the front door.

"How was the walk with Bobby?" Mom asks.

"Don't get your hopes up."

I join my mother, father, Joe, and Connie in the living room. They are dressed in wrinkled versions of their pressed funeral wardrobe from the morning. Joe has even loosened his tie. They look like a stack of deflated tires on their way to the junkyard.

"Everybody's gone?" I look around.

"Cousin Diane Palermo took Aunt Lil and her family home," Joe says.

"You want coffee?" Connie stands to go to the kitchen, and the doorbell rings.

"Just show whoever it is to the kitchen. We washed all the platters. They're ready for pickup," Mom says wearily. "When you die close to the holidays, everybody wants their serving platters back on the same day."

I answer the front door. Two well-dressed people around my age, whom I have never seen before, greet me.

"Good evening. I'm Detective Campovilla. I'm here to speak with Giuseppina Baratta of Capodimonte Marble and Stone."

I can't speak. My mind races. What do they want with me? I haven't had time to think about the business.

"Giuseppina." My mother pushes me aside. "Louis Capodimonte died. I am the deceased sister. Campovilla? Is that Italian?"

"Filipino," the detective clarifies.

"I'm Giuseppina Baratta," I admit.

"I'm Agent Trent." His partner, an attractive Black woman in her thirties, holds up her badge for me to inspect.

Dad, Joe, and Connie stand.

"Please come in," Mom says as she shoves Joe in the FBI's direction. "Our son, Joe, is an attorney."

Campovilla looks at my brother, then at me. "You may have an attorney present. No problem." He turns to me. "We've been calling you."

"Was that *you*? I thought it was a company out of Trenton trying to sell me car insurance. Forgive me. I've been a little overwhelmed with the funeral and all." I'm shaking. I've never dealt with the law, and I'm frightened, or maybe my blood sugar has plummeted after scarfing a slab of the Texas sheet cake.

"We need to speak to you about Louis Capodimonte," Campovilla says.

"I would like to understand what information you're looking for before my sister answers any questions." Joe speaks slowly, as if he is being paid to speak by the word.

Joe invites the detectives into the kitchen. Mom, Dad, and Connie follow us. Joe turns to them and says, "I'll take it from here," closing the kitchen door.

"Please," Joe says, offering them a seat at our kitchen table.

THE NEXT DAY, Joe meets me after work at our parents' house. We walk in lockstep in silence to Uncle Louie's as the bright autumn sun sinks in the sky. A great night for a run around the lake, a brisk walk at the beach, or collecting evidence for the FBI.

The large, empty canvas duffel bag on my shoulder flaps against me like the sail on a clam dinghy. I plan to fill it with checkbooks, files, and paperwork that will be useful to the FBI as they sort out Louie Capodimonte's business dealings.

"I appreciate your help, Joe." This is a new phase in my relationship with my brother. I need his professional expertise.

"Did you have any idea about Uncle Louie?"

"None." I lie to my brother because I remain loyal to Uncle Louie because he was loyal to me. But I can't avoid the truth entirely. "Uncle Louie told me some things before he died."

"You can't lie to the FBI, Jess. Did you handle the books?"

"No." I answered all the questions Detective Campovilla asked me honestly. Uncle Louie may have had an accountant, but the truth is, he kept his figures in his head, where only he had access to them. I told the FBI that Uncle Louie had his own way of doing business and I was not privy to it.

"You didn't go to the bank for him?"

"Nope."

"That's hard to believe," Joe says kindly.

I can see that my brother is worried for me. "Would I be living in our parents' basement had there been some grand financial scheme here? Uncle Louie liked money. He liked making it. That just makes him a regular American businessman."

"You knew him better than I did."

"Uncle Louie loved marble. It connected him to Italy."

"What was working with him like?" Joe asks. "You know, day to day."

"Uncle Louie and I were like mismatched detectives in a 1990s crime show on the verge of cancellation. We had an intergenerational friendship. He remembered the Beatles on *Ed Sullivan*. I remembered when Taylor Swift dated Harry Styles. I may have ridden shotgun in the Impala for sixteen years, but I was never his equal. Cap Marble and Stone was his baby. It wasn't like he'd go off for a couple of weeks and hand the business over to me. He'd close down when he went to Florida. But at the end, when he was in the hospital, he made it clear that he wanted me to take over."

Joe stops. "Do you want the business?"

"Right now, I just miss Uncle Louie."

I follow Joe up the yellow brick walkway at Aunt Lil's. Joe turns to me and says, "I will handle Aunt Lil. You know what you need to do." Joe tries the door; it's open. "Aunt Lil?" he calls out.

Aunt Lil pokes her head out from the kitchen at the end of the hallway. "Back here," she says.

The cheerful kitchen is done in white subway tiles with black trim. The appliances are apple red. The kitchen table is cherrywood, with seating for four. Aunt Lil is wearing a lounge robe in teal blue with matching slippers.

"I wish I still smoked. I hate the morning after. Coffee?" she offers.

"Sure," Joe says.

"I'm good, Aunt Lil." I slip the duffel bag onto the back of the chair. "May I use the powder room?"

My aunt waves to the door next to the kitchen.

The powder room off the kitchen has a bold wallpaper of palm fronds, green on white, an homage to Miami. Italian American interior décor is often inspired by where we vacation. That may be why you often find our interior decoration in the palette of saltwater taffy and mai tai umbrellas.

I slide the medicine cabinet open. Uncle Louie wasn't kidding. Aunt Lil has the ultimate vintage Avon collection. The narrow shelves are neatly loaded with finger-sized delicate opaline, frilly porcelain, and milk glass bottles. There are unopened boxes of perfume. I flush the toilet to cover the sound of the sliding door of the medicine chest. I open the boxes quickly, one at a time, searching for the hard drive. Summer Dew, Somewhere, Here's My Heart, Field of Flowers. I could be here all day in miniature hell. I can't remember if Uncle Louie said Avon's Sunsplash or Hayride, but it doesn't matter, because there's no hard drive in any of them. I'm taking too long in here! I reach for a box that says Sweet Honesty, open it, and peer inside. Boom, the hard drive. How's that for irony?

"Everything all right in there?" Lil asks from outside the door.

"I'll be out in a second." I place the box back on the shelf, slip the hard drive into my pocket, and gently close the medicine cabinet.

"Jiggle the handle. It'll stop running," Aunt Lil says from outside the door.

"Can do," I say through the door. I wash my hands and join them in the kitchen. "Joe, please fix the toilet."

"Louie used to fix everything around here that was broken." Aunt Lil begins to cry. "I don't know what I'm going to do. I keep thinking he's going to come in that door. I'm alone. You can't imagine the terror."

"You're safe," Joe says. "You have ADT, and Mom and Dad are right down the street."

"Don't forget Cousin Carmine," I tell her. "You have a state trooper six houses down."

"I'm not afraid of someone from the outside; I'm afraid of being alone on the inside."

I give Aunt Lil a hug. "Uncle Louie loved you so much. He always said he was the luckiest man in the world because you married him."

"He did?"

I nod. "When he wasn't talking marble, he was bragging about his Lil."

"Do you think he knew how much I loved him?"

"Yes!" Joe and I say in unison.

"He went first because he couldn't bear the thought of losing you." I reach for her hand.

"Thank you, Jess." Aunt Lil wipes her eyes. "He loved you like his own daughter."

"Jess, why don't you get the paperwork you need from Uncle Louie's office, and I'll sit with Aunt Lil."

"Jess, I wish I could help you, but I knew nothing about Louie's business." Lil holds up her hands as though resisting arrest.

"I won't be long."

"Take whatever you need," she says to me.

I sling the empty duffel bag over my arm and climb the carpeted stairs to Uncle Louie's home office. A marble sculpture of *The Birth of Venus* is softly lit in the alcove at the top of the stairs. To her right, Uncle Louie's office. And to her left, the master bedroom suite.

I tiptoe into the master bedroom. The ornate crystal chandelier overhead is lit to dim.

An emerald-green satin coverlet on the California king, thick wall-to-wall carpeting to match, and elaborate draperies in a tasteful green-and-white silk stripe tied back with white tassels. This is where Saint Patrick's Day and shag carpeting came to mate and die.

I open the closet door by lifting the decorative knob in the shape of a lion's head. I'm hit with a blast of White Diamonds. Wrong closet. I close it and lift a second lion's-head knob on the adjoining door. The scent of Woodhue cologne comes at me like a meteor. I turn on the light and step inside Uncle Louie's closet. His size 32 three-piece suits hang neatly as though they are fresh out of the

Jos. A. Bank showroom during their annual sample sale. His shoes, Italian loafers with gold chain links, are lined up on a ceiling-to-floor rack, with sneakers and flip-flops on the bottom. There's a photo of Aunt Lil in a sexy blouse on the accessories shelf; below it, a photograph of his parents, looking stern on a bocci court in Paterson in the 1950s. They must have lost.

I open drawers. Pressed handkerchiefs. Socks. Briefs. Men's bikini briefs. Didn't need to see those. Undershirts. No laptop. I open a cabinet. A spinning rack is loaded with silk ties. Hats on shelves. One shelf for summer holds a few straw palmettos stacked; beneath them, his winter hat, a navy blue Borsalino fedora. I begin to panic, then I ask myself, *Where would Louie hide a laptop?*

I get down on my knees and peer under the suits. I feel the carpet inside the cabinet on the floor. I follow the seam of the carpet around the inside of the closet. I have a memory of Uncle Louie having me hide cash under the carpet in the Impala when we stopped for lunch once in Ocean City. I didn't think anything of it because our customers often paid in cash. I pat down the edges, then I feel something hard under the shoe rack. I peel back the carpet and aha! I put the laptop in my bag and make sure that I place everything back where it was.

I back out of the bedroom, leaning down to erase my footprints on the wall-to-wall carpeting with my free hand, remembering that Aunt Lil is particular about impressions in the carpet pile once she has vacuumed.

I hear the drone of my brother and Aunt Lil's conversation downstairs as I go into Uncle Louie's office. The draperies are drawn. The walnut desk is polished. Behind the desk is an impressionist painting of the Lake Como boardwalk. On the shelves behind Louie's desk, on a mirrored display case with glass shelves, are more framed photos of Aunt Lil. On the top shelf, a black-and-white eight-by-ten of Uncle Louie at the Playboy Club in Las Vegas in 1975. A Panatela stogie, half-smoked, juts out of his mouth, while his smile is due east of pervy.

I sit down at Uncle Louie's desk and open a drawer. Rolling Writer pens. The file drawer is filled with order forms, letters, and contracts. I lift them out and place them in the duffel bag on top of the computer. I open the small drawer at the top and pull it out as far as it will go. I find a leather case holding Uncle Louie's kept marble samples—"tiles," he called them, to entice customers. When I was a girl, we were allowed to play with the tiles anytime we wished. Calacatta gold is my favorite; it looks like vanilla ice cream with gold swirls through it. The translucent tile glitters when I hold it up to the light.

Uncle Louie explained that the great Italian sculptors chose Calacatta gold because it was porous; they could chisel with ease like it was soft clay. I imagined the quarries in Tuscany as he described them, where the Apuan Alps were hollowed out, leaving open white rooms with walls of Calacatta marble so tall they pierced the clouds. I'm sad all over again when I think he is not here to show me the mountains. There is never a good moment to give up a dream; I'm going to hold on to going to Italy until I can't.

I find Louie's address book. Most of the contractors listed don't have last names. Omar. Dusty. Hiram. There's a page with the header *Carrara*. I find a treasure trove of contacts listed with notes. Family names I may have heard once or twice but would not remember: Tasca, Cellini, Trombetta, Milani, and Apugliaetta. I place the book in the duffel.

Stacked neatly in the drawer in an upright position are fat envelopes of photographs developed at the drugstore. A pocket holds the strips of negatives. I lift out a stack of black-and-white photos framed in a frilly white edge.

Uncle Louie was handsome when he was young and single and on his own in Italy. He would gloss over memories of the arduous work in the quarry; instead, he talked about the food, the family, the camaraderie, the old motorcycle he used to get around, and, of course, the beautiful women. I never knew Uncle Louie to be unhappy, but in these photos, he is blissful. There's a photograph of Uncle Louie with a young woman I don't recognize. She has a tumble of black curls and red lips, and she isn't Aunt Lil. I tuck the photographs into the duffel. My aunt doesn't need to find old photos with Uncle Louie and a pretty girl that isn't her.

I save the large drawer under the desktop for last. I lift out leather-bound ledgers and the company checkbooks. A few bills fall out of a ring binder as I place them in the duffel. I scoop the envelopes off the floor when I see an envelope with Uncle Louie's handwriting: *Italy.*

I open the sealed envelope carefully, knowing Uncle Louie is the last of a generation of Italian Americans who still put cash in envelopes. But there's no cash and no note, just two open round-trip plane tickets from Newark Liberty International Airport to Milan Malpensa Airport on Italia Trasporto Aereo. One in my name and one in his. I hold the tickets to my heart. We were really going to go to Italy; it wasn't a dream.

"Jess?" Joe calls to me from the bottom of Aunt Lil's stairs. "We gotta go."

I clutch the duffel, bulging with files, receipts, bank statements, and checkbooks, close to my chest as though it's a baby I must protect through a war zone.

"Jess?" Joe calls out again.

"On my way!"

Uncle Louie used to say, *Trust no one.* Yet, he moved through his life as though every person he met was his best friend. He embraced the outcasts, the misfits, and the occasionally nefarious just like family. Everyone has secrets, but I hope the extent of Uncle Louie's are the eye lift he had in 2010 and the seventeen kids he adopted around the world through Save the Children since 1987. He was a tough guy, but he would weep openly when the kids sent him their annual letters. I don't know if the FBI knows *that* Louie Cap, and I don't care. I hold everything in my arms to prove them wrong, clear his name, and restore his reputation. Someday, when I'm on the other side and find Uncle Louie in the afterlife, I will tell him what I really think. I'm angry at him for putting me in this position, but it's nowhere near how sad I am at having lost him.

8

The Big Secret

After I ransacked Uncle Louie's home office with Aunt Lil's permission, Joe and I returned to our mother's kitchen. We'd helped Aunt Lil get ready for bed and made her a cup of tea. She was exhausted and went upstairs to sleep. Now I'm the one who is spent. I drop the heavy duffel near the top of the cellar stairs.

Mom claps her hands together. "You're back! I'll put on a pot of coffee."

"No, thanks. Had a cup at Aunt Lil's," Joe says.

"I'll have a cup," Connie says as she slides into the booth close to Dad, who sits in his chair at the kitchen table.

"If I drank, I'd swear this was an intervention," I joke.

"We need a debrief," Mom says pleasantly.

"Maybe tomorrow. I need to sleep." What I really need to do is go through Uncle Louie's laptop.

"We should talk," Dad says.

"Why?" I joke. "We've done so well avoiding one another, why ruin it?"

No one answers. They look nervous. Joe slides into the booth next to Connie and indicates that I should sit in the straight-back chair on the other side of the table.

"Ma, why are you crying?" Connie asks.

I turn to look at my mother. "You can't make a decent pot of coffee with salt water," I remind her. She shakes her head. I start to get nervous. *What is going on here?*

"We love you, Jess," my father says.

"What exactly is there to love about me?" I stand back and look at my family.

Not a peep as my mother makes herself busy measuring Chock Full o'Nuts out of the canister and scoops the coffee grounds into the strainer of the percolator.

"Dad, you want to take a swing at an answer?" My father looks down at the table. "Joe? No? Connie? Mom? All right. Allow me. I am your loser child. The almost thirty-four-year-old with nothing to show for a third of her precious life. I am alone. I don't own anything. Well, my car. But even when I left the keys in it with the note *She's all yours*, no one bothered to steal it. The only job I ever had, in an undistinguished career, turns out to be a front for a second business in the Cayman Islands run by a man I loved and trusted who died suddenly and didn't leave instructions. He did, however, leave me his companies, so let me amend my comment. I do own *something*. And now I'm either going to be held responsible by the FBI and IRS, or the creeps Louie Cap associated with will do the job for them. The anxiety I experienced in the past is nothing compared to how frightened I am in this moment."

A hush falls over the kitchen until Connie says, "Your therapy is working."

How would Connie know? It doesn't matter. In Exercise 3, Dr.

Mohammed schooled me about an emotional place called *a position of strength.* I assume the position. I sit down at the table and lean in.

"Going forward, let's be clear." I place my hands on the table.

My mother makes a plate with the last of the sfogliatelle. "Here." She puts the pastries in front of me. "Eat."

"They're stale."

"They don't get stale," Mom argues with me. "They stay moist from within. The filling doesn't get hard."

"Ma, when I say something is stale it's because I believe it's stale and therefore I will not eat it. I don't want your three-day-old pastry!" I shout. I shove the plate toward my father.

"You took the starch right out of them. Lost my desire." Dad pushes the plate of sfogliatelle to the center of the table.

"Stop," Connie says softly.

"Stop what?" I turn to my sister. "Have you had a bad day?" I ask with a twist of sarcasm.

"Yes, I have had a bad day," Connie says defensively. "My head is pounding. I drove over here because Dad called an emergency family meeting, and I would prefer to be putting my kids to bed." Connie pats my hand. "But I'm here for you."

The percolator releases a shot of steam, indicating the coffee is ready. My mother sheepishly removes the stale pastries from the table as though they are the actual cause of my anger. She serves cups around, filling the awkward silence with an observation. "Louie Cap was a complicated person."

"He wasn't that complicated," Dad says as Mom pours him a cup of coffee.

"Oh, it's complicated," I assure them. "The FBI broke it down for me. Joe, please jump in when you have something to add." I turn to my parents. "Uncle Louie secured an EIN number and used my name on the incorporation of a second company where he off-loaded remnants from Cap Marble and Stone for profit."

"He was double-dipping?" Connie asks.

"Evidently. But why is my name on the paperwork?"

"Because it's hard to spell," my mother says quietly. "And it wasn't *his* name."

"You knew about the Elegant Gangster?" My voice catches as my heart races. "Did you also know he paid no taxes on the income?"

Mom and Dad look away as though they are guilty of something but aren't sure exactly what, and even if they knew, they would not share it with me. Instead of choking, I shout, "Come on, tell me everything you know." I don't need a paper bag; all I need is the truth.

Mom throws her hands in the air. "That's all I know."

I don't believe her. "Are you telling me he just sent the cash to the Cayman Islands?"

"Louie said he was diversifying. I went along with it. What do I know? I didn't know he was using your identity in a shady fashion. Would we live like this if we broke the law? I'd have an in-ground pool! And a housepainter."

"Hey," my father warns her.

Mom continues. "Louie already had your information for the payroll, and he told us he was making you the sole heir to his and Lil's estate. So I didn't see anything wrong with letting him use this address and your name and information on the paperwork. It was to benefit you."

"Why didn't you tell me?"

"Louie asked for it when you left Bobby. You were fragile. I didn't want to pile on."

"Ma, you invented the pile on."

"The FBI showed me incorporation papers where Uncle Louie used a stamp with your signature on the papers," Joe says. "Where did he get that?"

"I have a signature stamp I use on my designs," I explain. "I kept it in the Impala. In the glove compartment."

"Louie said he was putting together a trust for your benefit," my father says. "I believed him."

"You too?" I turn to my father, whom I have trusted all of my life. He may not have always given me the answer I wanted, but he told me the truth. I am stunned. "You're involved?"

My father flails his arms around like he is choking on seawater while summoning a lifeguard off Como beach. "I'm his insurance guy. He was a business associate! What was I gonna do?"

"Stop him?"

"How is leaving his niece a trust for her future a crime?" Dad shakes his head.

"Criminality has yet to be determined," Joe reminds us, as though this is a free consultation in his law office. Why do I feel I am getting exactly what I pay for?

"We thought Louie was being generous. He and Lil always liked you," Mom says.

"Jess was their favorite," Connie says. "The daughter they never had."

"And on the face of it, it sounded like a good idea," my father reasons. "Your mother and I were concerned that you would need money down the road. We were looking out for you. For your future."

"Especially after the divorce. You walked out on Bobby and took nothing," my mother reminds me.

"I didn't need anything! I was no longer a wife, and the role of maiden aunt was waiting for me right here in your house. I started cooking and cleaning and dressing your wounds. Every family needs a maiden aunt who will give up her life in order to give her family a better one." I pick up the sfogliatelle and throw them in the trash.

"Those were good!" Mom yells.

"Not anymore," I shout.

"Please. Jess. We know you have your own life; we respect that," Connie says calmly.

"Do you? Where were you when I was crying my eyes out in the cellar?" I turn and face my parents. "Connie and Joe have less of an anxiety level about your welfare because they know I'm here to take care of you, and I'll do what needs to be done. Like Mom's knee replacement and Dad's shoulder ordeal."

"We are ambulatory!" my father barks.

"I am good for everyone but me." I drop my voice. "When you say you have my best interests at heart, I don't believe you. You use me and expect me to be grateful for that privilege."

"You make us sound horrible," my mother says. "I lay this all at Louie's feet. He left us in emotional disarray! If he were alive, I'd put him on the Island."

"Of course you would, Ma. He knew exactly who you were."

"I was his sister!"

"His fragile sister," I clarify.

"Fragile? I'm married to a regular Zamboni," Dad says quietly. "At work they call me Flat Joe."

"And there it is. The one thing we do really well in this family is role definition. So, let's say it: I am the maiden aunt. I've become Zia Giuseppina."

"I wouldn't go that far," Dad says.

"Isn't that the plan?" I look at my brother and my sister. "That I get so bitter and angry and comfortable in my loneliness that I calcify like a barnacle on the cement walls in the basement and never leave?"

"I Sheetrocked them," Dad says sheepishly.

"Don't worry, Jess. We plan to participate in the care of our parents down the line," Joe says calmly.

"Really? Couldn't get you two to cover for me when Lisa Natalizio invited me for a girls' weekend in Bermuda." I turn to Connie. "You had gymnastics." I look at my brother. "And you had tickets to basketball homecoming at Notre Dame. I didn't go on the trip because there was no one here to help."

"You could've gone," Mom says.

"Only to return and find you sitting in your own filth?"

"We're all better now," Dad says.

"Let's look at this situation honestly," I begin. "You both live an hour away, longer in traffic. Your kids will be in high school and college in ten years, when Mom will be pushing eighty and Dad will be older. You won't have time to take care of them."

"Oh, just put us in the Little Sisters of the Poor Home and call it a day!" my mother cries.

"We're not going to do that, Ma," I promise her.

Connie looks at me. Joe looks at Connie. Despite our differences, we grew up with the same parents. I understand how they feel. In many ways, we are three strangers who witnessed the same car wreck and arrived at the same conclusion about who was at fault for the accident. We may argue, but we have yet to send one another to the Island. We are pretty good problem solvers and possess the cool heads that skipped our baby boomer parents.

"You have a point, Jess." Connie sighs. "We don't think ahead."

"We aren't thinking at *all*," I insist. "We are unprepared for the future. And I don't know what will be left of Uncle Louie's money when the FBI and the IRS settle up the bill, so I may not be able to help. I have a feeling I will end up with less than I had when I started." I would cry, but it would take too much energy. My life has never been my own, and today, it's even less so. Mrs. Cartegna is waiting for me to drop off the deposit check for my apartment in Hoboken, but with the company under investigation by the FBI, I may no longer be able to afford my own place. Instead of admitting this to my family, I go on. "I've saved some money, but I wouldn't rent out the cellar just yet if I were you."

"You still have your sense of humor." Dad shakes his head sadly.

"That will go too," I assure them. "You see, I knew I was Uncle Louie and Aunt Lil's sole heir before he died—"

"So why are you punishing us because we knew?" Mom interrupts me, mystified.

"Because you kept secrets from me and made decisions on my behalf without my input. You treat me like a child or an adult who has to be protected from herself. Joe? Connie? Am I right?"

They nod in agreement.

"Here's the fundamental problem. You don't see me."

"I'm looking right at you, Jess." My father sounds pathetic. "What are you talking about?"

I turn to Connie and Joe. "Your parents didn't offer up your private information in exchange for an undisclosed future sum of money without your knowledge."

"Sixteen years with Cap Marble? You deserved something."

"I would be all right, Dad."

"Tell her everything, Philly." My father is resigned. "She's going to find out anyhow. She hauled home a sack of intel from Louie's. She'll know what we've done."

I sit down, afraid my legs won't hold me.

"We changed our will," Mom begins. "It was always a three-way split." My mother reaches across the table and takes my hands in hers. "But your father and I went to your brother and sister and asked if we could leave the house to you."

I turn to my mother. "Why would you give me the house?"

"Because we used your college money to pay for Joe's law school," Mom blurts out.

I go numb. Joe stands up.

"What?" my brother, who never raises his voice, shouts. "I thought you loaned me your savings. I paid you back! Where did that money go?"

"The roof. The materials for the renovation of the basement. Philly's car died. Our parents' funerals. Four of them. Connie's wedding. Jess's wedding. What can I tell you? It mounted up fast. We found ourselves buried in unexpected bills; I hit sixty-five, and instead of negotiating a raise, they offered me the same job for half the salary. I took the bad deal." Dad's face is flushed with embarrassment, but he continues. "We were going to give Jess her savings when she graduated from high school so she could go to Rutgers. That was the plan. But you got into law school, Joe, and we had to choose."

I can't believe what I'm hearing, but I focus, because I want to understand how they could do this to me.

"But there was a rainbow." Mom looks to heaven. "You began commuting to Montclair State and seemed happy. And it was just a little while later that you took up with Bobby Bilancia and we figured, she'll want to spend time with Bobby close to home, so it was all a win-win."

I put my hand over my mouth so I won't scream.

"It's a family pot; that's how we look at it. What's there, we share. It belongs to all of us." My father clears his throat.

"That's when we came up with the house idea in our will." Mom looks at my father. "So instead of giving you the money when you got divorced, we paid off the mortgage with what was left from the money Joe repaid us for law school and our portion of the sale of Grammy B's house to Cousin Carmine. That's when we decided to ask Connie and Joe for their permission to put this house in your name. Someday, you will have all of this free and clear. Unless we live too long and need a reverse mortgage."

"We will never do that, Phil. Stop it."

"I *wanted* the opportunity and the experience of going away to college. I *needed* it." I let go of my disbelief, which makes room for my anger.

"Going to college, sleeping in those coed dorms, things go on. And you weren't cut out for all that," Mom insists. "You had anxiety issues! How many paper bags have we gone through in this house?"

"Maybe standing on my own two feet would have cured my anxiety. I had only seen this tiny corner of the world and I wanted more. I wouldn't have married Bobby if I had been exposed to the world."

"Don't say that. You were nuts about him."

"We are not going off topic, Ma. That was *my* money! I worked summers. Babysat horrible children. One bit me and it left a scar. Mowed lawns since I was twelve. Every time I received a cash gift, birthday, confirmation, whatever, you snatched it out of my hands and it went into my college account. You told me my money was safe. When you came to me to borrow against my savings, you told me Dad needed to pool my savings with your account to get a home loan to do the roof and furnace."

"First I've heard of this." My brother looks at my parents. Joe is as stunned as I am at their betrayal.

"You meant to keep me here in the cellar like they keep our cousin Marina Bustagrande in the attic!" I shout.

"Marina has crippling shyness," Mom explains. "Entirely different pathology from your issues."

"You treated me like I needed protection, when what I needed was adventure. What made you think I couldn't cut it at Rutgers when I graduated magna cum laude from Montclair State while working full-time? I am talented!" I can't breathe. My mother jumps up and goes for a brown paper lunch bag she keeps in the drawer. She hands it to me.

"Breathe into the bag!" Mom commands.

I close my eyes and hold the bag. I don't open it. Instead, I inhale on my own. I cannot show weakness in this moment.

"Forgive us. We knew it wasn't ideal"—my mother puts her head in her hands—"but we wanted to protect the family name."

"What name?" I stand in my fury. "Stop with the airs! The only place you can find the Capodimonte name is on the side of a gravel truck. It wasn't on the Magna Carta. Your maiden name didn't secure the bond to raise Saint Patrick's Cathedral. Your people didn't build the Verrazzano Bridge. We are not a family with a name anyone remembers, much less can spell, unless they happen to be in a secondhand store looking for a lamp covered in ceramic flowers! The Capodimontes busted rock in a quarry in Italy for generations and then came over here and busted slate until we figured out how to sell the marble. We are hardworking Italian Americans who have done all right. There was a time when *all right* was *enough* because we had each other. I didn't think we were held together by our bank accounts, or our lust to fill them. I believed we had a mission. To . . . to love one another." I look at my family. Their expressions are frozen until my mother decides to scream at me.

"Dear God! Fine! We decided to help your brother." My mother gets louder, more vehement. More defensive. "We saw an opportunity to do better. To finally have a professional in the family. And didn't it come in handy when the FBI showed up at our door?"

"Let me understand this. The market crash excuse was a myth! I was in a money market. They bounced back! The money was never gone; you *took* it."

"Jess, you will get all the money back and more someday when we're dead and you sell the house," Dad offers.

"What's mine has never been mine. You took my future and handed it off to your son because he is more important than me. You're misogynists!"

"Hey," my father says in a warning tone.

"You do for your son and not your daughters!"

"They paid for my wedding," Connie says softly. "I am grateful for that."

"And mine, but only half. Mom caved and split it with the Bilancias, so I'm in their debt until the Rapture for that ice sculpture of a giant heart over the raw bar, which we didn't need and could ill afford."

"I thought I paid for the raw bar." Dad glares at my mother. "I knew nothing about this." My father leans back in his chair.

"Whatever flimflam deals ensued! The point is: You put *my* resources behind *your* son when they weren't even yours to give! To think I've been living in that hole at the bottom of the house without complaint."

"No rent," Mom whispers. "You paid not one dime."

"You live down there, Ma. You wouldn't last the night. You should be paying me to stay down there. Grandma Cap died instead of moving into that apartment."

"Don't say that!" Tears stream down my mother's face.

"I tried to make the cellar nice for her, then I tried to make it nice for you," my father says sadly.

My heart starts to break for him. I shake my head. *This is how they get you, Jess. Pity.* "Dad, you did try. Ma, not so much. You are quick to say what you do for me, but you don't acknowledge what I do for you. Kindness cuts both ways."

"I definitely feel the knife," Mom says. "You might as well plunge it directly into my beating heart."

"Did Aunt Lillian know?" Connie asks. "About Uncle Louie?"

"Lil didn't care what Louie did as long as he took his shoes off before entering the house," Mom says wearily. "That plush 1986 Karastan Deluxe is as new today as it was when they installed it."

"Aunt Lil has her own money," Joe confirms. "She told me she didn't trust Louie's 'business style,' she called it. She put her own money aside through the years and she's set."

"She was the top Avon saleslady in New Jersey in 1977," Mom says. "Lil is her own woman. I'll give her that. My brother had his quirks, so I did what I had to do in order to deal with him. It wasn't easy. I am done being criticized for putting Louie on the Island for a few weeks here and there."

"Ma, it was five and a half years," I correct her.

"Look at the facts. Louie took care of you." My father pinches his fingers into small bouquets. "Jess. You were an Italian studies major. What were you gonna do with that?"

"Italian *culture*, Dad. Marble! Design! Antiquities! Art! The family business! My major made it possible for me to design installations for customers. I work hard."

"No doubt. But when you blew up your marriage, Louie saved you," Mom insists. "Don't forget. Your divorce was the cause of all of this. You gave up your life and for what?"

"I didn't give up my life; I started over. Dr. Sharon said the divorce was actually positive—it was the only decision I could make to save myself. And it was the right one. Leaving my marriage didn't make me sick. This!" I wave my hands in the air like my father did. "All of this made me sick!"

I get up and go down into the cellar, hauling the duffel with me. I have no idea how long I've been lying on the bed when I open my eyes to find Joe and Connie standing over me.

"I didn't know it was your money, Jess," my brother says softly.

"I believe you."

"You can't catch a break," my sister says.

"Connie, your name didn't even come up tonight. They don't pay attention to us in the same way they do Joe."

"Joe is a firstborn son. I wanted to work in retail and have a family," Connie says. "I got my dream. You should have your dream too. Is there anything we can do for you?"

The basement stairs creak as my parents descend the narrow staircase. Dad almost bangs his head on the low ceiling even though he installed it. They stand back, waiting to be invited into the conversation. My father is seventy-two and my mother is sixty-nine and they look every second of it and then some in the beam of the garish overhead light.

"May we join you?" Mom asks.

Dad looks down at the linoleum floor. "I'm sorry, Jess. I see you could have handled your affairs—past, present, and future—on your own without our interference. We should have come to you about the college fund, but we were cutting and pasting our children's needs in the moment. Kind of like that dream board thing you put together. A piece here. A piece there. Sometimes we held this family together with nothing but prayer and glue. Sometimes as a parent you do that—you do for one at the expense of the other—it's a juggling act. But in all of this, we underestimated you. This is, frankly, inexcusable behavior from your father, who makes his living assessing the value of things."

"Dad, I'm holding you accountable. Mom, I am holding you accountable too."

"I'm so sorry," Connie cries. "You haven't been treated with respect."

"I feel awful." Mom clutches her stomach.

Never underestimate the revelation of the truth to change the power grid of a family. I feel my lungs open. "When you respect a person, you assume they will make the best decisions for themself that they can with the information they have at that time. When it was my turn to go away to college, you needed the money to send Joe to law school. If you knew me, you would know that had you come to me, explained the situation, and asked me for the money, I would have given you my last dime. No further questions asked. But you didn't think enough of me to ask. All these years, I thought I wasn't worthy of my own dreams because they never seemed to come true. Now I know why they didn't."

We sit in silence until Mom says, "Giuseppina, I want you to sleep upstairs."

"I'm okay."

"You won't be for long." She turns to Dad. "She's right. This is a hole and I smell fumes."

Dad inhales the air. "I stored the engine from the push mower in the utility closet. It's just motor oil. Nothing that could kill you."

Mom and Dad go up the stairs to the kitchen.

As I watch them go, I know what I have to do.

I look at Connie and Joe. "Don't let them rent out the basement. It's awful down here. Sometimes a cellar should just be a cellar."

Joe sits on the end of the bed. He looks at Connie, who sits in the lawn chair and scoots it toward the bed. They look at me.

"Where will you go?" Joe asks.

"I'll let you know when I get there." I lean back on the pillows and inhale the faint scent of motor oil, which will fuel me out of this cellar and into my new life.

9

Il Coraggio

I'VE BEEN IN constant motion in the weeks since Uncle Louie died. As the sole heir to Cap Marble and Stone, I followed Uncle Louie's mandate to take care of our customers. I delivered a new base for the baptismal font to Saint Catharine's, followed up with our clients, met with the accountant, and paid all vendors and workmen on outstanding invoices. Cap Marble and Stone is now on hold while the Elegant Gangster is being investigated by the FBI and IRS. I surrendered all of Uncle Louie's business files to the detectives, but I asked Detective Campovilla if I could keep the photographs of Uncle Louie's time in Italy. He let me.

I signed up for a Pimsleur course to refresh my college Italian, connected with Conor Kerrigan, and put several calls in to Googs, who has returned none. I went to Lisa's for a bangs trim and had my nails done, and I've been writing journal entries faithfully in my notes app. I have ascended to Exercise 4 with Dr. Pamela.

I also took care of any loose ends for Aunt Lil, including sending the thank-you notes from the funeral. I cleaned out the basement and packed up my old clothes (anyone who wears a size eight and prefers an all-black wardrobe is in for a haul at Goodwill). I bought some new clothes at T.J. Maxx and Target and donated my car to Kars4Kids. (I figured if their annoying television jingle is true, they deserve the heap.) I didn't make the rounds to say goodbye to my relatives because I'd just seen them at Uncle Louie's grief buffet. I haven't seen Bobby since we took a walk after Uncle Louie's reception; it's as though I left him in the mist on Lake Como forever. But the truth is, I have so much to sort through, I can't think about Bobby right now.

THE CELLAR WINDOWS have a thin layer of ice on the glass like the white frost on a cocktail shaker. I check the clock: 4:10 a.m. I zip my suitcase closed. I pull my tote over my shoulder. I don't look back at the neatly made bed, where I have slept for a total of ten percent of my current natural life; instead, I climb the stairs to the kitchen. As I go, I tuck a letter, stamped and addressed to Aunt Lil, in my pocket, which I plan to mail from the airport.

October 23, 2024

Dearest Aunt Lil,

It's almost time for your trip to Florida with Carmel and Marina. Uncle Louie would want you to head south. Get in the ocean once you're there; it's the great healer. Uncle Louie taught me that, among the many lessons I learned from him. He loved you with all his heart. I will let you know my plans when I've made them. I don't want you to worry about a thing. I love you for understanding and so much more.

Your niece,

Jess

My mother has left a small lamp in the kitchen window on, a habit from when we were teenagers. By the glow of the lamp, I roll the suitcase through the shadows of the dining room, through the living room, and out to the foyer. I order an Uber on my phone and step outside. I lock the door behind me and leave my keys under the front mat.

The breezes off Lake Como are downright frigid at this hour. I look down the street to Grandma Cap's dark house. It's sad to see it that way when it was once a home full of life. I look in the other direction to Aunt Lil's. The glamorous house shimmers in the dark, illuminated by garden lights staggered throughout the prim landscaping. Her home has always made me feel secure. I snap a photo of Aunt Lil's house, one of the lake, and a third one of our front yard. I post them: *Big changes.*

I hear the click of the lock behind me as my mother opens the front door. She wears a coat over her bathrobe and a twisted look of worry on her face. "I wish you'd let us drive you to the airport."

"It's okay. I got an Uber." I pat the cross-body purse on my hip and look down at my suitcase.

"It's bad luck to have a stranger drop you at the airport," she says.

"You're making that up."

"You want me to take you, Jess?" My father joins my mother in the doorway. He yawns. He wears a Phillies baseball shirt and sweatpants. His unruly hair comes to a point on his head, like a party hat.

"I wish you would talk to us. We meant no harm," Mom says sadly.

"And even if you had, the results would have been the same."

Mom winces. I'm half Cap and I know how to land a punch, but the Baratta side is ashamed that I hurt my mother's feelings. But this is not the time to indulge and buckle under the weight of my filial guilt. As far as I'm concerned, my parents are on the Island. The Uber pulls up in front of the house.

My father carries my suitcase down the walkway and places it in the trunk of the Uber. He opens his arms to me, and I give my father a quick hug—an awkward moment for both of us. For whatever reason, I don't blame him as much, though Dad was half of the team that approved the scheme that hurt me. He breaks the silence. "What about your mother?"

I choose not to argue with my father. I turn, walk back up to the porch, and embrace my mom.

"Will you tell us where you are when you get there?" Mom cries.

"Okay." I am lying. No one in my family ever sent postcards to the Island. It's just not done.

I walk back to the car, where Dad holds the Uber door open. "I love you," he says.

I climb in, closing the door behind me.

"Confirming the airport. Newark? Terminal C?"

"Yes, sir," I tell him. We drive off in the predawn darkness, one last half loop around Lake Como. The sun is coming up over the water in a ribbon of gold along the horizon. I look to the light, and I don't look back.

10

Crying on Airplanes

I CLASP MY HANDS in my lap in seat 32E on Italia Trasporto Aereo flight 987 to Milan, Italy. When I called the airline to book the flight, I turned in Uncle Louie's ticket and gave Aunt Lil the refund. I asked her to keep my plan a secret, and she agreed. I am trying my best to be brave. I summon a bit of courage knowing Uncle Louie would want me to take this trip.

There are three seats across on either side of the aisle in economy. I'm in the middle seat on the right side of the plane in the back row. The smells of cafeteria beef stew and hot coffee waft from the galley behind me, oddly comforting scents, like a potluck in the church basement. A few overhead reading lights are on, smattered through economy like a defective string of white lights on a Christmas tree.

There's a fidgety man to my left in the aisle seat and a sweaty woman wedged into the window seat; at her feet, a large purse, an oversized carpetbag, and a paper bag stuffed with whatever didn't fit into the purse and carry-on.

Suddenly alone, with enough distance between my hometown and me, I am free. I feel tears on my face. They freeze on contact in the frigid cabin, causing my skin to itch, but I don't care because I'm crying at last! I remember what Dr. Raymond said when I Zoomed with him. "The reason you cannot cry is because you are furious. When you understand the weight of all that you have lost, and that includes your uncle, you will find release." The doctor was right!

I rub my eyes, but the tears flow. I look around at the rows of passengers through my glassy tears. Is anyone else having a breakdown in economy? A long airplane ride is like church, specifically, being trapped in a pew between people you've never met. I'm having a spiritual unraveling in a sea of seat-belted strangers. I have seven hours to examine my conscience inert in this seat; it's not just an airplane, it's a confessional flying at the speed of sound.

I search my pockets for a tissue. I can't find one, so I pull the cloth sleep mask out of the amenity packet and cry into it. Tomorrow is my thirty-fourth birthday. I am so old, if I were a fossil, archeologists would have to carbon-date me. The tears flow as I heave for air at the loss of my youth. I can't breathe, I am ancient ruins, and what is left of my life is nothing but rubble! I sit rigidly, trying to take up as little space as possible, ceding the armrests, attempting not to be a bother, but instead I hope to disappear in the middle seat. I tap the screen on the seatback to check how much of the trip remains. *Hours* to go. I sob over Greenland. I couldn't find Greenland on a map before I got on this plane. I trace the map on the screen with my finger, tears streaming down my face, when I feel a hand on my arm.

"Come with me," the flight attendant says.

"Oh no, what did I do?" Can they eject a passenger over the ocean? Do they turn back?

"It's fine," he reassures me. "Do you have anything in the overhead?"

I shake my head that I don't. I'm ashamed that I can't stop crying.

"Is that your bag?" The flight attendant points to the midnight-blue leather tote I picked up at T.J. Maxx a week ago tucked in the space under the seat in front of me.

I nod.

"Bring it with you," he says.

I unclasp my seat belt. The shaky passenger in the aisle seat gets up and drops back, making space for me to go. I follow the flight attendant up the aisle to the forward galley. The flight attendants have drawn the curtains; he opens them to let me inside, closing them behind me. Their workspace is brightly lit, stinging my swollen eyes.

He unfolds a cocktail napkin and hands it to me to wipe my tears. His brass name tag shimmers: L. ANGELINI. One of my tribe, evidently.

"Are you ill?" he asks.

"No. But I've lost everything."

He smiles kindly. "I'm going to have you move your seat. I only have one available; it's in first class."

"I can't afford that."

He looks to the other flight attendants, who are busy preparing the meal carts. They say nothing, but their expressions show amusement. "You don't fly much, do you?"

"This is my first trip overseas."

"Once the plane takes off, we make the decisions."

"Maybe someone else would like to move?" I cry into the cocktail napkin. He hands me another.

"I've never met a passenger less willing to give up a middle seat," Mr. Angelini says.

"It's a first." A blond flight attendant with a warm, bright-white smile winks at me. "Take the seat, honey."

"But I don't mind the middle seat. Really."

"I recommend a come-apart in first class," she says. "You can weep until you can't."

"And there were complaints," Mr. Angelini whispers. "So you understand why I have to move you. Follow me."

Mortified, I follow Mr. Angelini through the second set of curtains up the aisle. The front of the plane, in contrast to the back, has the scent of lilies and champagne. He seats me in the front row, in a first-class pod. It's a space-age seat on an angle. A white down-filled comforter and pillow rest on the plush leather seat. I move them aside and sit down in the high-tech cocoon. I unzip my tote bag and pull out a copy of *A Room with a View*. Mr. Angelini takes my bag and places it in a compartment inside the cocoon.

"E. M. Forster? What? No Kristin Hannah?" he jokes.

Mr. Angelini explains the menu. At first glance, there's a filet, tortellini, caprese salad, and poached pears, among other delectables. He shows me the movie list and how to use the headset. He explains the remote used to recline the soft leather seat into a bed. He rolls the privacy screen into place.

"You can rest now," he says kindly.

For someone who believes in accidents, this is *not* one. *Il destino.* I lean back in the seat, hit the button to raise my feet. I slide the window shade open and look out into the light. Nothing but an orange sun and pink clouds as far as I can see. It looks like the landscape of a Tiepolo fresco. A sense of calm comes over me. Is it possible that I can fly far enough away from New Jersey that the past can no longer claim me?

"Are you sure about all this?" I am not used to being pampered.

"My pleasure." He leans down so only I can hear. "When you've lost everything, the least the universe can do is provide first class." He turns to go.

"Mr. Angelini? Thank you." I am nothing but grateful to this kind stranger.

"Please. Call me Louie."

I reel back. "I don't believe it."

"Let me guess, your father's name?"

"No. My best friend."

Louie Angelini smiles. "Everybody knows a Louie. Is this your first trip to Italy?"

"Can you tell?"

"Prepare to be transformed." Louie chuckles and walks away.

If only, I hope. Have I built up Italy in my imagination too much? That's putting an awful lot of pressure on a country to become home to a woman who is without one. But I remember who came before me. The Caps and the Barattas did all right when the worst things happened to them. They were made of something indestructible, and maybe I will find out that I am too.

The flight attendant with the white smile appears and offers me a glass of champagne the color of a silk stocking. I thank her, wrap the comforter around me, and lean back in the chair.

"*Cent'anni.*" I raise the glass to no one and sip. I have an angel looking out for me, or maybe all the good-hearted, imperfect guys in this world just happen to be named Louie.

PART TWO

Sing It Away

11

Sweet Home Carrara

Conor Kerrigan and I sing "Flowers" at the top of our lungs with the windows down as we drive through the hills of Tuscany. Miley Cyrus sings in our key (or we sing in hers), which delights both of us. An auspicious welcome on my journey! I have pushed the passenger seat as far back as it will go to match the driver's side in Conor Kerrigan's compact powder-blue Fiat. Conor is over six feet tall, so he needs as much leg room as he can get.

Conor is a robust American of Irish descent, with thick sandy hair (needs a trim), observant hazel eyes, and a warm smile. His nose is straight and in proportion to his strong jawline, the Italian American ideal. (This is the model nose that my Spedini cousins ask for when they go to Dr. Salgado to get theirs "fixed.") No FaceTime image could capture the scale of this man, his presence. Conor is a bit like Italy in that way; you must meet him in person to fully appreciate the magnificence.

Everything changes at the starting point. The air, the light, and my mood are new to me as the road to Carrara twists through

Tuscan forests dotted with squat, full chestnut trees with thick trunks. The rows of trees hem the base of the mountain like ruffles of green silk taffeta on a ball gown. The scent in the air is cool cedar and sweet lemon, pungent earth and possibility.

"You're falling in love, Jess."

"Am I?"

"Good thing I put in for your two-year work visa at the embassy. I think you might be a keeper."

"Pull over!" I holler.

Conor drives off the road onto the shoulder, brakes to a stop, turns, and looks at me. "You don't have to stay two years; that's just an option."

"This is not about the visa, though I am eternally grateful. The chestnuts are down!" I announce as I pull a ziplock bag from my purse. "This will only take a minute." My mother was right. Travel with empty plastic bags because *you never know.*

"You're serious."

I climb out of the car. "Be right back." I follow a footpath into the forest.

"You're not going into the woods alone." Conor gets out of the car. "I can't lose you on the first day."

The floor of the dark forest is carpeted with ripe chestnuts; their shiny black shells glint in the sunlight through the branches. I am careful to tiptoe through the snarl of sticks and leaves without smashing the yield.

I kneel and examine the plump chestnuts individually, giving each a quick shake to make sure the meaty center is present before placing it in the bag. I look up at Conor. "Gold!"

"I thought you were kidding." Conor folds his arms, stands back, and watches.

"Never leave a chestnut on the ground if you can help it," I tell him. "It's called survival. Grandma Cap's law."

Once the bag is full, I follow Conor back to his car.

"I think you're going to make it just fine in Italy," he says as we pull back onto the road, leaving the moody woods behind. My first connection in Italy to the life I left behind is humble chestnuts. Grandma Cap would roast or boil them to pound into a dough to make gnocchi. I like to think the chestnuts are a sign that my grandmothers are with me in Italy.

We drive into a clearing, following a narrow road lit by the low orange sun. The Tuscan countryside rolls out before us in waves of soft gold. We pass an ancient walking path seared into the earth like a stamp on marble. I wonder where it goes, as its veins disappear high into the forest. I take it as a challenge. The answers are not going to come to me; I will have to *climb*.

Conor swerves onto a wide road that unspools in a straight line, the last lap toward our destination. I know we are close because I see the white summit for the first time. "Is that marble?"

"Did you think it was snow? First time I saw it, I thought it was." Conor slows down and points to the horizon that hems the sky. "They're quarries." The white peaks shimmer as though they are drizzled in diamond dust. I lean out the window to take in the peacock-blue hills that cascade from the mountaintop to the autostrada.

"How could anyone ever leave this place?"

"Did you ever ask your grandparents?"

"They were hungry," I tell him.

"The sooner you find what fills you up, the better. The day I landed in Italy, I knew this was it for me. When my dad died, I came here temporarily to run the operation. I thought about selling the business, but then I fell in love. First with the country, and then with my partner."

"And if she won't go, you won't either."

"*He.*" Conor smiles.

"*Sei bello da impazzire.*"

Conor laughs. "You'll have no problem meeting great guys over here. People say this is the land of the Ferrari, and it is, but the Italians' greatest invention is not the race car. Are you looking?"

"I don't know. I've never looked for love. I married a man who I met when we were kids in kindergarten. He was part of the fabric of my life, like the family I was born into; I didn't question it."

"There's your trouble. You've got to question everything."

"It's not how I was raised. I was taught to obey and serve. I thought if I made other people happy, that would make me happy. I'm in therapy to sort it all out. Online."

"Is the therapy working?"

"I got on the plane, didn't I?" I say cheerfully.

"Louie Cap believed in you. He assured me that you could run the business without him."

"Did he? Did Uncle Louie also tell you that he was running a second operation where he resold marble he didn't use on jobs, banking the profits in the Cayman Islands?"

"Louie was not enthusiastic about paying a lot of taxes," Conor admits. "But who is?"

"He *paid*; he just didn't pay double. This is according to the FBI. They believe his operation, called the Elegant Gangster, owes the government back taxes."

"How much money are we talking about?" Conor asks.

"Enough that it's worth the investigation to find out."

I have plenty to leave behind, not just my marriage, but matters at work. Typically, I'd be anxious at the thought of all that lies ahead with the FBI, but I find that I'm not. Instead, I have a sense of peace as we drive toward Carrara. Uncle Louie often spoke of the serenity of Italy, how it soothed him and shored up his soul. If I experience either of those on my journey, I just might figure out what makes me happy.

Conor turns off the autostrada. The village of Carrara is tucked into the blue-green velvet folds of the Apuan Alps like a rare sapphire. It is just as my grandmother described it, but even her stories cannot compare to the thrill of seeing her hometown for the first time.

Sensing my wonder, Conor slows down and turns onto a narrow side street dappled with glistening cobblestones still wet from rain. I jump out of the car and run to the piazza. The sun is setting; the last of the light illuminates the amber, mustard, and coral painted stucco facades of the buildings. The vivid colors are framed in a glossy black trim like works of art.

"I don't want the sun to go down."

"It'll be back in the morning," Conor promises.

Piazza Alberica fades into the blue in the last moments of daylight. I stop to inhale the sweet air. "Take a deep breath."

Conor takes it in. "What is that?"

"Petrichor. The scent of rain on stone. Uncle Louie liked to watch when the stonemasons cut marble because they'd douse it with water as they cut. Had the same scent. Uncle Louie would close his eyes and say it reminded him of Carrara." *The rain is a sign*, I tell myself.

Our heels tap against the marble tiles like sticks against a snare drum as we cross the serene town square. I look up, beyond the town square, where a ring of foamy clouds has settled over the mountaintop like a halo.

A regal statue of the Duchess of Massa in the center of the square oversees the town.

"Say hello to the duchess. Maria Beatrice d'Este," Conor says.

"She's a beauty."

"It only mattered that she was rich."

Maria Beatrice's hooded eyes look up to the white hills where the marble from which she is sculpted was mined. The folds of her opulent alabaster robe and the crown anchored in her smooth curls are proof of her stature and the wealth she inherited from her lucrative family business. There's a lion guarding his mistress at the base of the pedestal. Above the lion, the duchess holds a scroll in one hand, a staff in the other. A menacing bird at her feet protects her, even though it doesn't appear that she needs it.

Conor leads me across the piazza, past the statue, to a white brick building set behind a black wrought-iron gate.

"This is the place I texted you about," he says. I follow Conor inside the entrance garden. "If you don't like it, there are options," he says as he knocks on the door of number 19, apartment 1.

A youthful woman in her fifties, her brown hair tied back in a low ponytail, answers the door.

"Conor! Come in, come in," she says. Signora Laura Strazza wears khaki pants belted at the waist with a white dress shirt half tucked, pale blue loafers, and gold hoop earrings.

I follow them inside through the small foyer and into the living room. Signora Strazza has decorated the place in the rich blue tones of a Francesco Albani painting, with none of the whimsy. This is an uncluttered and modern flat where every object in view has a purpose.

We hear laughter. An attractive woman and a good-looking man (both around my age) chat as she cuts his hair beyond the open French doors that lead to a garden. The woman is lovely, with shiny black hair to her waist, while the man, with a thick head of brown hair, is draped in a beach towel. A girl around six or seven years old sits cross-legged on the green-and-white-striped settee, oblivious to her parents. She colors with crayons in a book.

The woman lifts a small section of his hair and cuts, shearing a curl before it falls to the garden floor. A feeling of desire peels through me. Conor is right; in the land of the Ferrari, this guy is a Lamborghini. He is a stranger to me, and yet he's familiar. I am drawn to him, until the man looks up at me and through me as though I am the Uninvited.

Signora Strazza introduces us. "*Questo è mio figlio, Angelo. Dalia si sta tagliando i capelli, e quella è Alice.*"

Angelo nods. Dalia smiles, and Alice looks up from her book and gives a little wave.

Signora Strazza closes the French doors. "My garden is not always a barbershop."

"This is Signorina Baratta from New Jersey," Conor introduces me. "Signora Strazza has an apartment available for rent."

"Aren't I a *signora* if I've been married?"

"Technically, yes," Conor says, shooting me a look. Evidently, divorce carries the same stigma in a traditional Italian village as it does in my hometown in New Jersey.

"*Signorina* is fine," I tell them.

"Signorina Baratta. You're American." She places her hands on her hips.

"Yes." What is this, an inquisition?

"Your people are from Puglia. The south." Signora Strazza puts her nose in the air.

"I'm also Tuscan."

"On her mother's side," Conor adds.

"Capodimonte?" I offer up my middle name like it's an envelope of cash New Jersey supers are offered in exchange for first dibs on a nice apartment. Signora Strazza is not impressed. Conor and I follow her up the stairs to the third floor. She fishes for a key on a ring of them she wears around her wrist like a charm bracelet. She unlocks the door of apartment 7.

The furnished studio apartment is a large attic room, decorated to Signora Strazza's aesthetic. The walls are painted the palest blue, almost white. There's a prim double bed in an alcove, neatly made with a white coverlet. A set of French doors, propped open, leads to a balcony overlooking the piazza. The organza sheers catch the breeze and flutter inside the apartment like wings. I brush them aside and go out onto the terrace. The view of the town in the last of daylight rolls out like a priceless Aubusson. The town square is empty, making it easy to see the artful pattern of the inlaid stonework that extends to the edge of the piazza.

"*Lei piace?*" Signora Strazza asks from behind me. "Satisfactory?"

I nod. "*Grazie mille, signora.*"

Back inside, Signora Strazza shows me the galley kitchen, the alcove, and the bathroom; she's chattering about the amenities but I'm not listening. My eye is focused on the terrace. The light. The air. The local color of piazza living. This apartment would put the memory of my cellar room behind me for good! And the high-rise in Hoboken? Keep your Hudson River and the Manhattan skyline; I've got the mountains, the sea, and Renaissance architecture.

"*Ho un appartamento più grande da offrire nella porta accanto,*" Signora Strazza offers.

"Signora Strazza says there's another apartment, a one-bedroom available. Do you want to see it?" Conor asks.

"No. No. I love this. I'll take it! I want to live here." I turn to Signora Strazza. "*Perfetto!*" I assure her.

She shrugs. She leaves the key to apartment 7, my new home, on the dining table.

Before she goes, I offer the bag of chestnuts. "*Castagne. Per Lei.*"

She takes the sack as a smile crosses her lips. "*Grazie, signorina.*"

"*Prego.*"

Conor closes the door behind her. "The chestnuts were a nice touch."

"Who's the family in the garden?"

"That's her son." Conor shrugs. "I just met Dalia and Alice for the first time with you."

"Married? Too bad. He's cute," I tell him. "I'm starving."

"Me too. I know a place. Settle in. I have a couple of calls to make. I'll meet you downstairs."

The first thing I do is place my passport in the cupboard in the kitchen. Before I snap the leather sleeve shut, I open it and look at the circular red stamp awarded to me upon my entrance to Italy. I have arrived.

I lift my suitcase onto the bed in the alcove and unzip it. I hang my good jacket, dress, and coat in the closet. I take my toiletries into the bathroom. I'm glad I bought the good stuff at Nordstrom's autumn blowout. A fresh start begins with self-care. (Thanks, Dr. Rhoda.) The last time I bought this many new toiletries was when I packed for Rutgers. I line up the pretty containers on the glass shelf over the sink as if they're on display in a posh boutique. I run the bath. Steaming-hot water pours out of the faucet and into the four-legged white marble tub.

A stack of fresh white towels is folded on a stool next to the tub. I return to the main room to finish unpacking. Shoes on the rack in the bottom of the closet. New undergarments and pajamas in the bureau. Keeping things simple will be the foundation of my new Italian life.

I place the snacks in the kitchen cabinet. I take my phone into the bathroom and set it on the shelf. I need a clock. Instinctively I go to dial my mother's number, to tell her that I landed safely. I remember they're on the Island, so I text my sister and brother instead.

I'm here. Carrara. Bellissima. All is well.

I slide the phone back onto the shelf and undress. I sink into the hot water in the tub. Every muscle in my body releases its tension after the long flight and drive from Milan. I wash my hair and rinse it. I run my fingers through my clean hair. Hallelujah. My hair agrees with the water in Italy. The soft water soothes me. The tub is so large, I practically float in the bubbles.

I wanted a marble bathtub like this my whole life. I will write in my journal later, but while I'm partially submerged, I remember when Bobby Bilancia found our first apartment.

"YOU'RE GONNA LOVE this place." Bobby picked me up on January 9, 2020, and carried me through the front door of apartment 3 before he gently placed me on the floor.

"Is it *us* or what?" He was giddy and spun around. The Shore Drive complex on the outskirts of Lake Como was for the newly married or nearly buried.

The empty apartment smelled of fresh paint. The front door opened into the living room, which I would not have chosen. The galley kitchen to the right of the living room was small and seemed like an afterthought. Bobby put money down on the rental; evidently, every newlywed on the Jersey Shore saw this apartment, and there was sure to be a bidding war.

"Let's see the bedroom." I followed Bobby through the living room to the back of the apartment.

"Most important room in the house," he teased, taking me into his arms.

"It's not a house; it's an apartment." I sounded like my mother, who believes nothing, no matter how significant, is good enough.

Bobby is undeterred. "This is our starter place. We'll get a house someday. We just need to save up some more money."

"But the interest rates are good now. I checked online, and Belmar has some affordable homes."

"I want our children to go to Saint Rose School like we did. I like a low rent and shoring up our savings," Bobby said firmly. "It worked for my parents, and it'll work for us."

"But our money will grow if we invest in a house instead of renting."

"We have a money market." Bobby sighed. "This is a quick commute to the butcher shop. I could bike to and from work. Save on gas. Leave the car for your needs."

I bit my lip. It was true. I could use his car.

"Okay." I gave up because there was no point in fighting. Bobby was on track to run the butcher shop while I remained Uncle Louie's draftsman and assistant. There was no comparison between our salaries. But I couldn't help but think this wasn't just about the commute. Bobby wanted to be close to his parents—close like *across the street.*

Bobby opened the door to the en suite bathroom. A gargantuan walk-in shower with sliding glass doors and all the wall-attached Swedish gizmos took up half of the space. There was a double sink, and the toilet was behind a glass brick wall.

"How about that shower?" Bobby said proudly.

"There's no tub."

"Soaking in a tub is a waste of time." Bobby could see that I was disappointed. "You want a tub?" he asked, hoping the answer was no.

"I love to soak in a tub."

"Since when?" His tone turned impatient, and I felt myself backpedaling.

"I don't know. Just an idea." I wanted him to be happy, even if it meant I didn't get a bathtub. "The shower is fine."

"The shower is state-of-the-art. It's more than fine. It's brand-new. You'll love it!" Bobby went inside the walk-in and fiddled with the showerhead. "The floor heats. Look. You just hit it on this panel over here."

"Fabulous." I forced a smile. The bathroom might be the newest room, but it had the least personality in an apartment that had none.

"Then we take it?" Bobby asked eagerly. "The Bilancias move in?"

"The Bilancias move in."

Bobby kissed me. This apartment would be our first home. Did it really matter where we were as long as my husband was happy? I figured I could make anything warm and cozy, and if I couldn't, we could always sleep on the shower floor.

12

The View from Maria Beatrice's Head

I STEP OUT OF the bathtub of my dreams and wrap a towel around myself.

I open the closet door. The new clothes I brought to Italy include every color but black, subconscious proof I want a new start, out of the basement and into the light! As I dress, I remember when Uncle Louie and I listened to *Walden* on audio. Thoreau wrote, "Beware all enterprises that require new clothes." Uncle Louie thought Thoreau was a little harsh ("Who doesn't like a snazzy new outfit?" he said at the time), but I thought there was wisdom in it. I packed nothing but new clothes, so I plan to embrace every single enterprise that requires them, starting with my first Italian dinner with Conor. After all, a new start means everything should be new, not just my attitude.

I walk up to Conor, who is in conversation with Angelo on the piazza.

"You don't look like the woman I dropped off here an hour ago,"

Conor says while Signora Strazza's son looks at me, his expression softening a bit.

"I had to get the stink of free first class off me."

"New jacket?" Conor asks.

"How could you tell?"

Conor grabs the sales tag attached to the back of my sleeve and gives it a yank. He hands the tag to me; I slip it into my pocket. I have no fashionable allure. Now Conor knows I live for a discount.

I put out my hand to officially introduce myself to Angelo.

"Ciao," Angelo says, keeping his hands in his pockets.

I awkwardly pull my rejected hand away and clutch the strap on my shoulder bag.

Angelo is tall like Conor. He has dark brown hair (cropped short from the recent haircut), a strong nose, and a nice mouth. No idea about the teeth because his lips are pressed into a straight line like a zipper that's stuck. He wears a crisp white button-down shirt and jeans rolled at the hem. Timberland boots. The national shoe of Italian men. I know this for sure because there was a time when Googs and Uncle Louie shipped a supply to Milan for a hefty profit.

"You rented the apartment from my mother." His English is excellent; it would be nice if his attitude were too.

"Your mother left me the key, and I was baptized in the tub, so yes. I think we have a deal."

"*Va bene,*" Angelo says, studying me.

Angelo's gaze unsettles me, so I attempt to fill the awkward silence. "You look like your mother."

"Unless you met my *papà*."

"Oh, I'm sure I'll see him around." I smile.

"He died seven weeks ago."

"I'm so sorry," I say.

Angelo nods and walks away.

"Sorry," Conor apologizes. "I didn't think to tell you about his father. I didn't know you'd love the first apartment you looked at."

"That guy just ruined my birthday."

"Happy birthday." Conor takes my hand. "I wish you would've told me sooner. We'll have to turn this evening around. I think I can. There's a wonderful restaurant on Via Mafalda Spolti."

I look back over my shoulder. "I hope I didn't offend Signora Strazza and her son."

"You were fine. Angelo didn't want his mother to rent the apartment."

My heart sinks. I knew apartment 7 was too good to be true. Nobody is this lucky. "Does he want it for himself?"

"No, he doesn't live in the building. Signora Strazza and her husband converted the house into apartments a couple of years ago. He handled the rentals, and they've had problems with previous tenants. But I assured them you are a solid citizen. And I just paid the first three months of your rent to prove it. In the meantime, we'll wait for your long-term work visa to go through. If you decide to go home sooner, no problem."

"What if I fall in love with Italy?" I ask, thinking about what awaits me at home.

"Then you stay and apply for your dual citizenship or fall in love and marry somebody from around here and live a perfect life."

"Let's not count on that. I will need work to pay for my room with a view. I'll Venmo you."

"E. M. Forster. Great novel." Conor grins. "Better movie. You up for your first gig in Carrara?"

"Yes, please."

"I have a client in Bergamo who wants a drawing of the piazza. Your terrace has the best view."

"I accept the job. Thank you."

"It's not a very good birthday gift."

"Are you kidding? It's the best. I'm hitting the ground running." I take Conor's arm. "What does Angelo Strazza do for a living?"

"He's a gilder. He specializes in gold on marble."

That's the attraction, I think to myself. He works with his hands. He's an artist.

"I've worked with him," Conor says. "He's a perfectionist."

"And he's the kind of guy that if he had a good personality, he'd be dangerous," I say.

I've met my first Italian man from *the other side*. Now I understand why Grandma Cap warned me about them.

THE MORNING SUN drenches Piazza Alberica in a blanket of tangerine velvet. The sky has been a different color every morning since I arrived, or maybe I'm just looking at the world differently. I sit at the small table on the terrace and draw the piazza as Carrara comes alive.

I put down my pencil and pick up the cup of hot coffee. I close my eyes and sip. Why is my morning coffee more delicious in Italy? Italians, whether you've just met them or known them a lifetime, know the importance of a good cup of coffee. I found a shop on the piazza where they sell finely ground beans. The cream is fresh from a farm near town.

A small brown sparrow drops out of the sky and lands on the table. He looks at me.

"I'm sorry. I have nothing for you to eat."

The bird cocks its head and flies off. *If you want a man to stay, feed him*, Grandma Cap used to say in Italian. I remember the day her bird Oscar Hammerstein flew away. I tuck the pencil behind my ear and reach for my phone. I write.

"Grandma?" I called out. The aroma of fresh coffee wafted from the kitchen. "I got the bread!" I moved through the living room to the kitchen. "A bag of rolls from Kohler's."

A full cup of coffee in a saucer was set on the kitchen table. It was cold. I took it to the sink. A tiny blue flame sputtered underneath the coffeepot on the stove. I turned off the stove and moved the pot to a cold burner. When I looked inside the pot, it had simmered down to a thick brew at the bottom. It had been on the stove for a while.

"Grandma?" I called out again as I moved through the kitchen to her bedroom in the back of the house. "I'm here."

Grandma Cap was asleep on top of her bed, made with a pink chenille coverlet. She was fully dressed in a pressed white blouse with navy slacks cinched with a slim red patent leather belt. She wore navy loafers, even though she was lying on her bed. The windows were open; the white sheers danced in the breeze. I went to the window and closed it because I didn't want her to catch a cold.

She opened her eyes. "Jess?"

"I brought you rolls." I went to her side and pulled up the tuffet covered in pink bouclé and sat.

"Grazie," she said.

When I was little, the tuffet was my favorite piece of furniture.

"Oscar Hammerstein got out of his cage," she said.

"He's probably in the drapes. I'll find him."

"No, he's gone. I opened the front door to check for the mail and he flew out."

"I'll look in the yard."

"It's too late." She smiled. "He took off like he's been waiting to escape since Louie brought him home."

I didn't correct my grandmother. The current Oscar Hammerstein was the fifth (or sixth?) parrot she'd kept in a cage in her kitchen through the years. The first parrot she owned was one Uncle Louie won in a ring toss at the Feast. She bought the current Oscar at the pet store in Belmar. I took her hand. "Oscar was happy here."

"Was he?"

"Very. We'll find him, and he can move with you. Dad is almost done with the basement."

She made a face. "I don't want to move in with your parents. Cellars are not for people."

I had argued with my parents about the importance of keeping Grandma Cap in her house, but Mom wanted her closer, even though Grandma Cap was just a few steps from my parents' front door. I hadn't told my mother half of what I'd found when I checked on Grandma Cap. I didn't tell her that Grandma Cap left the burner on in the kitchen. I let my father know so he could disconnect the gas.

"How's Bobby?" Grandma Cap asked.

"He's fine," I lied.

"He's a nice young man," she said. "But not for you."

How did Grandma Cap know I was leaving Bobby? I hadn't told anyone yet, not even my husband.

Grandma Cap pressed her delicate pink lips into a soft smile and closed her eyes. She took three sips of breath, and without any struggle, she stopped. I watched her color change as her soul left her body. I didn't panic; instead, I was filled with gratitude that I was with her. This was her passing as I imagined it, just the two of us.

"God bless you, Grandma." I said the Hail Mary aloud so the Blessed Mother might meet her on the other side. It wasn't a coincidence that Oscar flew away; he had completed his mission. Italians believe that birds appear to accompany our souls to heaven.

Outside the window, the light changed. The grim, rainy day grew darker under a heavy canopy of gray clouds over the lake. It was so dark, I turned on the lamp on the bedside table. I heard my mother at the front of the house calling out for us; Oscar wasn't the only one around here with intuition. I let go of my grandmother's hand and placed it gently across her waist.

I met my mother in the hallway. Her raincoat was wet. "Mom, she's gone."

"What do you mean?" My mother was stricken as she looked past me and back to the open door to the bedroom.

"I was holding her hand."

Mom pushed me aside and ran into the bedroom. She dropped to her knees and threw her arms around her mother. I ran out of the house and into the rain to find my father.

I PUT DOWN my phone and wipe my eyes. I miss my grandmothers; somehow they seem closer to me in Carrara, even in memory.

The therapist told me to push through my feelings and stay in the moment I live in, but the past is potent, and it has a grip on me.

A few well-dressed folks crisscross the piazza on their way to work. Soon they are joined by a young mother with wet hair pushing a pram with a crying baby inside. A shopgirl unfurls the awning over the entrance of her store. Someday, I hope to know all of their names, just as I know the names of the folks in Lake Como. A gaggle of schoolgirls runs together under the loggia, their backpacks bouncing as they go. A deliveryman pulls an Amazon cart piled with boxes (*Et tu, Italia?*), passing two older men as they have a spirited conversation beneath the statue of Maria Beatrice. A shopkeeper sweeps the portico and eavesdrops on their conversation. The scent of freshly baked bread wafts up to my terrace. I see a line of folks outside the bakery. My kind of people. I go back inside the apartment and throw on clothes.

I join the line at the bakery. I am completely unknown, except for the occasional stare acknowledging my status as *una sconosciuta*. This is the first time I've been a stranger anywhere in the world, living in a place where people don't know me and I don't know them. Even when the Jersey Shore swelled with summer tourists, I could always find Lake Como locals in the crowd, and they could find me. *Embrace the anonymity*, I tell myself. *You always wanted it and now you have it.*

I place my order to the baker in Italian, who appreciates my efforts at speaking the language. I studied traditional Romance-based Italian with Latin roots in school, but there are more than thirty dialects in this country. If I live here for the rest of my life, I will never learn all of them.

I carry the *cornetto*, a buttery layered pastry, hot from the oven, back to my apartment. Everything in Italy is fresh. I haven't slept in fresh air since I can remember, and I haven't woken up to the sun since I went on a Girl Scout camping trip in the Poconos when I was nine years old.

LA CAVA DI MICHELANGELO
(or Michelangelo's Quarry)

I began working for Uncle Louie when I was eighteen years old. My job brought me a sense of purpose that nothing else could. So Conor understands that the sooner I earn a paycheck, the better I'll feel about the future. He texted that he has already gotten me drafting work, which pays the rent, but I am required to share any information about salary to the FBI until the matter of Uncle Louie's offshore accounts is settled. I am taxed in Italy *and* in the United States for my salary. Uncle Louie was right about most things, but he never mentioned two Caesars. I have gone from one constricting marriage to another: first with Bobby Bilancia and, second, a marriage of inconvenience with the US government and now the Italians. Once a week I get a text from Detective Campovilla, keeping me in the loop on their investigation.

"Sorry," Conor apologizes, gripping the metal bar on the back of the seat of the van as we ascend the winding Canalgrande Alto from Carrara to the quarries at the top of the mountain. We slide into one another as the road swerves. I clench my teeth when we hit a deep pothole. There is one truth that binds all of humanity together around the globe, and on this we can agree: there is no such thing as a comfortable ride in a van.

"*Perdonatemi. Questa è una strada di merda.*" The driver looks up at us in the rearview mirror.

"He says it's a bad road," Conor says.

"I can't talk right now. I don't want to break a tooth."

"*Piove.*" The driver blames the heavy rains.

"LaFortezza needs to fix the road," Conor groans.

"Who's LaFortezza?"

"Mauro. He is one of the last local quarry owners on the mountain. When he meets you and gets to know you, I think he'll recommend you for projects."

The van hits another pothole. The driver grunts.

"Thank you. Not for the ride, the recommendation," I tell Conor.

"*Se vuoi mordere, morditi la lingua,*" Conor says.

"Is there an Italian saying for everything that happens in life?"

Conor laughs. "*Tutte le riposte si trovano nella saggezza della vera amicizia.*"

The van tilts close to the edge of the cliff as the driver hits a curve. I stifle a scream, but Conor cries out in fear loudly enough for both of us.

The driver chuckles. "*Non sono mai andato oltre la montagna.*" The driver's reassurance that he's never gone over the mountain does little to comfort us.

The van hits a stretch of paved road to the peak, smooth at last, and easy. The driver presses the accelerator to the floorboard on the final ascent to the quarry.

"To the left is number 35, where my dad and Louie Cap worked in the seventies. We're going next door to 36," Conor says.

"*Infine!* I may survive to make a living in Italy." I wipe my sweaty palms on my pants.

The gate to the official Massa-Carrara operation swings open. We drive into the worksite cluttered with flatbed trucks and heavy equipment. In the distance, a group of miners sits on the rock wall eating lunch.

The main office trailer is propped against the mountain, a short walk from the entrance of the mine. Just for fun, or so it seems, our driver proceeds to hit every pothole in the gravel lot before he parks, jumps out of his seat, comes around, and slides the van door open for us.

Conor and I climb out.

"There's got to be a sherpa guide around here that can lower us back down to town on ropes. And if you can't find one, just throw me off the mountain," I joke.

"Come on, I'll show you around," Conor says, handing me a blue hard hat. "It's dangerous. Stay alert."

The ground is covered in a thick white dust that clings to my boots. Gigantic blocks of pale white marble form the exterior walls of the mountain. Slabs of Calacatta are lined up in orderly wooden sleeves awaiting transport down the mountain to the sea. Looming behind us is the majestic face of the mountain, carved smooth from raw white stone so massive it pierces the clouds with its sharp edges. I find myself holding my breath at the sight.

Conor leads me through the mouth of the quarry. As we walk past the entrance and more deeply into the mountain, I realize the ceiling of the mine raises to several stories high. We stand in the white cathedral as I run my hands over the marble wall. The stone is cold and smooth like the surface of water. I trace the cursive swirls of gold in the white stone with my finger.

"This is Michelangelo's quarry?" I ask Conor.

"Yep. That little endorsement from the master of the Renaissance has helped me sell marble in six countries five centuries later."

I follow Conor back outside. The view from LaFortezza's quarry is as delicious as the detail inside the mine. He points to the rolling caramel-colored tile roofs of Carrara that look like they're made of toffee. We walk along the edge of the bluff. Conor shows me the competition, quarries in operation across the top of the mountain range. Glaciers of white stone form a jagged line to the horizon. Below them, on the ground, bulldozers leave a trail of black zigzags on the white ground while the forklifts dig arabesque grooves in the slag. The face of the mountain is sliced flat, a white canvas of stone that throws a light of such intensity, the sun itself seems dimmed by its reflection. A system of pulleys and diamond ropes used to cut the stone dangles off the marble wall outfitted with hooks and handles used by the stonemasons to mark the stone for cutting. The slopes of Carrara marble that extend down the mountain in swirls of eggshell with slender veins of pale gold resemble Burano lace.

"There's Louie Cap's wall." Conor points. "Fifty years later and they are still cutting marble from the face of it. In a hundred years, they will still be at it."

The thought of eternity and Uncle Louie's role in it moves me. I wipe away a tear on my sleeve. Conor doesn't notice and I'm grateful. He may believe that the mountain is forever, but when you chip away at anything, whether it's a vein of marble, a slab of wood, or a person's self-esteem, bit by bit, day by day, and year after year, eventually it will cease to exist no matter what the experts say.

"LaFortezza's operation is one out of about thirty," Conor explains. "Underneath us across the Apuan Alps, there are more than one hundred and fifty deep mines."

I follow Conor up a set of stairs made from marble blocks to a lookout that reveals the western vista. Tucked into the blue hills are clusters of small towns, including the gumdrop-colored rooftops of Porto Venere. The villages of Cinque Terre are scattered along the coastline like confetti while the rocky bluffs of the Gulf of La Spezia tower over the shoreline like parapets. The distant waters of the Ligurian Sea are a rich midnight blue, topped by foamy white waves that turn emerald green as they lap close to the shore. Except for the rooftops below and the white quarries above, it is one brushstroke of blue from the sky down the mountain to the sea.

"Marble formed sixty-five million years ago in the ocean. Below sea level," Conor says. "Do you think people appreciate that science when they bathe in a marble tub?"

"They do in New Jersey." That's something Uncle Louie would say because he believed it.

"At quarry 36, the LaFortezzas extract mainly luna marble. The pagans of ancient Rome named it. They looked up and saw the moon and thought it looked like it was made of stone."

"When I was a girl, I used to hold marble tile samples against the sky through my bedroom window. I'd close one eye to see if the tile matched the moon."

"Ciao, Kerrigan!" a voice thunders from below our perch.

"Make a good impression," Conor says quietly. "If he likes you, you're in."

Mauro LaFortezza is a big, sturdy man, around fifty years old. His black hair has streaks of white, like my mom's when she allows the gray to come in. His broad shoulders and large hands indicate that he hasn't spent his career behind a desk. Either this man was a stonemason or he was a starting tackle for the New York Giants.

"I'd invite you in, but I have a meeting in Carrara," Mauro explains. "I understand you draft?"

"Yes, sir."

"I would like to see your work. *Quando vedo il tuo lavoro capisco l'artista,*" Mauro says.

"*È vero.*" I agree with the big man. The work is the artist, and therefore the artist is the work.

"This is the first time my American friend introduced me to another American in the marble business," Mauro says.

"*Italian* American," I offer.

"You consider yourself to be an Italian?" Mauro asks with a twinkle.

"*Conosci i tuoi fiori dalle loro radici.*"

"My *nonna* died twenty years ago and yet you know her." Mauro laughs.

"They are all the same," I assure him. We agree that you know your flowers by their roots. An auspicious start for a friendship or, fingers crossed, a commission.

"Can we grab a ride with you to town? We can talk business on the way down," Conor says cheerfully.

"*Andiamo.* It's a better trip in the truck," Mauro says.

"I hope so," I say.

"Bigger wheels, better shock absorption."

"You could always fix the road," I offer.

"The government owns the road. Let them fix it," Mauro says, sounding a lot like Uncle Louie.

Once I'm settled in the back seat, Mauro makes eye contact with me in the rearview mirror. "Tell me about your company," he says.

"It's called Capodimonte Marble and Stone. I am the third generation to sell and install marble in homes and buildings in New Jersey. How about you?"

"My stepfather bought the quarry around the time he married my mother in 1974. He trained me to use the diamond cutter himself."

"You were one of those men hanging off the face of the mountain? I could've guessed it. *Forza!*" I tell him.

"We stopped using explosives and went back to the way the old artisans worked. We measured and cut; that's why the mountain looks like a wedding cake that is cut one thin slice at a time instead of a pile of slag. Without explosives, the quarry looks like it did during the Italian Renaissance."

"You took your mining technique back to its roots."

"We had to. We try to preserve the mountain for environmental reasons and yet extract what we need to sell. We do our best in that regard. We have machines now, of course. Automated hoists, cranes, and instead of ropes made of hemp, we use steel."

"I'm trying to imagine what the work was like when my uncle was here in 1971."

"I wasn't born yet. But they were still blasting then. Every excavation had a team of stonemasons, *la compagnia di lizza*. They blasted the stone and cut it away from the mountain. The man in charge is called *capolizza*." Mauro explains, "He leads the team of men called *mollatori*. They're the quarrymen in charge of the hawsers—the ropes. They were strong men, tough, deft—they had to calculate how to move the haul; they controlled it with the ropes. We move about four tons of stone down the mountain a month. It takes tremendous skill. It is a great honor to be part of the *mollatori*. They say the *mollatori* know the mountain better than God, who created it."

"It also took guts. *Coraggio*," I offer.

"*Sì*. The job that required the most courage was the job of the *legnarolo*. He had to be a fast runner. His job was to run ahead of the marble block that the *mollatori* were sliding down the mountain. The locals used to gather on the *via di lizza* to watch the transport."

"How can a man outrun a block of marble?" I ask.

Mauro's expression changes. "There are times he can't. You must pray that the hawsers don't break. I lost my father in an accident, so I know something about it. He died before I was born. So, you see, I have a love-hate relationship with the mountain. I make my living from it, but it came at a cost."

When Mauro drops us off at the piazza, we thank him and promise to return to the quarry.

"Bring me those sketches, *signorina*!" Mauro says as he drives off.

"I will!" I call after him. "How'd I do?" I ask Conor as I walk him to his car.

"He liked you."

Conor gives me a quick kiss on the cheek. He gets into his car to drive home to Lucca while I cross the piazza as the sun sets. When I reach Signora Strazza's building, I race up the stairs and into my apartment.

I have vowed never to miss a sunset in Carrara. I pour myself a glass of wine and go out on the balcony. I sit and rest my feet on the railing. Today, I expanded my view because I went to the mountaintop.

I sip the earthy wine, a rich red. Soon, the mountains recede into shadow as darkness falls, and the marble peaks emerge, catching the last of the light. The peaks become the glittering points on a crown that appears to float on the horizon. Here below, I live where Michelangelo, the duchess, and my ancestors once walked. There is so much to learn because so much is hidden. I didn't know the quarry would conjure such an emotional reaction in me. People have secrets, but places have them too.

13

Clues

I'LL HAVE TO remember to close the balcony doors before I leave for the day, as winter arrives in Carrara. I snap the latch shut and flounce the curtains. This is the first time in my life that I have lived alone. I went from my family home to my husband's apartment and back to my parents' cellar when my marriage ended. I planned to move to Hoboken before I lost Uncle Louie, but instead of proceeding with my plan after he died, I changed course. No one was more shocked than me when the world didn't end because I took a chance. I am grateful that Uncle Louie left me the ticket to my new life.

I have discovered that my great fear of living alone was completely unfounded; solitude is a gift and an essential pillar in an artistic life. Michelangelo said, "Genius is eternal patience." Perhaps he was referring to the time it took to create a masterpiece; for me, it was about the patience it took to live in a house with people who didn't share my need to be alone. I have, for most of my life, gone into bathrooms and closets to work. I knew in my soul that I needed to be alone to create, but I never had the guts to ask for what I needed. I guess Uncle Louie wasn't the only one who lived life on two levels.

I pull on a sweater and shiver anyway. I put on a pot of coffee and sit down at the table. As I wait for the coffee to percolate, I click through the black-and-white photographs I found in Louie's desk, which I scanned onto my computer.

I enlarge an image of Uncle Louie standing outside the quarry on the mountain. His thick eyebrows and the prominent nose, the smile with the strong Capodimonte teeth, are familiar, but not as I remember him. This was my uncle long before I was born. I did not know him with a big head of curls and the swagger of youth. Louie was just emerging in the world; his high hopes are captured in his warm smile and open arms.

I wish I had asked more questions about Uncle Louie's time in Italy. Maybe he tried to share his experiences and I changed the subject, wanting to talk about whatever book we were reading or a problem with an installation at work or my own agita, which was constant the last couple years of my uncle's life. I thought we had more time, lots more of it.

A notification sounds on my computer. I open the email.

Dear Ms. Baratta,

We are working with the Internal Revenue Service to resolve back taxes and fees owed by the Elegant Gangster to the United States government. We will reach out when we have further information. Please provide your current address abroad to us for all official correspondence.

Sincerely yours,

Detective Campovilla

Detective Campovilla is like a member of my family; he's solicitous yet irritating at the same time. There are moments when I am furious with Louie Cap for putting me in this position. But then I remember that it was his idea for us to come to Carrara together. There can be no redemption without forgiveness. I'm trying. I don't know if I learned that from one of my doctors on rotation at Thera-Me or from Sister Theresa at Saint Rose confession prep during Lent. I was raised in a family where we often ignored problems, hoping that they would disappear, or, even better, denied their existence in the first place. Denial worked for generations in the Cap and Baratta families. But I have learned that time does not heal the pain; only people can.

In a life where no one thought I could do anything on my own, including breathe, where every decision I made was challenged because I had made the wrong one, Uncle Louie put his money on me. Well, some of it. He believed I could do the impossible. And here, I'm doing it. Alone. Without him.

ACCADEMIA DI BELLE ARTI DI CARRARA

The Palazzo Cybo Malaspina is a twelfth-century stone castle built for a wealthy Tuscan family who filled their opulent home with fine art, music, and children. The gardens, when they are not fallow, are manicured plots of red roses, night-blooming jasmine, and gardenias. Spindly lemon trees, fragrant with white buds, will bear fruit by next summer. I identify the plants by snapping photos of their leaves to track them on my phone. Anyone can be an amateur horticulturist, even me, and even in Italy. I film a video of the fallow plants. *By spring, roses*, I post.

I walk under a garden arch into a marble breezeway. Students loll on benches, a few sketch, others check their phones; in this way, the academy could be like any school of art in America. A spider-web of outdoor loggias leads to the interior of the palazzo, which houses a theater, a grand ballroom, and a chapel. When Italy cancelled royalty, the *contadini* were the beneficiaries. Sometimes it pays to be a peasant.

I flip open my notebook and quickly sketch the design of the inlaid marble floor of the foyer. Triangles of gold marble offset midnight-blue stars in a pattern that sweeps the visitor inside, as if walking through clouds on a starlit night. The doors are carved of thick wood from the local forest and inlaid with gold gilt. The Malaspina family crest, intersecting lines staggered with the thorns of roses, is mounted on the wall. It's an accurate rendering of any complicated Italian family, including mine. Mauro LaFortezza has hired me to draft a series of floor designs for a private company in Rome. I am officially on the clock, *stile Italiana*.

Inside, the grand corridor and wide staircase are constructed of blocks of Carrara marble in coral and black. It is cool inside the palazzo, *gli e di accio marmaho*, yet the feeling of warmth, *caldo come l'oro*, flows through the colors of the antiquities. The intensity of the colors of the original stone has faded, leaving a brushed-gold patina as if the palazzo had been dipped in honey. The brooding depths of the paintings of Ippolito Scarsella create a backdrop for the sculptures of Bartolomé Ordóñez, perched in alcoves like castle guards.

The ballroom of the academy is set for the lecture, filled with neat rows of white folding chairs facing a podium with a microphone and a screen unfurled behind the stage. I don't know if a lecture can distract me from the architectural magnificence of this theater. Mauro suggested I attend the lecture at the academy to get an overview of the history of the local marble industry. I'm also getting an art lesson in Italian history. We are surrounded by murals depicting scenes from Greek myths and Roman conquests. The vaulted ceilings are mirrored gold, making the room twice as grand in size. More mirrors are inset on the walls, reflecting the jewel tones of the art.

A cool breeze ruffles the hydrangea-blue silk draperies tied back with matching satin ropes. A table, properly covered in white linen, is set with a silver coffee service and clear pitchers of lemon water. I help myself to a cup of coffee.

"Make yourself at home," Conor jokes as he joins me.

"I wish." I give Conor the cup of coffee and pour another for myself. "When are we going back up the mountain? I am going to hit Mauro's deadline for the fountain project."

"He'll be so happy. The next time we go to the quarry, we go with Professor Adeel. She knows more about marble at Massa-Carrara than Michelangelo."

"Sounds like she's my girl," I tell him as we take our seats.

Conor points to the refreshment table, where Angelo Strazza pours himself a cup of coffee. "Should we invite him to sit with us?"

"Ugh." The sound escapes my mouth.

"I guess not," Conor says.

How rude of me. "Guilty Catholic going in." I hand Conor my coffee cup, stand, wave to Angelo, and indicate the empty seat next to us.

Angelo throws back the coffee like a shot, leaves the cup on the table, and heads toward us. His dark, observant eyes are intense and miss nothing. If you combined Rochester, Darcy, and Easy Rawlins from my favorite novels and rolled them into one six-foot grump, you'd have Angelo Strazza.

I sit up tall in my seat because good posture indicates the return of strength as the patient heals. Evidently, as your spine goes, so goes your resolve. Dr. Cynthia has suggested that I attempt to be direct in my communication with others. Inviting Angelo to join us is a solid first step.

An art historian from the academy introduces Professoressa Farah Adeel, the guest lecturer, an engineer from London who is an expert on marble excavation from the Italian Renaissance through the present. Her list of accomplishments is as long as the Via Grande. A lovely woman in her fifties, the professor wears a pleated brown skirt with a periwinkle-blue sweater, which brings out her dark eyes and golden skin.

Professoressa Adeel takes us through the history of mining in Massa-Carrara, displaying photographs on the screen behind her to dramatize her points and provide perspective.

A black-and-white photograph fills the screen. It's an aerial view of the marble quarry above Carrara. Quarrymen dangle off the face of the mountain, secured by harnesses attached to thick hemp ropes.

"The men are strong, but the mountain holds all the power," the *professoressa* says. "The old techniques have changed through modern automation, but the process remains a function of a man, a blade, and stone on that mountain. There's a personal aspect to stonecutting that will never be replaced by a machine."

Professoressa Adeel goes on to explain the typical workday of the men on the mountain. My mind wanders to Uncle Louie as images of young quarry miners through the centuries fill the screen.

Uncle Louie came to Italy at the invitation of his father's cousin, who promised him a job on the mountain. His parents liked the idea of their party-boy son learning the family trade. I try to imagine Uncle Louie, a slight, skinny kid in his early twenties, working side by side with skilled quarrymen on the face of the mountain with nothing but a harness between the wall and certain death. No wonder Uncle Louie was invincible when he returned from Italy. He had risked his life mining marble; maybe that's why he became the leading salesman of the stone in New Jersey. What's a little creative accounting compared to outrunning a block of marble down the mountain?

La professoressa receives an appreciative round of applause when she concludes her talk. Conor invites Angelo and me to the podium to meet her.

"Ah," Professoressa Adeel says when she takes my hand, "the three audience members who did not nap through my talk."

"I enjoyed it," I tell her appreciatively.

"You're American?"

"Brand-new to Carrara," Conor says. "Our families are in the marble business."

"Lovely." Professoressa Adeel smiles at me. She turns to Angelo and embraces him. "*Come stai*, Angelo?"

"*Bene, bene.*"

"You know each other?" I ask.

"A little. Angelo and I have been emailing about his work. He's the best gilder in Tuscany, I'm told."

"I'm interested in gilding too." I look at Angelo.

"*La professoressa* wants to see my work." Angelo shrugs. He looks at Conor and then at me. "You're welcome to join us."

STUDIO LA STRAZZA

This would never happen to me in Lake Como, New Jersey. It wouldn't be likely that an esteemed professor and a fine artist would invite me along with a friend on a casual evening to learn about gilding. I am falling in love with *mia dolce vita*. It's more than a new start on days like these. It's an Italian do-over.

Via Regina is a narrow side street off the piazza along the shallow banks of the Carrione River. In Jersey, the Carrione would be a stream; it's so shallow, you can cross it at certain points without getting your shoes wet.

Angelo's studio is a large workroom on the ground floor of a converted stable. When he unlocks the barn doors, we follow him inside. The scents of turpentine and beeswax greet us as Angelo turns on the lights to reveal a workshop of enchantments. Renderings. Tools. Sketches. Plans. "My dream," I say as I take it all in. The walls are built from fieldstone; the crossbeams on the ceiling are outfitted with hooks, from the days when this place housed animals. Three long worktables set on horses are positioned close to shelves overflowing with books. Open cans house the brushes. Blocks of marble are organized neatly on the tables.

"*Brava.*" Professoressa Adeel looks around. Conor looks through the titles on the shelves as I examine blocks of Carrara marble carved with a fleur-de-lis.

Angelo stands beside me. "For the museum in Florence," Angelo explains. "I am slow, and they wait."

"Your work is quite lovely." Professoressa Adeel leans down to examine the architectural ornaments closely.

Angelo brushes his cheek, then brushes the stone. When he brushes his cheek a second time, I ask him why.

"We use primers and sealers in the process for speed. But even when I use modern techniques, I brush my cheek once I have applied it; I wait for the primer to come to tack and then apply the gold. It's personal. My own humanity binds the gold to the stone before I burnish it."

"May I?" I open my sketchbook.

I sketch as Angelo applies gold to the stone. He taps the thin leaf to the carving in relief. He uses a tool that is a slim hammer on one end and a hook on the other. The points of the fleur-de-lis shimmer; as Angelo moves his brush over the inlay, the gold fills the embossing. Angelo stands back. "This is my own technique to seal the gold. Every gilder has his own style."

"Please demonstrate." Professoressa Adeel sits next to the work-table.

Angelo uses a knife to tap the gold into the grooves of the design. He brushes a liquid resin over it. The layers of color in the marble emerge through the resin as the gilt settles in the crevices and illuminates the design in brushes of gold. Every element in the design is enhanced by the presence of another, which is the essence of *simpatico*. I watch Angelo work and it reminds me of Grammy B's expertise with her paring knife.

I HEARD THE click of Grammy B's knife on her cutting board as I entered her basement kitchen through the cellar door. Grammy B's basement was cool without a fan or air-conditioning, even though it was sweltering outside. The scents of dank earth and flour hung heavy in the air. A mound of dough the size of a deflated basketball rested on the cutting board on the silver Formica table.

Grammy B was tall, and her white hair was pulled back into a low ponytail. She wore a sleeveless dress with an apron over it. The apron was like a vest with pockets; it buttoned up the front. The pockets bulged with clothespins. Sometimes she had a pack of Juicy Fruit gum in one of them and would treat me to a piece.

"What happened to Connie and Joe?" she asked.

"They went to the pool." I washed my hands at the sink. The metal faucet was pitted from age, and the white enamel sink was chipped. The fixtures may have been old, but everything was scrubbed clean. I dried my hands on a starched white dish towel. The fabric was as hard as cardboard and didn't soak up the water. I wiped my hands on my T-shirt before I sat down next to her in one of the red vinyl chairs with silver piping.

"Why didn't you go swimming?"

"Because I promised you I would roll the cavatelli."

"I wish you would have gone to cool off. You didn't have to come."

"We wouldn't have enough macaroni for Sunday dinner if I didn't."

Grammy B grinned and shook her head.

She cut a corner from the mound of dough and rolled it out thin. She set the rolling pin aside and picked up her paring knife, cutting ribbons of dough. She sliced the ribbons into uniform pieces, with precision, as if the point of her knife were the tip of a pen and she was writing a letter. She sprinkled a handful of cornmeal on the cutting board.

I rolled the small squares of pasta with two fingers and flicked the shapes of soft dough into the circle of cornmeal at the center of the table. Grammy B used her knife and got the same result, adding the small tubes to the pile. I played a game with myself and tried to roll the macaroni faster than Grammy B could cut it with her knife. Soon, we needed more dough, so Grammy B cut off another piece from the mound and rolled it thin. She sliced the pieces, and we rolled. The dough seemed to grow the more she cut it and the higher the mound of cavatelli became as we rolled them. I also had my own agenda. I wanted to get this chore done so we could go upstairs and have anisette cookies with sweet tea and watch TCM.

My mom's family and my dad's lived close to each other, but they were very different. Grandma Cap and Grammy B didn't appear to have much in common, but they both loved old movies, and they taught me to appreciate them too. Whenever Italy was in a movie, we made a date to watch it together. *Roman Holiday*, *It*

Started in Naples, and *Houseboat* are my favorites, but maybe they're my favorites because my grandmothers loved them first.

Grammy B looked at me and smiled. She saw an eleven-year-old girl at the table, but in my mind, I was already grown up because we were true partners in this pasta-rolling project. That afternoon, we were equals, but that dynamic ended when she rolled the last of the dough. There were boundaries in my family, and though I was just a kid, I already knew how to keep secrets, and I knew not to ask too many questions.

I had my own ideas about our lives on the lake, which I would not share with her or Grandma Cap or anyone for that matter. I was the youngest, and that meant I might not know as much as my brother and sister, but I did understand that I must pay careful attention and forget nothing so I could figure it all out later. I learned that from my mom, who can recall small details of an event that happened years ago and throw them like grenades into a fight when she and Dad argue. I saw them coming and couldn't understand why he didn't duck.

"You worry too much, Giuseppina." Grammy B continued to roll the dough expertly with the knife. She could make *chickadades* in her sleep. "Why do you worry?"

I smiled even though worrying is not something that brings joy. I didn't answer her, because if I did, I would have to tell her things she wouldn't want to hear. The question should have been: Why *wouldn't* I worry? My parents argued about money. There was never enough. Mom worked for Uncle Louie but wasn't happy about it. Dad got bad news at work and it caused a fight. When they disagreed, eventually they'd make up and everything seemed fine, until something else came up and there was not enough money. I wished we were rich so they wouldn't argue. If we had lots of money, the fights would end. I was sure of it.

"You can tell me anything," Grammy B said.

"I'm worried that Dad's company moved to Buffalo." What could possibly be better about upstate New York than South Belmar, New Jersey? "Dad says we have to move wherever he can get a job."

"Did he?" Grammy B was not ruffled in the least, which soothed me. "There are many insurance companies in New Jersey. He'll get a better job here." Grammy B rolled the macaroni so quickly, I barely saw the blade on the flat knife move. "Don't you fret. We are safe."

"Can I use the knife?"

"Someday. Right now, your hands are still small enough to roll the dough. When your hands are too big, I'll teach you the knife," she promised. "Soon."

Cavatelli are small tubes of dough whose edges touch but are not sealed. Once they're cooked, you can fit several on a spoon at one time, which always bothered me, because people ate them in less time than it took us to roll them. An entire afternoon of hard work was shot in ten minutes.

"I am southern Italian," Grammy B said proudly. She was born in America, so Puglia for her was a dream state, a faraway place without all the nice things we have in America. She was happy to relay the stories about her roots, but she had no interest in returning to Italy, even though she celebrated her southern Italian traditions. "My family doesn't call this macaroni cavatelli. We call them *chickadades*."

"Why don't the Capodimontes call them *chickadades*?"

"Because the Caps call them cavatelli," she said, smiling, "and it doesn't matter to me what we call them, as long as we have Sunday dinner together."

"And you don't want to get in a fight."

"No need. We can be different and get along just fine. The Barattas and the Cascioles are farmers, and the Caps are miners."

"You grow the food, and they eat it."

Grammy B laughed. "Does that worry you?"

"On the Cap side, a little. You can't eat a marble birdbath," I told her.

"No, you cannot. But you can sit on your porch and look at it. You can watch the birds splash around in it. Living with beauty is as important as the food you eat. Sometimes beauty sustains you more than bread."

ANGELO'S STUDIO REMINDS me of Grammy B's basement. The tools are clean and ready to be used. The shelves are organized with supplies. There is order. Conor and Professoressa Adeel stand back, as though they are observing an installation in a museum, when Angelo picks up a clean cloth and gently dusts it over the gilding. He stands back so we can see his work, the layers of gold in the carving of the stone.

"*Bella?*" Angelo asks.

"*Sì*," I agree.

Beauty sustains Angelo Strazza.

14

Gilt

Conor offers Professoressa Adeel a ride back to Lucca, where she lives part time at the university, leaving Angelo and me alone in the studio.

Angelo shows me the fragile sheets of gold he uses to gild the stone. The sheets are like loose pages from a book, except the patina of the gold is lovelier than any words that could ever be printed upon them. "Sicilian gold," he explains.

"Sicily is on my list."

"I'll take you," he says.

Is he flirting with me? Do I want him to be? Before I can reply, he is back to business.

"Let's see your work." He wipes his hand on a rag.

I surrender my sketch pad to Angelo and regret it the moment he flips the cover open. He studies a sketch of one of the fountains I am rendering for Mauro.

"Hmm," he approves before turning the page. He holds up my self-portrait. "Who is this?"

"That's me."

"It doesn't look like you."

"It's how I see myself."

"You're much prettier than that miserable woman," he says as he flips the page.

I don't know whether to be insulted that he finds me lacking in artistic talent or pleased that he finds me attractive. "I'm just fooling around." I take the sketch pad from him and close it. "That's why it's called a sketch pad." I tuck it under my arm. "Just ideas."

"If it were hanging on the wall of the academy, your self-portrait wouldn't be accurate. That's all I'm saying," Angelo says, speaking English slowly and deliberately.

Either my Italian is lacking in his opinion, or he appreciates the opportunity to practice his English, but either way, I feel like an ignorant expat. I dive into a well of self-doubt. I have not been alone with a man since Bobby Bilancia, and it shows. "I should be going," I tell him.

"When a man pays you a compliment, the proper response is *grazie*."

"*Grazie*."

"You don't mean it." He moves close to me.

"I meant—thank you." Whenever I'm nervous, I pile on. It sounds ridiculous, even in the glorious Italian language. "*Grazie. Grazie mille*."

"Now you've gone too far." He laughs.

This is the first time I've heard Angelo Strazza laugh, and it fills me with desire. It's the first time in my presence that I see who he is, and I want to know more. "I have a question."

Angelo folds his arms across his chest. "Anything."

"Where do you live?"

"I *show* you," he says, leaving out part of the verb in English. I don't point the mistake out to him. Instead, I follow him as he crosses the studio floor and opens a door, revealing a bedroom behind it. I look inside. The neatly appointed room is spare and white, with simple furnishings, like a monk's cell.

"Where do your wife and daughter live?"

"I don't have a wife."

I really need to listen more carefully when people speak Italian. I thought Signora Strazza said that Dalia was his wife and Alice was his daughter.

Angelo goes on. "Dalia lives with her parents and her daughter in Seravezza."

"Is that far from here?"

"It's not too close."

"I assumed you were married."

"We aren't. That's her mother's highest dream"—he smiles—"and my mother's too."

"Every mother's dream." At least the ones I know. The happiest day of Philly Baratta's life was my wedding day because she told me the saddest day of her life was when my divorce was final.

"Are you married?" Angelo asks.

"I was."

"Ah. You're one of those. You want everyone to be happily married but it's not for you."

"Your mother has a beautiful building. There's plenty of space for you and Dalia and her daughter should you choose to live there. Married or not."

"Would you want to live with your mother?" he asks.

I laugh. "You're right. I wouldn't. What am I saying? I did live with my parents. After I got the divorce."

"Children?"

"Not yet." I put my hand on my lips like the answer accidentally fell out of my mouth. A simple no would've done.

"You will have children. You will marry again," Angelo says.

"Are you a fortune teller?"

"Just a gilder." He shrugs. "I live alone because I'm married to my work. And I must get back to it." Angelo picks up my jacket and helps me into it. "Where did you live in the United States?"

"New Jersey."

"Where's your ex-husband?"

"He lives in Lake Como. The other one. In New Jersey. It's a beautiful town. It has a lake and the ocean. That's very rare. We call it the Italian American Riviera."

"Why would you ever leave a place of such importance?"

"I don't know if Lake Como is important, but all my memories are there. So it's important to me."

"Why did you leave a place you love?"

"I don't know." I am not about to tell a man I hardly know the details I share with my army of Thera-Me doctors, whom I hardly know.

"Italy is either a destination or an escape. It's been this way since Hannibal's army came over the Alps," Angelo says.

"Italy is neither of those things for me. When I took drawing in college, the professor spent the first class having us look at a blank page in our drawing pad. We weren't allowed to get out a pencil. We had to look at the paper. He said that we couldn't draw until we knew where we were going."

"Do you know where you're going?" Angelo asks.

"I've begun to hack away at the rock, like the *cavatori* or the *scarpellini*; like excavators and stonecutters, you don't know what you'll find until you dig deeply. Or you can choose to stay aboveground and be safe. I guess I am looking for a different kind of security."

"Why did your husband let you go?"

"I'm not sure he has."

"You're funny." Angelo opens the door. "May I walk you home?"

"No need. You know where I live. It's just across the piazza. I can see my balcony from around the corner."

"I know," he says, leaning against the frame of the old door. "I've seen you sketching as the sun rises."

Angelo extends his hand, and I take it. His hand envelops mine, and he gently grips my wrist, as if to pull me close. I let him. The thrill of his touch makes me shiver. It's been a long time since I felt a rush like this. I step closer to him. His skin has the scent of cedar and lemon and salt, like a warm Tuscan afternoon.

"When I met you, you wouldn't take my hand. Why?" I ask.

"I don't know," he says. "Maybe I didn't want to know if I would like it."

Angelo takes me in his arms and pulls me close. I've missed being held since I left Bobby, but thoughts of his embrace are as far away from me in this moment as Angelo is close to me. Angelo nuzzles my cheek and his lips find mine. He kisses me. I melt into him.

I pull away. "This is a bad idea." My voice breaks.

"Only if you don't like me."

"You have a girlfriend. I should go." I move through the door quickly and out into the street.

The cool evening breeze washes over me as I walk back to the piazza at a clip that could, from a distance, seem like a sprint. I'd break into a run if it didn't look like I was fleeing the scene of a crime, which I am. My heart beats faster at the thought of Angelo's touch, his tousled brown hair the color of chestnuts, his eyes the color of midnight-blue velvet, and hands so expressive and strong they rival Adam's in Michelangelo's creation. I sketched those hands a thousand times in Renaissance art class at Montclair State. Why is it that a man who works with his hands always has beautiful ones? I remind myself that Angelo is taken and that there's a sweatbox in purgatory for women like me who fool around with another woman's man. I should be disgusted with myself, but instead, I find myself ravenous.

Instead of heading back to the apartment, I stop for an espresso and a butter cookie (who am I kidding, I will request a double on the cookie) at the Caffetteria Leon d'Oro. Signorina LeDonne sees me when I walk in and prepares my espresso. Can it be? I'm a regular! This is a small but important victory for a woman living abroad. I will celebrate by sipping the hot espresso from a tiny ceramic cup instead of downing it like a shot. Civilized. I hold up my hand and give her the peace symbol, which in Italy means double on the side cookies.

A kitten with a fluffy gray coat enters the bar. She must belong to one of the kids on the piazza. She appears to be well kept and is comfortable around people. Her face markings include a black line down the center of her face, which gives her the appearance of wearing a Venetian mask. Maybe she's on the lam from an off-season Carnevale. She brushes along the stools at the bar before she scampers off. She must be a regular too; she seems to know her way around.

"*Il gatto,*" Signorina LeDonne says, shaking her head.

"Is it yours?" I ask.

"No. She came from the mountain. Something must have happened to her mother."

"That's terrible."

The *signorina* shrugs. "Everyone that comes into my bar is looking for love."

"Not me!" I blurt.

"Perhaps you already found it?" The *signorina* winks at me.

I walk toward my apartment under the loggia nibbling cookie number two. The stray kitten from the Caffetteria Leon d'Oro bounds out from behind the basin at the feet of Maria Beatrice and follows me. I walk aimlessly, because I can't shake my first kiss with Angelo or my last kiss with Bobby. The final kiss between Bobby and me happened in the parking lot of Thompson, Thompson & Thompson. I guess Bobby didn't want to end our life together on a sour note, or he hoped a passionate kiss would change my mind. It didn't.

"You have to go home," I tell the kitten. She rubs up against my leg. I kneel. "Somebody somewhere is missing you terribly," I tell her as she rubs her face into my hand. "You must be hungry." I pick her up and she snuggles into my neck. "Did the farmer tell you I bought cream?"

I pass Signore Parolo, who operates the bakery. "*Questo gattino di appartiene?*"

"*No, no. Quel gattino giovaga qui fuori da una settimana.*"

I look around the piazza; the kitten doesn't seem to belong to anyone.

Signore Parolo goes on. "*La stavo portando nel bosco.*"

"You're not taking this kitten to the woods!" I tell him. I'm about to translate what I blurted into Italian, but it doesn't matter. The *signore* gets the point and goes into his shop. Besides, the kitten has dug her claws into the shoulder of my sweater, clinging to me as if she understood our conversation. "All right, little one. You can come home with me."

The decision to adopt the stray kitten may seem like a small thing, but for me, it's as big a life change as it gets. I have always wanted a kitten because, somehow, I knew the company of a pet would make me a better person, a more loving one. Bobby is allergic, so I didn't even bring up the possibility. My mother was determined to live pet-free. I don't have to live her life; if I did, I would be back in Lake Como, married to Bobby, and about to give birth to my third child. I nuzzle the kitten into my cheek. She smells like talcum powder.

As the shops close on the piazza, the lights on the street level dim, and the lights on the second story turn on. I watch Signore Parolo take the steps up to his apartment over the shop. It's the sacred hour on the piazza, as families gather for dinner in their homes over the shops that provide for them.

I carry the kitten up the stairs to my apartment. I'm naming her Smokey, in honor of her gray coat. I open a can of *tonno all'olio* and feed her a little bit. She gobbles it up. She curls up next to me when I check my mail. Dr. Albert has left me a message. "When adapting to a new environment, be kind to yourself. Making friends and acclimating is a process. Seek comfort and familiarity but set a goal to talk to someone you don't know every day. You will be empowered to form bonds and make friends."

I pick Smokey up. "Hello, friend."

I google "litter box" and find that, in a pinch, shredded newspaper will substitute for kitty litter on a temporary basis. So I rip *L'Eco di Bergamo* in a plastic bin and place the kitten in it. She takes to the idea immediately. I am thrilled. Tomorrow, I will go out and get the proper equipment for Smokey.

Starting over has its challenges. The connection I have with Smokey is satisfying because she needs me. I like to be needed, and thanks to Dr. Rhoda—or was it Dr. Elaine?—I no longer consider being needed a weakness. I wonder if I am building a new life out of all the things I didn't have in my old one. Or is the acknowledgment of the pain of certain memories where the answers lie?

When the Feast finished in mid-August, the tourists left Lake Como soon after the carnival rides were disassembled and loaded onto flatbed trucks. The Ferris wheel was the last to go;

the carnies rolled it out of town like a giant pink Hula-Hoop. The end of August in a shore town felt like a final sale—everything must go—so everything did, including me. I was off to Rutgers for my freshman year.

Mom stood in the bay window of the living room, waiting for me. "I wish you wouldn't run at night."

"The sun isn't down yet."

"It's close. Somebody could pick you off that path and stuff you in the trunk of their car, and we'd never see you again. I put coffee on."

My parents were almost done renovating our kitchen. It seemed like it took Dad years because he did the labor, and he had a full-time job, so most of the work occurred on weekends. When Dad finished, the renovated kitchen would be sunny and roomy at last, with plenty of counter space, white cabinets, a blue marble island, and a blue subway-tile backsplash. Mom recovered the booth and seat cushions herself with a Sicilian lemon theme, an Italian chintz: a bright polished cotton print in white, hot yellow, and blue. But they were still covered in plastic until Dad finished painting.

"This came for you." Mom handed me an envelope.

"He and Aunt Lil could've walked it over. Saved a stamp." I opened the back of the envelope carefully. I slid out the graduation card. *To a special niece.* A little girl holds the hands of her aunt and uncle as they walk on the beach.

"That's nice," my mother said, but her tone of voice indicated she didn't mean it.

"Ma, it's a check for a thousand dollars."

"What?"

I gave my mother the check. "For my college account."

"He's trying to buy his way back in."

"You know what, Ma? I'm done with your stupid Island. I don't want any part of your feuds. I love Aunt Lil and Uncle Louie. They've been good to me. And they just sent me a check that will pay for my books and some of my tuition. I am nothing but grateful to them."

"I taught you to be grateful. I also taught you to consider the source."

My father entered the kitchen. His hair was dappled with yellow dots where the paint had dripped onto him when he painted the kitchen ceiling.

"Good God, Joe, I told you to wear a shower cap when you paint."

"How about *Good job, Joe. The ceiling is perfect.* Which it is."

Mom looked up. "Thank you, Joe. It looks good," she said tersely.

"You're friggin' welcome." Dad went into the refrigerator and took out a bottle of beer.

"Giuseppina, Daddy and I need to talk to you."

"You don't have to drive me up to school. Joe said he would. Connie said she'd come too."

My mother looked at my father. "Honey, there's a problem," she said to me.

My heart began to race. "Who has cancer?" My eyes darted between them.

"No one, Jess. We have a little issue," Dad said quietly. "The money we put aside for your college is not there anymore."

"What do you mean?" My voice broke. My heart pounded faster as my skin tightened up all over my body. "What happened to my money?"

"We lost your savings in the bad market." Mom looked at Dad and then at me.

"You have to get it back. I'm . . . I'm all packed. I'm ready to go."

"It's all gone, honey." My mother's eyes filled with tears. "We did not intend for this to happen, but it did. It's out of our control."

"I don't understand. What did you do?"

They didn't answer.

"I start a new job the first week of October," Dad explained. "We're strapped until then. It's just bad timing. Could you help us out?" Dad asked. "Could you delay your move?"

My father had never asked me for anything, so this was serious. "What do you mean by *delay*?" I'd already met my roommates. Gin, a lovely Korean girl from Seoul, and Isabella, a nice Italian American girl from Queens. We chose our matching bedspreads online at Target. Mine was upstairs in plastic wrap.

I snatched the check back from my mother. "Uncle Louie and Aunt Lil sent me a thousand dollars. I could go to them for a loan!"

"Absolutely not," my mother said. "We can't run down the street every time we need something."

"This isn't a *something*! I'm not a flat tire or a hole in the roof or a broken tooth or some unexpected expense! There was a *plan*!" I was frozen like an innocent bystander blindsided by the crime she had just witnessed. I'd been robbed, except in this situation, the thieves weren't strangers; they were family. My mouth went dry. "This is my future!"

"How about this?" Dad placed his hands on the table.

It was hard for me to take my father seriously when he had yellow paint in his hair. But this isn't funny. It feels like a setup.

Dad went on. "You could study at Montclair State and

commute. Just for freshman year. Live at home. Save all that money. And by then Mom and I will find a way to get you to Rutgers."

"I could get another student loan. The deadline passed, but maybe they'll make an exception."

"We looked into it, honey. We maxed out," Dad said sadly. "We are still paying off the loan we took for Connie's schooling. We need nineteen thousand dollars to send you. The dorm is more."

"Dad. Please. There has to be a way. Make Mom heal her rift with Uncle Louie. He would help me. I know he would."

My father wiped tears from his eyes. "I can't do this." He sat and put his head in his hands. This big and tall man who shopped at the big and tall men's store was suddenly very small.

"I will find a way to get the money. I will figure this out on my own." I chewed my bottom lip like it was rawhide. The truth was, I had no idea what to do, or where to turn, as the gravity of the situation set in.

I was ashamed that my parents were idiots about money. My father was covered in paint because they never had enough money to hire a proper housepainter or plumber or electrician. Our lives were held together with duct tape and despair. I was furious at my mother for severing the lifeline to my future because she couldn't get along with her brother. I had nowhere to turn, and they knew it!

Mom began to speak. This time, Dad cut her off.

"I don't want to hear a word about your brother either," my father said. "Louie Cap has always been good to my kids."

"Now I'm the bad guy?" My mother put her head down on the kitchen table and wept.

"Don't start, Philly. I told you, when you poison the well, you can't drink from it."

I heard them argue as I climbed the stairs to my bedroom; my legs felt like they were made of cement. I pushed the door open, closed it behind me, and locked it. I looked at everything I had packed to take to school. I had borrowed my dad's leather suitcase with his initials on the lock. His parents had gifted it to him when he graduated from high school. There were large plastic shopping bags filled with bedding, a smaller one with toiletries, a hot pot, and a blow dryer. I had collected every item they listed as essential in the freshman manual and packed them to take to school. However, I didn't have the tuition; a lot of good boiling ramen noodles was going to do me now.

I made it to my bed.

I cried into my pillow for so long, it was soaked, like it came in with the tide on Lake Como beach. How could this have happened to me? I was ready for college. I worked hard, got good grades, and saved. None of it mattered. Money had always been a problem in my family; there was never enough of it, and it ran out, right on schedule, just in time to ruin my life.

15

Ravioli Revelation

La Camelia Ristorante of Carrara is owned by two sisters who prepare local delicacies from their garden to *la tavola.* They make their own wine, hand roll their pasta, and serve cheese made from the milk of their own goat. Their restaurant has the scents of flour and vanilla, like Grandma Cap's kitchen, where we hung strands of fresh pasta on wooden laundry racks. The sister-chefs have prepared a feast of delicate tortellini in a light cream sauce. They stuffed pumpkin blossoms with a filling of sweet pepper and duck.

Professoressa Adeel pours me a glass of wine and one for herself. She examines the bottle. "Oh my, this wine is twenty years younger than me! I'm fifty-three years old. Ancient ruins."

"My mom says never tell your age because then people think you look every day of it. It's a thing in my family. Instead of pitting women against one another, we're taught to pit ourselves against ourselves. At least in the end, we know who to blame for our misery."

"Familiar in my culture. I'm Muslim."

I raise my hand. "Catholic."

We laugh.

"Do Muslims get the guilt-and-shame platter to go? They hand it to us with our diploma when we graduate from Catholic school."

"Oh yes. I own that platter." Farah laughs. "You see, I am convent trained. I had the Maryknoll Sisters in my school in Pakistan. We had our religion, they had theirs, and they taught us everything else."

"The nuns pushed me toward perfection. You can never achieve it, but they insisted I try. When I draw a rendering, the first thing I do once I get up in the morning is revise it as the sun rises. There's something about that early morning light that helps me see the flaws," I tell her.

"That's how it is on the mountain," Farah says. "There's a reason the quarries are close to the sun. God could see what he was doing."

"Will you show me the quarries? Conor says you go up quite a bit, and I wondered if I could go with you sometime."

"Of course. It's the only family business in the world that has lasted for centuries. The Massa family owned most of the quarries until about ten years ago. The Vatican purchased most of the marble from that mountain. You know the stories of the great sculptors who went to the mountain to choose their marble. Today, productivity is as it was during the Renaissance, except instead of building cathedrals, we're building mosques. Some of the quarries have been sold to my people in the Middle East," Farah explains. "Tell me about your work."

"I'm in the family business. It's in flux at the moment."

"I was curious about why you came to Italy."

"The truth is, I had no place else to go. I had run out of options in New Jersey."

"What do you hope to find here?"

"Everything."

Farah smiles. "You said you're renting a place?"

"From Signora Strazza on the piazza. Angelo's mother."

"Is that how you found my lecture? Angelo invited you?"

"No, Conor knew of your reputation."

"He's a good man. Not a lot of those to go around," Farah says.

"Men are so strange sometimes."

"Do you think so?" Farah smooths the napkin on her lap.

"Don't you?"

"I used to be one."

I put down my fork. "I don't understand."

"Eleven years ago, I became a woman. Although, I assure you, I was a girl from the beginning; I just wasn't allowed to be one."

I shouldn't be surprised; there is something about Professoressa Adeel that is so calm and centered, it could only come from an inner knowingness, an irrefutable belief about her place in the world. She knows who she is, and the self-knowledge seems to come from her soul. "Forgive me. I would have never guessed."

"That's because it's my true nature. You can't fight what you are, what's in you. People try, and God bless them, but I couldn't. The girl won."

"How did you ever find the courage?"

"At first, it was so awful. My expectations were so high. I thought the change would make me happy right away."

"And it didn't?"

"Not at all. I wasn't the woman I pictured myself to be—at first. But I didn't give up. I stayed with it. And day by day, the person I saw on the outside began to look like the person I was inside. I began to look like the secret dream I had from the time I was a child. I had to let my soul settle in because I knew it held the wisdom to guide me through. One day, a few years after I transitioned, I woke up and my gender wasn't my first thought of the day. I was comfortable. I fit in my own life. Just in time to become a middle-aged woman and render myself invisible to men, by the way. Now, how's that for irony?"

I'm impressed by Farah's insistence to live on her own terms. "You couldn't know that it would turn out all right," I tell her.

"I didn't. But I had to change if I was going to live a life that mattered to me. I found moving through the world in my old identity was so much work. It kept me from my real purpose, which is teaching. All that effort to be someone I am not. Now I don't care what anyone thinks," Farah says.

We take a walk after dinner to the duomo as the sun sets. It was built in the eleventh century and has withstood changes in architectural styles, from primitive to Romanesque to Gothic. Constructed entirely of marble, the interior of the church is as cool as the stone itself; only the polished wood pews, red sanctuary lamps, and votive candles, lit by penitents, provide warmth.

The Altar of the Blessed Sacrament has tone-on-tone Carrara marble blocks on the walls. The sculptures of putti dance overhead; below, larger angels announce the Holy Spirit. A dove carved at the center of a marble monstrance looms over the Blessed Mother holding the baby Jesus. The saints in their alcoves balance the altar beneath the floating sculptures, all carved from Calacatta marble from the mountain. The candlelight throws shadows on the altar as the moonlight streams through the dome, throwing a peach glow on the gold and enamel tiles.

"I'm going to light a candle," I whisper to Farah.

"Light one for me, please." Farah takes her seat in the back pew.

I kneel at the shrine of the Blessed Mother and light a long matchstick. I light a candle for my family and one for Farah's. I close my eyes to pray. The sweet scent of beeswax and the tender curl of smoke from the matchstick remind me of Sunday Mass in

Spring Lake. A wave of sadness peals through me. I slip into the pew next to Farah.

"I sent up a flare for your family," I tell Farah.

"Thank you. But it may take more than a candle. I've lost them. I think of my mother every morning when I wake, and she's my last thought before I go to sleep. You see, she was the person who believed in me when no one else did. She understood why I wanted to go to school. She knew I outgrew my village before I did. She saw it coming. She told me I had to fly. She insisted that I get out of there. Home wasn't going to be the setting of my happy life. And so I listened to her. I went to school in London, and I still live there. Except when I'm here."

"You've built a great life."

She nods. "I have everything I ever wanted. Wonderful friends. I travel. I'm in Italy in a church that has survived since the eleventh century, built by artisans with marble from the mountain. I read about it in books, and here we are. This is a miracle to me." She looks up at the cross timbers over the nave. "I am most at home in history because it is bigger than I am. Bigger than my dreams and bigger than my problems."

"It turns out you didn't need your family's approval."

"But I wanted it. The irony of my life is that I wouldn't have been able to leave home and seek an education if I were a girl. We don't educate daughters in my family, only sons. I think about the old me sometimes and remind myself that without him, I wouldn't be an engineer. He became an engineer so I could become one."

"If I may ask, what was your name, when you were a boy?"

"Mohammed."

Farah and I laugh but hold back; we're in a church and laughter is not a sound at home among the pious.

"My mother gave her firstborn son the most sacred of names to live up to, and when I didn't, I'm sure I was nothing but a disappointment."

"You don't know that. Why don't you just get on a plane and go and see your mother?"

"I think about it," Farah admits.

"You should do it."

"You don't know my village."

"I understand when your hometown turns on you. You can't find one person who has known you all your life who believes you made the right choice. It's awfully lonely," I tell her.

"What do you do about the loneliness?"

"I got a cat."

"There's always a cat." Farah smiles. "It hurts to be estranged from my family. But there is worse pain."

"What is it?"

"Pretending."

Farah is onto something. The worst lies are the ones we tell ourselves. Those lies keep us in jobs we hate, in marriages that suffocate us, and in places where we cannot thrive. It takes guts to change. If Italy is the great teacher, and if she's going to be mine, I have to accept that there are no accidents. Professoressa Farah Adeel came into my life for a reason; beyond her knowledge of engineering and stonecutting, she is also in the mirror business. Reflective glass.

When Farah goes outside to take a call from the university, I open my notes app and write.

Uncle Louie and Aunt Lil were coming over for the first time in *months*, according to my mother (but in truth, it was *years* to the rest of us, who actually kept track of Mom's feuds). Nothing was more important to me than healing the family rift once and for all. It was 2009, and it was time to move Uncle Louie off the Island.

I worked for Uncle Louie on weekends when I wasn't in school. It was awkward when we ran into Mom when he picked me up in the morning. I was nineteen years old, lived at home, and had started my sophomore year at Montclair State that fall. I had hoped to transfer to Rutgers and live on campus, but I decided that my class schedule at Montclair worked well with my job at Cap Marble and Stone, and I wanted to do both.

My mother didn't know that during Uncle Louie's various internments on the Island, I would sneak down the block to see my aunt and uncle. I would visit, have a chat as Auntie served a latte and a slice of cheesecake. Sometimes I would stay long enough to watch *General Hospital* with Aunt Lil or play cards with Uncle Louie. When the fun was over, I snuck out their kitchen door, walked through the Parthenon in the backyard, went down the alley to Grandma Cap's house, swung through, checked on her as she watched *Jeopardy!*, walked down the street, and arrived at home in time for dinner. I always made sure to tell my mom I had visited her mom, because that part of my ruse was true.

Mom had done all the cooking for the reconciliation dinner because I was swamped with schoolwork deadlines. I agreed to serve as waitress and clean up the dishes afterward.

"Did you light the Sterno?" Mom asked.

"Yup." I returned to the kitchen and lifted the pan of stuffed artichokes out of the oven and carried it into the dining room.

"Connie, fill the water glasses, please."

"On it." Connie was in her senior year of college at Saint

Elizabeth's, our mother's alma mater. College had turned my sister preppy; she wore fruit cocktail colors like hot pink and lime green together and refused to leave the house if there was so much as one curl in her hair.

"Giuseppina, please call your brother to the table."

I went into the living room, where my brother was studying. Usually, no one was allowed in the all-white room, but for Joe, Mom made an exception, because he was in the thick of his second year of law school and needed a quiet place to study. It appeared the future of the Baratta family was in Joe's hands, along with our reputation. My parents were proud of him, but there seemed to be more riding on my brother than just the family honor. Connie and I were proud of him too; we just didn't understand why law school was so taxing and why he had been in a bad mood since he started. Wasn't being a lawyer his goal? Wasn't the pursuit of a dream supposed to bring you happiness, a certain lightness and joy? Joe was slumped over a book, making notes on a legal pad, when I interrupted his thoughts. "Joe, Mom sent me to tell you dinner is ready."

He didn't hear me. I repeated myself, loudly.

"Thanks, Jess." Joe looked up at me, bleary-eyed. He followed me to the dining room and sat down next to Uncle Louie.

"Where'd you get the artichokes?" Uncle Louie asked.

"Billy on the Shore," Mom said.

Their banter was way too cheery for two people who couldn't stand to be in the same room with each other as of yesterday. Was it me or were my mother and uncle overcompensating for their estrangement? Even Grandma Cap was giddy at the reunion of her children.

"Let's raise our glass to my nephew, Joe, who is changing the course of our family history. The Caps used to bust rock and now we bust books." Uncle Louie went on. "And to Connie, with her internship at Lane Bryant on Fifth Avenue! Congratulations, kiddo."

"Thanks, Uncle Louie." Connie blushed. "It's not a big deal."

"It's a very big deal to the big girls who shop there." Uncle Louie rapped the table.

"To Dad!" I held up a glass. "He has a new job at Nationwide Insurance."

"For the record, I was always on your side." Dad toasted the family and sipped.

"I'm proud of our family," Uncle Louie said. "Nothing but good news. Jess is pulling double duty at college and in my office. She is the future of Cap Marble and Stone."

"Sure, Uncle Louie." It was hard to accept a compliment in front of Mom, because she hadn't cut it at the company. I had hoped my part-time job wouldn't be discussed, because you never knew what would trigger my mother to send Uncle Louie back to the Island. One slip or a bad joke and this Sunday dinner could derail our good intentions. "Thank you, but I'm just a runner in the organization."

"You're so much more. You have real artistic ability," Uncle Louie insisted. "Have you seen her renderings?"

"I think it's wonderful," Grandma Cap said. "A family business should stay in the family."

"We're going for another century, Ma," Louie assured her.

Grandma Cap joined her hands in prayer. "That would be marvelous. Continuity! I remember growing up in Carrara. When the men went up the mountain to work in the quarry, my mother kept the house and milked the goats. The Montini family provided milk and cheese to the village. Mamma worked as hard as any man. We were so poor, but we were proud of our work. I would look up at that mountain and know that my father and his brothers mined the marble that built churches."

My grandmother holds up her glass. "I'd like to make a toast, to my daughter, Philomena, and my son, Louis. I am proud you could put your differences aside for the sake of our family."

"To peace and prosperity!" Uncle Louie said.

"To the lot of you with love!" Dad raised his glass.

"Spoken like an in-law," my mother joked. *"Cent'anni."*

"To the outlaw!" Aunt Lil toasted the family and winked at me.

I had been operating inside my family like a secret agent, carrying information between the warring sides hoping to find the path to peace. Now it was their turn to sustain it. I was done with all that. It was time to grow up—not just me, but my mother and Uncle Louie.

16

Saint Dymphna

I PROP MY LAPTOP on the folding table in Signora Strazza's laundry room in the basement of number 19. I review a rendering for Mauro LaFortezza. I am about to press send when the wringer washing machine shakes. I turn off the water, reach inside the machine, and rejigger the drum as Signora Strazza taught me to do.

The wringer washing machine is so old it was probably used by Elizabeth Barrett Browning during the Risorgimento, but I am nothing but game to try it because my landlord explained that the traditional machine is better for the environment. As I feed each article of clothing through the rollers, I notice this machine gets the clothes cleaner, a revelation from someone who lived in a basement with a silent state-of-the-art front-loading washer from Maytag. I am piling the wet clothes into a basket to hang on the indoor clothesline when Signora Strazza pushes the door open.

"*Signorina?*"

"You know, you're right about the wheel. It got jammed and I turned off the water and gave it a twist and now it's fine!"

"Do you have a cat?" Signora Strazza stands back and folds her arms.

"Yes! *Perdonami, per favore!*" Her glare tells me it's too late for forgiveness. "I meant to tell you about Smokey," I say sheepishly.

"Absolutely no pets in the building."

"She followed me home."

"*Nessun gatto!*" Signora Strazza's face flushes with anger.

"But she has no place to go."

"*Signorina.* There are cats everywhere in Carrara. I don't want them in my building."

"But she's quiet and small; she's just a kitten. She won't be a problem. I promise."

"Get rid of the cat. If you refuse, you will have to find another place to live." Signora Strazza slams the door behind her.

I've been evicted.

SMOKEY CHASES A small rubber ball across the floor. I get up, pick up the ball, and roll it in the opposite direction. Smokey chases it, pounces, and rolls onto her back and wrestles with the ball.

I text Conor about the eviction. As much as I love this apartment and the view, and all it has done to heal me with air and light, I love the kitten more than I love the apartment. If this makes me sound crazy, then I'll find a Thera-Me doctor to confirm the self-diagnosis.

I get up from the floor and go into the kitchen to put on a pot of coffee. I've been evicted just in time for my two-year work visa to come through. In true Baratta fashion, I was also evicted before my paycheck cleared. Evidently, I inherited my father's lousy financial timing, along with his unruly hair.

There's an urgent knock at the door. I hear Angelo call my name from the other side. I throw the *mopeen* over my shoulder and open the door.

Angelo's face is as white as the wall behind him. "Can you come downstairs? It's Mamma."

I follow him down the stairs at a clip. When we get to his mother's apartment, we find Signora Strazza sitting at her dining room table, struggling to breathe.

"Do you have a paper bag?" I ask Angelo.

"What?"

"A paper bag. You know. From the pharmacy. Small paper bag." I make a rectangle shape with my hands.

But Angelo freezes, so I tell him to stay with his mother. I go into the kitchen and search through the drawers. Every Italian woman since the Tuscans sacked Rome saves bags, so I know Signora Strazza must have a stash. I look under the sink. Found them! I blow into a paper bag to inflate it.

"*Qui. Soffia nel borso.*" I demonstrate breathing in and out of the paper bag, inflating it, exhaling, and inflating it again. "*Te.*"

I give the bag to Signora Strazza. She breathes in and out of the bag, her eyes full of fear. After a few moments, her breathing settles into a rhythm.

"Better?" I sit next to her.

She nods.

"A panic attack is nothing more than letting fear get the best of you," I explain. "Can you breathe with me?"

She nods that she can, covering her mouth with the opening of the paper bag.

"Close your eyes. Take a gentle sip of air. Breathe. That's it. Not too much. Exhale. Keep your eyes closed. Take a sip of breath, this one a little more deeply than the first."

Signora Strazza complies.

"Exhale. Gently. Your lungs are soft, like sponges. Your breath fills them. Slowly. Slowly. Inhale. Now exhale, slowly, blow all your anxiety out to sea. That's right. Picture yourself standing on the mountaintop. Exhale over the treetops, all the way to the shore of the Ligurian Sea. Let your breath take you over the waves and out to sea."

Signora Strazza's brow relaxes as she breathes in and out.

"Close your eyes. Repeat . . . *ripetti*: Bobby Bilancia Breathe. Bobby Bilancia Breathe." Funny how my past pierces my present through the silver arrow of Bobby Bilancia.

"*Chi è Bobby Bilancia?*"

"*Non è importante,*" I tell her. "*Fidati di me.*" I'm asking a woman who is nothing but suspicious of me to trust me. And my cat.

Signora Strazza furrows her brow and concentrates as she breathes in and out, filling the paper bag with the force of gale winds. Slowly her color returns. She transforms before our eyes.

Angelo stands against the wall with his hands on his hips. "Should I take her to the doctor?"

"No need for a doctor. It was just a panic attack. Plain old anxiety." I place my hands on Signora Strazza's hands gently. "Do you get these often?"

"Once in a while."

"They're frightening, aren't they?"

She nods.

"I get them too. You'll be all right. You need to rest now. Put your feet up." I pat her hand and turn to Angelo. "Take your mamma to the garden and let her rest in the sun. Before it rains again."

It's been raining on and off in Carrara for a few days. Maybe that's contributed to Signora Strazza's struggles. She's been confined more than usual, even though I catch her walking back and forth underneath the piazza loggia for exercise. Angelo helps his mother to stand.

"Take this." I give him the paper bag. "Just in case."

Angelo puts his arm around his mother's waist and accompanies her to the garden. He turns to me through the garden door. "*Grazie*, Giuseppina."

I take the blanket from the sofa and bring it to Signora in the garden while I recite a silent prayer taught to me by Sister Eugenie, a nun at Saint Rose School.

Saint Dymphna,
Fill my lungs and heal my breath,
Make me calm and help me rest.

The nuns had a prayer for everything. My first panic attack gripped me in kindergarten, or maybe that's the first episode I recall. The nuns kept a stash of paper bags handy for kids who might throw up, or for kids like me who would get so anxious, they would hold their breath until they turned as blue as the Blessed Mother's mantle. A fretful person can usually spot a fellow anxious person in their midst, but I did not see the signs with Signora Strazza. If anything, I was afraid of her. That's something to explore in Thera-Me. Am I afraid of people who are just like me or only those who have power over me?

I see Signora Strazza for who she really is, in her most vulnerable state. While I empathize with her anxiety, I have my own, some of which she has triggered. I have to find another place to live, and yet, it didn't send me looking for a paper bag. Am I evolving? Am I better? Is this the moment when my emotional grid lights up in recognition of the hard work I have done in therapy? Is this what it means to heal? I am going upstairs to make some follow-up calls on apartments in Carrara. I am not afraid of anyone anymore, not even Signora Strazza. I choose the comfort of my rescue kitten over the view of the piazza. Priorities! Thank you, Dr. Jean, wherever you are.

I watch as Angelo makes his mother comfortable on the chaise longue. He pulls up a wooden stool and sits next to her. A mother and her son in a private moment of understanding can be as inspiring as a painting by Tiepolo or as exquisite as a sculpture by Brunelleschi. How can there be beauty in suffering, and why do I see it so plainly? The love of a good mother might be the highest form of art because there is line, form, and revelation. And now that the cloud cover over Piazza Alberica has lifted and the pattern of swirls of lavender toile have drifted away, there is light. I slip out the door quietly. Mothers are either holding us together or falling apart themselves. I record a few thoughts about Signora Strazza in the notes app before revisiting a day I return to in order to understand it.

Mom had texted me her grocery list. I had one final stop before I had every ingredient I needed to make Sunday dinner. The bells on the door jingled merrily as I slipped inside Croce's. I imagined the scent of buttery dough and sharp cheese was the scent of Italy, and I couldn't wait to find out for myself. It wouldn't be long before Uncle Louie and I were in the motherland. I walked through the narrow aisles and loaded the basket. I splurged on small, exotic jars of tapenade, sun-dried tomatoes, and green olive paste on my way to check out. *Crostini per tutti!*

"Jess? I almost didn't know you."

My heart sank. "Mrs. Bilancia."

"You can call me Mom. Always. Or even Babe, if Mom seems like too much." She looked me up and down. "You've gotten so thin," Babe marveled.

Mr. Croce had set out a free tray of focaccia by the cash register with Olio della Donna to sample before purchasing. Mrs. B made no secret that she had been on a diet for the bulk of her sixty-seven years of life, but like me, she couldn't resist a carb. We dipped the soft bread in the olive oil, which I thanked God for because I couldn't talk when I chewed.

I couldn't recall a single conversation with Babe Bilancia that didn't involve weight. Hers. Mine. Anyone's. She'd cornered Lisa Natalizio, Debi Martinelli, and me at the crowning of the May Queen in sixth grade and assured us that we'd slim down when puberty hit.

She picked up a napkin from the stack next to the bread and daintily wiped her hands. "I'm glad to run into you. You know there are no accidents. This was meant to happen."

"Mrs. Bilancia, we live within a two-block radius of each other in a small town."

"Jess, my son is a fine young man. But Bobby is a broken boy. You really took a piece out of him when you left him. I don't know what happened with you two and I don't ask because, frankly, he is a person of good humor and he has a lot of responsibilities at the shop now that my husband retired, and I don't want to pile on. But I wish you two would work it out.

Divorce decrees are signed on paper for a reason. They can be shredded or burned or flushed; you can even line a birdcage with them. You move back in together, and we'll all pretend that none of this happened."

"I am so sorry for causing you any heartache. You were a wonderful mother-in-law."

"I tried." As her blue eyes flushed with tears, she looked like she was swimming underwater. "It's so nice of you to say so. Your mother and I have agonized about you two. We pray. We scheme. We try to think about what we can do to help get you kids out of the ditch and back on the track."

I leaned against the counter because if I didn't, my legs might have buckled, and I would fall into the barrel of pickles next to the checkout. "My *mother*?"

"I'm grateful that we have each other to commiserate. To share our pain. We're grieving. I gave her a podcast to download to help her cope. Anderson Cooper's. It's been a Godsend."

I felt violated—I listened to the *same* podcast as my mother and former mother-in-law.

"Is this all?" the cashier said to me.

"Yes, yes. This is it. And the ravs. Under Baratta."

The cashier disappeared to the back room.

I got up on my toes and looked after her. *Come back. Don't go. I'm being eaten alive out here.*

"Your mother and I tried to stay out of your business. We aren't meddling mothers-in-law, you know. We just love you both and want the best for you. Your mother did mention that the basement doesn't suit you and she's terrified you'll leave the house and get an apartment all alone and end up like one of those women who joins too many book clubs and shares cat videos on TikTok at all hours of the night."

"I don't have a cat." My head pounded. Was she done?

Babe went on. "If Philly had her way, you'd get back together with Bobby and stop all this nonsense."

The cashier returned with the sleeves of ravioli and slid them into a paper bag.

"Did you order enough? I can't get away with less than ten sleeves." Babe looked off into the middle distance. "Sunday dinner isn't the same. We want you back, honey. Bobby is like a lost ball in high weeds without you." She held up her hands like she was under arrest. "You are always welcome to come back to us. No questions asked."

"I don't have any questions," I whispered.

"Well," Babe said, "I said what I needed to say, and you know how I feel. Your mother has been so good to Bobby. Makes him chicken cutlets and drops them off in his freezer. We're all praying for a reconciliation."

I nodded, because if I spoke I would throw up. I handed the cashier my credit card.

"Thank you," I whispered. I picked up my bags and rushed out the door as though the shop were on fire. Once outside, I climbed into my car and set the ravioli sleeves on the front seat. I placed two fingers on my carotid artery. This was what a stroke must feel like. My veins were exploding inside my body. I looked out the window and tried to remember where the new urgent care facility was in Lake Como. I took my fingers off my neck to answer the phone.

"Did you get the ravs?" Mom asked pleasantly.

I could barely speak. "Yes."

"I can't hear you. Are you all right?"

"No! Mom, how could you?"

"What did I do now?"

"You drop off chicken cutlets for Bobby Bilancia?"

My mother's voice broke. "He likes them." She sounded scared. "He used to steal your lunch, and now I head him off at the pass." She forced a laugh.

"I am done," I told her. "You hear me? Done!"

—

IT'S TIME FOR my Thera-Me appointment. I swipe on some lipstick and open the Zoom.

"Nice to meet you, Dr. Nora." I prop up the laptop to get a better look at the doctor. She's around my age.

"I'm up to speed on your file; let's dive in. How are you coping in your new home?"

"I was pretty good."

"Until?"

"I have agita. Do you know what that is?"

"A kind of dyspepsia?"

"Can be. I get it when I think of my family, even though I'm not communicating with them. But that might be causing it. I'm guilty because I don't talk to them. That might be making me sick."

"Sometimes we have to let go of relationships that do not serve us."

"You mean put them on the Island?" I sit up.

"I don't know what you mean."

"It means I put them away on an imaginary island and don't communicate with them."

"That's exactly what I am suggesting. Sometimes it is best not to engage with the people who know how to hurt us. We have to eliminate them from our lives."

"I can't banish them forever. I want to learn how to manage these feelings and be a part of my family."

"Maybe you need to build your strength first and see where the process takes you."

"That's too vague, Doctor. I would like you to give me the tools to make this better."

"This is up to you," she replies.

"No, it isn't. It's up to *you* to tell me how to handle *them*. I want to learn to navigate the difficult relationships, not tank them. I want to be able to be in a room with my family and not feel resentment. I want to love them without the anger."

My phone buzzes on the nightstand.

"I've got to go, Dr. Nora."

"But you have eleven minutes left in our session."

"Yeah, well, I have the FBI on the other line. Punt my file to the next therapist and we'll meet up later."

"To be continued." Dr. Nora signs off.

I pick up the phone. "Detective Campovilla?"

"Ms. Baratta, I have a couple of questions about Rolando Gugliotti."

"Googs?"

"Yes. Is this a good time?"

I take the phone and go out onto the terrace. The piazza is serene. The Apuan Alps have fallen into shadow. The white caps along the horizon flicker as the night clouds pass over the bright moon. "How can I help?"

"We're having trouble establishing a paper trail for the Elegant Gangster and wondered if you might be able to help us locate Mr. Gugliotti."

I scroll into my contacts. "I'm texting you his phone number.

Keep in mind he hasn't responded to any of my calls since Uncle Louie died. It's always hard to say what could be going on with Googs. He's mysterious."

"Got it," Campovilla says. "When did you see him last?"

"On a pier in Perth Amboy sometime in the spring. With my uncle Louie."

"We have Mr. Capodimonte's phone records, but it appears that Mr. Gugliotti changes phone numbers frequently. Did your uncle ever give you any insight about him?"

"Uncle Louie said Googs had diverse business interests. Through the years he was a middleman for all kinds of imported products. Marble, of course. Olive oil. Wine. Kitsch. Aprons. Fireworks. Oh yeah, Timberland boots. You name it. I once bought a necklace for my mom out of the trunk of his car."

"Will you let us know if you hear from him?"

"Absolutely."

"And if you have plans to return to the United States, would you let us know?"

There's no running from the feds. They know where you live and ring the doorbell. Even if you're in Italy. I have been honest with the FBI because it's the right thing to do, but will it set me free? After all, Uncle Louie, who got me into this mess, said, *You only get cuffed when you spin a tale.*

As a practical business matter, had Uncle Louie lived, I might have been able to convince him to put the Elegant Gangster on the books. I'm not sure about that, but in my fantasy mind, I like to think my uncle thought enough of me to listen to reason. Sixteen years is a long haul to work at one job for one boss, and I paid attention. I knew my uncle as well as anyone did except for Aunt Lil. His associates? Hardly at all. Maybe it's because I was his niece, or maybe being female was enough to bar my entry into their boys' club. I will never know. I did not sense my uncle was close to these men, but he was always cordial. He got things done with them, on time and on a handshake. It appeared that all parties benefited from the handshake.

My brother, Joe, picks up his phone on the first ring.

"Jess!" he shouts through background noise. "Lemme go outside. How are you?"

"I'm all right." I feel better hearing the sound of my brother's voice. "Joe, why is the FBI calling me about Googs?"

"This is just a guess, but I assume they are having trouble seizing the money from the offshore accounts."

"I don't even know what's there," I cry out.

"They can see everything."

"Then why are they asking me?"

"They want to know if they're missing anything."

"Joe, how much is in the Cayman Island accounts? If you had to guess."

"I don't know. A few million."

I sit down. I had no idea there was this kind of money anywhere in the vicinity of or adjacent to Uncle Louie. "There wasn't that kind of money in Cap Marble! Not ever."

"Because Uncle Louie paid his taxes, salaries, and expenses."

"But he didn't with the Elegant Gangster?" My heart races. "What are you saying? Am I liable?"

"Unfortunately, you inherited all the assets and therefore any debts and liens incurred by Cap Marble, according to his will. You are the sole heir and that leaves you open for whatever Uncle Louie left unresolved. The FBI and IRS are treating the Elegant Gangster like a legitimate business. As long as they do, it opens up the paper trail to deal with the banks. And tax law. That's their hope."

"They want their money." I wipe my forehead on the sleeve of my pajamas. "I should have known. Joe, please. I need your help. I'm trying to—" I try not to cry. "I just want to be free of this."

"Understood. We can make the argument that Uncle Louie intended to pay the taxes eventually, that he was just holding the money there."

"Can you do that?"

"I will try." Joe sighs. "Can you do something for me?"

"Anything."

"Mom and Dad miss you. They're worried."

The longer I'm in Italy, the easier it has become to leave Lake Como behind.

"Can you send Mom and Dad a text, a note? Anything?" Joe asks.

"I will think about it."

I thank my brother and hang up the phone. The cold air reminds me of autumn in New Jersey a year ago. I open the notes app to write what I remember when I was with Uncle Louie and Mom.

Uncle Louie, Mom, and I stood on the wet ground in front of the Capodimonte plot at Saint Catharine's Cemetery. The family stone was high-polish Calacatta Nero embossed with gilded letters. The stone itself was shaped like a door, a door that leads, I was told when I was a girl, to heaven.

"Do the right thing, and paradise is yours," Grandma Cap used to say.

My Capodimonte ancestors, Philomena, Luigi, Maria Luisa, and Zia Giuseppina, lay behind the family marker. Uncle

Louie's and Aunt Lil's headstones were already in the ground. Our patch of this hallowed ground was manicured like the back nine at the Upper Montclair Country Club.

"Even in death, appearances matter," Uncle Louie said as he and my mother stood at the foot of their mother's newly installed headstone, made of coordinating black onyx marble with gold matte letters. Uncle Louie brushed a few stray fall leaves off the tombstone. "What do you think?"

"It's lovely, Uncle Louie," I assured him.

"Philly? You approve?" Louie asked gently.

"She was a saint." Mom dabbed her eyes.

Whenever a family member in the Cap and Baratta families died, once the funeral Mass was over, we submitted the deceased for sainthood. We threw out all facts and rewrote their life story. Villains became heroes, heroes became saints, and once you were a saint, we prayed to you to intercede for us in heaven. You were assigned a role on the other side as surely as you had one here.

Uncle Louie stood back and squinted at the new marker. "I think Ma would like it." His eyes filled with tears at the thought, and a breeze kicked up. The dried leaves on the ground took flight like winning lottery tickets in a drum. My macho-ish Uncle Louie could blame his tears on the cold wind. I didn't need an excuse. Soon it would be Thanksgiving, a reminder of all we had lost, including my grandparents. Whether Baratta or Cap, we had a hard time letting go of those we loved, almost as much as our anger.

"I want you two to make up," Uncle Louie announced out of the blue, as though the idea had fallen out of the lavender sky like a paper star. "I am tired of the fighting. Life is too short. It's time. Right out here, in the open air, in this sacred place with no one but Ma listening to you. *Talk.*"

Mom spoke first. "I don't know how you could still be mad at me when I am grieving the loss of my mother."

"I am grieving the loss of my grandmother too."

"I'm sorry for all of us," Mom said quietly.

"But Grandma Cap didn't go behind your back to Grammy B when you were having trouble with Dad. She remained loyal to you. Her daughter."

Mom turned to me. "Your father and I had our issues. I do not deny that. When I was a newlywed, I had a nervous breakdown."

"What?" I was not happy to hear that there was a history of mental illness in my family, though I shouldn't have been surprised.

Uncle Louie patted his hands as though he was kneading imaginary dough, encouraging me to take down the temperature and listen.

Mom nodded and reached into her coat and under her bra strap to retrieve a fresh tissue. "I went to see Father Rausch and he said he'd get me an annulment." Mom flashed her black eyes my way. "Did you apply for yours yet?"

"I am not spending five thousand dollars on an annulment when my car won't start."

"In the end, your father and I stayed together. Obviously. We pushed through a very dark time, and eventually, we loved harder than ever on the other side of my breakdown. I had Joe and Connie, and then you, the surprise."

"I thought your dream was to have three children."

"I wanted you to feel included in the master plan, but the truth is, we didn't see you coming. But there you were, and you brought us nothing but joy—once you were out of the NICU and could breathe on your own."

"What NIC Unit?" I glared at Uncle Louie, who looked down at the ground. "I was in an incubator?"

"For a month," Mom remembered.

"It was seven weeks, Phil."

"You were there every day, Lou. I'll give you that."

"Every day?" I turned to Uncle Louie. "Why didn't you tell me?"

"Not my story to tell."

"Ma. Why didn't *you* tell me?"

"Because I was advised against it. Those months in the plastic bubble may have led to your anxiety issues, but that's just a theory," Mom said.

"Why are you telling me this now?"

"Because we're putting it all out there!" My mother waved her hands impatiently. "I've always been afraid for you, okay? Before you blame me for not telling you, I would have, but the pediatrician advised me not to tell you about the incubator after your first panic attack. He said it would add to your anxiety. I went to doctors too! Plenty of them. Believe me. I was in and out of Belmar more often than a beer truck. What did I know about anxiety? And it wasn't easy back then. One doctor told me to ignore it and you'd grow out of it. You didn't. Where was I to turn?"

"I'm sorry." Why did I apologize? It was not from a place of weakness. I apologized from a place of relief. It took this revelation to understand why she held me back, raised me risk averse, and discouraged me from going to *sleepaway* college. She feared I would die.

"I want you to be happy," Mom said.

"Do you? Then stop pushing for a reconciliation with Bobby Bilancia."

Mom took a deep breath. "It's none of my business, but the things that are none of my business are the things that matter the most to me as your mother."

"Mom. Please. Stop gossiping with Babe Bilancia."

Uncle Louie made the okay sign behind my mother's back, approving of my tone.

"I don't know what you mean by *gossip*. We became one family when you were married to Bobby."

"We were not *one* family. They were in-laws. To *me*."

"What is your point?" Mom makes jazz hands in the air in frustration. "What do you want me to do? How should I proceed? Tell me what you want me to do, and I will do it."

"I want you to stop making chicken cutlets for Bobby."

Mom looked up at the sky; her eyeballs crossed over the clouds as though she was reading the message on a blimp hovering overhead. "I will not fry another chicken cutlet for Bobby Bilancia."

"Thank you."

"Okay, but I have to live in this town. How do I do that? Babe and I are old friends all the way back to kindergarten. We thought we were being very adult about your divorce. We didn't let your problems come between us. Lifelong friendship is not a spigot I can turn off."

"You can do whatever you want with your two-way flow of information; just make sure I am not part of the conversation. Ma, look at me. I don't want the Bilancias to get the wrong idea. I do not want to hurt Bobby. I am not vacillating. I am not going back. I am moving forward. Your only message to anyone outside of our family should be, *I support my daughter.*"

"That's fair, Phil," Uncle Louie said, tapping the straw on the ground with the toe of his brown suede Gucci loafer.

"I support you. You took shelter in our home!" my mom cried out, her voice ringing out across the cemetery. "But where is my support? I can't do anything right. I don't want to be like this!"

I recalled a post on Instagram that I shared on my feed. It said, *When pulled into the whirlwind of chaos, remain calm, and remember who you are and the result you seek*. I gave it a shot. "Ma, are you asking for my forgiveness?"

My mother stamped her foot on the straw-covered mud. "With all my heart."

"I forgive you," I told her. And I did.

"Now, hug it out, girls. Hug it out," Uncle Louie said, his arms outstretched as though he held the entire world in them.

I embraced my mother. I didn't want to fight with her. I buried my face in her neck like I was five years old and I didn't know where the Shalimar perfume ended and she began. This time, though, I comforted her. We stood in the place that serves as a reminder that she will never see her mother again in this lifetime. Whatever questions she failed to ask Grandma Cap, whatever secrets they held, whatever went unsaid, will never be revealed. It's over. But I still have my mother, and as long as I do, there's a chance we can learn to communicate.

I CLOSE OUT of the notes app and go back inside my apartment. I flip the latch on the French doors and draw the curtains. I slide back into bed and pull the covers over me. Smokey jumps up on the comforter and marches through the thick folds of the down squares until she reaches my face, as is her routine.

Exhausted, I'm almost asleep when my phone lights up in the dark. It's a text from Angelo.

I hope it's not too late to thank you. My mother is not easy.

I smile and text him back.

You haven't met Philly Baratta.

I've been apologizing for my mother all my life, so I know how Angelo feels. But I always had Uncle Louie, who was the balm.

I envy Angelo's small family. It must be simpler to navigate. Is my family too close? Is that the issue? Did we insert ourselves into one another's affairs without invitation? Did we believe that a secret would stay that way forever, harming no one, even if your own child was once the girl in the plastic bubble and you didn't bother to tell her? Is it even a problem if your parents fail to share that you almost died when you were born? What good will it do you now?

I may never figure this out and it doesn't appear that my landlord and her son will either. The therapist encouraged me to sever all ties, at least until I had answers. If I had to guess, Dr. Nora isn't Italian. She can't understand how I could love these people and occasionally hate them too. In my next session, I will explain that the Caps and Barattas were in each other's pockets, but those pockets, for my money, were filled with gold.

17

Pisa

A MARIGOLD SUN BURSTS through the clouds and illuminates the marble cathedral, the duomo, the baptistry, and *il più famoso*, the Leaning Tower of Pisa. I snap a photo of the tower and post it on Insta: *Just what Insta needs #AnotherPicOfTheTower.*

The tower looks like a wobbly stack of bone china plates in a fancy hotel kitchen that could crash to the ground with a nudge. The layers of eggnog marble are separated by arched windows that let in the light. The field around the tower has turned to a drab brown, like a tapestry that has aged, its vibrant colors drained over time to a soft patina, with only a few gold threads remaining that glisten in the sun. Conor and I stroll through the statues of saints and ornate marble urns on pedestals, treasures of the Italian Renaissance.

"*Prato dei miracoli,*" Conor says.

"I don't need a field of miracles. One would do. And I hope it comes with keys to my new apartment that allows pets."

"I'll help you look."

"You've done enough for me. I love my place at Signora Strazza's. But I'm not giving up Smokey. 'Women and cats.' I'm on the team now. I never had a pet growing up because my mother *skeeved* animals. What are the chances I move into a building where the landlord feels the same?"

"The same issues follow us around until we solve them," Conor says.

"It's my fate to be pushed around, have you noticed? I can't even get closure with the FBI."

"Why don't you close down Cap Marble and start over?" Conor suggests.

"Because I don't want to be the person who closes down a family business that's a hundred years old."

"That's how they get us. The *L* word."

"Love."

"Legacy," Conor corrects me.

I take his arm as we walk. "You've done all right with your dad's company; maybe I can too."

"My solution was to grow the company after my dad died. My dad was the greatest, but he was cautious. I'd say, 'Pop, I'm over here. I know Italy. Use me. Let's expand this thing,' but he didn't get on board with it. When he died, I figured while I'm exporting marble from Carrara, why not expand to include other products? Now we export stone from Scotland and wine from Puglia."

"You're turning into Googs. That's not for me. I love what I do. Marble and stone are enough. I love drafting. Thanks to you, I'm doing it. I haven't needed to breathe into a brown paper bag since I arrived in Italy."

Conor squints up at the tower. "Do you want to climb it?"

"Not really."

"You don't like heights, do you? Trust me. It will not topple."

"With my luck it would."

"When the engineers began construction, they didn't know the ground beneath it was soft. But it was too late, so as they continued to build the tower higher, they constructed a way to keep it in place even as it leaned. Sometimes the builders would get creative and try and weight one side to stabilize it. Whatever they did, it kept leaning."

I tilt my head and follow the line of the tower. "Why did they keep working on something that didn't make sense?"

"Because to them, it did. According to them, the strength was in the flaws."

"You didn't know me when I was a pushover. My mother tried so hard to toughen me up. When we were little, my mom took my sister and me to Radio City to see Cyndi Lauper in concert. Mom wanted us to see a brave Italian girl in action. When I got married five years ago, I was willing to blow the entire budget on a Sylvia Weinstock cake because I wanted a Leaning Tower of Pisa cake like Cyndi Lauper had at her wedding. When my fiancé and I went for the tasting menu at the hall, and it came time to talk about dessert, I proposed the Leaning Tower cake. I printed a picture off the internet and everything. But Bobby wanted a traditional cake with the buttercream frosting and the plastic bride and groom on top. Just like his parents had."

"What did you do?"

"I caved." I sigh in regret. "If I'm honest, that's when I knew we were doomed. I'd lie in bed and think, how can a cake be a problem? It's a *cake*."

"So you gave up your dream."

"Because I was afraid to insist on what I wanted."

"Straight people." Conor shakes his head. "How about the next time you get married, you have whatever cake you want?"

"How about we climb the tower?"

"Aren't you afraid of heights?"

"I choose to be brave."

—

THE WINTER SUN over Carrara is a pearl in a white sky. I hold Smokey in my arms and look up at the mountain.

"This is *it* for the view, Smokey. We can't stay where we aren't wanted." I kiss the kitten and put her in the basket for her morning nap. "Don't worry. I got you. Whither I go, you will whither with me."

Signore Fabrini has an apartment for rent on the ground floor of the building next to the Caffetteria Leon d'Oro. Signorina Le-Donne gave me the tip over a free espresso because she is a cat lover. No view, but at least I'll have espresso on tap.

I grab my purse and jacket and keys. I stuff the phone in my back pocket and open the door. There's an envelope on the mat. It's from Signora Strazza. She must really want me to go. I tear into it. Accepting bad news is a superpower. Getting evicted is not as frightening as being under investigation by the FBI.

Signorina Baratta,

You may keep the cat. But I don't want to see it wandering the hallway.

Signora Strazza

Thank you, Saint Dymphna! I am retiring the "Bobby Bilancia Breathe" mantra and replacing it with "Jess Baratta Stay," because, as of this official letter, I will! I peel off my jacket, sit at the table, and open my laptop. I log in to the journal section of Thera-Me.

Note: I have spent my life compromising on the big and small things, as if compromise is a goal or a path to happiness. It's quite the opposite. Pleasing other people is the hardest work of all because there's no end to it. Why is being honest so hard for me?

TRUFFLE HUNTING IN SIENA

Conor and his husband, Gaetano, along with Farah and I, boarded the train early this morning at Carrara-Avenza for the trip to Siena. The train cars sway, rattling to the beat as the metal wheels click on the tracks. The straw-colored hills of Tuscany, drenched in the golden light of morning, form a patchwork quilt of contour-farmed parcels of land dotted with an occasional stucco farmhouse painted the color of a glazed doughnut.

If you offered me a view from anywhere in this moment, including a perch on the moon, I would still choose to experience Italy from this train. It's as if we move through the map of history, when Italian provinces were small countries divided by disparate dialects, mountain ranges, silver lakes, and smoky green rivers. I take a video out the train window. I open up Instagram and post it. *On our way to the hunt, but first, the train.*

I scroll through. Connie has posted my family at dinner for Thanksgiving. Oh wow. They invited Carmel and Marina, Aunt Lil's sister and niece. I zoom in to see my nieces and nephews, who wear felt pilgrim hats. I get a wave of homesickness; the kids are growing up fast and I'm missing it. I move the image around and land on my mom, who doesn't have anyone there to remind her to refresh her lipstick. She's got the suction-cup look going on with her lip liner; only a bright red rim remains.

I am so far from home, and it is still hard to accept that I ever had to leave. It's Thanksgiving in America (the first without Uncle Louie), and the final weeks for truffle hunting in Tuscany. Connie sees that I'm online and sends a message: *Love u.* I send the same message back to her.

I believe Conor and Gaetano set the date for the hunt to distract me from the holidays underway back home. I went all in. I bought a pair of navy wool trousers with suspenders for the excursion. I wear a short puffer vest in orange and matching hiking boots. I've never worn an article of orange clothing in my life, but we're spending the day in the woods, and if I happen to get lost, maybe I'll be easily found before Christmas in this getup.

"Who's hungry?" Conor is dressed like Abercrombie in brown cords, while Gaetano, like Fitch, wears a black sweater and jeans. (The pair of country squires and two women in wool are taking the truffle hunt seriously, or maybe just the costumes that go with it.) "What have we got?"

"I packed enough food for a spin on the Orient Express." Gaetano laughs. His black hair is cropped; his brown eyes sparkle. He is around five foot ten and slender; his fine southern Italian features remind me of the Baratta men. "And plenty of wine." He holds up two bottles.

"What are you waiting for? Pour. *Per favore.*" Farah holds out a plastic cup. She wears a Scottish plaid wool skirt with a red leather bomber jacket. Her hair is a loose ponytail cascading out of the back of a black baseball cap. Farah has joined our Italian friend group. My little community is growing. I close out of Instagram. I want to stay in the moment in my new life.

CONOR TAKES THE seat next to me. The train has rocked Gaetano and Farah to sleep.

"I heard from my accounts in Jersey. A couple of guys that work with Googs reached out to me. They're concerned. Googs is looking for money to retain an attorney. The feds picked him up in Brielle."

"No way. They'll be coming for me next," I say quietly.

"If they had something on you, they would've never let you leave the country."

"I gave them everything I had," I tell him.

Unresolved business issues are like problems in a marriage; the longer you ignore them, the worse it is when you go to solve them. And sometimes, you never do. Conor leans back in his seat and closes his eyes. Instead of sleeping, I write. I remember Bobby's and my final meeting at Thompson, Thompson & Thompson.

I poured myself a glass of ice water from the pitcher placed on a silver tray in the center of the conference table at my divorce lawyer's office in Spring Lake. I saw Bobby through the glass partition and waved to him.

"Hey, Jess." He kissed me on the cheek before he sat down.

I poured him a glass of water and placed it in front of him.

"We're really doing this?" Bobby sipped the water. He looked sad, which hurt me. Bobby Bilancia had never done bleak and now he was living it.

I had to stay strong, so I nodded in the affirmative. This way, I wouldn't cry.

"This is crazy. I still love you. We'll buy a house. I know you hate that shower. We'll move. I'll get you a tub as big as Lake Como. Whatever you want."

I sat next to Bobby and took his hand. "It's not about a

house. Or a bathtub. I don't think I'd be happy anywhere. Not yet anyway."

"What was wrong with us? We're just getting started. There are always problems, but we work them out. Okay, we had a setback—"

"It was not a setback, Bobby; it was a *sign*."

"I wish you wouldn't look at our life together as though we were doomed by some *strega* on the boardwalk." Bobby sat back in the chair and folded his arms across his chest.

"It's not your responsibility to make me happy."

"Now, there we disagree. As a husband, that's my job. To seek happiness for my wife is part of why I got married in the first place."

"And what if you can't make me happy?"

Bobby turned away from me, which in all of our time together, he had never done. "Then we do this," he said.

PIAZZA DEL CAMPO

The city of Siena sits peacefully on a Tuscan peak covered with flimsy clouds that float over the rooftops like a veil of sheer organza. Siena is an amber fort constructed of medieval brick from the twelfth century. As we enter the piazza, the charcoal sky overhead breaks open, allowing a cylinder of coral light to fall upon the town, illuminating the operatic, fan-shaped piazza, which resembles a stage after the curtain rises. This is the Italy of Shakespeare, of medieval pageants and parades, with displays of colorful coats of arms, bold flags, folk music, and dancing in the streets.

As we disembark from the train, we're greeted by our guide, Raphael, a *trifolau*, a local truffle hunter, accompanied by his energetic beagle, named Forza. Raphael, from San Miniato, is a robust Italian, small, sturdy, and quick, with a bottle-brush mustache and lively eyes. We load into a truck with them to drive up into the hills above Siena. I am going to forget Googs, the FBI, and my troubles to focus on the truffle hunt.

"The important thing to remember," Conor says, "is how good the truffles taste once we find them." The truck sways back and forth on the dirt road as we climb to the spot where the truffles grow. "Any suffering will be worth it!"

"Keep telling us that, Conor," Farah says.

Raphael follows Forza, and we follow them along a narrow path deep into the forest. The men leap over a small creek; Farah and I take our time walking over the stones to the other side.

We've been climbing for about half a mile when Forza begins to bark. She circles a tree a few feet from the path. Raphael asks us to stand back. Soon, Forza scratches at the base of the tree, kicking up sticks and leaves with her paws, until she clears a spot, revealing the bare, black earth underneath. Like a grave digger, she goes deeper, making a wall around the center. Raphael kneels and roots around the hole. He pulls a spade out of his pocket and gently glides it along the walls of the hole that Forza dug. Soon, he pulls out a black bulb with stringy white veins. "*Brava*, Forza!"

Raphael holds the truffle up for us to see. "*Tartufo! Splendida!*" he says before placing it in the cloth sack tied around his waist. "*D'oro.* I was here a month ago. No truffles. We came on the best day! Who wants to dig?"

"I will," I volunteer, pulling on my work gloves. I kneel next to Raphael. Forza barks.

"There may be another here," Raphael says.

I move the dirt aside, feeling for the bulbs.

"No, no. Dig!" he commands.

I try to follow what Forza did, and Raphael is still not pleased. "Show me." Using his hands, Raphael pushes deeper into the ground. He closes his eyes and feels his way down to the roots. "*Se non scavi in profondità avrai sempre fame.*"

The lesson is simple: if I don't dig, I will always be hungry. I don't know what comes over me, but I plunge my hands into the cold earth. Once I break through the mesh of roots, there's a layer of soft mud. "Wait!" I shout. I make a deeper well in the ground, pushing aside the dirt until I feel the smooth texture of a rock buried deeply in the earth. It's not a stone; it's a bulb. With two hands, I yank the truffle free. Forza barks. I stand with the truffle and hand it to Raphael. "*Non voglio avere fame!*"

Raphael brushes the earth off the truffle and hands it back to me. I place it in the linen sack tied around my waist.

We follow Forza and Raphael deeper into the woods. Forza leads us to tree after tree. We settle on one with obvious roots that cover the ground like a spiderweb. Raphael guides us to dig, and we work hard at it. Farah is persistent and she, too, finds a small truffle beneath the roots of a tree with the help of Raphael. She is jubilant and we're exhausted. We agree to hike back down the mountain to town. The return trip is filled with surprises, a silver creek, a blue lake, and a purple sky that turns lavender on the horizon as the sun sets over Siena.

On the train ride home, Conor, Gaetano, and Farah play cards. I'm reading when the phone buzzes in my backpack. There's a new text from Detective Campovilla.

We need to speak with you regarding Rolando Gugliotti at your earliest convenience.

I UNLOCK THE door to my apartment. Smokey scampers to greet me. Why didn't anyone tell me how delicious it is to return home to a pet who loves you? I place my tote bag on the sofa, turn on the lights, and open the windows and terrace doors. I unlace the hiking boots and slip my feet out of them. I pull off the socks and leave them on the floor. I'm on my way to run the bath when I notice a bouquet of sunflowers on the kitchen counter.

Grazie mille, Giuseppina.
Signora Strazza

I post a photo of the flowers—*Pavarotti's favorite flower*—when there's a knock at the door.

"My mother would like to invite you to dinner," Angelo says the moment I open the door. He takes in my hiking ensemble.

"Truffle hunt," I explain.

"I see that. How about dinner?"

"That's so nice of your mother. She's done enough for me. She let me keep the kitten. What could be better? Jake Gyllenhaal rents the apartment downstairs and falls in love with me? A rent decrease?" I rub my hands together.

"I don't think Mamma will lower the rent." Angelo leans against the door and smiles. "Is Jake Gyllenhaal your type?"

"Could be." Angelo has a girlfriend, but I like flirting with him.

Angelo's work clothes are patched with splotches of turpentine and streaks of dust from filing stone. His shoes look like pointillist paintings where the paint has dripped in tiny drops. Angelo Strazza is growing on me. So I say, "I'd love to come to dinner."

"You will make my mother very happy."

"How about you?" I blurt.

Angelo is surprised. "I always enjoy your company," he says.

"Good. What time?"

"An hour?"

"*Perfetto*," I tell him.

Angelo stands and looks at me. The water in the bathtub is rapidly rising. I need to close the door, but he's not making a move to go.

"*Va bene.* See you in an hour." I begin to close the door.

"*Va bene.*" He closes the door.

I slip out of my muddy clothes and into the tub. Smokey jumps up on the sink and looks at me.

"What? I'm going to dinner."

Smokey doesn't shift her gaze. She steadies it.

"Angelo is taken, okay? He has a girlfriend. He is off the table. I kissed him but it wasn't a big deal. It was a goodbye thing. This is strictly a social call. Dinner with no strings."

Smokey doesn't believe me. She jumps off the sink and goes to the living room. I sink into the steamy water and suds up to my chin. I float, weightless in the bubbles. I've taken more baths in Carrara than I had in total for my entire life in Lake Como, New Jersey. I missed something I never had. That's a topic for my next therapy session.

"I am a bath person," I say out loud. "Not a shower person."

I send a return text to Detective Campovilla as I float in the tub.

As much as I would love to talk to you tonight, I have plans with a truffle I dug with my own hands out of the earth in Siena. I appreciate your patience. May I speak to you about Rolando Gugliotti at another time?

I place the phone on the fluffy towel and sink back down into the water. The bubbles pile up on the surface of the water in silver mounds. What was I doing all these years, denying myself a soak in a hot tub with Calabrian orange bubble bath, as if soap, soaking, and pleasure have to be rationed? Installation after installation, I would marvel at a bathtub's beauty, then walk out of the customer's home and return to my deprivation state as though it was what I deserved. I must view life as a slog, a pain parade like the Crusades, where beating myself up eventually earns me a spot in paradise. Why would I wait? Catholic girls suffer now so we don't have to pay later, I remind myself. It took me thirty-four years to realize that a desire I had all along was, in fact, a need.

I get out of the tub, dry off quickly, and go to the therapy notes I keep on the phone. I type: *I need a bathtub wherever I live. Non-negotiable.* I write.

Uncle Louie and I were stuck in traffic on the Jersey side of the Lincoln Tunnel. We were headed to the D&D Building to pick up a gold spigot and matching handles, levers, and hose for a posh bathroom installation in Franklin Lakes. Uncle Louie seized the opportunity to counsel me on the same day my final divorce papers arrived from the attorney's office. I carried them in my work tote as though they were renderings for a job. I was reading through them in the car when Uncle Louie said, "You can go back to Bobby, you know."

"Why would I do that?"

"Maybe he doesn't get you, but he doesn't hit you either."

"That's a low bar."

"I dated a girl out of Newark who used to beat me with her umbrella. The drought in Jersey in spring 1969 was a true Godsend. We got along so nice in dry heat."

"I can't believe you went all the way to Newark for a date."

"There is no distance too far when a man wants a woman. He'll stand on a bus for six hours just to get to a girl. And he won't complain about it. I would know. I didn't have a car."

"She must have been quite a girl."

"Had her charms. Until they weren't so charming. No regrets." Uncle Louie took his hands off the wheel and made praying hands before returning them to steer. "How about you?"

"I need a storage locker for my regrets. I did everything wrong. I wish I would've lived somewhere besides Lake Como before I got married. Don't care where. Or how far. Sea Girt. Philly. Somewhere. My view of the world was not so different two blocks over with my husband than it was from my bedroom window of my parents' house. Maybe if I'd had some perspective, I would have made better decisions."

"You'd have made different ones. Not necessarily better. We can all go back and try to rewrite the past, and of course, if we could, we'd try to fix it and have things go our way, but who knows if that would have made us happy? Do-overs are a crapshoot. Snake eyes."

"You told me that the time you spent away from Lake Como helped you appreciate it when you came home."

Louie nodded. "Italy changed me for sure. But it was no Perillo tour. It was hard work, and I got my heart broken over there. But I guess that was meant to be. Never look back. It only hurts your neck and breaks your heart." Uncle Louie tapped his wedding band against the steering wheel.

"Do you ever feel suffocated by your choices?"

"I have days where I feel a little snug. I have obligations. Trying to live up to my father's dream. Tradition is a weighted blanket. It feels secure, but it limits your movement. It always worried me that you went to school with Bobby Bilancia, then you started going with him when you were in college, and then you married him. I think you needed a little exposure to a wider world and different people."

"Now you tell me?"

"You didn't ask."

"I wish I would've known what I was looking for."

"How can you know until you try it? It didn't work out. Sometimes things don't. When it works out, you stay. All I know about marriage I learned from my wife. Lil is on my side. Always has been. You give up some things and you get some things when you make a commitment. Who needs *unpleasant* after a day of working with customers? Agreeable is important to me."

"*Agreeable.* Jane Austen's favorite character trait. Rosamund Pike gave *Pride & Prejudice* a great read. I'll download it."

"Only if you want me to fall asleep behind the wheel. Those books are a snooze on tape. Too much letter writing and delivering mail on horseback. Plus, the sad girl always gets the guy in the end. And the guy always has money." Uncle Louie thought. "Not that a happy ending is a bad thing."

I SLIP INTO a sweater and jeans. I run a brush through my hair. I put on lipstick. Lipstick to the Baratta women is what the Mighty Isis bracelet is to Wonder Woman: a power tool. I take a bottle of wine out of the cupboard. I kiss Smokey and turn to go, then I remember the truffle. I grab the cloth bag and head down the stairs for dinner with Angelo and his mother.

18

Tartufo Nero Uncinato

Signora Strazza opens the door. "*Sono felice!*"

"*Come sta, signora?* For you." I hand her the bottle of wine and the cloth sack.

"*Tartufo!*" she squeals as she peers inside.

"I dug it out of the ground myself."

"*Grazie mille.*" Signora Strazza clutches the sack near her heart.

"No, no. It's a gift. *Grazie mille* to you—for letting me keep Smokey. It's not good for a woman to be alone. It's in the Bible." I realize I just said the word *alone* to a widow who feels lonely every second of the day. "You know what I mean, don't you, *signora*?"

Signora Strazza nods and extends her hand like a woman presenting a refrigerator on a game show. "Do you know Dalia?"

Angelo's girlfriend comes around the corner holding her phone. Her long black hair is braided down her back. She wears a white T-shirt, jeans, and a cropped red jacket. I could never pull off a cropped jacket, but Dalia is a woman who can rock equestrian style even though she's probably never been on a horse. The sight of this beautiful woman fills me with shame. I think about that stolen kiss, which was not mine to give or accept.

"Nice to meet you. *Officiata*," I say to Dalia, happy that she isn't looking at me to see me blush with embarrassment.

The dining table, which I last saw when Signora Strazza was in crisis, is now covered with a lace tablecloth. The table is set for four, with delicate pale blue china and crystal wineglasses. Cloth napkins match the eggshell-white tablecloth. I might as well be in New Jersey for one of my mother's Sunday dinners, though my mother would criticize the fresh-cut flowers at the center of the table for being too tall. The flowers are, in fact, way too tall. Evidently, I remain my mother's daughter. I take a photo of the table setting. "Do you mind if I post?" I ask Signora Strazza.

"*Va bene*," she says.

Only eat truffles at an elegant table, I post. The photo reminds me of @CasaDePerrin, when @JerseySidePhil pops into the comments.

How are you, G? My mother, who is @JerseySidePhil, reaches out to me with the single tear emoji after her comment.

"Everything okay?" Signora Strazza asks.

"Fine." I stuff the phone into my back pocket. "I'm starving." I take a seat at the table. Dalia sits down across from me. Angelo pours her a glass of wine. Without looking up from her phone, she pats his rear end before he comes around the table to pour a glass for me. Was that pat for me or him or both of us? Dear Lord, this dinner cannot be over fast enough.

Angelo has brushed his hair and tucked in his shirt; evidently, the shower before dinner is the Strazza version of the Baratta lipstick routine. He and Dalia probably have a date later, I think, as he pours me a glass of wine. He is so close, I catch the scent of his skin, fresh cedar and a Sicilian tangerine.

"You sit," Signora Strazza says to her son. She goes into the kitchen and returns with a soup tureen. She ladles the soup into our bowls. Steam rises from the fluted bowls with the scent of butter and lemon. Hand-rolled bow ties of pasta are delicate and dense in the broth. Signora Strazza grates paper-thin slices of the *tartufo* onto my soup. She does the same for Dalia, Angelo, and finally herself. The earthy slices of *tartufo* are a fragrant complement to the pasta *in brodo*. I taste the soup; the *tartufo* melts on my tongue like a snowflake.

"*Un tartufo.*" Signora Strazza samples the soup. "*Delicioso?*"

"*Sì, sì,*" I tell her. "What do you think, Dalia?"

"It is—*difficile* to find *tartufo* this year." Dalia speaks in English with a determination that I had this afternoon when I was digging for truffles.

"That was my first truffle hunt, and you're right. It took five hours and a three-mile hike to find this one. So, everybody, do me a favor and eat slowly."

Dalia's phone buzzes. She makes an excuse and leaves the table to answer it.

"Did you grow up in Carrara?" I ask Signora Strazza.

"We lived in Avenza, not far from here. On the Ligurian Sea. My father worked on the trains. He transported marble to the port."

"I used to ride the route with him," Angelo says.

Dalia returns from the other room. She leans down over Angelo, speaking softly in dialect, which I can't understand. Angelo pushes his chair back from the table. Dalia turns to Signora Strazza and apologizes for having to leave. She looks at me and gives me a half smile. Angelo walks her to the door. More conversation ensues between them.

Angelo returns to the table. "Dalia's daughter, Alice, needs her. She is sorry she had to leave the dinner."

"I love the way you say Alice in Italy. *Ah-lee-chay. Bella.*"

"That child rules the household," Signora Strazza says under her breath.

"Mamma," Angelo warns.

"I can't say anything!" Signora Strazza gets up and goes into the kitchen.

I don't look at Angelo. As a veteran of family arguments at the dinner table, I don't want to encourage this one. Signora Strazza returns with the main event, the entrée. "I hope you like spaghetti with peas and cream." She places it next to Angelo to serve it.

I twirl a few strands on the end of my fork. The light cream sauce on the spaghetti is buttery, and the capers and peas are tart and crunchy. Conor was right; Signora Strazza can cook. She drops her voice and speaks to her son in a local dialect, which I couldn't translate if they offered me every language app on Google. It sounds like it's about Dalia and her daughter. Signora Strazza is like my mother: she can't let anything go, and when she attempts to, it's just another version of passive-aggressive behavior. Angelo and his mother's conversation is so spirited, I am certain a fight will break out any moment. I continue to twirl the spaghetti and eat it. Truthfully, I don't care what they do, as long as I can have a second helping of this pasta.

"How do you make this?" I interrupt their conversation.

"I bake the peas with garlic and fry the capers before adding them to the sauce," Signora Strazza explains.

The old Philly Baratta dodge always works. When my mother worked herself into a gale-force cyclone, I could always bring her back to center with a diversion. Sharing a recipe is a fail-safe.

"Do you cook?" Signora Strazza asks.

"I love to cook. I learned everything from my grandmothers. I roll my own pasta. I learned that from my Grammy B; her people were from Puglia. But I learned the rest from Grandma Cap. She was a Montini from Carrara before they emigrated."

Signora Strazza puts down her fork. "The Montinis. They lived on the river."

"My grandmother told us about the river! They must be *my* Montinis."

AFTER DINNER, ANGELO makes espresso. He brings three cups of vanilla gelato to the table and pours the spicy, hot espresso over the ice cream. "*Affogato*," he says.

"My favorite," I tell him. I taste the creamy vanilla gelato with the espresso finish and savor it. Sometimes, when I came home from work, I'd skip dinner and Dad and I would have this dessert instead, the elegant version of an Italian milkshake. Italy and New Jersey are never far apart, at least when it comes to dessert.

Angelo and I clear the table. I attempt to help Signora Strazza with the dishes. She takes the *mopeen* from me and hangs it on a hook in the kitchen.

"You go. You and Angelo. *La passeggiata*," Signora Strazza says, fluttering her hands. "Go!"

"*La passeggiata*," he offers.

"Sure."

I follow Angelo outside; we walk under the loggia around the piazza.

I can't be certain, but Signora Strazza was nice to me and aloof to Dalia. Something is up, so I ask Angelo, "Did you tell your mother we kissed?"

"Who would do that?"

"The same guy who invites his girlfriend to dinner and doesn't tell his tenant in the attic when he invites her to the same dinner party."

"You think I'm up to no good?"

"Did you tell Dalia you kissed me?"

"No."

I stop in the middle of the piazza. "Angelo, I think you're playing me."

"What does that mean?"

"You're one of those guys for whom one woman isn't enough."

"Let me ask you something. You ended your marriage. Did you wake up one day and decide the relationship was over?"

"No, I did not."

"It took time?" he suggests.

"Yes. It was a process."

"Ah. Are you the only person who ever loved that is entitled to a process?"

I don't answer. Dr. Veronica taught me that one should never answer a question for which there is no answer.

He goes on. "I was offered a job in Milan. An excellent position. It's not easy with Dalia. She wants a commitment, but it means I can't take the position. The truth is, I'd be gone already except for Mamma. I feel guilty leaving her so soon after my father died."

"If you wait for the right moment to start your life, it never comes." I bury my hands in my pockets as we walk.

We don't talk much. We walk, down the side streets and past the academy, but the fresh air feels good, and I'm glad to work off the spaghetti with peas and cream. Soon, we cross the piazza to the house. Angelo holds the gate open for me.

"Thank you for the company." I skitter away to avoid any physical contact with Angelo. I'm climbing the steps two at a time to the landing when he calls out to me.

"I'm not what you think I am," Angelo says.

"None of us are," I tell him, and I keep climbing. Once I arrive back inside the apartment, I take my phone out onto the balcony. I put my feet up and write.

Mom was waiting for me when I came in the front door. I didn't bother with the basement entrance because I'd only have to climb the stairs when Mom called me for a debrief of my evening. This had been our routine since I was a kid. She'd make popcorn after a party or a night out with my friends. We'd sit at the kitchen table, and I would spill my guts and tell her everything I knew: who snuck a fifth of gin into the prom, who smoked a joint in the locker room, and which couples were having sex and bragged about it. Mom was a good listener; that came with the territory of being a blowfish. All that information I fed her expanded her database, and the rest she sucked up from the streets of Lake Como on her own.

"I put coffee on." Mom smiled. She wore her robe, but she still had on her makeup and good gold hoop earrings. This only meant one thing.

"You had Sodality?" I asked her.

"What do you think?" Mom placed the sugar and creamer on the kitchen table. "Tootie Filingo was voted president."

"What about you?"

"Recording secretary. I got what I deserve. The worst job in the club. That's what I get for ditching my hours at the *pizze fritte* stand at the Feast. You pay for everything in this life."

"Did you at least score some cookies at the meeting?"

"I made a plate." Mom placed the cookies at the center of the table. "You don't want to miss Andreana Comensky's seven layers."

"Hit me." I pulled the tinfoil tent off the paper plate. The scents of chocolate, peanuts, caramel, and coconut made my mouth water. Mom served us each a cup of coffee.

I placed my hands on my mother's. She scheduled her manicures with her Sodality meetings at the church. Her hands were soft; the French tip manicure was pristine, white stripes on pink nails. The small diamond my father gave her when they were engaged was joined by her grandmother's when she died. Mom wore a new ring made of two round diamonds set together like owl eyes.

"When I die, you split up the ring. One diamond for you, one for Connie. Fifty-fifty. No fighting."

"Ma, leave the ring to Connie. We're not going to bust up your jewelry after you die."

"But this is my best piece! The rest of it is just so-so." Mom's eyebrows knitted together in one black line like a dropped stitch when she crocheted. "I want everything to be fair. I don't play favorites as a mother. You're all equal in my heart."

"I love you, Ma."

"I know."

"You're crazy, but I love you."

"Why do you say things like that, Giuseppina? I'm not crazy. I'm a passionate individual who does the best she can."

"You worked hard. Dad started at the bottom every time he moved insurance agencies, so you had to take all those crappy side jobs to give us the extras. You bought our prom gowns and saved up for a car for Joe, which he refused to loan to Connie and me."

"He needed the car once he was in law school. But we didn't favor him. The car was a necessity. That's why I want to split the diamond ring. My daughters deserve something special too. We sacrificed plenty, but there's no need for you to continue the family tradition of sacrifice. And I'm not leaving the good diamonds to Katie. She came into this family fully loaded. Her great aunt worked at Tiffany, don't forget."

"I remember."

"So, you and Connie carry on with my diamonds. I'll give Katie candlesticks or something."

"Give the ring to Connie. She has three daughters. Two diamonds; at least you have two of the girls covered."

"I never have enough of anything to go around." Mom dunked a seven-layer cookie into her coffee. "I'm a grandmother. I hold the traditions. It's my responsibility to spread the family jewels around. I still have to worry about Mackenzie. What to give that kid. I'll have to come up with something."

"Be creative, Ma. We hold on to traditions whether they serve us or not. I tried to give Bobby his engagement ring back, but he wouldn't take it."

"Where is it?"

"In my sock drawer in the basement."

"A one-and-a-half-carat diamond and you keep it in the sock drawer?"

"One and a *quarter*. And yes, it's in the sock drawer. Who is going into the basement to look for a diamond ring?"

"I see your point." The elevens between her eyes relaxed.

She appreciated that I could foil any potential burglars with a good hiding place.

"So, Ma, you see? Do not split your ring. I can't be trusted with diamonds. Or the man that goes with one."

"You'll keep the one from Bobby?"

"Not likely. A diamond ring from a man you divorced is like a plot of scorched earth upon which nothing will grow."

"You could sell it. I don't understand you kids. You don't care about the finer things, the stuff I aspired to have when I was your age. You kids want experiences, trips, adventures, instead of Paul Revere silver and Lady Carlyle dishes. What is wrong with a gracious home? Sunday dinner? Holidays?"

"Nothing."

"When we stop with Sunday dinner and the holidays, it's all over. We'll turn into a pack of Protestants. Lose our Italian natures. Promise me you will hold on to Bobby's ring like a Christmas club account at New Jersey Federal."

"You and Dad and those Christmas clubs." I shook my head. "No interest and by December twenty-fourth you have saved up fifteen bucks to spend."

"You laugh, but we tried to teach you to save even though we rarely had anything left over to put away ourselves. Look. Families have all kinds of problems, who drinks, who gambles, who sneaks around. We didn't have those particular crosses to bear; we had a cash-flow problem. But I'm not complaining." She made a face. "Besides, you don't need the money right now. You're living with us."

"I've saved my money, Ma. I have a little nest egg."

"Good. Because the day will come, and you will want something to show for all these years working for my brother."

"I do have something to show for it. I am a fine draftsman."

"Whatever you say," she said. "But I know my brother, Louie. My advice? Have a plan."

—

I BRING UP my mother in my session with Dr. Rex. I lay it all out for him. I want to learn how to communicate with my mother, and I want to let go of her issues, which have somehow become my own. My mother feels she never got a fair shake in the family because she was a girl. Except for the college money—and admittedly, that's a doozie—in general, the opposite has been true for me. Uncle Louie gave me an opportunity, which I grew into a career as a draftsman. When he died, he could've left the company to my mother or sold it outright to a corporation, but he didn't. I knew how Louie felt about my mother, and wisely, in leaving the company to me, he knew she wouldn't object because I'm her daughter. Dr. Rex says I should examine my mother's views regarding religion, sex, health, money, and beauty. Dr. Rex requests that I be completely honest, because I have spent a lifetime defending my mom. This was the hardest assignment of all.

PHILLY BARATTA'S HIT LIST

Religion: The patriarchy offends her. Mom left off with the Annunciation.

Sex: Fear-and-shame platter to go. Mom left the story dangling about the fate of her high school friend Monica Spadoni, who was sent away when she got pregnant second semester of her junior year and no one ever saw her, the baby, or her family again. Monica's story, as imparted by my mother, was like falling asleep before the end of a Movie of the Week. You wake up not knowing the ending and living in fear that the same fate might befall you.

Health: Never go to the doctor, and pray the symptoms disappear. Don't look up any diseases on the internet because the internet is a disease.

Money: Slippery. Elusive. If you get a couple of bucks, hide them. Keep an account on the side for emergencies. Mom once said, *You watch. When you get a little bonus, the first thing that happens: you break a tooth. There are no bonuses, always get cash up front.*

Beauty: You must work with what you've got no matter the raw material. A manicure, an eyebrow wax, and a spray tan are the keys to self-confidence.

I feel so sorry for myself after this exercise that I don't bother to review it. I hit send, pressing the key like a button that detonates a bomb. *Coming at you, Dr. Rex.* I am compelled to call Aunt Lil. I have missed her but have avoided calling her because it would bring my mother pain to know that I was communicating with Aunt Lil instead of her. But I don't care anymore; I miss my aunt.

It's noon in New Jersey, a couple of hours before *General Hospital* goes on the air, so I'm sure to find Aunt Lil at home. She picks up.

"Aunt Lil? It's Jess."

"Oh. My. God. Honey, how are you?"

"I'm Italian now."

She laughs. "Good for you."

"How are you?"

"Oh, I miss my shadow. Me and my shadow, you know. My Louie. I'm heartbroken as I ever was, but I'm trying to get to the other side."

"You will, Auntie."

"I keep hoping Louie will visit. But he hasn't yet or maybe I just don't remember the dreams. I was going to go to a psychic, but she was arrested, an online scam or something or the other, so I thought if she didn't see *that* coming, how would she know what's going on in my spiritual world?"

"Trust your own gut, Auntie. I feel close to Uncle Louie here. Why don't you come visit?"

"Thank you, sweetie, but I don't ever want to get on an airplane again. I love my house. My sister wants me to go to Florida this winter, but I'm just not interested. It won't be any fun without your uncle."

"I know what you mean."

"Tell me about you. I don't know how you found the courage to move out of the cellar."

"Did it take courage or was I just tired of the dampness?"

"Lake Como is still buzzing. And there's plenty of chatter over in Bilancia Land. But you know, there always is."

"How are my parents?"

"Since you left, we have been together for every Sunday dinner. Your mother cooks, and I schlep over. I bring something. Connie makes a dish. It's not like when you did it and all I had to do was get dressed and show up at your four-star meal. It's all-hands-on-deck now." She chuckles. "I miss you."

"Thanks, Auntie." I'm sad when I hear about the dinners; I may have resented it from time to time, but there were parts of being useful that I enjoyed.

"Your mother is a piece of work. She always was and she always will be. You can't change the spots on a leopard. And why would we? We love an animal print in this family."

"Leopard. The Italian neutral."

"Beats beige. The *Amerigan* essential. Your folks are just fine. And honestly, even if they weren't, I wouldn't tell you. You stay put over there. You put your time in, above and beyond, in the Baratta clan. As far as I'm concerned, they owe you."

"I want to thank you for all you did for me."

"Oh, look, that's just being an aunt."

"No, it was more than that. You were my refuge. You and all those criminals and crazies in Port Charles."

"Are you watching? You cannot believe what Sonny Corinthos is up to. I've been watching for fifty years, and honestly, I don't know how they come up with this stuff."

My aunt catches me up on her soap like she is blood family to the cast of *General Hospital.* "Isn't it funny? For one hour a day, I watch my story and it's the only hour of the day I don't miss your uncle."

"I miss you, Aunt Lil."

"Everyone misses you, Jess. But you'd better not come home. You stay away until you build up the hide of a rhinoceros. You are only allowed to come back here when you can tell them all to go to hell. Am I making myself clear?"

We laugh.

"They're good people or your uncle and I would not have lasted. But I know they had a little fun at my expense behind my back.

Part of that is just the status of in-laws in Italian families, and the rest of it was just fear. Your mother probably knew your uncle was on my side, so she didn't have a chance. Yet she tried to make her points anyway. I was Diamond Lil. But I never minded because I know who I am and what matters to me. I loved my husband and you kids, and even my sister, Carmel, though she can drive me nuts. But my niece, Marina, is a peach. I got more than most, you know. I lost my husband too soon; though people say that fifty years is a long time, it wasn't to me. It was like a blip. Someday, when you fall in love again, you'll remember what I'm telling you. Time stands still when you lose the love of your life, because it has nowhere to go. You just *are*, and it just *is*. Your life becomes something else entirely without someone to love. When there's nothing to do, you don't even need to wear a watch. And if you're like me, you don't care if the clock ever starts ticking again. Life just stopped and I'm on pause. Waiting."

Aunt Lil wants to get to the grocery store before *General Hospital* starts, so we say our goodbyes and our *I love you*s, and I promise to call again soon. I'm wiping my tears on my sleeve when there's a knock at the door.

"*Ciao, signora.*"

Signora Strazza has a look of concern on her face as she takes in my bloodshot eyes and runny nose, but she doesn't pry.

"I called my aunt in Sestri Levante," she says. "She was so happy that somebody was interested in the Montini family. She knew all about them and even remembered that when the Montinis left for America, the little girl left a wagon behind and gave it to one of my aunt's cousins. They must be your Montinis. She said it would be a good idea to show you their old homestead; it would give you a true picture of your people. I can take you."

SNOW DAY

Signora Strazza and I walk under the loggia of the Piazza Alberica. She has pulled the silk scarf from around her neck, put it over her head, and tied it babushka-style under her chin. A few lazy snowflakes flutter through the air. We make our way past the Caffetteria Leon d'Oro to the street beyond the piazza.

"Looks like we're getting a dusting," I tell her.

"My husband used to say that snow was lucky."

"That's funny. In New Jersey, it's a curse. We have to shovel out from under it."

"This way." Signora Strazza points to the Via Sorgnano, which leads out of the piazza to the countryside. "It's not far."

I take her arm. "Tell me about your husband."

"He was handsome. A very kind man. Quiet. Angelo is like him."

"It must be hard. So many years together."

"I'm grateful, but my life as I knew it is over. There's no place in the world for a widow."

"That's not true. You have friends. You have Angelo."

"Widows wear black not because we're in mourning; we wear it to disappear."

Uncle Louie hated when I wore black because it was all that I wore. "*Signora*, in America, we wear black because we look thinner."

She laughs. "You Americans. You take the worst thing that could happen to a woman like me and turn it into a fashion statement."

"It's not deliberate. Believe me. Americans are nothing but practical."

Signora Strazza stops and takes a turn onto a small side street. "This is Santuario Madonna delle Grazie a Carrara." Signora Strazza leads me up to the facade of the church, a Romanesque cathedral built of local marble. She points to Via Carriona, which cuts in front of the church steps. "This road is as ancient as marble itself. This is the path they used to transport the marble to the sea."

We walk until we reach the end of the road. An abandoned two-story farmhouse, made of fieldstone and wood, sits back from the road on the hillside.

"Here we are," she says as we reach our destination. "The Montini farm."

The frame of the Montini farmhouse still stands, but time and weather have gutted it. We can see through the first floor to the field behind it. I imagine my grandmother as a young girl, playing in the field. Standing here, where she once stood, makes me miss her even more. I snap photos of the old house. I post one photograph with this message: *Simple beauty.*

Signora Strazza points. "The Montini family lived upstairs. The bottom part of the house is where they kept the animals. When my mother was a girl, they had two goats that provided milk for every family in Carrara."

"Grandma Cap told me about the animals sleeping beneath them in the house. She said they kept the house warm."

I peer in through the window frames, where there once was glass. Inside, I see a dirt floor with thatches of brown grass growing through it, a broken trough, and columns of wood that hold up the house, outfitted with rusted gear, hooks, chains, and prods. The wooden doors to the stalls have collapsed, their hinges holding what is left of the planks that once kept the animals safe inside. Only the ceiling beams appear uncompromised, though the stucco between them has worn away.

Signora Strazza and I walk around the outside. A set of rough-hewn wooden stairs climbs to the second floor of the farmhouse. The wood is peeling and splintered; rusty nails jut through the wood where it has worn away.

"I wouldn't go up there. The property was abandoned so long ago. The steps might not hold you."

"It's not that far to fall," I assure Signora Strazza. She stands back and tries to talk me out of it, but I carefully take the steps to the top. The door is gone on the landing. I look inside. A stone fireplace on the far wall is all that is left of the room. The mantel has rotted away. Half the roof is gone, which explains the ceiling in the barn below. There is no furniture. Nothing left behind, not a bucket, a stool, or an old tin cup. From the doorway, I can see through the floorboards to the stalls below. I make my way down the creaky stairs.

"Satisfied?" Signora Strazza says. "You could have fallen through."

"I had to see it, Signora."

Her expression softens. "I miss my grandmother too."

"That's because they taught us how to be women. That's an art we never master."

"I don't know about that," she said. "It takes time."

The snow begins to fall in large, soft flakes the size of coins. I'm cold, but I don't feel it so much because I'm thinking of Grandma Cap, which fills my soul with the warmth of my memories. This is where she was born and grew up. It's a gift to pull the thread from her life in Carrara to the present moment. This was the place she longed for all her life, though she made her home in Lake Como warm and cozy for us. Now I understand why she was so particular. We'd drive all the way down to Eden Farm in southern Jersey for fresh eggs when she planned to bake a cake. The Montinis raised chickens, so she only knew fresh eggs as a child. She wanted whatever she baked to taste like it had in Italy. And even more important, she wanted us to experience the taste, so we would carry Italy from her table into our lives. She kept a garden because there was never a doubt that the family would eat as long as she grew our vegetables. We would always have marinara as long as we grew our own tomatoes and canned them ourselves. She built her life, the life I observed from the start, from all she learned in Italy. This was her foundation. The old farmhouse might be in ruins, but to me, it's a palazzo because she lived here.

Signora Strazza hands me a tissue.

I dab my eyes. "I'm sorry, *signora*."

"She sees you. She knows you're here."

"I hope so."

"We cry because we are lucky to have known them."

"I should've brought her back here. We should have brought her home. But, as families do, we were busy growing up and going to school and trying to make something of ourselves, when the truth is, I would have learned everything I needed to know from her, right here, where it all started."

"You can't have both?"

"I'll never know," I tell her.

"The story of the Montinis in Carrara is simple. They were humble people. *Contadini.*"

"Peasants," I say.

"That's not a bad word in Italy. *I contadini* filled the table and our stomachs. It was their hard work that sustained us. Every year, the Montinis did something special. During Holy Week, they made a particular cheese you could only get during Eastertide. It was fresh mozzarella with a paste of figs and other sweet things rolled inside. When you cut into them, the slices became lovely pinwheels. My mother would make an Easter platter with fresh fennel and the Montini pinwheels. It was a beautiful thing. Delicious too."

"And then they went to America."

"I didn't hear about them beyond the stories my aunt shared

when I called her. That was typical. There were a few families that left our village and that was that. My parents would keep up with them for a while, letters went back and forth, and over time, the correspondence was more and more infrequent, and eventually, the letters stopped. The old world faded away. America must be *magnifico*, because when our neighbors went there, they forgot Carrara."

"I promise you. They did not forget Carrara."

I take Signora Strazza's arm to make the long walk back to the piazza. I turn back to look at the Montini farm in the snow; the fieldstone and mottled wood are covered in icy pearls through the haze of falling snow. Pearls. My treasure, my people, my home.

PART THREE

Love It Away

19

An Italian Christmas

I STAND ON MY TERRACE in my coat, mittens, and hat as the local dignitaries place a holiday wreath at the statue of the duchess in Piazza Alberica. It's the week before Christmas, cold enough that I can see my breath in the air as the sun sets. The Tuscans are engaged in their version of the holiday rush, which is more of a saunter and stroll. A few locals stop to listen to the *sindaco* dedicate the wreath, but most just nod at their mayor as they pass.

The holiday decorations in Carrara are elegant. The loggia is lit by a row of twinkling spheres of white lights that resemble crystal chandeliers. The locals decorate their doorways with swags woven from evergreen branches. There are no blow-up characters, musically timed to blinking lights or animatronics, and while I miss them, they don't belong here in Italia Vecchia. A historic piazza requires little adornment when the passage of time whispers around every corner. Besides, Maria Beatrice's stern expression doesn't invite tinsel and lights. She wouldn't approve and they wouldn't dare.

The holiday decorations back home are a show, a *carnevale spettacolare*. If you stand still long enough in the month of December anywhere in New Jersey, someone will wrap you in strings of twinkling lights. New Jersey is where glitz was born. Our house is drenched in colored lights from Saint Lucy's Day on December 13 through the Epiphany on January 8.

The day after Thanksgiving, Dad secures a large plastic Santa and sled to our roof by hanging himself out of our bedroom window, his feet hooked to the windowsill. Connie and I stand by to grab his feet, terrified he might slide off the roof and break his neck. He has placed Santa on the roof for so many years, he's mastered the chore like an aerial stunt. In honor of my dad, I've placed the star of Bethlehem on the terrace in Carrara. I light it and take a seat at the café table. I've pulled out my phone to call my sister when there's a knock at the door.

Signora Strazza leans against the doorframe catching her breath from the climb. "Would you like to go to Milan for Christmas? Angelo invited us."

I think for a moment before answering. Angelo has been gone for a month and I haven't heard from him, so I say, "I have big plans. I was going to read a book and eat chocolate."

"You must see Milano at Christmas," Signora Strazza insists. "We'll take the train."

I don't have to think about it. I don't want to be alone on Christmas, and the thought of a train ride is bliss. Don't I always feel better after a train ride to anywhere? I put aside my ambivalence about my feelings for Angelo. The connection has faded now that Angelo has moved to Milan. Do I really want to stay in Carrara alone? Wouldn't I love to see the cities in the north at this time of year? So, I do something I never would have done before moving to Italy.

I am spontaneous. I look at my landlord and smile. "When are we leaving, *signora*?"

THE TRAIN CHUGS north to Milan from Bologna. The Italian countryside in late December falls away from the tracks in sheets of charcoal and white like newsprint. The prattle of the wheels and the sway of the train car are soothing, so much so that Signora Strazza has fallen asleep across from me. She reminds me of my mother: selfless, yet happy to complain about all she has to do. And like my mother, Signora Strazza wears herself out until she is so exhausted, she could fall asleep anywhere.

I left Smokey with Signorina LeDonne for the holiday and I miss my kitten already. I have more than a twinge of guilt that I am with Angelo's mother at Christmastime and not my own. I spent every Christmas of my life with Philly and Joe Baratta, a tradition I kept up even after I married. Bobby agreed to Midnight Mass with the Bilancias and Christmas Day with the Barattas.

My family needs a workhorse this time of year. I wonder if Connie or Joe took up the challenge. When I was home, I bought the Christmas tree, sawed off the trunk, put it in the stand, and decorated it. I'm worried about my mother going up and down those creepy cellar stairs to haul the strings of lights when she's had her knee replaced. I don't want my dad on that rickety ladder to the attic retrieving boxes of ornaments when he has a bum shoulder. Truthfully, I don't even want them wandering the mall to shop for presents. I had them make their lists, then I went out and bought the gifts, wrapped them, and placed them under the tree. I doubt Connie has the time. But what about the cookies?

When I was growing up, baking holiday cookies was a production. We learned from our grandmothers by watching our mom bake with them. Connie and I were adept at rolling coconut balls, twisting *S* cookies, and icing cutouts long before we mastered cursive handwriting. We stacked cookies on trays, wrapped them in cellophane, tied them with ribbons, and delivered them up and down the street. Who will do the baking and deliveries without me? Will they even bother? When the tradition of the holiday cookie tray goes, so does civilization.

I thought about sending my parents a Christmas card to break the ice, but I fear if I did, the veneer would crack and I'd plummet through the surface, drowning in a pool of my own unresolved issues. Therapy has given me floaties to swim against the tide, but they're not effective long term. I am committed to change, and that takes work. More than one therapist has told me that I must forgive my parents in order to move forward. I haven't been able to do that just yet, so until I know what to say, I will say nothing at all.

Therapy has taught me to think about how I communicate. My resolve doesn't make being away from home on Christmas easy; in fact, it breaks my heart, one memory at a time. The happy holidays shared with my family are lovely memories until they overwhelm me and they're buried in a blizzard of guilt like silver glitter in a snow globe. I long for home, but not enough to get on a plane. Besides, if I flew home, Uncle Louie wouldn't be there to pick me up at the airport. It's better if I don't pretend that I can be happy under any circumstance this Christmas.

I scroll through my phone.

CONOR: Googs got two years.

JESS: Jail? OMG.

CONOR: Banking malfeasance and RICO.

JESS: He and Uncle Louie would've been in bunk beds.

CONOR: LOL.

Uncle Louie put me where I am today, and there is nothing tackier than making jokes at the expense of my uncle's reputation. In my defense, I have justified moments of anger toward Uncle Louie. He put me in this position and died before he could fix it. Despite all that, there isn't a day that goes by that I don't ask myself, *What would Louie Cap do?* I miss him and the work we did together, but I can't move forward until the tax situation (which he created!) is rectified. The operation of Cap Marble and Stone is suspended, like a slab of marble in midair between the boat and the Perth Amboy dock. I am lucky to make my living in Carrara drafting projects, but I miss working directly with the marble, the customers, and the installations. If I questioned my career path when I was working with Uncle Louie, I don't anymore. I loved my job and I miss it. The FBI reached out a few weeks ago; they had questions about the deposits they found on Uncle Louie's hard drive. I didn't have any answers for them then and still don't. I sigh loudly but Signora Strazza sleeps through it.

Outside the window, the landscape changes as we leave the hills of Tuscany behind and roll into the pewter fields at the foothills of the Alps. I remind myself why I came to Italy. I came here to escape my situation in hope of a better life: in fact, the old switcheroo of what my ancestors did when they emigrated to America. No matter how lonely I feel, as any expat abroad during the holidays would know, there are plenty of distractions to keep my mind off my troubles. I'm in the heart of my place of origin, and my life has not worked out as I planned, but I remain hopeful. I either have to accept the risk that comes with change because that's where the lessons are, or I retreat into the cellar from whence I came.

"What did I miss?" Signora Strazza asks as she awakens.

"I'm solving all the world's problems," I joke.

"So, I will go back to sleep." She grins.

"Let me ask you something. Are you sure I'm welcome at Angelo's? I don't want to be the weird extra girl during your family holiday. I can get a hotel room."

"Nonsense! Angelo insisted I bring you along."

A warm holiday feeling floats through me. Maybe this won't be the worst Christmas of my life.

"You like my son?"

"He's very nice," I reply cautiously.

Signora Strazza nods knowingly.

Another meddling mother with an agenda? I can't shake them.

"Will we see Dalia and her daughter?" I ask.

"Who knows? Those two. On and off like a spigot."

"It isn't any easier when the spigot is off and the water supply dries up. That's what it's like to be divorced."

"I am sure you had your reasons for getting a divorce," she says.

"I couldn't breathe. Does that count?"

Signora Strazza nods. "So much of happiness is circumstances, and that is a matter of luck. *Fortuna.*"

"Or is all of life mapped out before we arrive at the destination?" I wonder aloud.

"I am an Italian mother," Signora Strazza announces for an audience beyond just me. "Fate and I are not friends. I went through so much to have my son. I named him Angelo because I prayed so hard when I found out I was expecting him. I had two miscarriages before him, and I almost stopped trying altogether. And then, *miracolo.* You're young. You don't understand this yet."

"I understand, *signora.*" And then something I vowed to keep to myself for the rest of my life would not stay buried. I leaned forward and said, "I lost a baby too."

Signora Strazza looks at me, her eyes full of understanding. "I am so sorry."

We ride in silence until I explain. "It was very early. I cope with it, I'm still dealing with it, and maybe this sounds dramatic, but it destroyed me. I was surprised at the depth of the heartbreak. My own mother doesn't know. I couldn't tell my sister; she was happy with three healthy daughters and I didn't want to upset her. My brother and I have never shared pain on that level. So I turned to my Aunt Lil, who couldn't have children herself, knowing she would understand my grief. I still wrestle with how I could love a soul I had never met. But you can. You do. Aunt Lil understood. She tried to have a baby too, but it wasn't to be because she had an ectopic pregnancy, and that ended her chances of ever having her own child. I found out I was pregnant one day, and it seemed like I lost it the next day. It happened so fast I hadn't yet told my husband I was pregnant when I miscarried. I hadn't had a chance to share the good news when I had to deliver the bad news. The look on his face. I couldn't bear it."

"You didn't try again?"

"Not with my heart in it. And now, *signora*, I don't want to talk about it."

Bobby *was* understanding, as he was about everything, but my heart and view of him changed when we lost the pregnancy. He moved on very quickly, it felt to me. Bobby struggled with why I would hold on to the loss when we could try again. You could surmise that Bobby was a positive person, and it was a loving suggestion to encourage me to let go of the sadness, because he could see how it consumed me. But I wasn't ready to let it go. I wanted him to understand how unbearable it all was for me. I wanted him to help me move through it, but he didn't know how.

"I feel badly that I was so hard on you," Signora Strazza says.

"You weren't *that* hard on me. I'm from New Jersey, and we can take it. But I hope this helps you understand why I need the kitten. I need continuity somehow. I mean, she's not a baby, or a husband, or a person, but she comforts me."

Signora Strazza reaches for my hand. "We share this. I wish we didn't. I'm sorry."

I know she is truly sorry. I am too. I learned to keep my troubles to myself because sharing them would only deepen the pain, or at least, that was my perception. I pull a book out of my backpack and settle back in the seat. I try to focus on the words on the page, but I can't.

I close the book and excuse myself. Signora Strazza nods and shuts her eyes. She will be asleep again in no time. She's grieving her husband, her first Christmas without him, so her sleep is sporadic, like all those with broken hearts who wake up and wonder if their pain is just a dream and find themselves sickened when it is not. I still have those dreams, less as time goes on, but they are never truly gone.

I get up, and holding the luggage shelf, I work my way through the train car. I bypass the ladies' room and open the door between the cars. A cold wind cuts through me. I need air, as much as I can inhale. I breathe in and out until my breath matches the rhythm of the turn of the train wheels, metal on metal.

I grip the door handles and stand between the cars and cry. I mourn everything I've lost, my old life, my grandmothers, my marriage, Uncle Louie, and the pregnancy. I ask the Blessed Mother to help me leave my sadness behind on the tracks that disappear in the mist as if they were never there in the first place. Time becomes a thick fog; there is no looking back through it. *Take away my pain*, I plead. I can't outrun my sadness for the rest of my life, but I don't want to carry it either.

Signora Strazza is asleep when I return to my seat. I sit and open my phone. It's almost Christmas Eve as I remember the Feast of the Seven Fishes. I wipe my eyes and write.

I was eight years old as I stood at the bay window in my parents' house and watched the biggest snowfall of my lifetime blanket the neighborhood on Christmas Eve. The snow was so heavy I couldn't see the lake. I had all the fears a child might have about Santa Claus traveling through the storm and down a chimney. I was afraid the holiday would be ruined. On the Baratta side, in our southern Italian tradition, Christmas Eve was a night of fish, family, and faith that culminated in Midnight Mass at Saint Catharine's. The Cap side threw themselves into the tradition because they would never stand in the way of a good party. Furthermore, a blizzard would not cancel the Feast of the Seven Fishes. We would proceed and persist. Mom lined up our Wellies by the door and placed scarves, mittens, and hats on the bench for each of us to brave the trek from house to house. Dad put chains on the tires of our station wagon so we would not slip into a ditch on the way to Spring Lake for Midnight Mass. Despite my doom, I felt safe, as though no harm could come to us.

The feast had been planned for weeks. On Black Friday, the day after Thanksgiving, the women of the family gathered in

Grammy B's kitchen and drew the fish they would prepare out of a hat. Nobody wanted to draw the smelts, because the scent of the fried sardines stayed in the curtains until Easter.

Connie even drew a map so the families on the block would move in order from house to house, appetizer through dessert. Seven homes, including ours, would serve one fish dish, with the eighth stop, Aunt Lil and Uncle Louie's garage, for *il finale,* the Venetian dessert table.

They transformed their immaculate garage into a party room, with lights, a tree, and a dessert spread, including a chocolate fountain, a build-your-own-sundae bar with hand-cranked gelato, and a stuff-your-own-cannoli table. Anything your heart desired, you could have, but what we didn't know was that we had *la dolce vita* all along. We were together, every side of the family, in-laws including extended family that included Sicilians, Neapolitans, and the random Irish, all celebrating together. Our southern Italian side celebrated Christmas Eve, but the Tuscans, instead of fasting, as was their tradition, went along for the ride. The feast was a tradition long before Mom sent Louie to the Island, and yet beautiful memories of Christmases past weren't enough to save it. The Feast of the Seven Fishes was abruptly canceled whenever my mother feuded with her brother. And, as these things go, the feast was reinstated when Mom decided to make up with him. The loss of those holidays was never addressed. We were expected to rewrite history and move on as though the pain had not been inflicted in the first place.

"*Buon appetito!*" Uncle Louie raised a glass of eggnog in the garage to toast. "To *la famiglia*!" He sipped along with the rest of the grown-ups. "Tastes like Carrara."

"Carrara. Carrara. Louie talks about that place like it's

nothing but heaven. I wouldn't know. Never been there." Aunt Lil sipped her eggnog. "And don't ask me, Lou. I don't want to go traipsing all over the world. I like New Jersey."

"You're Sicilian, Lil. A different set of traditions altogether. Island people."

"I go along with yours, don't I?" Aunt Lil said pleasantly.

I went up on my toes and dipped a spoon in the chocolate fountain as Uncle Louie told a story about his time in Italy. The family gathered around him on their folding chairs, leaning in to listen.

"There I was, in the same quarry as Michelangelo. Blinding white-hot light as far as the eye could see. I'm not kidding, the exact same place where Michelangelo got the marble to sculpt the statue of David. I'm a kid from New Jersey on hallowed ground. I do whatever they tell me, and soon they see I'm serious, and they teach me to cut the stone. I'm on the mountain, dangling off the face of the marble—not just me, there were maybe a dozen of us. We are suspended in air, wearing these leather harnesses. They told me to hold on to my tools; if you drop one, you're screwed. You have to wait for another guy to swing over to you, which can take hours because we're up there to measure and cut. The sun is beating down hard on us; we're frying in the heat. But the marble is always cool, it doesn't heat up, so in a way, you learn to love the marble because it gave us comfort. My Italian wasn't great when I got there, but I learned quickly. There was a brotherhood on that mountain. Now, you all know I love my sister, but there was something about being accepted by these guys who had no reason to take me in that taught me the meaning of family. And maybe a little about courage."

"You are so lucky to have been born a man," my mother

piped up. "You got to go to Italy and have an adventure. The summer you were gone, I washed cars, cleaned my mother's house, and put up raspberry jam."

"That's how it was for girls back then, Phil. Don't blame me; I didn't create the system," Uncle Louie said.

"Women were burning their bras. I was months away from emancipation. Timing is everything," Mom complained.

"I don't know about all this feminism stuff," Aunt Lil said, "but my husband would rather be hanging off that mountain cutting stone than installing marble tubs in those mansions in Ridgewood. Believe me."

"I'll take all the danger in the world, if you give me Italy." Uncle Louie winked at me.

I was eight years old and didn't understand the adult conversation, or why their jokes were funny, or not, but something happened that Christmas Eve that took root in my subconscious. I was certain that a place called Italy and a man named Louie would conspire to give me my dream, even though I wasn't sure exactly what it was or how to make that dream come true. I had no vision, no proof, just a Capodimonte hunch, one I would hold on to through all that lay ahead.

MILANO

Milan is statuesque, a Gustav Klimt creation; tall, slender, swathed in beige, and left out in the rain. Spires and spheres, marble bell towers and sculpted gargoyles define Milan from the ground. La Scala opera house, built of cladded stone, is all arched doors, windows, and pediments as ornate as a wealthy patron who wears every priceless jewel she owns in order to turn heads on Via Emmanuel when she attends the opera. Heavy gray clouds hang low, turning the pavement wisteria blue. Milan is in a mood, and she has painted herself shades of purple.

Angelo waits for us at the train station. We find him easily in the crowd; his intense eyes cut through the mist when all else recedes into the haze. He pushes through the throng toward us. His mother lets out a sigh of delight and points to him. This is not the Angelo Strazza of Carrara who works in a studio in an apron. He's Milanese now; his new job is one of commercial design and customer relations. Angelo has acquired *sprezzatura*, an effortless elegance. The artist has become a work of art himself. He wears a cashmere topcoat thrown over a brown wool blazer and navy slacks; his brown-and-blue-striped tie is loosened at the collar. He embraces his mother. She reaches up and tightens the knot on his tie before he turns to me and kisses me on both cheeks.

I haven't seen Angelo since he left Carrara. He recently sent a couple of texts, but they were more about his mother than our friendship.

Angelo takes my backpack and throws it over his shoulder. He takes his mother's arm with one of his and her luggage with the other. I roll my own suitcase beside them.

"Mamma, I got you tickets to La Scala. Zia Bette is going to take you."

"But what about you?"

"I'm going to take Giuseppina up the mountain."

"Bergamo?"

He nods. "Valle di Scalve."

"You're not going to take her to see your father's lunatic friend."

"Yes, I am."

"Beppe Novelli is crazy." She turns to me. "Stay in Milan if you know what's good for you."

"I promised Conor I would show you the gilding studio." Angelo winks at me. "It's business, Mamma."

"Another time," Signora Strazza pleads. "You'll ruin Christmas."

"Nothing can ruin Christmas, *signora*," I insist.

"Beppe will ruin Christmas. You don't know. Everything is a joke with that buffoon. And watch his hands. That's my final word of warning. Nobody listens to me, but you will see."

Does every Italian mother play guilt like a round of pickleball? Or is it their go-to when they want to control their children? "*Signora*, when it comes to new friends, the crazier the better," I tell her.

"I won't let anything happen to Giuseppina," Angelo assures her.

"You two are alike," Signora Strazza says. "*Pazzo.*"

We're not crazy. There is a much simpler diagnosis. I know it, and eventually Angelo will understand it too. We were raised by the same mother.

BEPPE

Grotto D'Oro is a gilder's workshop on the mountain in Città Alta, an Elizabethan-style village above the city of Bergamo. The piazza is Italian, but the details are old-world English: wrought iron, curlicued gates, and fussy architectural ornamentation on the buildings. No saltwater taffy colors here, only neutrals, white and beige with a touch of pink that comes from the light. Even the winter birds play along, circling overhead, jet-black slashes in the sky that drop onto the piazza, tuck in their wings, and skitter on the stone tiles searching for crumbs.

"If Bergamo's Città Alta were a woman, she would be Jane Eyre,"

I tell Angelo. "It's a fortress. It reminds me of Thornfield Hall. It's set on the mountain, remote, and it feels like it's got secrets."

"Is everything you see in the world from a story in a book?" Angelo asks.

Beppe's workshop is off the piazza, in a single-story stone building, tucked into the mountain with rounded edges, which may be why it's called a grotto. We enter through a pair of wooden barn doors with brass rings for knobs. Inside, the workshop is one large room with a long farm table cleared for work. Against the walls are piles of marble blocks, stacks of stones, planks of wood, and granite sheets resting against the walls like mirrors. The stools are so old the wood is worn on the seats and slope where Beppe sits, pitched forward to do his work.

Beppe Novelli, the master gilder, looks up and smiles. He gets up, throws his arms around Angelo, and keeps his eyes on me. Angelo introduces us. How could this robust and compact man around five foot five be any trouble at all? What was Signora Strazza thinking? Beppe, in his sixties, has youthful energy. He kisses both my hands before he buries his own in the chest pocket of his overalls, underneath the apron. He steps back and sizes me up.

"This one has a good shape," Beppe decides. "Not like the other one."

"Who are you talking about?" Angelo asks.

"The broomstick."

"Dalia?"

"I was going to say Diana, but she is far from the Greek huntress. I don't know what I would call her besides *stuzzicadenti*."

"Why don't you start with *nice woman*," I snap, "instead of comparing her to a toothpick?" I find myself in the odd position of defending Angelo's girlfriend.

"Women stick together," Beppe exclaims. "Good for you. Always know which side you're on."

"And bad for you," I reply.

Angelo pats imaginary dough with his hands. Uncle Louie must be floating around in the grotto.

"Forgive me, Giuseppina." Beppe doesn't seem particularly contrite.

"I broke up with Dalia," Angelo explains. "My friend Beppe is concerned for me. That's all."

"She was not for you!" Beppe says.

I don't know what to say; Angelo is single. When he moved to Milan, and I was invited north for the holiday, I thought I would assume the role of the extra guest, like Carmel or Marina at our Christmas table. I even packed two pairs of new mittens, in anticipation of Dalia and her daughter showing up at the last minute for the holidays. I didn't want to be caught without gifts for them.

"How is Laura?" Beppe asks Angelo as he rocks back and forth on his feet.

"Mamma sends her regards."

"Impossible! She loathes me."

Angelo laughs. "It's Christmas, Beppe. Mamma is being charitable."

"What happened between you two?" I ask Beppe. "Why does Signora Strazza make a face when your name comes up?"

Beppe looks at Angelo, who looks at me.

"I'm curious," I tell them. "It will go no further."

Beppe begins. "I tell you the story. Many years ago, I was seeing Laura's sister. Bette was my *innamorata*." He whistles. "We were young."

"Zia Bette," Angelo explains.

"And one day, poof! I disappeared. It wasn't a match. Bette was too much for me. And I didn't know how to handle it. I knew the *romanza* was *pfft*, but I didn't want to tell her, so I became a vapor. When Bette came to the shop to find out why I disappeared, I acted like I had lost my mind so she would fall out of love with me. It worked. Bette believed I had gone crazy because she would never understand why any man would leave her. She thought very highly of herself." He whistles and makes his hands outline the dimensions of a curvy bass fiddle. "Perhaps she was right."

"Zia Bette is a great beauty," Angelo agrees.

"So was I." Beppe winks at me. "Everyone thought that I was *pazzo* except for Angelo's mother. Laura knew I was . . ." He whistles again. "A *scungilli*. So she sent her husband to Bergamo to set me straight."

"My father was sent to restore the family honor," Angelo explains.

"Your mother wanted your father to beat me."

"When my father got here to defend Zia Bette's honor, you already had another woman in the back room. *Scungilli* is right."

"Is that true? I don't remember. Anyway, I told your father to go home and tell his wife that he beat me with stick and I learned my lesson. Your father did as I said and she believed him."

"Why didn't you just tell the truth?" I ask. "You were with the wrong person. That's no crime."

"The truth has no place in matters of love."

"*Non è vero*," I tell Beppe.

"*È vero.* Truth is truth." Beppe looks at me. "I am not a good husband. Boyfriend. None of it. I am in love with gold. She is my lover. I explained this to your father, and he didn't disagree. So we went for dinner and drank wine and became friends. Now I have two problems. I am friends with your father and enemies with his wife. And then your father went to heaven, and I only have one problem. Your mother. Now you know everything about me. I want to know about you, Giuseppina *bella*." Beppe pinches my cheek.

"I came here to see what you do." I sit on the work stool and look at him. "Not to get pinched."

Beppe sighs. "Work. Work. Work. What I do is simple. But only if you have done it for forty-eight years."

Beppe lifts a small square of marble off the pile. It is carved with cherubs and rosebuds in relief. In its raw state, it is a lovely block of Carrara blue. "I show you."

Beppe opens a sleeve of gold leaf sheets. He picks up a knife and, using the same motion one might when slicing a very thin piece of cheese, lifts the gold off the sheet and applies it to the carving, the stem of one rose. He taps the knife and returns it to the table. He picks up a brush and caresses it against the gold and marble.

"Why didn't you brush the bristle against your cheek?" I ask. "Like Angelo. You taught him, didn't you?"

"I am a bad teacher!" Beppe throws his hands in the air. "It's an old technique. Sometimes I use it, sometimes I don't."

"In America, we use a machine to gild stone."

Beppe makes a face. "In America you eat out of Styrofoam. I don't recommend that either. I have changed my technique over time. Maybe another artist chooses another way. We learn." He shrugs.

"But I would hope we hold on to tradition," I say.

Beppe shakes his finger at me. "Tradition can only exist in a state of change."

Could that be true? I thought tradition and change had nothing to do with each other. Haven't I learned that the tighter the grip I have on my life, the less I control it? It seems, from the old master himself, that change is the key to moving forward, not holding on to what once served me.

Beppe cannot be convinced to attend Midnight Mass with us; he says he would spontaneously combust and turn to ash if he entered a church. But he wished us a *buon Natale* before crossing the piazza to spend Christmas Eve with his new girlfriend. Lucrezia is forty-two and a *bombolona*. His word.

Once Angelo and I are outside the shop, on our way to his car, he takes my hand.

When I came up this mountain with Angelo, I thought he was in a serious relationship, and now I know he's not. This doesn't change anything, I tell myself. I live in Carrara. Angelo lives in Milan. We are miles apart.

20

Midnight Mass in Vilminore

As Angelo drives up the mountain on the Passo della Presolana through the Italian Alps, small stars sneak through the winter clouds, making pinpoints of silver light on the black velvet sky.

Angelo swerves off the road and enters Vilminore di Scalve, a village with narrow cobblestone streets that twist through rows of two-story houses built of cross timbers and stucco. The shutters on the windows are painted shades of caramel and licorice, draped in white Christmas lights that twinkle in the dark.

Angelo parks outside the Parrocchia Santa Maria Assunta e Santo Pietro Apostolo, a baroque cathedral. The stucco is painted a soft gold; in the dark, it looms against the black mountains like a fortress. The steep steps of the entrance are lit by squat candles, whose flames sway in the winter wind. I snap a photo of Angelo climbing the church steps; his wool scarf unfurls behind him in the wind. I post it quickly with the message *Buon Natale*. I put my phone in my coat pocket before my mother can post her reaction.

Inside the cathedral, braided garlands of fresh fir are draped along the pews. The scents of frankincense, beeswax, and pine saturate the air. The inlaid marble floor is a *pietra dura* masterpiece of carnelian, black, and turquoise stone. The side altars that line the outer aisles had been added over centuries by families of the village. These artful alcoves honor their patron saints. They are filled with statues carved of Calacatta marble.

The frescoes create a backdrop behind the main altar, depicting the life of Jesus. They are lit by crystal chandeliers that throw light on the mosaic of gold.

The main altar shimmers with the flames of candles set among branches of fresh pine. But tonight, it is the crèche that creates an intimacy in all the grandeur that surrounds it. A primitive, wooden stable filled with straw with characters depicting the Holy Family is set off to the side. A family welcomes a new baby. A simple idea that has inspired artists for centuries.

"It reminds me of home," I whisper as Angelo guides us to our seats. We kneel. "One difference. I'm starving." Evidently, no Feast of the Seven Fishes north of Rome.

Angelo smiles. "Tonight, we fast. Tomorrow, we have a banquet."

Christmas Day in New Jersey was an open house. Cousins stopped in, Grandpop Cap was at one end of the dining room table, and Grandpa B on the other, equal in stature and power. The women worked in the kitchen, while their husbands tended the fires, smoked cigars, ate, and napped afterward. The roles were easily assigned, and no one questioned them.

Mom prepared a buffet with roast turkey, platters of salami, capicola and prosciutto (from Bilancia Meats, of course), focaccia, hot rolls, and salads. There were cookies for dessert; whatever we didn't deliver up and down the street, we saved for Christmas Day. Mom made coffee in a silver urn that she received as a wedding gift. It was the only time of year she used it, because the brass spout was delicate and she wanted the urn to last her entire lifetime. My parents, for all their flaws, anchored us in the importance of making memories. I long for our traditions, but I hope to reinvent them too. If only it were as easy as the eraser I use when I draw. I take away what doesn't work and draw what I believe might. Mistakes are part of the process, so we fix them and move on, if we can. What would Christmas be without regret?

The Gregorian chants, written by monks many centuries ago, fill the breadth of the cathedral with rich harmonies. The voices of the choir soothe me as the candlelight throws beams of soft light on the marble altar. I rest my head on Angelo's shoulder and close my eyes. He takes my hand. We listen.

As Angelo and I drive back down the mountain to Milan, I am reminded the Passo della Presolana is no New Jersey Turnpike. There are only a few safety reflectors posted on the curves to illuminate the roads that turn off into the villages buried in the folds of the mountain. If I'm honest, I miss the wide lanes, glittery exits, neon signs, and rumble strips of our American highways. This is Alpine reality; you have to have grown up in this terrain to navigate it. Angelo spent his summers with the Strazzas on the mountain and it shows.

The road requires all of Angelo's attention, so I try not to talk. He navigates the stone overpass fenced in by low guardrails with confidence. The beam of the headlights illuminates the road ahead, a black patent leather ribbon that hugs the side of the mountain. I resume our conversation once we make it to Clusone, a hillside town with A-frame houses and a wide main street.

"I just had the best Christmas Eve of my life," I tell him. "And I've never had a bad one."

"Did you miss your American Christmas Eve?"

"I miss the people."

"Tradition," Angelo says. "A gift and a noose."

"For the first time, I wasn't standing over a hot stove making shrimp scampi or boiling lobster tails to make sauce. I had nothing to do but pay attention to the Mass and listen to the music. Maybe my Italian is improving. I don't know. I am beginning to feel at home in Italy, and more Italian than I did before I got here."

"I like your American ways," Angelo says. "Don't change too much."

"When I was growing up, I always thought whatever the Italians did was better than the Italian Americans. Maybe that was Uncle Louie's influence, or Grandma Cap's, who told me how much better everything tasted on the Montini farm. Blueberries were better in Italy, even though New Jersey is famous for its blueberries. This great Italian yearning in me was placed there by my elders, who knew better about everything."

"Is Italy your dream or theirs?"

"It's mine." I say this with confidence because I believe it. "Definitely."

"And your ex-husband? Is he part of your future?"

"I don't know." How do I explain to Angelo what Bobby Bilancia meant to me? We were once family.

"You had feelings for him once, and you could have them again?"

"Uncle Louie used to say a relationship is like a crab on the beach; it will either go forward or backward but never sideways."

"Or they stand still."

"Bobby and I are sideways."

"I broke up with Dalia because I have feelings for you." Angelo doesn't take his eyes off the road.

"Oh no." My stomach drops.

"You don't like me?" he teases.

"I'm here."

He ponders this and asks, "Has your time in Italy made you happy?"

"In so many ways." My heart goes to the moments that have given me peace of mind. The sound of the trains. Riding through the Italian hills on those trains. The scent of bread baking on the piazza in the morning. The polenta served hot and sliced on a board. The white marble face of the mountain in the moonlight. Smokey when she's curled up asleep in her basket. I turn to Angelo. "I slept through the sunrise when I went through the worst, and it was a mistake. I couldn't find peace in the dark. Then I moved to the piazza to wake up to the light."

Angelo shakes his head. His eyes remain on the road. "I was not expecting you," he says softly.

To be *unexpected*, in a life where I have tried so hard to meet every expectation of me, is a gift. I lean across the seat and kiss Angelo on the cheek, breathing in the sweet scent of orange and pine. Angelo Strazza smells like Christmas.

We don't talk after I kiss him. There doesn't seem to be anything left to say.

Milan in the early hours of Christmas Day is tranquil, except for the crunch of the wheels on the ice as Angelo parks the car. It was snowing and cold in the Valle di Scalve, Vilminore, and Città Alta, but the light dusting in Milan will be gone by morning. We left the holiday magic behind in the Italian Alps. To be fair, there is a white Christmas every year in Milan because it's built of Carrara marble. I squeeze Angelo's hand and thank him for taking me to the mountain. Angelo gets out of the car, comes around, and opens the door. He helps me out. I dust a few drops of water—melted snowflakes—from the shoulder of his overcoat.

Angelo takes my hand as we climb the stairs to the entrance of his building. I like the feeling of my hand in his; sometimes I think holding a man's hand is more intimate than a kiss. He unlocks the door, and we go inside. We tiptoe into his dark apartment. His mother is asleep in his room; the door is ajar, and we can see her in the shadows, asleep under the coverlet in the moonlight through the window. I put my finger to my lips and tiptoe into the guest room. Angelo will sleep on the pull-out sofa in the living room. Before I close the door, I return to the living room. I hold him close. "*Buon Natale.*" I let him go.

"Maybe for you," he says.

NEW YEAR'S ON THE ORIGINAL LAKE COMO

I take the bus from Bergamo to Cernobbio and arrive on Lake Como alone. Angelo and Signora Strazza asked me to stay on in Milan, but three days is long enough as a houseguest. I loved spending time learning about the city from two women who know it well. Signora Strazza and I toured the city with her infamous sister, Bette, after which Angelo joined us for dinner. There was lots of laughter around the table, but Angelo's feelings for me were like low clouds overhead, lots of fog and no clarity. One time, he reached under the table to squeeze my hand, but it was more friendly than romantic. I can't complain when I'm the one who placed the guardrails, but my feelings are confusing. I just knew I had to get out of Milan. So I went online to reserve a hotel room. Lucky for me there were last-minute cancellations, so I booked the smallest room in the best hotel, the Villa d'Este, with a view of the original Lake Como. I am happy to be alone, though everywhere I turn, I see happy couples and families, and I had hoped to start the new year without reminders of all I've left behind. What's a New Year's Eve without regret? *Arrangiarmi.*

I have wanted to visit Cernobbio since I studied Renaissance architecture in college. The Villa d'Este is an ornate palazzo. Glorious pediments and trims outline panels of sunflower-gold walls; inside, stately arches define marble corridors and staircases. There are layers of gardens carved into the hillsides and regal statuary overlooking the Lago di Como, known for its midnight-blue water.

The lakes in Tuscany and Lombardy are of the deepest blue india ink. The Italian skies are any color they want to be; sometimes the clouds are cotton-candy pink, and other times, swirls of Arabescato or folds of pale blue silk. Today, the sky is ribbed with clouds that appear to be skeins of white wool from the lake to the mountains. I'm here to find solitude, like Caroline of Brunswick before me, on the shores of Lake Como on a cold holiday weekend where I will find warmth inside the pages of a good book. I haven't finished my current reread of *A Room with a View*, and I can't think of a better companion on a cold winter holiday in Italy.

Classic Italian art and Renaissance architecture typically began with a commission by the Holy Roman Church. The Villa d'Este is no different; it was built as a residence for the Cardinal of Como five centuries ago, and since has been inhabited by a royal family, sold to various private families, and now is a hotel for people like me, who hope to immerse themselves in the history that lives throughout the rooms, connected by ornate marble staircases and wide, shimmering floors. Outside on the grounds, I will walk through the fallow gardens, designed to emulate the Tivoli Gardens and Hadrian's Villa in Rome. I know before I set one foot in them that they will be my refuge. I am falling in love with the idea of this solo holiday, an adventure all my own, with only myself to blame if

I don't find my bliss. How could I not? Snowflakes flutter through the air on my way inside the hotel, dusting the shore of the lake with glitter.

I JOIN A group in the grand lobby to tour Orrido di Bellano. After studying Stendhal's tour of Italy, I've wanted to see the glorious waterfalls that feed into the lake.

Evidently, I'm not the only one. There's a lot of enthusiasm in the van for the tour. I'm attempting to understand French (which I should be able to speak after three years of study in high school) when I receive a text.

FARAH: I want to send you a photo.

JESS: Please do. How is London?

FARAH: I'm not in London.

JESS: Dove? Where?

FARAH: Took your advice.

A photograph of Farah and an older woman, both smiling, arms around each other's waists, pops up.

FARAH: Mamma and me.

JESS: She looks happy!

FARAH: Not easy for her.

JESS: But you're working it out?

FARAH: Mamma said, I loved my son and now, I love my daughter.

JESS: Bellissima!

If Farah's traditional mother can accept her daughter, there may be hope for Philomena Baratta and me. I'm tempted to text my mom but instead focus on the tour guide, who explains what we are about to do.

The van takes a turn onto the road that encircles Lake Como. The islands in the middle of the tranquil lake are set in the blue like emeralds. I unload from the van with three Germans, two French ladies, and a Sicilian couple on their honeymoon. It's so cold, we pull on hats and gloves as we follow the guide. I'm relieved there are so many languages spoken in my group that I don't have to talk. Today, I want to *see*.

We follow the guide single file into the wintry woods. I breathe the spice of the pine and the green, crisp cedar. Eventually, we find ourselves between two towering stone arches, made smooth by water and time. As we pass under the arches, we hear the deafening roar of the waterfall as it tumbles over the rock wall. Silver ribbons of water flow from its peak, so high above us, its origin is hidden in the clouds.

As we make our way up to the suspension bridge, stretched between two stone formations, I want to turn back. I don't think I can cross the old bridge that sways over the precipice. I've always been afraid of heights but never bothered to test my fear. It was just something I believed to be true about myself. The thought of this is overwhelming, so I make the decision to go back, but the Germans are stacked up tight like a roll of nickels behind me. I'm trapped. Too ashamed to make a scene and too meek to ask them to let me go back, I gather my courage. Before I take the first step, I make the mistake of looking down. The pool beneath the falls is gray and foamy, and evidently so deep, scientists still study its mineral content because they discover new elements all the time.

I keep my eyes forward and take one step, followed by another.

I grip the ropes so tightly, I practically shear the leather off my gloves, yet I hold on. The weight of the other tourists ahead on the line throws me, but instead of resisting the sway, I move with the bridge. One. Two. Three. One. Two. Three. I mentally dust off my ice-skating lessons from childhood, shifting my body weight from one foot to the other to maintain my balance. It helps to picture myself in control. Soon enough, I make it to the platform on the other side. I am filled with a sense of accomplishment as I join the group. I raise my hands in the air once I am on solid ground. I spin around, ecstatic that I made it across. A French lady pats me on the back. I mop the sweat from my brow with my sleeve. I want an Olympic medal for this, but self-satisfaction will have to do. This must be how astronauts feel when they walk on the moon and make it back to Earth to talk about the experience.

I take in the majesty of the waterfall at eye level. The falls are so loud they drown out any conversation. We find ourselves smiling and nodding, knowing that we will only have this moment and one another in it to remember what we see. The falls are both powerful and *serena*; these two truths exist in the same natural state, and together, they are bigger than my terror and were worth the risk of crossing the old bridge.

The other tourists have their phones out, snapping away at the beauty. I text Aunt Lil a photograph of the falls with this message:

Oh, Aunt Lil. I found peace on earth.

She texts,

You deserve it. Happy New Year, honey. Hope to see you sometime. Love you.

I experience a wave of guilt, so I send the same photograph to my sister and brother and their families. My heart is heavy. Once I'm back in the van, I post a photograph of the falls on Instagram and caption it: *The View from Lake Como.* I share it with the hope that my family, who celebrates an ocean away on the other Lake Como, will see my view of this one. This is my imaginary cannon shot of confetti, a New Year's revelry sent across the Atlantic Ocean. This is a sincere first step toward healing that may not lead to a second, but I hold nothing except hope in my heart on the cusp of the new year.

The tour group and I disembark from the van and are led to a pier, where we board the boat from a dock on the lake. I take a seat by the hull and place my phone in my pocket. I'm not going to take pictures; instead, I will pay attention and remember every detail. No need to record, to sketch, or to snap. The captain of the skiff, a handsome man of around twenty, looks at me and winks. I'm old enough to be his aunt, but I smile back at him.

I sail on the original Lake Como as the skiff bounces over the blue satin waves, cutting the surface with barely a ripple. It is cold, I'm hungry, and yet, I am at peace. There is nothing but whipped-cream clouds overhead, the water beneath us, and the winter air, sweet with bayberry and nettle. The icy water mists my face. I close my eyes. This is what Uncle Louie meant when he told me to be happy. Pay attention to the moments you live in and find your place in them. Be content with your portion. I'm a very small part of something beautiful on this Italian lake, and that's enough.

A year ago, I couldn't imagine a holiday away from home, and this year, I'm happier than I ever have been in my life. As the boat sails along the shoreline of Lake Como, the houses look like rows of sweet pastel macarons in shades of butter yellow, pale green, and pink. It's as though the world itself has been wrapped as a gift just for me. There is nothing for me to do but dream.

THE OTHER MICHELANGELO

The waves of the lake lap against the shore. My feet are submerged in the cold water. I shiver when I feel a man's arms envelop me; soon, I'm bathed in warmth. I'm lifted out of the water. I turn and place my arms around his neck. His lips find mine. The curves of his shoulders and arms are smooth and defined. I lean into him; his chest is broad and strong, as though the heart within it could not break. He takes my hands in his; there is power and strength in them. As we kiss, I long to tell him everything I feel, but this is no time for conversation. He found me here, and I might have been here forever had he not come along.

"Giuseppina, why do you wait?" he asks before kissing me again. His lips are sweet; he kisses my ear, then my cheek. He whispers in my ear, "I belong to you."

He helps me into a rowboat with a gold lamé sail that billows in the night wind. The moon lights our path on the surface of the water; there is barely a ripple as the boat moves across the lake. "Come here," he says. He puts down the oars and pulls me close from behind; we look out over the lake in the light of the moon. I reach up, and he kisses my neck and wraps his arms around me. I run my hands over his; they are the hands of a man who has worked with them all his life. His hands are rough and calloused and purposeful, and in their use they hold a beauty that can only come from strength. I kiss his hands and lace my fingers through his. The boat falls away as we float over the water, like a cloud or a mist or a square of fine silk caught up in the breeze. I turn to kiss him. His mouth finds mine.

I wake up on the edge of the bed curled like a croissant. I forget where I am and soon remember. The bedsheets are twisted around my legs like bandages. The pillows have fallen on the floor. The room is freezing cold. I peel off the sheets and blanket. I run to the window to close it.

A low moon over Lake Como throws shadows over my view of the shore, where boats bob along the pier in the dark. The lake beyond the shore is a black pit that undulates under the moon. *Where did he go?* I wonder. *Was it him? The wild curls. The lips. Was it Michelangelo? Was it David? I didn't see the face. Was it Angelo Strazza? Or was it Bobby Bilancia?* I crawl back under the covers, finding the warmth beneath the blankets.

I WAKE UP with the crazy feeling that the dream I had the night before was real. I need proof that it wasn't, so I get out of bed, open the drapes in my hotel room, look out the window, and make sure the storm that blew over Lake Como had actually happened. I'm relieved when I see charcoal clouds peppered over the lake and the wet, bare tree branches dipped in silver ice outside my window. There had been a storm!

I dress for breakfast. I put on a dab of face cream but find I don't need much of it this morning. My skin is radiant from the trek to the waterfalls the day before, and any tension I felt in Milan has melted away. I swipe pink gloss on my lips and like what I see in the mirror. I am ready for anything the world might send my way. I have a feeling of anticipation, for no other reason than it's almost a new year, and with it comes hope. The unwritten has all the power. So instead of grabbing a coffee and roll to go, I plan to sit alone in a pretty corner of the dining room under the windows and enjoy the view with my breakfast and a book. Eating and reading, a perfect pairing. The ultimate romance! How very Lucy Honeychurch from *A Room with a View.* I will be the heroine in my own novel, at least before lunch.

I descend the grand marble staircase, imagining myself in a brocade gown over a skirt thick with crinolines. I walk across the lobby to the garden pavilion, where breakfast is served. I am almost to the maître d's station when I inhale a blast of fresh peppermint and I hear my name.

Bobby Bilancia steps in front of me.

"Bobby." I'm confused. Bobby Bilancia on Lake Como? How did he get here? Why is he here? My thoughts remain muddled from the dream I had the night before, and I've yet to have coffee, so I question my judgment. But Bobby *is* here. I am happy to see him, someone from home whom I know, loved, and who knows me. My instinct is to throw my arms around him, so I do. There it is. More peppermint.

"I didn't want to scare you," Bobby says, wrapping his arms around me in return.

"I'm not. I'm surprised that you—" Before I finish, he interrupts.

"I had to see you."

"Is something wrong? Are your mom and dad all right? The family? My family?" Bobby Bilancia is the type of guy who packs a toothbrush when he has a meeting in Avon-by-the-Sea. He would never cross an ocean unless he were delivering news of some importance.

"Everybody is okay. They're fine," he says.

Bobby holds the black leather duffel that I spent the better part of an afternoon deciding to buy in a small Greenwich Village shop for his wedding gift. Bobby takes care of his things, so I had no problem splurging. He took it to Las Vegas on our honeymoon. The bag looks new; it is as supple and shiny as the day I bought it. Bobby wears jeans, a white button-down shirt, and a navy-blue wool bomber jacket that he's had since high school. When we were married, once in a while, in cold weather, I'd borrow his jacket and walk around all day smelling like a candy cane. "You look good, Bobby Bilancia."

"So do you."

I wish I had put on a little something more than lip gloss, but then I remember I didn't need it. It doesn't matter anyway; he's seen me with less. "How about breakfast?"

Bobby and I never disagreed about food. One of us was always hungry, and the other would eat to keep the famished one company. We settle at a table for two in the window of the hotel restaurant overlooking the lake. I tuck the book I was going to read under the chair.

The waitress places a basket of *cornetti* on the table, hot, fluffy rolls shaped like horns, fresh from the oven. She brings us a crystal bowl of strawberry *marmellata* with a tiny gold spoon next to a soft, yellow ball of *burro*. The waiter, a trim Italian man with a mustache, around my dad's age, brings us a pot of coffee, two cups, and a pitcher of fresh cream. The sugar is already on the table.

"So, this is the original Lake Como," Bobby says, looking out over the lake. "It's huge."

"Crazy, right? I thought our Lake Como was big, until I saw this."

"Nothing wrong with our lake at home." Bobby smiles.

"Not a thing." I unfold the napkin and place it on my lap. "How did you find me?"

"Your brother gave me your address in Carrara. Don't get mad at him; I told him I was sending you something for Christmas."

"The gift is you."

"Kind of." Bobby blushes. He pours a cup of coffee for me and one for himself.

What else would the gift be? Bobby is not one for surprises, and I can tell he would've rather been invited to join me in Italy instead of just showing up. My heart melts for him. I know the effort that went into flying over here because I was the person in our marriage who made all the plans. I responded to the invitations and put them on the calendar. I bought the gifts and made sure Bobby's shirts and pants were pressed and his shoes polished. I don't recall a time when Bobby ever made plans on his own without someone's input. Evidently, I'm not the only person who is changing.

"Let me explain," he says. "First, I went to Carrara. But you weren't there. The building where you live was locked up tight—I couldn't even get inside the gate to leave a note. So I started asking around, and people on the piazza were very forthcoming. I went into shops and asked questions. They love you. They say that you sit outside and draw. You're like the town artist."

"They said that?"

Bobby nods. "I told them it's your job to draw, but they didn't seem to think that was true. They think you're like a Picasso or something."

"They really said that?"

"They did." Bobby prepares his coffee with a lot of cream. "A guy in a shop sent me to the café. Signorina LeDonne told me you were in Lake Como. She said she's your cat sitter?"

"Yeah. I adopted a kitten. Her name is Smokey."

"You know I'm allergic."

"I know. But you're really missing out."

"I'd only miss out on the hives," Bobby jokes, before appearing concerned. "Are you crying?"

I dab the corner of my eyes. "I'm just happy. I belong here."

"You belong in Lake Como, New Jersey. You are one of us, and everybody misses you."

"That's funny. I thought no one would miss me."

"Did you come all the way to Italy to see if you could fit in with new people?"

"Partly. Maybe. I don't know. Bobby, why are you here?"

"I guess I need to understand what happened to us. All these months later I still don't get it, and I'm not able to move on until I do."

"We had a couple of years to sort through everything."

"It didn't seem like it to me. I look back on that time, and I just did whatever you wanted me to do because you were in so much pain. Over the past year, I've been thinking about it. And I had time to think on the airplane."

"Did you cry?"

"I came close. I get it. You lose it because you're trapped in a flying tin can over the Atlantic Ocean. That's enough to make anyone cry," Bobby says.

We laugh.

"Jess, I don't think I tried hard enough. You know, I'm a hard worker. I don't shy away from it. But when it came to us, I had no clue. I had no idea what to do when the worst happened, and I didn't know how to comfort you. This has been nagging at me. I don't want to be that guy. The one who runs away when the going gets tough."

"I didn't let you in because I didn't know how."

"I should've been kinder to you," Bobby says. "More patient."

"You were fine. You handled things the way you could. I understand." I hadn't given much thought to Bobby's feelings over the past two years, because I was untangling my own. His pain is just as deep as mine. "I hope you're seeing people."

"Nothing serious." Bobby blushes. "If I did, it was because I tried to get over you."

Tried? Does this mean he didn't succeed? We are getting somewhere at long last. Away from Lake Como, New Jersey, we can be honest with each other. This is what it means to get distance. Truth is a pillar of forgiveness. We can't forgive each other unless we agree why we parted in the first place.

I'm slathering fresh butter on the warm *cornetto* when Angelo Strazza enters the dining room. I drop the knife when his eyes meet mine. Angelo frowns when he sees that I'm sitting with Bobby. A look of confusion crosses Angelo's face.

What is happening here? I think as he strides across the room toward us. Angelo's expression tells me he's thinking the same thing.

"Ciao, Giuseppina," Angelo says. "Who is this?" Angelo nods toward Bobby.

"Who are you?" Bobby asks.

Angelo ignores him. "What is this?" Angelo fans his hands toward Bobby like he's dealing a deck of cards.

Bobby sits up in his seat; his chest fills with air like a baboon on Animal Planet when his nest is invaded. "I don't like his tone. Do you know this guy?" Bobby refers to Angelo with his thumb.

"Yes, this is Angelo Strazza. From Carrara," I explain.

"What is going on here?" Angelo repeats, raising his voice slightly.

"Don't yell at her," Bobby says.

"This is Bobby Bilancia, my ex-husband," I tell Angelo quietly.

Angelo takes him in. No matter where Bobby Bilancia is in the world, he turns heads. His vibe is prince on horseback, ready to scoop up his *innamorata* and ride off into the mountains to make love by a campfire on a bed of roses. I observe that Bobby's strength and presence are as powerful a force outside the town limits of Lake Como, New Jersey, as inside them.

"So, this was your plan all along. Christmas in Milan with me, New Year's in Lake Como with your ex-husband," Angelo says.

Bobby stands. "You spent Christmas with him?" Bobby does the thumb thing again.

"We're no longer together," I remind him. "I can spend Christmas wherever I want."

"What kind of a woman are you?" Angelo raises his voice.

"Evidently, I like to break up my holidays." The joke drops like a raw meatball into a pot of gravy splattering everywhere. "Come on, guys." I encourage them to take down the temperature.

I've never seen Bobby Bilancia hit anybody, but I think he's about to. "Bobby, please sit down. You don't understand."

"Are you with this guy?" Bobby asks.

I don't answer and neither does Angelo, which I would find interesting if I wasn't concerned that Bobby was about to take a swing at him.

Bobby puts his hands in the air. "This changes everything. You're together?"

"No, we are not together," I insist.

"Are you with him?" Angelo points to Bobby.

"No."

"I don't believe you. You weren't ready to be in a new relationship because evidently, you're still in an old one," Angelo says evenly. "You didn't tell me the truth."

"Are you calling her a liar?" Bobby goes full Jersey on Angelo. I'd find this funny if Bobby weren't really angry.

I turn to Angelo. "Are you serious? You and Dalia just broke up. I have always told you the truth."

"Jess, you need to explain this to somebody," Bobby says.

Conor and Gaetano enter the dining room. A big holiday smile spreads across Conor's face when he sees me. The men join us at the table.

Conor claps his hands together. "Great. You found each other." Conor's smile fades when he hits the wall of tension. "Maybe not so great?"

"Who's he?" Bobby asks.

"Conor Kerrigan. And this is Gaetano," Conor says pleasantly.

"They're together," I tell Bobby.

"I don't usually lead with that, but happy New Year," Conor says as he shakes Bobby's hand.

The maître d' joins us; he looks nervous. "Is everything all right? *Cornetti? Marmellata? Caffè?*" He lists the items on the menu like it's an arms sale.

"No, thank you," Angelo says.

"Please. Bring," Conor says, pulling a chair from another table. He nods to Gaetano to do the same. "Sit down, Angelo. You said you were starving."

"I'm leaving," Angelo replies.

"Don't be ridiculous, stay for breakfast," I offer.

"I am not hungry."

"Then let me walk you out." I stand.

"I can find the door without you," he says.

"Or I can show you," Bobby says tersely.

"I would be happy to meet you outside," Angelo says quietly to Bobby.

"Guys, come on. We're a couple of miles from the Swiss border. Let's go neutral. Sit down. Have a roll." Conor breaks one open, offering half to Gaetano. "*Mangia!*"

"Most disputes occur when people are hungry." Gaetano takes a bite of the cornetto. "It's an Italian thing."

Angelo Strazza storms out.

"Sorry, Jess," Conor says, making sure Angelo is out the door. "He's jealous."

"Of what?" I fold my arms across my chest.

"I'm not going to take that as a slam," Bobby says.

"I didn't mean it that way. He and I are *friends*." One of the benefits of being thirty-four years old is knowing that it's never a good idea to talk about dating a new guy with your ex-husband.

"Sheesh." Conor searches his pockets. "I have the car keys." He goes to find Angelo outside.

"What are you guys doing here?" I ask Gaetano.

"We are on our way to ski in Cortina," he says.

Conor returns to the table. "Done. He's driving back to Milan. I'm sorry about all this. I've never seen his temper."

"He must have feelings." Gaetano shrugs.

"How are you going to get to Cortina?"

"The train," Conor answers. "Coming through Cernobbio was Angelo's idea. He was worried that you were alone on New Year's."

"Well, she isn't," Bobby interjects. He motions to the waitress to bring more coffee. Conor looks at me and mouths, *Whoa.*

VILLA DESTINY

Bobby and I have—what else?—macaroni for dinner. When Italians from New Jersey have any issue whatsoever, the problem-solving takes place over a meal of carbohydrates. The Villa d'Este makes a buttery pasta with a light cream sauce with shaved truffles. How can one plate of pasta sum up my entire life in Italy? But it does. I tell Bobby about the truffle hunt in Siena.

"I would've loved that," he says.

I know my ex-husband well enough to know that whenever he eats, the meal is followed by a walk. We follow the path that hugs the shore of the lake. The midnight-blue surface of Lake Como is still, except for the lone speedboat that leaves a trail of white foam, which forms a seam down the center of the lake.

"What are your plans?" I ask Bobby.

"I don't have any."

He takes me in his arms and holds me for a long while. He then kisses me; the familiar way our faces fit and our lips feel is comforting. But a spark is missing. The spark that had me marry Bobby in the first place.

"Happy anniversary," he whispers. "Five years ago, we were in Vegas on our honeymoon. Remember?"

I hadn't even thought of it. It didn't cross my mind all day, nor did it in the days leading up to New Year's. "What's the gift for married four years and divorced for two?" I ask as he holds me close.

"Wood?"

"Nope."

"Oven mitts?" he jokes.

"No. It's regret." At least, I believe it is for Bobby Bilancia and me. A long history means more memories than a heart can hold and the pain of letting them go.

"Should we try again?" Bobby asks as he kisses my neck.

I have to think. Regret, it turns out, is the knot in the gold chain that cannot be undone with the finest needle. Regret means we tried, failed, and lost hope. But it's only in the act of forgiveness that we can let go of pain. When it comes to Bobby and me, that means letting go of each other.

"New year? New us?" Bobby offers weakly, as though he isn't convinced he means it.

My heart aches for Bobby. He traveled all this way, which is not something that comes easily to him. He loves being home in New Jersey. He believes he's here to win me back, and he came this far to assure himself that I still might be. If I wanted to make Bobby happy, I would go back to him in this moment, but I know, even if I did, it wouldn't work.

"Will you forgive me?" I take his hand.

"If you forgive me," he says softly. Bobby has forgiven me just in time to start a new year.

"We'll always be family," Bobby says, weighing his words like they are cuts of beef.

I nod. "We have a love that is bigger than being married."

"I used to believe marriage was the greatest love," Bobby says, letting me go.

Bobby holds my past, all of it, and I hold his. "Bobby, this is like the Nativity at Saint Rose."

"I don't understand."

"You played Joseph in the Nativity. Remember? Your mom forgot the staff for your costume, so she wrapped your dad's golf club in burlap at the last minute to stand in for a real staff. They told you to hold it upside down. Remember?"

A look of recognition crosses Bobby's face. "Dad's favorite putter."

"The putter may have stood in for Joseph's staff, but in the end, it was just a putter. It was never a staff. Don't you see? Our marriage was a putter. It was a stand-in for the real thing."

Bobby nods as he thinks. I take his hands in mine.

"We wanted it to work because we were sure we could. But it didn't. You're a good man, and you were a wonderful husband. But

I want you to be happy more than I wanted our marriage to work. I learned something in Italy. It's called the art of the possible. Love is waiting out there for both of us."

Bobby ponders what lies ahead for us. Just as surely as Bobby needs to walk after a meal, he does not stay in a place for long, when he can be happy at home. We walk around Lake Como until the moon slices through the clouds and lights our way back to the hotel. Bobby and I had not ended our marriage properly, if there even is such a thing. This time we didn't slip past our feelings; we accepted them, and instead of rushing through them, we savored the goodbye just as we had embraced each other when we fell in love in the first place. Each step we took around Lake Como was in the direction of our future. Apart.

I TAKE THE train with Bobby back to Milan for his return flight. While I was happy to see him in Italy, I am also glad to see him go. I want to be alone to plan my goals. No resolutions, just an acceptance of the hard lessons that will become the foundation to build out the walls of my new life, which I hope will expand my view of everything that matters.

I return to the Villa d'Este hotel on Lake Como on the same train, climb the grand marble staircase to the second floor, and close the door to my room behind me. I open the draperies and tie them back. I open the doors to the terrace. I can hear the lake as its waves lap against the shore, but in the dark, I see nothing except the twinkle of lights from the houses on the distant shore. Soon, Bobby will be home in Lake Como, New Jersey, where we canoed and fed the ducks, the place where we grew up and fell in love and out of it. I change into my pajamas and get out my book. I slide under the fluffy down comforter and lean back on the pillows. I read myself to sleep.

When I wake the next morning, *A Room with a View* is open beside my pillow. I haven't dreamed, or at least I don't remember dreaming. No drama, no confusion, just a feeling of peace. I throw on clothes, grab my book, and stuff the key in my pocket.

When I get off the elevator, I follow the scent of fresh coffee to the dining room. The maître d' sees me and leads me to the table by the window. He fills the table with a basket of hot *cornetti*, *marmellata*, coffee, and cream. For one. The sugar is on the table. Happiness in the new year is on the menu, so I reach for my phone to text Angelo.

Miss you.

21

Primavera

I TAKE OFF THE protective plastic helmet and hang it on the board outside Mauro LaFortezza's quarry. I pull a baseball cap out of my backpack and put it on my head. The March sun burns hot on the mountain, but the breeze is cool. I remove my jacket and am tying it around my waist when Farah joins me outside the mine. Her students board the van to go back down the mountain. She hangs her safety helmet on the board.

"Mauro invited us to his mother's place for lunch," Farah says. "You don't want to miss this. The woman can cook."

Mauro waves to us from the road below. "Come to my office."

I spent the first three months of the year drafting new projects for Mauro. I'll take any excuse to come up the mountain to the quarry. The clean, white walls of stone and the surrounding grounds of the quarry, covered in rock dust, are a blank slate and therefore a good place to think. High on this mountain, I breathe deeply and feel close to my purpose.

I was in Bergamo a week ago working on a restoration when Angelo returned to Carrara for the first time since the new year, to visit his mother. Signora Strazza let me know her son had been home when I returned. Signora Strazza is like Babe Bilancia. She would like me to get involved with her son—Signora Strazza doesn't push, but she keeps me in the loop on his whereabouts and what he's doing. But it doesn't matter what Signora Strazza thinks; it's clear Angelo Strazza is no longer interested in me.

My texts to Angelo have gone unanswered. I sent him random articles about museum curations, nothing personal. I miss our conversations. It turns out I'm a miner too; I prefer to dig deeply but I don't expect any man to go into the excavating business with me. It's obvious that romance is not meant for me at this point in my life. I have plenty of work to do. And I still have to settle my family business. An email from Detective Campovilla says I should have their final report on the Elegant Gangster soon.

I follow Mauro and Farah up the ramp to the trailer marked OFFICIO. Inside the trailer is a command center for the operation of the quarry. A smart board with the excavation teams is illuminated on a screen behind Mauro's desk. File cabinets overflow with paperwork, books are stacked on the floor, and a small table is cluttered with photographs. Farah and I sit at the conference table.

"I need to check in with the foreman before we go. I will be back to take you to lunch." Mauro goes.

"Mauro needs an assistant," I joke when I stand and move through the stacks of stuff on the floor of the trailer. "Look at those photographs. It's a history of the quarry." I sift through them. There are pictures of young Mauro at work on the mountain. There's another, more recent, where he receives an award. In another, he's a boy sitting on a barge at the dock in Avenza. There's a group of photos with his wife and children on holiday on Lake Garda. A few older photographs are pushed to the back. I pick up a small silver frame with a black-and-white photograph and study it. My heart begins to beat fast.

"Are you okay?" Farah gets up and joins me.

I hand her the framed photograph. "I know him," I tell her.

Farah takes the framed photograph from me and studies it. "I can barely make out a face."

"It's my uncle Louie," I tell her.

Farah hands it back to me. "Mauro is family to you?"

"No. But why would he have a picture of my uncle in his office?" The picture in the frame is similar to the collection of photographs I took from Uncle Louie's office after he died.

"You have to ask him," Farah says. "I'm sure there's an explanation."

"Maybe it's not my uncle?" I unhinge the back of the photograph. I carefully remove the velvet stand, slipping it out from under the grips. I lift out the small square of cardboard holding the photo in place. The back of the photograph bears the stamp *4 Aprile 1971.* I begin to sweat.

"Take a photo of it," Farah suggests.

I scramble for my phone. Suddenly, I can't remember where I put it. I'm completely flummoxed.

"Here, let me put this back together." Farah takes the photo and frame from me.

Mauro pushes through the door. He sees Farah struggling to put the photo back into the frame.

"*Signora*, what are you doing?" He takes the photograph and frame from her.

"I was interested in the date of the photograph, for one of my presentations."

"Be careful, Farah," he says, putting the photo under glass.

"Who is the gentleman in the photograph?" Farah asks.

"My father," Mauro says.

FARAH GETS IN the front seat of Mauro's SUV as I climb into the back. They chat on the ride up the mountain, while I feel sick in the back seat.

"Your father was a handsome young man," Farah says.

"I never knew him. He died before I was born. On the mountain. Quarry work is dangerous, and there was an accident."

"What was his name?"

"Luigi."

Luigi is a common Italian name, so there's a chance this is another Louie. Or maybe Uncle Louie left more behind than secret accounts in the Cayman Islands. Is it possible he also left a son?

Mauro shares some of the same mannerisms of the Capodimontes and Montinis, which should have been a clue, but I'd chalked them up to general Italian traits. I wouldn't have assumed Mauro was from my mother's side of the family because he is tall and strapping, whereas the Caps are small and quick. We embody one another's characteristics, which weave through the generations like the pulley ropes on the hawses. If you are born in the same place, eat the same food, and do similar work, you will cut a similar *tipo di corpo.*

"Here we are! Mamma's." Mauro turns into the driveway. The Mediterranean-style home with a beige stucco exterior and red tile roof is tucked into the side of the hill like a leather-bound book on a shelf. "I hope you don't mind; I invited Angelo Strazza to lunch," Mauro says. He locks eyes with mine in the rearview. I manage a weak smile. This day just got worse.

Mauro's mother greets us at the front door. She is a petite blonde, with classic Tuscan features, a smooth brow, a straight nose, and a warm smile. She wears an apron over Capri pants, a silk blouse, and flat leather sandals. We follow her to the loggia, where Signora LaFortezza has set the table for our lunch.

"*Signora, grazie per avermi ospitato.*" I take her hand.

"*Per favore, chiamami Claudia.*"

"Your name is Claudia?"

She nods, surprised at my reaction. "Have we met before?"

"*Che bella nome.*" I compliment her name as a feeling of knowingness comes over me. This is Uncle Louie's tomato, his Claudia. I have been looking at photographs of her as a young woman, and she has the same smile, the same eyes. The hair is no longer dark, she's a blonde, but the smile is the girl in the photo from fifty years ago.

I'm trying to make sense of this when Angelo Strazza emerges from the house and onto the loggia. He looks handsome in a pressed blue-striped shirt and jeans. No paint splotches on his boots. He runs his hand through his hair, ruffling his curls. We compensate for the awkwardness of this surprise reunion with effusive greetings for one another, like long-lost friends. Angelo kisses me on both cheeks like a sister. The scent of his skin is cool and crisp, citrus in the heat. I want to jump off the mountain.

"Giuseppina, will you help me?"

"Of course." I follow Claudia into the kitchen to help.

Claudia's kitchen is orderly and neat, like Aunt Lil's. She takes a loaf of fresh bread out of the oven and hands me a knife. She gives me a clean dish towel to anchor the bread as I cut it so I won't burn my hand. I arrange the bread on the tray; Claudia drizzles the hot bread with olive oil.

She lifts the lid off the *conca*, a round white marble container, and lifts out the *lardo di Colonnata*. She cured the pork fat for months in the marble container, in a full immersion of herbs, garlic, and white vinegar. Claudia slices the lardo in thin strips, twists a ribbon of the delicacy on the back of the knife into a rosette shape, and places it on a slice of the hot bread. She hands me the knife and asks me to finish the job. She tosses a salad of mixed greens with a dressing of salt and fresh-squeezed lemon and drizzles olive oil over the top. It's hard not to compare Claudia to Aunt Lil. They're both lovely and good cooks. I wonder how either of them would react if they knew about the other. I'm dizzy, but I blame the heat, or maybe I'm just hungry. I follow her to the loggia with the tray of fresh bread and lardo.

Farah claps her hands together. "*Bellissima.*"

"Have you ever eaten lardo?" Mauro asks me.

"I remember Grandma Cap talking about it when she reminisced about growing up in Carrara." What I don't share is that every time Uncle Louie mentioned lardo, it sounded horrible to me.

"Try it," Mauro says, handing me a plate.

I take a bite and close my eyes. The ribbon of the herb-infused lardo on the hot bread with buttery olive oil melts in my mouth. The earthiness of the herbs and the tart vinegar cut the richness of the pork fat. The spices trip over my tongue: rosemary, sage, nutmeg, and clove, then coarse salt and black pepper, followed by grace notes of thyme and anise. I savor the bite because the dish is rare, and in it, my family history. I am connected to the past and especially to Uncle Louie. He told me stories about how the miners kept weight on in the heat. They ate the richest food they could find.

Lardo di Colonnata is a local delicacy, but it is also a superfood. The miners and stonemasons needed high-calorie food to function through long hours cutting and moving stone on the mountain, but they were also Italian, so whatever food they chose to sustain their strength had to be delicious. The curation of the pork fat is a family enterprise, and the *concas* themselves, carved from the marble of these mountains, hold the lardo as it marinates for months. This dish is of the farm, the earth, and the mountain.

"This is my last *conca* before the new season," Claudia admits. "I save it for Mauro. He is my firstborn and he loves lardo. I make it every year for him. My other children, they like it, but they don't have the love affair with this dish that he does."

"My mother would do the same for my brother," I explain, "but she would have her daughters do the work."

"The same in Italy." Mauro laughs.

"I say this as a visitor," Farah begins. "The Italian man, unless he ruins it for himself, has the best life. If he is lucky enough to have his mother by his side all his life, he cannot fail."

"My son is intelligent and a hard worker. I can claim no credit for that. In fact, as a mother, I control nothing. Mauro *è miracolo.* His story has a sad start," Claudia says.

"No one gets everything in this life," Mauro says.

"Mauro's father was a stonemason," Claudia begins.

Are they really going to do this? Are they going to talk about Uncle Louie like he's a character in a book? Or is this a story Claudia made up so her son would have one of his own to tell?

"Luigi had one of the most dangerous jobs outside the quarry. He was cutting on the mountain one summer, and they pulled him off the job to fill in as *legnarolo.* That's the man who runs ahead of the marble as it is lowered down the mountain. My father came home one day and told me that the young man I loved was killed in the transport."

"My father," Mauro says quietly.

Farah squeezes my hand under the table. I don't know what to do. How do I tell them that there was no tragic accident? The most dangerous thing Uncle Louie ever attempted was to light the fat fryers for the zeppole tanks at the Feast, and even then, the Belmar Fire Department stood by in case of an accident.

"I don't know anything about my father's family." Mauro shrugs.

"We know he was American," Claudia confirms.

Mauro goes on. "You can imagine how stunned I was when I heard your company was called Capodimonte. I thought maybe we were related. But you're a Baratta."

"But you're also a Capodimonte," Angelo says.

Of course Angelo would be of no help and make everything worse.

"Capodimonte is a popular name on the Ligurian coast," Claudia says. "Very common."

"How did you meet . . ." My voice breaks.

"Luigi?" Farah finishes my question and attempts to shore me up.

Claudia is oblivious to my discomfort and continues with her story. "Mauro's father came over from America to work in the quarry one summer. We met and fell in love. In those days, you didn't speak about such matters. It's a story of young love."

"And an overbearing father," Mauro adds. "My grandfather."

"Yes, it's true. My father was strict; he ran our family like an army. So, when I met Luigi Capodimonte from America, it was not to my father's liking."

"Mamma. Tell the truth. He hated your suitor."

"If Luigi had lived, I believe I could have changed my father's mind about him. Luigi was very warm and funny. But my father didn't want his daughters falling in love with any young man without his approval. When I was a girl, the parents chose the husband and made a match. A proper courtship would commence if the parents approved, even though the old ways were already on their way out fifty years ago. We knew it, but our parents did not."

"So how did you make it work?" Farah asks. "How did you manage to see one another?"

"At first, I thought Luigi was local, but soon, I learned his Italian was not so great when we had a conversation and he confirmed he was American. But we managed to communicate, and I found him charming. That summer, we fell in love and planned to marry. He promised he would stay in Italy because he knew it was the only way that we could be together."

"Oh, so you made a plan?" I can't believe what I am hearing.

"Of course." Claudia goes on. "I had not shared our plan with my parents. When Luigi died on the mountain, I found out that I was pregnant." She places her hand on Mauro's. "I was healed by the news, even though I had no idea what the future would hold for us. We made a happy story out of a sad one. I had my son, and two years later, I married Alberto LaFortezza. Alberto adopted Mauro and loved him like his own."

"He never made me feel like I was not his son. Mamma didn't keep the story from me either. She would tell me the story of Luigi when she put me to sleep. It was like a fairy tale to me. A faraway dream that happened to someone else."

"It's wonderful that Alberto's family accepted you." Farah looks at me.

"They did! Alberto was a wonderful man. We had three more children together, and soon, his quarry prospered. When he died, he owned several of the quarries on the mountain."

"We made you sad." Claudia notices the mood under the loggia has changed, especially mine. She chops the air with her hand. "It was so long ago."

"I understand why." Farah dabs her eyes with a tissue. "It's tragic when a mother or father never knows their child."

"My father didn't want to tell me that Luigi was killed," Claudia tells us.

"It's a terrible thing to have to deliver that news," Angelo says. "I don't know how your father did it."

"My father told me that he was going to come home and lie. He was going to tell me that Luigi went back to America so I wouldn't cry. But I am happy he told me the truth. I've been able to look up and pray to my angel."

"Dear God," falls out of my mouth, and it doesn't sound like a prayer. The guests around the table look at me. "I mean, wow. What a story."

"It is," Claudia agrees. "Mauro had a guardian angel from the moment he was born."

"Excuse me." I stand, but not upright and not well. The chair scrapes the slate floor, making the sound of a rusty knife on stone.

Claudia offers directions to the powder room. Once inside the house, I run inside the bathroom, close the door behind me, and lock it. I search through the cabinet for a paper bag. I find a small one filled with cotton balls under the sink. I dump the cotton balls onto the counter. I breathe into the bag, in and out, in and out, until my heart rate steadies. I put the cotton balls back into the bag and place them under the sink. I wash my face and hands. When I open the door, Angelo is waiting for me.

"What happened?"

I throw myself into Angelo's arms. "I'm sorry. I have trouble with sad stories." I pull away from him.

"Why don't you sit inside for a few minutes? Where it's cool," he says.

"No, I'm okay," I tell him. I'm going to motor through this nightmare like an American.

"Are you all right?" Claudia asks when we return to the table.

"*Va bene*," I assure her.

"The first time I had lardo, I overheated too," Farah admits. "It's so rich. But so delicious I can't stop eating it!"

Angelo looks at me with concern. "So, we eat just a little. In the village we call *lardo di Colonnata*, '*paté di povero uomo*,' the poor man's pâté."

"Well, the poor man's pâté is too rich for this American's blood," I tell them.

Farah toasts our hostess. We raise our glasses to Claudia. My hand is so slippery from sweat, I raise the glass and drop it. It shatters on the slate floor.

"I'm so sorry. I don't know what's wrong with me."

"No problem, *signorina*," Claudia says, and pats my hand.

"We only break a glass at the best meals," Mauro says.

"I've got it." Angelo gets up and goes for the broom. He sweeps the glass into the dustpan. "It's good luck, Giuseppina," Angelo assures me.

Is it? I wonder.

DR. SCOTT LISTENS attentively over Zoom as I share the details I learned about Uncle Louie at lunch. Thera-Me thankfully has an emergency feature that connects you quickly with a therapist when the patient feels in crisis.

Dr. Scott listens, then asks, "Miss B, how is something that happened to your uncle over fifty years ago your concern?"

"This is my family. We take care of one another. I found out that I have a cousin I didn't know existed, and my mother has a nephew.

I am the only person on the American side of the family who knows about Mauro."

"You say it will hurt your aunt. Your deceased uncle's widow?"

"I don't know for sure. Mauro was born before they met. But it would open old wounds."

"So, you are concerned about her feelings if this truth is revealed?"

"Of course. She wanted children and couldn't have them."

"So why do you feel compelled to bring your new cousin into the fold at all?"

If I had to bet, I'd imagine Dr. Scott is not of Italian descent. This therapist is starting to bug me. He either doesn't get it or I'm not explaining my family dynamic very well. Didn't he read my file? Family is the center of our universe, never mind if the center is a red sun or a poisoned meatball at *la tavola*. It's our reality, our truth, our facts—which belong to the group. Over these months, I've been working hard to come up with a plan that helps me embrace my kin, flaws and all, along with any dreams and hopes I have for my own life. This therapist is acting like I can't have both.

"Dr. Scott. The truth matters in this situation. I don't believe there are accidents. I came to Italy to find out *why* I am who I am. My cousin Mauro is part of the story now. He is a member of my family. We don't leave people in the street when we find out we're related. We welcome them inside to assume their place in the story."

I may need another therapy session to unravel the last one. Smokey sleeps on my lap as I study the series of photographs of young Claudia and Louie. It's crazy to admit, but I think Claudia and Lil could be friends—although I don't know if I want to put my aunt through any of this. Maybe Dr. Scott has a point. What good will come of revealing this story now? It's not my story to tell.

It was Uncle Louie's, but he didn't know it. What becomes of a secret when the person holding it never knew about it?

Mauro and his mother are at peace with the story they have agreed is true. But it's a fable, invented by Claudia's desperate father, who was afraid his daughter would do harm to herself if she knew the truth, or worse, a lie invented by a controlling father who didn't think an American was good enough for his daughter.

I text Conor.

JESS: Uncle Louie has a son.

CONOR: Double life?

JESS: Louie didn't know.

CONOR: Mic drop.

JESS: It's Mauro.

CONOR: No way.

JESS: Mauro LaFortezza had a photo on his desk. I have the rest of the photos here with me.

CONOR: Seriously?

JESS: Would Googs know anything about this? He knew Uncle Louie back in the day.

If Uncle Louie knew Claudia was pregnant, he would have married her. He was principled about that sort of thing. I can't imagine my mother knew anything about Mauro, because if she had, she would have used it as blackmail or another reason to banish Uncle Louie to the Island. I observed some intense arguments between Mom and Louie where my mother would throw every lousy thing her brother ever did in his face, and while there were some juicy bits, an illegitimate son conceived in Italy by a stonemason's daughter during a summer romance was not one of them.

I pull on a jean jacket and head down the stairs. I need to think. I've closed the gate behind me when Angelo emerges from his mother's apartment.

"Giuseppina? How are you feeling?"

"Much better. Thank you. I thought you drove back to Milan."

"I am not returning to Milan just yet."

"Whenever you do, have a safe trip." I walk away from him and across the piazza briskly. I'm almost past the statue of Maria Beatrice when Angelo catches up to me.

"Would you like some company?"

"Not really."

"You're angry at me."

"No, I'm confused. You ghosted me."

"I don't text my feelings."

"You could text information. 'I'm fine,' 'I'm not fine.' 'Don't text me.'"

"Why don't we try to be friends?" Angelo offers. "I'm worried about you. You could use a confidant. It worked for me when I had a problem. Conor helped me."

"What problem did you have?"

"You and your ex-husband. You never mentioned how handsome he was."

"Bobby Bilancia is kind of the gold standard on the Jersey Shore. He turns heads. What can I tell you?"

"What can I do to make this right?" Angelo asks.

ANGELO PICKS ME up in an American army jeep the next morning. Evidently, they are prized vehicles in Italy, like a Maserati or

Ferrari would be in New Jersey. Before jumping inside, I unzip the clear plastic window to address the driver.

"Is this the right thing to do?" I ask him.

"You can let the secret lie," Angelo says. "It's worked in my family for centuries. But if you want to know the truth, get in."

I climb into the jeep. The Canalgrande Alto is still loaded with potholes, though there were rumblings that the town of Carrara had plans to fix the road. Maybe a tire will blow out or the engine might fail, and I can get myself out of this situation before I learn too much. But, it's too late. I texted Mauro, requesting a meeting with his mother and him. I don't know if I'm doing the right thing, but Angelo convinced me I have no choice.

"Claudia has had a happy life. Mauro is a good man from a fine family. Why unearth all of this now?" I ask. "This is a terrible idea."

"Last chance." Angelo turns to me as we pull into the field next to Claudia's home. "Are you going to take my advice? Or would you rather run?" Angelo asks.

"Either way I'm going to blame you. Just so you know."

Claudia and Mauro meet us under the loggia where we had lunch. Mauro lowers the bamboo shades on the trellis to block the morning sun. Claudia invites us to sit.

"We had such a wonderful time in your home."

"I hope you're feeling better."

"I am. That's why we're here."

"Angelo said you have something to tell us."

"Before we came to lunch yesterday, you showed me a photo of your father, Luigi Capodimonte. I knew him."

"Impossible." She smiles. "He died long before you were born." Claudia looks at Mauro, then back at me.

"I don't know why your father told you Luigi died in 1971, but he didn't. He went home to New Jersey."

"No." Claudia's eyes fill with tears. "It can't be. Is he alive?"

"Mamma, let her talk," Mauro says.

"Your father sent him back to America. Luigi Capodimonte was my uncle. My mother's only brother. He died last October of heart failure. I was with him when he died."

"I don't understand." Claudia takes her son's hand.

"I worked for Uncle Louie in our family business. We imported marble and installed it in people's homes. He was funny and warm and a good husband. A wonderful uncle and my best friend. He didn't have any children with his wife. Aunt Lil is still alive, and I haven't decided how I'm going to tell her about Mauro. But I will."

"My father lied to me," Claudia says softly.

"I'm sorry he did. Fate would have played out differently for sure."

"I don't believe this could be true. It's crazy." Mauro stands and paces. "Why should I believe you?"

"Because I have proof. But first, Mauro, I'd like to tell you about Luigi Capodimonte. I don't think Uncle Louie knew about you. If he had known about you, he would have never left your mother. He was a Grand Knight Fourth Degree in the Knights of Columbus. He believed in rules and doing the right thing. He was a Catholic boy, Jesuit trained, who believed in God, with whom he shared a personal relationship."

"I can't believe this." Mauro looks to Angelo, who encourages him to listen.

"When I saw the photograph of him in your office, I couldn't believe it. I looked at the negatives; the missing photograph of the collection is the one in your office. Here is the negative of that photograph." I lay the photographs on the table carefully, like a tarot reader with her cards. I hold up the photograph of Uncle Louie and the young woman. "Is this you, Claudia?"

Claudia's hands shake as she holds the photograph. "This is me."

"*Signora*, who took the photographs?"

"My sister Rossella had a Leica camera. She took this photograph. I remember because when we came home, my father was angry that we had been gone all day. So when the film was developed, I gave the photographs to Luigi for safekeeping. I took one from the pile because I wanted a photograph of him. Later, when my father told me Luigi died, I went to the boardinghouse to pack up his things, because I wanted anything I could find to remember him, but I was too late. His clothes were gone. Everything. It was as if he was never there."

"If he was alive, why didn't he come back for you?" Mauro is angry.

"Who knows what your grandfather said to him," I say.

"Mauro, don't blame him. Luigi wanted to marry me that summer. I was so young. Just eighteen. I promised I would go with him to America when I turned nineteen. We were making plans when the accident happened."

"But there was no accident," I remind her.

"Mamma, you took me to the cemetery. Papà is there." Mauro is confused.

"My father placed a marker on a memorial for all the workers on the mountain who perished in the quarry. My father put the plaque there, hoping I would get through my grief if I had a place to go and cry. And I did. For about a year, and I didn't go back until you were ten years old. And then I never went again."

"But I go, Mamma. Every Sunday," Mauro admits. "I didn't want to forget him. Now it appears I didn't have to," he says. "This is a tragedy. Twice."

"I had been the perfect daughter, very obedient. You see, Giuseppina, Luigi wasn't the only young person who was brought up to follow the strict rules of the church—but after I fell in love with Luigi, I changed. I became my own person. Love freed me and made me defiant. I wanted to choose how to live my life, while my father was holding on to the old ways because he could not accept the new ones. But Papà was the final word. And he was until the day he died."

"It was difficult to make your own choices," I tell her.

"I had no choice. The world was changing, but not Italy. And girls had a role, and you did not venture beyond the boundaries that were set for you. That was that." Claudia dabs her tears with her handkerchief. Signora LaFortezza, like my mother, missed the cut-off date for feminism, for freedom. They aged out of the old ways and were too young to reap the benefits of the new ones.

Mauro gets up from the table. "I would have liked to have known my father. It was my highest dream to know him."

"I can share everything I know," I tell Mauro. "Whenever you're ready."

I feel terrible for Mauro and wish that Uncle Louie could have had both of us in his life, but fate did not play out that way. I was the beneficiary of Mauro's loss.

"Giuseppina didn't want to tell you, Mauro," Angelo says. "She was afraid she would hurt you, that you would be angry."

Mauro doesn't respond to Angelo. Instead, he asks me, "May I have the photographs?"

"Of course. Take them." I gather the stack of photographs and place them in the envelope. I give them to Mauro.

"I need to get back to work," Mauro says. He kisses his mother on the cheek and leaves without saying goodbye.

If I needed proof that Mauro was Louie's son, this was it. Uncle

Louie removed himself from any situation that made him uncomfortable too. Mom called it "Lou's vanishing act."

"I'm so sorry," I say to Claudia.

"The truth is worse than Mauro imagined. And it is terrible for me too. I didn't think my son would grow up and want to go anywhere near the quarry. Instead of avoiding it, Mauro used his grief about the father he never met to fuel his ambition. He wanted to be a *legnarolo* like Luigi, and today he manages the mountain. He always had something to prove to himself."

"We've taken enough of your time, Claudia." Angelo stands.

"Where is the cemetery?" I ask.

"It's on the road to Avenza."

"San Michele?" Angelo asks.

She nods.

Claudia does not walk us out, as she did the day of our lunch. Her mind is elsewhere. In the past.

ANGELO KNOWS THE way down the mountain to Avenza, an enchanting village that curls along the base of the Apuan Alps like a sleeping cat. Spikes of blue evergreen trees cover the hillsides as they protect the stucco houses clustered in pink stacks in the valley below. The sky, the color of circus peanuts, peeks through a veil of tufted white clouds. I lean out the window and take a photo. I post: *Candy-colored sky.*

Chiesa di San Michele is an ornate Romanesque church set in a field outside the entrance of Avenza. The bright noonday sun reveals the glittering gold veins in the marble, which ironically happened to be Uncle Louie's favorite cut of stone. Angelo parks near the entrance to the cemetery. Grand marble mausoleums anchor the perimeter of the cemetery, set among ornate columbaria, outdoor altars, stone crypts, and statuary. White marble angels loom over the cemetery plots like guards.

"You take that side. I'll take this one," Angelo directs.

We split up. I am intrigued by the altars, which form a fence line around the cemetery. Each has a different personality. I find an altar that celebrates the trade of the family business with gilded carvings of chisels and hammers. The Rillo family are evidently marble miners.

"Giuseppina!" Angelo waves. "I found him."

I climb over the markers and through the morass of marble memorials to join Angelo at the far end of the cemetery. A wall is filled with the names of the men who lost their lives on the mountain, carved on bricks of gray marble. Angelo runs his hand over my uncle's name.

LUIGI CAPODIMONTE
Legnarolo

I wish Louie Cap could have seen this tribute to his life, the testament to the stolen love story that kept him from his son. When I left New Jersey, Uncle Louie's grave was covered in the wilted flower arrangements from the funeral home and the church. A big pile of mums, roses, and gladiolas, Styrofoam rings, and, from the floral arrangements that honored him, wide ribbons glued with gold letters that defined him: husband, uncle, brother, K of C. Here in Avenza, he wasn't celebrated, but he was never forgotten either. Mauro carries the wound of never knowing him, and Claudia put him in the past because there was no place for Louie Cap in her new family. Only Aunt Lil, his sister, his family, and I know all that Mauro and Claudia missed. And they missed everything.

"Your uncle is important to you, isn't he?"

I nod. "Even in death."

"Why?"

"He understood me." I face Angelo. "The way you do."

Angelo takes me in his arms and holds me. "I'm just trying to make things better," he says. "Not that you need anyone to do that for you. I guess that's my problem, Giuseppina. You're the first woman I've ever met that had me wondering if I'm good enough. Do I deserve you? You have more joy than anyone I know. It's why I've fallen in love with you."

You'd think all that money I've pumped into Thera-Me would serve me in a moment like this. Hasn't the entire hayride been about communication? And here I am, I can't speak.

Angelo fills the silence. "The first time I saw you, I was in the garden, but the sun came out when you smiled at me. I thought, 'Oh no. It's *her*.' I didn't want to get to know you because I already knew what you would do to my life. I didn't want to be happy because I thought happiness was my studio and my cell, a dish of spaghetti and a glass of wine, and my judgments. I would never have to make a commitment because I was not interested in being needed. But then you showed up with your American joy and your innocence and your complete lack of fear. I took the job in Milan, not because I wanted it, but because you didn't stop me. I couldn't bear the thought of being near you without your love, so I ran. When you came to Milan for Christmas, I had such hopes, and when you left me a pair of mittens behind for Dalia and Alice, I believed it was your way of telling me we would just be friends. I decided to go to Lake Como to tell you my feelings, and when I got there—"

"Bobby Bilancia."

"Yes." A cloud crosses over Angelo's face.

"I'm not ready—"

Angelo places the tips of his fingers on my lips. "I know. But I am. I will wait."

"How can you be so sure?" I ask him.

"Because you left me with one choice . . . to love you."

The sun overhead is hot, but the air is cool, perfect weather for a fever.

"I'll take you home now," he says. Angelo takes my hand and leads me through the treachery of the old cemetery, the sharp edges of the marble, the claw feet of the oversized urns, the uneven markers that have shifted in the ground and the spring mud that has settled between stones. But I don't trip or fall, as long as I hold on.

AS SOON AS I'm back in the apartment, I call Aunt Lil to check on her. It goes to voice mail. It's time for me to share the story with her. Her years watching *General Hospital* were good training for the tale I'm about to tell her. I leave a message.

> Hey, Aunt Lil. Thinking about you! How are you? I'm doing fine, lots to tell you, but what else is new? Love you.

I feed Smokey and put on the coffee. My phone buzzes. It's my brother.

"I'm sorry," Joe says. "I only call if it's urgent."

Waves of guilt wash over me. "What's wrong? Mom? Dad?" I sit down. I knew the Island could be fatal. One of them died when I wasn't speaking to them and it's all my fault.

"No, Mom and Dad are fine."

"Thank God." I exhale.

"I have sad news, though. Aunt Lil died." A few moments pass, then Joe says, "Are you there, Jess?"

"I'm so sorry." I fill with regret. "I just left her a message." I wasn't there. Uncle Louie would have wanted that.

"We just saw her at Sunday dinner. She looked good. You just never know."

"I should go." I feel my heart break inside my chest.

"Jess. She talked about you. She made a point to tell everyone that you have been calling her. She said it meant the world to her that you were in touch. You did the right thing, Jess. It didn't go unnoticed."

"Thanks, Joe." But it doesn't make me feel any better.

"Come home," my brother says. "It's time."

22

Home to Lake Como

THE TAXI DROPS me off at my parents' house. As I step out of the car, two emotions, anticipation and dread, ricochet around inside me with equal force. I remind myself how far I have come. I am not here to settle scores or seek absolution or forgiveness; I am here to honor Aunt Lil.

I packed light, so it's easy to navigate my rolling suitcase up the sidewalk to the front door, the portal to my old life. This was the door I was carried through (finally) on the day I came home from the hospital, seven weeks after I was born. It is the same door I went through every morning on my way to school. This is also the door that opened to reveal me in my bridal gown on the day I was married, in the video my mother still watches from time to time.

The bay window is lit up like a department store display selling crystal. The cut-glass globes and collection of crystal bowls and vases shimmer in the light. Every time someone dies, another piece of their crystal lands in the window, a sparkling reminder of the beauty of inheritance. The grief wreath, fresh greens roped with a large black velvet ribbon at the base, hangs from the brass door knocker, a sign to all who live on the lake that we have lost a loved one.

This house and yard meant everything to me as a child; it meant that we had a stake in the land on the lake that we loved, that we were part of the Cap and Baratta clans, that we were part of something bigger than our small stretch of the loop around Lake Como. Whenever I looked up and down this street, I had a sense of security and belonging because of my extended family.

I look down the block at Aunt Lil's. The lights on the walkway are dark; the house falls into shadow. A small lamp is lit in the front window, no doubt a strategic decision to make it look like there was someone inside, if only to ward off looky-loos and burglars. The breeze off the lake is cold for spring in Lake Como, or maybe my sadness at the loss of Aunt Lil makes it feel that way.

The front door flies open. My mother comes out on the porch. She wears a black dress and bedroom slippers. She covers her eyes and squints, "Giuseppina? Is that you?"

"Yeah, Ma, it's me."

"Joe? Joe? Get out here. She's back!"

Soon the doorway fills with family: my father, my brother, his wife, my sister, her husband, their children. They jump up and down calling my name. Cleopatra had a less enthusiastic welcome into Rome, but I'll bet she didn't cry. Before I can roll my suitcase to the steps of the front porch, my family runs down the walkway and surrounds me, welcoming me home.

ON EAGLE'S WINGS

The altar at Saint Catharine's Church is decorated with baskets of pink and white lilies. Family came from all over to honor Aunt Lil at her funeral Mass. I pray with the white pearl rosary Aunt Lil and Uncle Louie gave me on my confirmation. I found it in the nightstand of my old room, where I had left it. The repetition of the prayers keeps my mind off the histrionics going on around me. As we lose more of our beloved relatives in my mom and dad's generation, our grief escalates to operatic. We don't get better at losing people over time; we get louder.

I pick a small fiber of lint off Lisa Natalizio's LBD. Almost six months later, it remains, hanging in the cedar closet of my old bedroom; at least Ma moved it up from the basement, though she was supposed to return it to the beauty salon. The good news? The dress fits without cinching now. Must be the truffle hunts, the hikes in the Valle di Scalve, and the long walks in Carrara. Life is better without a car. That's just the truth.

I relax into the ritual of the Mass of Christian Burial like a warm bath. My faith is something I can count on, even when I forget I can. The priest blesses Aunt Lil's casket, draped in white linen, with the holy smoke. I make the sign of the cross when the frankincense wafts my way.

I look down the row at my family, sitting erect in their black suits and dresses, like a flock of black crows balancing on a wire. Our funerals are as important as our weddings and baptisms and confirmations. Maybe more so. We're a family that can't let go; we fear that when we do, we will fall off the wire. This morning, we hold on tight to our sacrament and one another.

When Uncle Louie died last fall, I was a mess. I wanted to get up and eulogize him, but I couldn't. But today I am on a mission. I will honor my aunt and, in so doing, my uncle too. I had a plane ride to think about them and all they meant to me. I have learned to stand up for myself, but real strength comes in standing up for others. Aunt Lil, like me, was an *other* in the family. Today, I will let folks know who Lil really was, not just a lady who wore good jewelry and had the unlined face of a woman who did not raise children.

The priest nods at me and takes his seat near the altar. I make the slow walk up to the lectern. My heels click against the Carrara marble, reminding me of the foundation of my family life, indestructible builder's stone. I am surprised that my nerves have left me; instead, I am determined to share Lil's story. I stand tall in my three-inch black suede stilettos. I place my phone, which holds the eulogy I have written, on the pulpit and look out over the mourners. Their sad faces galvanize me. I read.

> Aunt Lil was the most dazzling woman in our family, and one of the most glamorous I have ever met. She stood at four foot eleven but moved through the world like a comet; in a quiet blaze of white light, she lit up the night sky like one of her beloved diamonds.
>
> Liliana Filippelli Capodimonte was born on August 15, 1948, in Hoboken, New Jersey. Her father, Sal, was a florist, and her mother, Tess, managed the home. Her mother was of Sicilian descent and her father Pugliese. She has a beloved sister, Carmel, and a niece, Marina, whom she adored. She had a fabulous childhood. Because her dad was the neighborhood florist, their dinner table always had a fresh bouquet of flowers. Aunt Lil's favorite floral combination was ruby-red roses and blue delphinium. She also appreciated a hearty pink lily in season, as you can see from the altar sprays today. She approved of greenery

but disliked baby's breath in any arrangement. She called them weeds. As girls, Lil and Carmel worked in the shop together and wove the rose crown by hand for the Blessed Mother statue for May Day. Lil took this job seriously, as her birthday fell on the Assumption of Mary. She took this as a sign and was devoted to the Blessed Lady all her life. I believe, when she passed, she was welcomed home and, once there, was cloaked in the Blessed Mother's blue mantle.

Uncle Louie used to say that every city was a woman. If I were to choose the woman that is Lake Como, New Jersey, it would be Aunt Lil. A classic beauty with an Italian American twist. She wore white after Labor Day, diamonds with a sweatsuit, and sequins when she was in the mood for sparkle. As fashionable as she was, Aunt Lil was not superficial. She cared about others. She often said nothing, which, in most instances, wisely says everything.

Aunt Lil loved New Jersey. She went to the wedding of one of Uncle Louie's business associates in upstate New York in the early nineties. When they returned from their weekend "abroad," I asked Aunt Lil how the wedding went. She said, "Every expense was spared."

The congregation laughs. Jess takes a deep breath and goes on.

Aunt Lil knew me from the day I was born. She and Uncle Louie didn't have children, but in a sense,

> she had sixteen of us, the grand total of cousins who lived up and down North Boulevard in what was then called South Belmar. We were welcome in her home anytime, day or night, without invitation. She was a better baker than a cook (according to her), and whether she created a Venetian table on Christmas Eve or made our birthday cakes into works of art, she understood the importance of making everyone she knew feel special. My sister, Connie, and I were the beneficiaries of her Barbie cakes. The skirts were made of frosting. Barbie had her hands in the air, in a V for victory, holding our names on a small gold banner. When Joe's birthday rolled around, she would bake G.I. Joe into a jungle motif.
>
> Who can forget her zeppole? They were light and sweet, and never dense. In her honor, we printed up her recipe to share with you today. This recipe was kept secret her entire life, and now it's yours. My nieces and nephews will hand the coveted recipe out to you now.

The children rise from their seats, and in school-test-day style, they fan out to the aisles with copies of Aunt Lil's recipe. They position themselves on the ends of the rows to hand the stacks of recipes across. There is chatter and laughter as the cards are passed through the pews and the mourners read the recipe penned in Aunt Lil's perfect Palmer penmanship.

Lil's Zeppole

HOBOKEN-STYLE

Makes 30–35 zeps

INGREDIENTS

For the batter:

1 cup whole milk

2 tablespoons granulated sugar

2 teaspoons active dry yeast

2 cups all-purpose flour

1 teaspoon salt

1 large egg, beaten

Splash of cold water

For frying:

1 quart vegetable oil

For drenching:

2 cups granulated sugar, to sprinkle on the hot zeps out of the fryer

HOW TO FRY THE ZEPS

Heat the milk in a pot, whisk in the sugar and yeast, and set aside. Sift the flour and salt in a large bowl. Make a well, place the egg and a splash of cold water in the well, and whisk until blended. Add the milk, sugar, and yeast into the bowl until a lumpy dough emerges. Stop whisking. Smooth dough makes for lead zeps. Put a large *mopeen* over the bowl and set it in a sunny window to rise in the heat. You want the dough to rise high enough to fill the bowl to overflowing (leave it for about an hour as it rises).

Heat the oil in a large pot until it's roiling at 375°F. Have a cookie sheet covered in paper towels close by. Using a two-spoon technique, make a mound of dough about the size of a tennis ball and drop it into the hot oil. Continue until you have six balls of dough in the hot oil. Gently turn the zeps with tongs until they are golden brown. Remove the zeps with a slotted spoon from the oil and place on the cookie sheet. Repeat the same until all the dough has been fried. Douse the warm zeps in granulated sugar. *Note from Lil: South of Naples, they prefer powdered sugar, but I never liked it. The granulated sugar looks like diamond dust, and you know I love a diamond.*

The kids return to the front pew and take their seats.

Aunt Lil kept an immaculate home. She told me she didn't need to travel because she had the world at her fingertips inside her palazzo. However, she enjoyed her annual vacation to Florida and her bus trips to see Broadway shows in New York City. She never missed Bernadette Peters in a show because she was a first cousin once removed to Bernadette and her sister Donna DeSeta. Aunt Lil was so proud of them and her theatrical connections.

Aunt Lil was certainly beautiful enough to have been in show business, but she told me that she was too shy to sing in public. She had a glorious singing voice, as those of you who attend this parish know. She sang in the church choir for thirty-six years. She said singing in the choir loft freed her because she knew no one was looking at her. High above us sinners, she could let it rip. No one could top her solo of "On Eagle's Wings." She got many a parishioner through their grief with that hymn. They couldn't see her, but they heard her, and through her voice, she lifted their spirits.

Aunt Lil was the top Avon saleslady in the state of New Jersey in 1977. She worked for Avon until 2005. We were the beneficiaries of her sales samples. Connie and I fought over the Pearls and Lace cologne and the Sweet Honesty soaps. Years later, when Aunt Lil admitted that she wore Elizabeth Taylor's White Diamonds, she explained it like this: "I was a Liz Taylor fan all my life. If Avon would've made a deal with Liz, I would have worn anything with her name on it. Until they do? White Diamonds all the way."

Aunt Lil was a proud Italian American; she reminded us of her roots whenever the topic came up. She brought Connie and me to see the revival of the musical *Nine*, based on the Fellini movie *8½*. She made us watch the film *The Agony and the Ecstasy* every Easter, introducing us to a fictional Michelangelo by way of Charlton Heston. She thought Heston was a "dish," so that might have had something to do with her devotion to the movie. Her love for Michelangelo got into our DNA. Though she was a Beatles, Steely Dan, Doobie Brothers, and Bruce Springsteen and the E Street Band fan, in recent years, Aunt Lil played Frank Sinatra records on a loop. She told me it was the best way to remember her parents, whom she missed terribly.

Her favorite song was “Fly Me to the Moon,” and now, she has.

How lucky we were that Uncle Louie married Aunt Lil. He married up and the Capodimontes and Barattas of North Boulevard knew it. This day would be too sad to bear if I didn't believe that Uncle Louie was waiting for her on the other side. They had the real deal: a lifelong love affair. No perfection, just loyalty. When I asked her the secret to her happy marriage, she said, “Don't ask questions.”

In her honor, today at three o'clock, I would like all of you to turn on Channel 7, that's ABC on your dial, for *General Hospital.* You do not have to watch it because Aunt Lil will be; just leave it on and go about your business. You see, she believed that heaven was the place where you finally get everything you want. I see her there, curled up on a celestial couch, with Uncle Louie. They're watching her favorite story on a loop without commercial interruption. Nearby, there's a bowl of jumbo salted cashews, a tall cold glass of Tab with a lemon slice, and a bowl of Gibble's Bar-B-Q potato chips. The key to happiness is to know your bliss. Aunt Lil knew it, and now she has it for all eternity.

I return to the pew. My mother reaches over to pat my hand as my father nods his approval. I may not have been with Aunt Lil for her passing over, but now I hope she knows how I felt about her. She must. That's the promise of eternity. Her life is part of our family history, like the diamonds, like the zeppole, like the marble.

TEA SANDWICHES AND SYMPATHY

Aunt Lil was popular. The lake side of the boulevard is lined with parked cars belonging to the guests of the funeral luncheon. The brown grass on the front lawn is giving way to tufts of green. The buds on the trees are the palest green; small shoots push through the bare gray branches. The air still holds the sting of a cold winter; the overhead clouds have the patina of tarnished silver.

My parents' home fills quickly with family, friends, and the entire roster of the Sodality membership from church. The ladies made the spread of casseroles, tea sandwiches, cakes, and cookie towers, displayed on the dining room table on my mother's shimmering silver serving dishes, which she, Connie, and I had spent the previous evening polishing.

The coolers on the porch overflow with ice and canned drinks, including cans of birch beer and Red Bull. Aunt Lil's passing is the end of an era, as cousins from as far away as Pennsylvania and Connecticut made the drive to honor her. Easter is a couple weeks away. We gave up Aunt Lil during Lent, a sacrifice we'll feel for the rest of our lives. In a matter of months, we lost Aunt Lil and Uncle Louie, both of whom were at the family table for Easter dinner only one year ago.

Father Belaynesh has another funeral in Bradley Beach. On his way out the door, he expresses his condolences for a final time to my mom and dad. He shakes the hand of every guest on his way to the front door before departing. The Holy Roman Church remains in the people business, which gives me hope on this cold spring day. The Sodality ladies make sure that Father leaves with a Tupperware drum full of tricolor cookies (his favorite) for the ride.

I am back on dessert and coffee detail, as though I never left Lake Como, but this time it's different, or maybe it's that I have changed. It's little things. I move through the rooms without anxiety. I stay in the moment and don't look for validation. (I remind myself, for what exactly?) I don't take random comments to heart. I listen. But there is a restlessness in me. As much as I love seeing family and friends, I long for Piazza Alberica and the Italian sunrises that marked my time there. Perhaps this is the biggest difference, the most seismic change: I have a new landscape for my hopes and dreams.

"Jess, it's so nice to see you. I wish it were under better circumstances." Carmel, Aunt Lil's surviving sister, looks a lot like Aunt Lil, with smaller stones in her jewelry settings.

"I'm so sorry for your loss. We loved Aunt Lil." I embrace her.

"She got a kick out of the Capodimontes. Your mother tells me you're in charge of everything."

I nod. "I haven't had a chance to go over to Aunt Lil's yet, but I want you to know, the jewelry goes to you and to Marina. That was Aunt Lil's wish."

"It's too much." Carmel places her hand on her chest.

"No such thing. Aunt Lil taught me that you can never have too many diamonds."

"I loved her." Carmel cries. "She was a wonderful sister. I mean, we squabbled, you know, as sisters do, but I always loved Lil. So many memories."

"Mom, do you need anything?" Marina, her daughter, joins us. Marina is in her early forties, shy and delicate; she looks like she's made of the same porcelain from which Mom's Lladró Madonna was poured.

"My sister left us all of her jewelry," Carmel says softly to her daughter. "Can you imagine that?"

"I don't have anyplace to wear it," Marina says sadly.

"Then wear it at home and let it be your inspiration to travel the world and meet interesting people," I tell her.

Marina is about to tell me something when Lisa Natalizio lopes toward us, holding the wall with one hand and her drink in the other. Lisa is three-quarters in on her second jumbo tumbler of rum and Coke. She lets go of the wall and throws her arm around me for balance. I hold her up. Aunt Lil's funeral reception is about half an hour away from turning into a sloppy ladies' night at the Stone Pony, where we drink until we can't remember the words to the Hail Mary. I'm already way behind, so I help myself to a swig of Lisa's drink.

"Loved your epistle," Lisa says.

Lisa hated religion class at Saint Rose, and it shows she retained nothing for her lack of effort. "Eulogy," I correct her.

"That too. Just keep the dress," Lisa slurs.

"No, it's yours."

"It looks better on you."

My father comes up behind me and puts his arm around me. "I missed my baby."

"I missed you too, Dad."

"Wonderful job on the eulogy," Dad says.

"I was just sayin' . . ." Lisa rolls her head around, attempting to nod like a sober person.

"Yes, good job, honey," Mom says as she offers us tea sandwiches on a silver tray. "Death has become a permanent resident on the lake. We're losing family right and left. Poor Lil. It was so fast. She had trouble breathing, went to bed, and was gone. I hope God graces me with an easy death when the Grim Reaper comes for me."

"I'm sure he's on the intersection of North Boulevard and Surf Avenue, Phil." My father shakes his head.

"Go ahead, Joe, make fun of me. But things are changing. Keep that big head of yours in the clouds and you'll live to regret it. Look at the street. More houses dark than lit. It's like a set of rotten teeth around the lake. Falling out one by one. Clink. Clink. Clink. Soon, the smile is gone, and we don't have a face."

"Good God." Dad shakes his head. "You make grief worse."

"Tradition can only exist in a state of change," I tell them.

"Who the hell said that?" Mom asks.

"An artist in Italy."

"Well, he can keep his lousy observation. Joe, put on the air."

"It's cold outside."

"I don't care. I'm sweating like a beast of burden in here." She lowers her voice to a threatening register. "I'm gonna get that Giuliani smudge-pot look if you don't cool this house off. I couldn't get to the beauty parlor. I had to use the root spray. It runs when I sweat. It's gonna be a meltdown worse than *House of Wax* if you don't cool this barn down."

"Ma, go freshen your lipstick and nobody will notice your roots."

"Do I need it?" Mom purses her lips.

"Your lip liner looks like the coral ring around Saturn. You need a fill-in."

"Do I? No one else in this family pays a bit of attention to me." She glares at my father and turns her attention back to me. "Honestly, they wouldn't notice if I had my bra on backward. I'm a nothing. It took you flying in from Italy to be seen. I don't know how I got along without you, Giuseppina."

"You do just fine." I take the tray from her.

"I try. You know I was with Lil when she died. Right before she went to sleep, the last thing she said to me was 'Pass the Gold Bond.'"

"Let's not put that on the tombstone."

"It's already engraved. You know my brother, nothing on layaway. He paid in full in advance. Poor Lil. No kids. Died alone with no kids of her own."

I haven't had a chance to tell my mother about her nephew Mauro LaFortezza. Maybe when everyone leaves and there's nothing left but stale sfogliatelle and a fresh pot of coffee, I'll break it to her. "Having children is not the only path to happiness."

"But still. It would have been nice. I still mourn that loss for my brother. He loved children. Ah. What are you going to do? That's life. Lou got the money and success, and I got the house full of children. Who won? Who lost? Who knows?"

Connie offers us crabbies on a tray from the count of five hundred Carmel made for the reception and dropped off in two wax-paper-lined shirt boxes from Saks Fifth Avenue. "I'm pushing these crabbies as though my life depends on it," Connie says. "Not a lot of takers."

"Push harder," Mom tells her. "Fish spoils."

"You can't make people eat."

"Yes, you can. You cajole. You push. You force. Stand there and glare at them until they take one. They'll eat." Mom moves off to talk with a cluster of non-Italians from Aunt Lil's Avon days.

Connie and I laugh. "Mom is so intense."

"Our mother who art on North Boulevard, Brutal is her middle name."

Aunt Lil's doctors stand by the buffet. When we die in this family, we include every human being who ever encountered the deceased over the course of her natural life. We even invite the medical team, EMS, doctors, nurses, and caregivers to the funeral and reception. It's an international coalition of the healing arts, a rainbow of humanity from every corner of the globe. And even they know not to touch the crabbies.

I follow my sister into the kitchen to reload the tea sandwiches. "Con, what's the matter with Lisa?"

"She seems fine," Connie says.

"She's acting weird. Like she's on medication."

"Maybe she is. Everybody is on something these days." Connie bites her lip nervously.

The kitchen door swings open behind me. "Jess." Bobby Bilancia kisses me on the cheek. "How are you?"

Weird. I didn't smell Bobby coming. I sniff the air like a bloodhound for the scent of peppermint.

"I'm doing well. How are you?" Bobby no longer combs his hair back off his face; he has a side part. The cut is spiky too, very Ryan Gosling by way of Newark.

"I'm okay."

"Good. Good," Bobby says.

What is wrong with him? He never says a double *good*. Something is off. I thought we were fine at the Milan airport in January. We haven't communicated much since then, except for a couple memes about Jersey we sent back and forth. I thought we were good/good. Something has changed.

"I'd like to stick around later to talk to you," Bobby says. Connie skitters out of the kitchen.

"Sure, Bobby. You can help me with the dishes."

He tries to smile but his mouth turns into a squiggle. He's not going to help me with the dishes later. I know that expression; it's a firm no. Evidently, we didn't cement our future friendship in New Jersey in Italy.

"No presh, Bobby Bilancia. Thank you for being here."

Bobby follows me out of the kitchen and back into the dining room as the front door blows open. A blast of frigid-cold air peels through the house, which hopefully will cool off my mother, who descends the stairs with a fresh schmear of bright red lipstick and a dusting of face powder so thick, she looks like a powdered doughnut. The bulbs must be out on her makeup mirror.

My mother, along with every guest in the room, turns toward the front door. The dull chatter in the room suddenly fades, as sound will do when you slip into a coma or pull the lid shut on a tanning bed or two unexpected guests arrive at a funeral reception in a small town in New Jersey.

In the fading silver afternoon light stand two tall men, appearing like Randolph Scott and Joel McCrea on the horizon in a Western I watched a hundred times with Grandma Cap, except these are not cowboys. They're Italians from the other side.

23

Surprise, Surprise

THE MOURNERS FALL silent at the first glimpse of the men. Mauro LaFortezza enters the house first, wearing a well-cut blazer, tie, and slacks. Angelo Strazza follows him in a bespoke suit; the tie is loosened. Sometimes when you take a man out of his habitat and place him in a new one, he fizzles. Not Angelo. A gold Tuscan coin just rolled in. Desire peels through the loins of every woman in the room at the sight of him. You can hear the gentle snaps of their shapewear and bra straps as they make adjustments to look their best for the handsome strangers. In Bilancia Land, the incoming are known as fresh meat.

As for me? I'm having an out-of-body experience that is a combination of déjà vu and lust. My family, both sides, and our friends and neighbors recede like the outgoing tide on Lake Como beach to make room to ogle at the strangers.

"Is Giuseppina here?" Angelo asks, looking out over the crowd.

"She's back by the coffee server," my mother answers loudly. "And who might you be?" she asks suspiciously.

"Angelo Strazza." He extends his hand to her. "And who are you, *signora*?"

"I'm her mother." Mom takes Angelo's hand. "And this is?" She cocks her head toward Mauro.

I push through the mourners, but I can't get to my mother fast enough.

"I am Mauro LaFortezza. I am your nephew."

A second hush falls over the crowd, as though a tarp has been dropped on them and they are slowly suffocating under the weight of it. In my family, we have no unknown relatives. We don't have to spit in a cup and send it to a lab in Texas to know who we're related to—we can spot our DNA from fifty feet like a blue flare on the turnpike in the dead of night. We identify our people by their physiques. We clock shoulder span, high waists, low hips, strong yet sturdy legs, good hands, and suspicious natures as proof of blood ties.

"Joe?" My mother calls out for her husband. "There's a man here to see you from the Baratta side. Says he's our nephew."

"Why does he have to be a Baratta?" My father overheard the exchange.

"You're part of that crew up in Toronto," Mom says to Mauro as she forces a smile before turning to Dad. "Your people to the north." She snaps her fingers. "You know who I mean."

"The Roccafortes?"

"Of course, *the Roccafortes.* Your cousins with the big heads. Physically big I mean, not snobbish, though there are a couple of them who are borderline." My mother addresses my father as though there's no one else in the room. She goes on. "Who knows where the Barattas have blood relatives lurking? Your family has a rogue member pop up from time to time. You have that cousin in Philly. Pasquale?"

"*Patsy.* He's not rogue," my father fires back. "We're just not close."

"I don't think this fella is from Pennsylvania." My mother makes a judgment call as she looks at Mauro from head to toe. "He has an Italian accent as thick as my compression stockings."

"*Signora*, you don't understand. I am related to *you* on the Capodimonte side," Mauro says.

"I don't know *how*," my mother says dramatically. "My brother and his wife, may she rest in peace, didn't have children. We buried her this morning."

I finally make it to my mother by plowing through three of her Sodality members; luckily, they're tipsy and fold like two one-eyed jacks and the Man with the Axe. "Mom, we have to talk."

"Now you want to talk? After months abroad, you're ready to talk? Well, Giuseppina, guess what? We're in mourning. I don't feel like talking."

"Mom."

"I don't like the look on your face. Joe?" She looks at my father. "Giuseppina has lost all color. She's crestfallen. Look at her."

"Do you need a bag?" Dad asks.

"Eat something," Connie says nervously. "Crabbie?" She shoves the tray in my face.

"Didn't you tell her?" Mauro looks at me.

"I haven't had a chance."

"Ah." Mauro nods his head slowly.

I turn to Angelo.

Before I can say hello, Angelo says, "You left without saying goodbye."

"My aunt died suddenly."

"No note? No text? No call?" he says softly.

The women sigh, aligning themselves with Angelo. I ignore them.

"I left Smokey with your mother."

"You didn't tell her where you were going either."

"Who the hell is Smokey?" My mother fans herself with a stack of cocktail napkins. She turns her back to me and faces Angelo. "And how do you know my daughter?"

I keep my eyes on Angelo. "I have a rule. I don't leave death announcements on phones. Didn't Conor call you?"

Conor and Gaetano come through the front door.

"I parked in Weehawken," Conor grouses. "People, when it's over fifty guests at a party, you need a valet. Jersey rule."

"Who are these people?" Mom cries out. "They're multiplying in my house like sea monkeys. This luncheon is invitation only. And there's plenty of parking on the lake side," she says to Conor defensively.

"Jiminy, Phil. There's enough food. There are two boxes of crabbies in the kitchen. All are welcome," Dad says to our guests.

"You should answer your texts," Angelo says to me as though all of Lake Como isn't listening. "Are you returning to Italy?"

"She has made no decisions," my mother says loudly. "Can't you see we're in crisis here?" She turns to her Sodality chums and mouths, *The nerve.*

The guests move closer to the Italians from the other side and into formation. They lock arms as though they are waiting for the downbeat to perform an Apulian folk dance and snap dish towels to the drum.

"Is that true?" Angelo looks at me. "You're not coming back?"

"Who are you again?" my mother asks Angelo. "We have no idea who you are."

"This is Angelo Strazza. He's an artist."

"The guy who said the stupid thing about tradition?" Mom sneers.

"No, he's a gilder from Carrara."

"You make picture frames?" My mother makes a face.

"I was worried about Giuseppina," Angelo says quietly.

Mom turns to me. "You didn't tell me you were making picture frames."

"I'm not. And neither is he," I explain.

Angelo pulls me close. The guests make a coo sound, like a bunch of pigeons waiting for crumbs in Saint Peter's Square.

"Oh my God, you've found someone." Lisa barrels through the crowd, drunk. "I'm so happy for you! He's a looker." Lisa sizes Angelo up and down Jersey girl–style. "Jess, I've been going out with Bobby since Ash Wednesday. We met on an app. It's called the Clasp. I wanted to write to you or call you, but your mom said to leave you be, that you had put everyone in Lake Como on the Island. Including me." Lisa begins to cry. "I wanted to tell you, but I respect the Island."

"Don't fob this off on me, Lisa Natalizio," my mother says. "I told you that Giuseppina would let us know her life plans in due course. We were giving her space. Naturally, she chose the longest distance between two points on any map, with an ocean in between, but who am I to judge? It's her life and she's living it. We stand by and await instructions like the *stunods* we are."

I can hear the syncopated breathing of every mourner in the room. I look around. They anticipate my reaction. And why wouldn't they? Any family gathering on our street is an excuse for an impromptu barbecue or a roadhouse brawl. I choose neither and face Lisa.

"I think it's wonderful," I tell her.

"I thought you'd be mad at me. At Bobby. At both of us."

"Why would I ever be mad at you? You gave me a haircut that transformed my life. I'm just sorry Uncle Louie wasn't here to see it.

I'm happy for you." I embrace Lisa. "Does this mean you want your dress back?"

"You can keep it," Lisa says, holding me tightly.

"Might as well keep the dress; she got your ex-husband in the deal," Mom says wryly as the entire membership of the Sodality nods in agreement with her.

"Ma. Why didn't you tell me about Bobby and Lisa?"

"I didn't have a chance," she says. "So, we're even?"

"Don't get mad at Mom. I knew too," Connie says.

"We all knew!" Patti Ciliberti, vice president of the Sodality, raises her glass, toasts herself, and sips. "We want our butcher to be happy. How can we make a decent Sunday dinner without Bilancia Meats? Get real, people. Some of us have to live in this town."

Bobby Bilancia joins us from the kitchen. "It was completely accidental. I meant everything I said in Italy. At the time. I came home, and I wasn't looking. Lisa wasn't looking."

"Except online." Patti toasts herself and sips.

"Cut off Patti's liquor, please," Mom orders. "When she's plastered, suddenly she's the *Star-Ledger*."

"I am not *drink*. Drank. Drunk," Patti says. "Are these gentlemen on Clasp?"

Mauro, Angelo, Conor, and Gaetano go the bar.

Patti ignores their migration and, using her cocktail glass as a conductor's baton, she says, "I would like to know how this all unfolded."

"We all went to school together," Lisa says slowly, trying to sober up.

"We all loved Bobby Bilancia," I admit. "But Lisa the most."

"Is that true?" my mother asks.

"Not then. *Now.*" Lisa goes on. "I wrestled with this. I almost started smoking again from the guilt." Lisa wipes the tears from her eyes on her sleeve. "I was so scared to be happy. I was afraid you'd be angry. I don't want you to be angry. But I *do* want to be happy."

"I am not angry. I am happy for you. Both of you." I hug them. I think back to when we were kids, and when I picture my childhood, Bobby was always there, and so was Lisa. It's natural that they found each other. They are the last two singletons in their mid-thirties left standing in Lake Como. Their relationship makes as much sense as the annual Feast, the swell of summer tourists in July, and the inevitability of beach erosion. It was bound to happen.

"I told you Jess would understand," Bobby assures Lisa.

Lisa looks up at him with her beautiful green eyes, the color of martini olives.

"Jess is a good girl." Bobby smiles at me.

Good girl. The most prized compliment in all of Lake Como. One I have hopefully outgrown.

"No need to smoke, Lisa," I tell her.

Lisa takes my hands in hers like we're about to skip rope double Dutch, the way we used to do in the schoolyard on the macadam at Saint Rose. "Are you sure you're not upset with us?"

"I want everybody to find their bliss." I open my arms wide, like the statue of Jesus of the Sacred Heart in Cousin Carmine's backyard.

"We did," Lisa says quietly. "But what about you?"

"I want to be like that lemon slice you put in the sambuca. I want there to be nothing left of me at the end of my life except a peel, because I've squeezed everything I am into a life that mattered."

"Oh God. Are you becoming a nun?" my mother shrieks. "Joe, she's contemplating becoming a religious! We must stop her."

"I don't think that's an option." Dad winks at me.

"What are you going to do?" Lisa asks.

"Everything. I have so much more to see. I want to see Puglia, Sicily, Capri, and Sorrento. The Adriatic. I want to go to Montenegro. The Blue Danube. Greece."

"You want to be a travel agent?" Bobby asks.

"No, Bobby. I don't."

We laugh. Lisa and I look at each other in the way we did whenever Bobby said something dumb in school. The three of us. Three kids who have known each other since we were five, and one of us remains perpetually slow on the uptake, who just happens to be a man.

"I want to build things," I tell them. "And I will."

"I'm a travel agent," Marina says loudly. Her mother pushes her forward to address the crowd.

The room turns in her direction. This is a young woman who in forty-five years has barely ever spoken above a whisper. Marina finding her voice is somehow perceived as more shocking than my ex-husband and best friend getting together.

"She works for American Express," Carmel adds loudly.

"I think everyone knows, Carm. Why don't you just put it in the church bulletin already?" Mom says on her way to the living room as she takes Mauro by the arm.

"She should," Patti speaks up. "It would be good for biz-wiz."

"I think you mean *business*, Patti?" I clarify.

Carmel calls after my mother. "Philly, people travel somewhere every day. Maybe they could use the concierge service. When you're in a people business, you let people know. That's all I'm doing."

"I can get you deals," Marina announces. "I know where the bargains are."

"Italy?" Patti barks.

"Yes. And in addition I have wonderful travel opportunities to many countries around the world. I can get you a good deal on a cruise."

The room explodes with excitement. News of a discount cruise in Lake Como, New Jersey, is bigger than any scandal. The light in the room seems to change as the patter escalates. The bartender mixes the gin in the gold cocktail shaker. The world goes on around us, with Mauro, Angelo, Gaetano, and Conor folding into the din; only Bobby, Lisa, and I remain as we once were.

Bobby and Lisa look at each other.

"This is how the story was supposed to go," I assure them as I let them go.

I stand back, inhale slowly, and let go of the fear and anxiety I once held so tightly because, at the time, I believed if I didn't hold on I would lose everything. But my heart doesn't thump and my throat doesn't close. I breathe.

Bobby puts his arms around Lisa, who could not be more thrilled to be his. The guests congratulate them on their new relationship.

I made Bobby's life my project and my purpose. Now Lisa can have the job if she wants it. There is value in growing up with a man you knew as a child, because you knew him before he was locked into the idea of what it means to be a man. I've learned that a boy can be as vulnerable and fragile as any girl.

Lisa and Bobby will live together in Bilancia Land after a High Mass at Saint Catharine's and a wedding reception at Mallard Island Yacht Club in Manahawkin. One of the guests will break a tooth on the Jordan almonds in the confetti bags, but it will be considered a lucky sign for the couple. No one will remember that Bobby and I were once married. Our marriage will become the Molly Pitcher Service Area on the Jersey Turnpike, a nice comfort stop on a long drive, but not the destination itself. Life in Lake Como will go on.

Bobby Bilancia Breathe.

Bobby Bilancia *Release.*

I look across the room. On this grim day, the scent of Calabrian orange wafts through the room. Angelo Strazza is entertaining the Sodality members at the bar. They gather around him, plying him with their baked goods, their version of flirting. (That would have been me someday, if I hadn't left.)

"Your mother wants you in the living room," Dad warns me.

I nod. Perhaps I found inner peace a moment too soon.

Dad looks around to the guests. "Please. Enjoy the open bar."

"I don't think you need to remind them," I say quietly to Dad.

"I'm sorry," Connie says, following me out to the living room.

"It's all good," I assure my sister. Good ole Lake Como, a vat of secrets, stacked through the generations like our great-aunt's lace doilies in a breakfront. Indestructible. This town will never change. A non–Italian American once made the crack, "What's at the bottom of Lake Como?" expecting a nefarious answer; instead the answer he got was "Fish."

Mom and her nephew, Mauro, stand in the formal living room, the small room off the real living room. This is the room we never use, which has the Lladró Madonna illuminated under a ceiling pin light, two white upholstered chairs, a white sofa, and a white rug. The décor feels like you're drowning in a milkshake floating with religious relics.

Mom gazes at Mauro, holding both of his hands ring-around-the-rosy-style as she studies him. My father flanks them, like a minister at a shotgun wedding. Angelo joins us, taking a seat on the white couch. Conor stands with me.

"This would never happen in an Irish family. We'd just pretend that all this wasn't happening," Conor whispers in my ear.

"Mom, can you believe it?" I ask.

"That sonofabitch-bastard brother of mine." Mom shakes her head. "Just like him. He saved the best for last."

The doorbell rings.

"Joe, can you get that?" my mother says through her veil of tears.

My father answers the door.

Detective Campovilla of the FBI enters the living room behind my father.

My mother looks at me wearily. "Does a bell ring at FBI headquarters in Philadelphia every time someone in my family dies?"

"Sorry to interrupt, Mrs. Baratta."

"I'm sure you are. Connie, get the man a cup of coffee. Angelo? Mauro? Come with me. Joe, get your son in here. I don't want to leave Giuseppina flailing without an attorney."

"It's fine, Ma," I tell her, offering the detective a seat. "Detective Campovilla and I have kept in close touch."

Mom covers her ears. "I don't want to know about any of this!" She leaves the room.

"Would you like me to stay?" Angelo asks.

"You should go. We'll talk later. I'd like to keep the veneer of my perfect character intact as long as possible."

Angelo and Conor go.

"Good afternoon, Detective." My brother enters the living room, closing the door behind him. Joe and I take a seat across from Detective Campovilla on the settee.

"How are you?" Campovilla asks.

"I'll be better when you tell me where I stand with Uncle Louie's business."

"We have Mr. Gugliotti in custody. But we've had a difficult time tying him to the Elegant Gangster. We'd like you to wear a wire at the prison to help us close out the matter."

I look at my brother.

"Is this necessary?" Joe asks.

"It's in your interest, Ms. Baratta. If we can prove that Mr. Gugliotti was in some way tied to the accounts, the money may be freed up. Ms. Baratta can claim the funds, pay the taxes, and be done with this enterprise entirely. You have been cooperative, and the paper trail indicates you told us the truth. What's left is the matter of the disbursement of the funds."

"May I speak with my brother alone?"

"Absolutely."

Campovilla stands and goes outside the door to wait.

"I like the deal. You should get something out of this after all you've been through," Joe says.

"I need to think about it," I tell him. "Let him know I'll be in touch. There's one more thing I need to do before I close the books on the Elegant Gangster."

THE ENTIRETY OF the Saint Catharine's Church Sodality membership encircles Angelo like he's the homecoming bonfire at Pope John High School. All it takes to turn these Italian American women into a pack of sex pistols is hearing the accent of their motherland coming from a fine-looking man with a full head of hair.

"Ladies, may I borrow Signore Strazza?" I take Angelo by the arm.

"We're in love with him," Patti Ciliberti says, twisting a lock of her hair like a bread tie on a loaf from Del Ponte's in Bradley Beach.

I lead Angelo through the dining room to the kitchen, which is packed with more women. We squeeze through them to the cellar door. I take Angelo down to my old apartment. My father has parked two window air-conditioning units and a leaf-sucker bag where my bed used to be.

I put my arms around Angelo. "Why did you come to New Jersey?"

"I know you don't need me, Giuseppina."

"I do need you. You're a good friend."

"I hate that word in English or Italian," he says. "I don't like it at all when it comes from a woman."

"It's a word of honor."

"It is a word without romance," Angelo says.

"Then I will never call you my friend again."

"You promise?"

I kiss Angelo Strazza. His lips caress my cheek until he finds my mouth once more. We can hear the footfalls overhead, and the occasional peal of laughter from the ladies in the kitchen.

"Can we go?" he asks, looking around the room. "What is this place?"

"I used to live down here."

"It's horrible."

"Not to worry," I tell him. "Mom is putting you up down the street at Aunt Lil's. It's the best house on the block. All the accoutrements of gracious living."

"Whatever you say." Angelo pulls me close and buries his face in my neck. I hope he likes the scent of mothballs.

"And where will you be?" he asks.

"Not in the basement."

I release him. I go to my old dresser and open the small drawer at the top. I feel around for the sock where I hid my engagement ring. I place it in the pocket of my dress. "We can go," I tell him.

"Not until you tell me where I stand with you."

I take Angelo's face into my hands and kiss him again. This time with more urgency. "Now do you understand? Or do you need Google Translate? Come on. Let's find Cousin Mauro and get you settled."

"I want to stay with you."

"Well, that's not happening. Have you met my mother?"

We enter the kitchen, which is packed with women. They turn to look at us.

"Someone needs a lipstick touch-up and it's not me," Mom says quietly. She circles her finger around the outside of her lips. "Ring of fire."

The kitchen door from the back porch swings open. Babe Bilancia pushes the screen door aside with her hip as she carries a Nordstrom gift box filled with cookies, her signature sesame dunkers. "Did I miss anything?"

FOR GOOD

I nest the last of the party platters in its place on the shelf in my mother's kitchen marked FOR GOOD. These are the platters and utensils used for Sunday dinner and holiday parties, never in ordinary time. They're mainly the serving pieces Mom inherited as a daughter-in-law from Grammy B and the spoils of whatever she and Uncle Louie split when Grandma Cap died. On the Baratta side, Dad's sister, Pamela, got the dishes; Mom offered Aunt Pam the serving pieces, but she said, "No, no, Mommy's wishes." Once in a while, in my family, on either side, someone actually honors the wishes of the dead. There are more stories about my ancestors wandering the afterlife looking for the platter from Deruta they were promised, because somehow, it wound up in the wrong hands. I will make sure to follow Uncle Louie's and Aunt Lil's instructions to the letter of the law.

Nothing changes in Lake Como; we live, we die, and those who remain polish the silver for the next reception. There is a part of me that will always find comfort in our traditions. A cup of hot, fresh coffee in my mother's kitchen is more comforting than all the pharmaceuticals ever invented in the science labs of north New Jersey. I pour my mother a cup.

"There's cake." Mom pushes the pedestal holding three-quarters of a lemon Bundt cake toward me. "I don't know what I'm going to do with all these desserts. The freezer in the garage is full."

I cut a slice and taste it. "Who made it?"

"Elena Nachmanoff. It's her best cake, you know. Always popular." Mom sips. "You're the only child I birthed who knows how I like my coffee."

"I'm the only child who paid attention. Because I had to. That's what good servants do."

"Not true. My Joey steps up. And Connie in her fashion."

"Yup. We are all equal," I say sincerely, meaning it. I learned in therapy that sarcasm is a wall of defense used by bright people who sense danger. Since I am no longer in danger, I can afford to be kind.

"Are you okay with Lisa and Bobby?"

"I am. I gave Bobby his diamond back."

"Giuseppina! Why did you do that? You'll need that money someday."

"I don't think so."

"No matter how hard I try, this family just can't hold on to money. We are not meant to be rich," my mother cries.

"Every family can't be Vanderbilts and Rockefellers."

"No, because they're not Italian. It would've been nice, though." Mom sighs. "What the hell. I give up." Mom looks at me and offers me a cookie. "You look good, Giuseppina."

"Thanks, Ma. So do you."

"Italy agrees with you."

I take my mother's hand. "You must see Italy."

"I follow you on Instagram," she says. "I take whatever portion is given to me."

"I'm serious. You have to see Italy for yourself. My biggest regret is that we didn't take Grandma Cap. We should have."

"We were lucky to make it to the Poconos. The Caps and Barattas are not bons vivants."

"We are the ultimate world travelers. We're immigrants."

"What's the story with this Angelo fellow? Is he looking for a green card?"

"Ma!"

"There's my answer. You like him. Are you happy, Giuseppina?" Mom asks.

I sit back in my seat, stunned, like a bird that flies at full speed into a sliding glass door.

"What's the matter?" Mom asks. "You look like you've been slapped."

"You've never asked me that question."

"How is that possible?"

"Oh, it's possible, Ma." I give her question some thought. "I'm happy." I think of Dr. Darlene, who encouraged me to mirror my responses, so I ask my mother, "Are *you* happy?"

"I don't know. I'm aware that I caused my children unhappiness even though it wasn't my intention. I pushed you to marry Bobby because I knew that he would never take you away from me. When your child leaves you—and it doesn't matter how old they are—it's like losing a thumb. Maybe both of them."

"I didn't leave home to hurt you. I left home to grow up. Maybe I'm a little old for that, but it had to happen sometime and I'm glad it did. I needed to teach you how to treat me." I may send Dr. Darlene a bonus for offering me this insight, when my mother's face falls like a soufflé. "It's all right, Ma."

"Is it?" She is confused.

"Remember Grandma Cap's bird?"

"Which one? She had several."

"Oscar Hammerstein the fourth, I think. Grandma fed him fresh lettuce from her garden."

"They all got fresh lettuce," Ma says. "I *skeeve* birds. They're worse than turtles. But that didn't keep her from having them. Nobody ever listened to me."

"Whenever anyone went in and out of her house, Oscar would squawk at them: *sonofabitch-bastard*. Remember?"

She nods.

"He cursed at everybody but me. When that parrot saw me coming, he'd say *sweetie*."

"We thought it was your hair. He thought he could nest in the curls."

"No. Oscar Hammerstein already had a home. A very nice birdcage with a view of the garden. Oscar Hammerstein liked me. It wasn't anything I said or did; he understood me."

"Is that some kind of victory?"

"Just an observation. I don't blame you for not seeing me for who I am. People put you in a cage or a box or a role because they hope you will stay there. It took Italy to teach me that life is not supposed to be a struggle; it's supposed to fun."

"But there are responsibilities, sacrifices! That's how I was raised. Oh, what does it matter? It's just me and your father now, a pair of old Florsheims at the bottom of the closet. Everyone else is gone. My mother. Father. Lou and Lil. Even that birdcage is empty."

"You have to make a space to fill it, Ma."

"Do I?"

"Your brother, Louie, taught me. When we change, sometimes it makes a path for something wonderful. The problems in life are real. But they shouldn't bury the fun. It's a mistake to make all of life a slog. Balance. In all things. That's the true Italian way. It's why the Leaning Tower of Pisa doesn't fall. It's why Italian men can still have sex in their eighties."

"Tell me about it." Mom makes a face.

"It's why if you eat a portion of food at a meal the size of your fist, you'll never be hungry."

"Is that true?"

"Leonardo da Vinci lived by it. And he taught that wisdom to Michelangelo. Live abundantly but know when to put down the glass and get up from the table."

Mom sits back in her chair. "You've outgrown us, haven't you?"

"Does it help if I tell you that I got homesick for the Feast of the Seven Fishes?"

"I don't know if you heard, but Carmine Baratta did the smelts this year. Charlene left the windows open in zero-degree temperatures to air out the house."

"That cleared the stench."

"Nope. Got in the walls." Mom nods sadly. "And their pipes burst."

I look at my mother; she's getting older. How do I let go and hold on with the same pair of hands? We don't have much time. "You were a wonderful mother."

"Was I?"

"You pushed me."

"Did I?"

"Just enough."

"Do you think my brother loved me?" Mom begins to cry. "Louie was so hard to love because I wanted to kill him half the time."

"He loved you, Ma. He always came back when you let him off the Island, didn't he?"

"We'd pretend that nothing had ever happened. That was the best part." Mom looks off and smiles as if she sees her brother coming through the door for Sunday dinner. "The sonofabitch-bastard."

24

Italian French Toast

My mother sets the dining room table like William and Kate are stopping by for a bagel. The silver Italian cutwork lace, English china, and French crystal look like a yard sale in *Bridgerton*. After a funeral, our kitchen becomes an open all-night diner, with three squares served around the clock for guests, drop-ins, and family.

My father is in the kitchen making French toast from the leftover bread Mom didn't use to make the tea sandwiches. This is a family that wastes nothing, including the ends of Pepperidge Farm bread. Mom has put out the best silver to impress our guests from Italy. Mom made the beds for Angelo and Mauro at Aunt Lil's. Conor and Gaetano stayed in Sea Girt with his sister's family because I nixed the notion of anyone staying in the cellar.

Mom looks out the dining room window. "Connie and Diego are here. They're early," she grouses. "For once, I'd like to have my table just so before the crowd descends."

"Ma, it's just French toast. Relax." I close my eyes and inhale the scents of butter, cinnamon, and vanilla wafting in from the kitchen as Dad flips the bread in the pan. Thera-Me has taught me to stay in the moment. I find whenever I do, I make a memory.

"We dropped the girls at school," Connie says as she enters the dining room. "I'll finish the table." Connie takes the stack of dishes off the sideboard and sets them around the table. "Ma, Diego and I want to talk to you about something."

"Do we need your father?" Mom calls for him.

Dad joins us in the dining room. "What's up?"

"We would like to buy Grandma Cap's house," Diego says, looking at Connie. She nods supportively.

"It would be a good investment," Mom says. "People flip houses in Lake Como and make a lot of money. Just don't flip it to someone who would be a lousy neighbor for us."

"We want to live in it," Diego says.

"No kidding," Dad says.

"You want to live in Lake Como?" Mom looks at Connie.

"The kids go to Saint Rose, and it would be closer."

Mom smiles. "I would love to have you and the kids down the street. I'm still cleaning out the house. What are you thinking?"

"As soon as our house sells," Diego says.

"I will give you a very good deal. *As is* because the house needs work." Mom follows Dad and Diego into the kitchen.

"What happened? Why the move?" I ask my sister.

"Diego was let go," Connie says quietly. "The fund he was working for collapsed. He needs to find another job. We put everything we had into our house. It's a good time to sell. The kids are getting bigger. We have three college funds to save for. Honestly? It's overwhelming. We need to scale back."

"I think it's great. Grandma Cap would be thrilled that you're going to raise your children in her house."

"I'll be here for Mom and Dad too." Connie bites her lip. "When do you plan to go back to Italy?"

"I have an open return." I like the way that sounds. Open. Can it be I'm getting it right at last? Stay open. Stay in the moment.

I follow Connie into the kitchen.

"I smell French toast." Joe and Katie enter from the foyer.

"Did you tell Katie and Joe yet?" I ask Connie.

She nods that she has. "Joe is helping Diego with his exit contract."

"Isn't it great?" Katie says. "I think you will love it on the lake. The kids have the lake and the beach. What could be better?"

"Nothing," I assure her.

The doorbell rings.

"I got it," I call out on my way through the dining room. I throw open the front door. Angelo and Mauro are on the doorstep. "*Ciao!* Italians from the other side!" I call out, and lead Angelo and Mauro into the dining room.

"Zia Philomena," Mauro greets my mother.

"I still can't believe I'm an aunt," Mom says.

"And I can't believe I have an American family from this side." Mauro beams. "When Angelo said he was coming to New Jersey, I knew I had to meet you all."

"We are so happy you made the trip," my mother says. "We have many points of interest here in the Garden State to share with you."

"I am all yours," Mauro assures her.

"I like your name," Katie says to Mauro.

"*Grazie.* I am named for my mother's father."

"I like the name Maura for a girl." Katie looks at Joe.

"Don't tell me." My mother puts down her fork.

"Yes, baby number three!"

My parents cry out with joy. We all do.

"We were also thinking of a family name this time," Joe says. "Giuseppina."

Katie smiles. "After you, Jess. Who better? A girl needs guts in this world."

"I am honored, but please do not name that child Giuseppina."

"What's wrong with your name?" my mother cries. "It's Italian, isn't it? And didn't you end up in Italy? Give me a little credit. Maybe I'm psychic."

"Josephine?" Katie counters.

"That's the French translation. In honor of my French toast," Dad jokes.

"A new baby brings good luck." Mauro raises his glass.

Angelo is oddly quiet. I serve him French toast and continue with the platter around the table.

"What are your plans, Giuseppina?" Mom asks.

"I'm afraid I have to skip the local tour. I've got some business I need to take care of," I tell her.

"That's fine. We'll take Mauro and Angelo around," Dad says.

"I appreciate it," I tell him.

"I thought we'd do dinner here tonight. With our guests. The kids. Does that sound good?" Mom asks.

"*Perfetto*," Mauro says.

I get up to remove the dishes. Connie and Katie get up to help me.

"No, Katie. You rest. Connie and I have got this."

Joe joins Connie and me in the kitchen. "Need help?" he offers.

Connie clutches her chest. "No way! Is this real or am I having a heart attack? My brother never picked up a dish in his life."

"All right, Con, knock it off. I need a word with Jess."

Connie puts down the *mopeen*. "Fine. Call the scullery maid back in when you're done."

"No. Stay," I tell her. "I made a decision about the Elegant Gangster. I'm not going to wear a wire. I don't want the money."

"Are you sure?" Joe asks.

"They gave me an option to pursue a lawsuit to get the money in the accounts, or I could sign off on the accounts and be cleared of all liability. I signed off. It was a big day for Caesar."

"The money could have changed your life."

"I wish that were true. But it turns out, the only thing that can change my life is me."

"But money helps," Joe insists.

I don't know about that. It seems to me that any time a family member got sent to the Island, it was over money. More families have lost their way in pursuit of a windfall, and we were no different. My hope for the new generation is that they lose the address of the Island altogether and work things out when there's a problem. The Caps and Barattas hold on to secrets, but never cash. But even with all our flaws, if I need something, the first place I will turn is to my family. They're my judge and jury and I accept their verdict because they're all I've got. I used to think when someone in my family said, "It's about the money," it wasn't. But it *is*. It's about taking care of one another by any means necessary. And if we can do that, surely we can hold this fragile band of insane people together with the love that made us family in the first place.

THE ELEGANT GANGSTER

The sky overhead is a peachy pink, which means rain is coming in from the sea, an insider's weather tip from the Jersey Shore. When I was a kid, I constantly checked the colors of the sky in hope of a sunny day. When I went to Italy, I looked to the sky to connect me to home.

The walk to the entrance of the federal prison in Fairton, New Jersey, is a neat configuration of bluestone pavers hemmed with square separators of sandstone and brick. The walk could be aesthetically pleasing, but I don't imagine that beauty is a priority in the federal penal system. Fairton is a minimum-security prison, with the brick facade of a community center. Except for the guards and the metal detector and the purse search, you would never know it was a jail.

"Giuseppina Baratta," I tell the guard, handing over my driver's license. "The officer at the front desk sent me. I'm here to see Rolando Gugliotti."

"Family?"

"A friend. Googs is my uncle's friend, actually. I signed up to visit online."

"Wait here."

The visitors' room reminds me of a school cafeteria. There are round pressboard tables centered around the same orange and turquoise bucket chairs we had in our lunchroom at Pope John High School. There must have been a truck with faux Eames chairs that dumped a surplus on the turnpike. Every school, church hall, and civic club in New Jersey has the same bucket chairs, it seems.

Googs enters the room. I wave. He stands up a little straighter as he walks toward me. His khaki pants are fitted, except the pant-leg portion, which is rolled to break over his shoes. He wears black Merrell loafers and an untucked blue button-down shirt. He invites me to sit at the table by the window.

"You look good, Googs."

His thick white hair is cut short; his eyebrows are as black as licorice. "I'm glad you came to see me. Thank you."

"I want to thank you for the flowers you sent when Uncle Louie died. We didn't know where to send the note. You're a tough man to find."

"Forget it. I sent them from a place of affection. No acknowledgment necessary."

"Googs is an original name. Short for Gugliotti?"

"Actually, your uncle gave me my name. He said Rolando didn't suit me. I wasn't an actor or a movie star. Besides, he said I had the eyes. Googly eyes. It's my thyroid. Hyper. You get the whites around the iris. Looks like a golf ball floating in a sink. I've been on meds since I was seventeen. It gives you a corneal bulge. See?" He opens his eyes wide. "I was Googly, until he shortened it to Googs. Did he name you too?"

"My brother did. He couldn't say Giuseppina, so Uncle Louie made sure everybody called me Jess. Evidently, he felt that there was only one Giuseppina in the world who could carry that name, and that was his aunt. Sometimes he called me the letter *J*."

"Your uncle was a cut-to-the-chase guy. Unencumbered."

"He was."

"My condolences on the loss of Louie, and of your aunt. I met Lillian down in Miami several times over the years. Met them for dinner. Your aunt would turn in early and your uncle and I would hit the all-night card games. Good times."

"I'm sure."

"Here we are. You said you had some questions for me. Ask me anything. I'm an open book. Your uncle and I were as close as close can be. Very tight. I was mainly his traveling buddy, on trips to Vegas, Atlantic City, Miami. And we did business together."

"My uncle led a compartmentalized life."

"Doesn't everybody?"

I understand why Louie and Googs were close. They think alike. *Simpatico.* "How long are you in for?

"Two years."

"How old are you?"

"Seventy-eight. I'll turn eighty a few weeks after I get out of here. Looking forward to it. A clean slate. Birthdays with zeros are starting guns.

"You look good."

"It's the genes. You can't really mess up good genes. Smoking, drinking, nothing makes a dent in them. It's like your cells have a Mylar shield on them. Impenetrable." He looks at the field out the window and squints. "I guess you want to know about my business with Louie."

"I would appreciate anything you could tell me." Now that I have given all the marbles to the US government, I want clarity. Since the money is already gone, I would like to restore Uncle Louie's reputation and find a way forward with Cap Marble and Stone.

"I said everything in court. Came clean."

"I read the transcripts."

"So you know what I did. I moved money around and didn't report the taxes, but it was not our intention not to pay them. We wanted to build up the kitty overseas, and when we used the money here, we planned to report it. We used a bank that was known in business circles, but it turns out they weren't on the up-and-up. And of course, Uncle Sam wanted the dough now, and that led them to break the operation, the bank folded, and they came after your uncle and me."

"You helped put them away."

"It was a trade-off. I sang and got minimum and they got maximum intel in the deal. I meant what I said to the judge. I was truly sorry. If I had it to do over, I'd declare the profits. Naturally. Render unto Uncle Sam what is Uncle Sam's. Caesar can go screw himself. Excuse me."

"But the profits themselves, that you didn't pay taxes on, were not legal in the first place. They came from the resale of marble that had already been paid for?"

"That's still an open question, and I don't want to venture into that arena. I do know this. You sell something—you set the price, right? You bought it for *x*, you sold it to *y*, and *z* gets pissed off about it. *Z* is not my problem until he is. If a customer agrees to the price, how is that illegal?"

"You have a point. Unless the goods are stolen."

Googs makes bouquets with his fingers. "I never stole. We were moving marble. Rock and stone. That's it. That's all."

"Where did Uncle Louie come up with the name the Elegant Gangster?"

"That's a funny story." Googs chuckles. "That was me. I am the elegant gangster. I wouldn't use that phrase to describe myself, but we thought it was funny. They were called Johnny Carson suits, because he was the spokesmodel for them. You're too young to remember him, or his suits, but they were these drip-dry polyester pants and jackets, under which I would wear a Qiana shirt. Also drip-dry. Those shirts came in wild prints. Very chic. No tie. Wore it open at the collar. I had a chest like James Caan at the time and it behooved me to show off my taut neck and Adonis pecs. You should've seen me back then. I needed little embellishment, believe me. One day, your uncle picks me up in Hackensack on our way to Atlantic City and I'm waiting for him, outside some restaurant, and I'm wearing an aqua leisure suit with a Qiana button-down in a cockamamie print of hydrangeas or something like them all over it, and your uncle pulls up, leans out the window, and says, "One Elegant Gangster to go, please." And we laughed our asses off, I got in the car, and that was that. We called the company the Elegant Gangster because, let's face it, we figured naming our company in such a fashion was like hiding in plain sight. We figured if the IRS nailed us, we had enough money set aside to pay the shortfall. Our attitude was, "Oops, we didn't report everything, we'll cut you a check now." That was our prix fixe strategy if we got caught. You see, we didn't count on getting caught because we paid taxes stateside every year and on time. They just wanted more from us."

"You needed to pay the taxes on the foreign money."

"You read my confession. I apologized and now I'm serving my time," Googs says defensively. "How many times am I gonna apologize? I'm getting bored over here already."

I lean back in the plastic chair. "Do you get many visitors?"

"My daughter. My son, not so much. He's in pharmaceuticals and can't associate with convicted felons, or so he says. Not for nothin', I said, 'Gio, you're selling Ozempic for five hundred and change a pen, who's the gangster here, me or you?'"

"That's too bad."

"Kids. That's another hayride of crazy. I could choose to be miserable, waking up on a foam mattress the thickness of a waffle every morning, but I tell myself, 'Googs, find something.' Find one thing that makes it worthwhile to get out of bed in the morning."

"Have you found it?"

Googs nods. "I get to the cafeteria early before anyone else. I take one of those thick white regulation mugs off the stack. I hit the tap and fill it with fresh, hot coffee. I add cream. Two sugars. I stir. I sit down at a table by the window and sip. By the time I'm done with that cup of coffee, I almost believe I can face anything, conquer any foe, right any wrong. I believe in myself again. That first cup of coffee makes life worth living."

Googs says goodbye; he's due to work in the prison candy store. As he walks away, he resembles Frankie Valli on the reunion tour in Vegas. There's a slight catch in his gait—either his hip or his knee is acting up, or maybe both. But even with the limp, he's still got it. Italian men may lose a little something here and there, make mistakes and misjudgments, but no matter what, they retain the swagger.

Once I'm outside the building, I realize I've been holding my breath. I survey the pale green fields around the prison. The world looks washed-out, faded on the cusp of spring instead of coming to life. I have spent a good deal of time trying to understand Uncle Louie and his business dealings since he died. My uncle wasn't a crook or a thief, but he wanted to make as much money as he could in the time he had.

Googs may like the feeling of importance that money brought to his life, or maybe he was in desperate need of it. He had so many obligations: ex-wives to take care of and children to support. Imagine the energy it took to juggle the funds going out with what came in. Imagine the energy it took to keep those interested in his finances off his trail. It could not have been easy. He constantly changed his phone number because no sooner had he made contact than he had to give the person the slip. I've had the same phone number since I bought my first phone.

But this doesn't explain Uncle Louie. He made enough money with Cap Marble and Stone to provide a good life for Lil and himself. Why did he need the second company? What value was it going to add to his life? I check my pockets for Uncle Louie's keys. I drove the Impala over here today. It wasn't like the old days because he's gone, but in some small way, I wanted Uncle Louie with me.

I am thinking of my uncle when the sun blasts through the clouds. I see Uncle Louie inside the car in the driver's seat. He's waiting for me. I stand before the hood ornament on the Impala like it's the prow of a ship. I am afraid, and yet I have so many questions for him.

"Why, Uncle Louie? Why the Elegant Gangster?" I ask.

A wind kicks up in the parking lot. Clouds move in overhead and reflect on the windshield, obscuring him. Uncle Louie takes his hands off the steering wheel and speaks to me through the glass. He wears the Fourth Degree sash over his Knights of Columbus tuxedo. The Napoleon hat with the white marabou feather is perched on his head like a bird.

"Ah, Jess, don't make me say it," he says.

"Say what?"

"I was squirreling. The dough. You know, the money. I was worried about you kids. Philly and Joe were always underwater. Holding on to the house. Something was always breaking over there. You kids were growing up, and you were smart, and how were they gonna send you to school? How were they going to give you the necessities? Your father was a smart enough guy, but it's never about brains. It just isn't. He never took chances because he felt he couldn't. He stayed in insurance all his life because it was a steady paycheck. He never ruffled any feathers, and in this life, you get nowhere unless you agitate. Joe Senior needed to push but he didn't have the courage. He was afraid he'd lose everything if he made demands. Your father's dream was having a family, and he got that. Beyond that, Joe Baratta Senior did not aspire. My sister is a good woman, but she can't get along with people. She was put-upon from the day she was born—she blames everything on the pink crib. She was an Italian American girl, and while she might be a princess, she believed she was a second-class citizen. Nothing worse than royalty that doesn't trust the crown. My sister moved through life like a porcupine, looking for any reason large or small to give people the needle. Despite all of it, she gave me my nieces and nephew, so I forgave her for everything. I loved you kids like my own and I got a little peek into what it might have been to be a father. A father will do whatever he has to do to take care of his children. You kids motivated me to work hard. You gave me a purpose. I owe everything to you."

I rush to the driver's-side door and throw it open. I look in the front seat, I check the back seat, but Uncle Louie is gone.

I go to the trunk of the car and open it. His K of C regalia is gone. No sash, no hat, no tuxedo. No sword. He took them to eternity. I snap the trunk shut.

I get in and start the car. I grip the steering wheel. The scent of Woodhue wafts through the car. "I got this, Uncle Louie," I say aloud.

But do I?

25

The Impala

I PULL INTO AUNT Lil and Uncle Louie's garage. The automatic door closes behind me, and the car practically parks itself in position, as though it has sense memory. They say people have souls. Houses have souls. But no one ever says cars have souls, and they do. Uncle Louie's 2018 Impala was his tabernacle. I press the automatic button to recline the driver's seat. I lean back and fold my arms across my waist. I look out the pristine windshield. The garage is like a showroom. A worthy home for the Impala. Uncle Louie's car was his baby, waxed on the outside and polished on the inside.

When Uncle Louie told me stories about his uncles and aunts, he'd bring them to life in unforgettable detail. Sometimes, I'd request a particular story. Tell me the one about Uncle Shooky or Uncle Hap or Aunt Gus, and he'd repeat it. They became so real to me in the telling, I almost thought I had lived them. Once I asked Uncle Louie, "How can I love someone I've never met?"

"We *are* them, Jess. We are *them*," Louie would say.

Perspective is the gift you receive when you leave home. The only way to make yourself whole is to understand what shattered you to pieces in the first place.

Angelo taps on the car window.

"Get in," I say through the glass.

Angelo goes around the front of the car and opens the passenger door. "You've been gone all day. Your mother took us to the Paramus Mall."

"I am so sorry."

"Why are you sitting in the car?" Angelo asks.

"Thinking. Where's Mauro?"

"Your mother took him to see Saint Catharine Church. I begged off," he says.

"But it's built of Carrara marble. There's all kinds of gilding inside. You would appreciate it."

"I couldn't spend one more hour with your mother. Forgive me." Angelo puts the passenger seat back on recline. "This is very plush."

"Uncle Louie only drove the best. You're in my seat. *Shotgun*, we call it."

"I see. Have you thought about what we talked about before you left?"

"All the time."

"Are you coming back to Italy?"

"Will you miss me if I don't?"

"Yes."

"I'm coming back."

"Mamma wanted to know."

"Oh, now it's what Mamma wants. She sent you all the way to America to confirm my plans?"

"It's almost the first of the month," he teases.

"Tell your mother not to rent my apartment."

"Why did you go to Carrara in the first place? You could go to Milano or Roma or Firenze. Why our village?"

"Some girls grow up on fairy tales. I grew up on family stories of cutting marble, surviving on chestnuts, and being so poor you had to leave the place you loved to survive. I had to be a part of it. I didn't know if I would be accepted or if I would like it. I went to Carrara looking for love. Not the kind of romantic love that sweeps you off your feet, but the other kind. The love of life, where you can't wait to get up in the morning to see what the day will bring."

"Did you find it?"

I don't answer. Instead, I ask Angelo, "Why did you come to America?"

"I came to America looking for the love of a good woman."

"Have you found her?"

"If she'll have me."

Angelo takes my face in his hands. His mouth finds mine. I put my arms around him, and soon we're entwined in a kiss that seems to last for the entirety of a rainy afternoon. There's tapping on the window. I turn and let out a silent scream when I see my mother's face pressed against the glass. She attempts to peer through the car's fogged-up windows. We lost track of time. I clear a circle of fog from the window with my sleeve.

Outside, Mom makes the rolling motion with her hand, just like Uncle Louie. I roll down the window. My father, brother, and Mauro stand behind her like the Untouchables perusing the scene of a crime.

"This car has not been inspected since Louie died."

"Ma. Please."

"It's dangerous. But nobody listens to me. You could be sucking carbon monoxide in there unaware and you'd turn blue and die and you wouldn't even feel it."

"I don't think she was having a hard time breathing in the Impala," my father says.

"Dinner is ready down the block." Mom makes a face. "Whenever you two are otherwise not engaged. But hurry. My stuffed shells will dry out and dinner will be ruined."

"We'll be there shortly," I promise her, and roll up the window.

My mother, father, Mauro, and Joe leave the garage.

I gather the keys and go to open the car door when Angelo pulls me close. "Is there someplace we could go?"

"I . . . I . . ."

"There's no one upstairs. They're at your mother's about to sit down for some dry shells. They won't even miss us." Angelo kisses my neck.

I make a face. "Too weird."

"What about right here?"

"In the car? Hell no. The car is a cathedral. I think we should wait."

"That's a terrible idea," Angelo says.

"I know. It's awful. Brutal! There's the basement at my mother's, but they'd be overhead."

"I can't." Angelo shakes his head. "Worse than a landfill."

We laugh. We kiss. The thickness of our jackets makes them feel like medieval suits of armor that keep us from each other, from our bodies, which ache to be one.

"Wait. I know a place," I whisper.

Angelo unbuttons my jacket. He kisses my ear. My legs turn to *marmellata*; I melt into him like hot butter.

"I've never been there," I say breathlessly. "It's a Motel 6 on Route 11. It's off the Jersey Turnpike. Somewhere."

"I don't need directions. I have a GPS." Angelo's voice is husky; his heart is racing.

Angelo kisses me. There's a knock on the window. Angelo and I separate quickly. I rub the fog on the window. My father stands with his back to the car. "I see nothing," he says loudly. "Your mother sent me for the Parm wheel." He goes into the house through the garage.

"Why do you keep your cheese in this house?" Angelo asks.

"Storage. We can always use more refrigerator space."

Angelo nods. "So Motel 6 is dead?"

"For now." I give him a quick kiss on the cheek.

We pull on our jackets and get out of the car. Dad comes out of the house with the half wheel of Parmesan cheese. He grins.

"Oh good. We can walk together." He hands Angelo the wheel of cheese.

I hit the automatic garage door remote. We walk out into the dark, the three of us, my father, my would-be lover, and me. We take the turn down North Boulevard.

"Mom ironed the dollar bills. We're going to have a big night of Uno," Dad says.

"What is that?" Angelo nudges me.

"It's a lot of fun, Ang," my father offers. He must like Angelo; he's already shortened his name.

In the distance, we can see Mom on the porch in her house slippers and dress. "Joe, go back. Get the nut bowls!"

Dad sighs and stops. "You guys go ahead," he says.

Angelo and I take the turn onto my parents' walkway. My mother has left the front door wide open. We can see the family gathering at the table inside.

Angelo places the half of the Parm wheel on the sidewalk and turns to me. "I can't. I can't go in there."

"You said you didn't mind the wait."

Angelo hangs his head. He slides his hands up inside the sleeves of my coat, warming my arms up to my elbows. It might be the sexiest move any man ever made on any woman in all of history.

"There's only one thing to do," I tell him.

"Eat the shells? Iron the money? Play the card game?" Angelo sounds like he might cry.

"No."

Angelo slides his hands out of my sleeves. I take his hand. "Run!"

26

A Year Later

I AM UP WITH the sun as it rises in ribbons of hot pink and incandescent orange over the Montini farmhouse. The renovations are almost complete. How I will love my room with a different view.

This is Carrara off the piazza. I am close enough to the action to be a part of it and far enough away to be on my own. If Carrara were this woman, she'd be a sculpture by the great modern artist Jago. She would maintain her classic lines in a modern form sculpted of lustrous Calacatta marble from the mountain. The buttery light would play over her smooth skin, falling into shadow where she holds her secrets.

I open the window and breathe in the air from the pine, fir, and myrtle trees that hem the property.

I stuff a copy of Elsie de Wolfe's *The House in Good Taste* into the front pocket of my overalls. I sit down and take a moment to record the swell of what I am feeling, scrolling through the journal entries I've made over the last few months. This enterprise that once was a chore has become a habit. I have also learned there is wisdom in brevity. I write.

The Big Five:

1. Epiphany. I am as happy alone as I am in love.

2. I don't have to please anyone to find my worth.

3. A job is not just a job; it's a creative expression of the journey of the soul.

4. It's not where you live; it's how you live when you get there.

5. I am a person of the world, not just my small corner of it, and I own all she is.

I SET THE phone aside. Smokey sits next to me on the floor as I fill my bookshelves. I pull *The House in Good Taste* out of the chest pocket of my overalls and place it on the shelf. I run my hand over the cover; the line drawing of the facade of a house and simple title font speak to me. I have dog-eared the pages, underlined de Wolfe's wisdom, and written notes in the margins. I could not have renovated the Montini farmhouse without her. I open the storage box of my books and lift out the volumes, one by one.

I add Viola di Grado next to *Italian Ways* by Tim Parks, the DVD of Pietro Castellitto's *The Predators*, Domenico Starnone's *The House on Via Gemito*, and Margaret Mazzantini's *Don't Move.* I place Melania Mazzucco's *Vita* and *The Betrothed* by Alessandro Manzoni next to *Browning's Italy* by Helen Archibald Clarke. *Cross-*

ing the Alps by Helen Barolini gets its own placement, front cover out, because Helen has never received enough recognition for her work.

Some of the books are in Italian, others translated to English. I float between languages like a jellyfish, and not very well. I hold words and images in Italian like gold leaf attaches to impressions in marble. *A Room with a View* takes its place next to Barolini; in this way, it will never be lost. I will always find it.

"Giuseppina!"

I hear my mother call my name from the front yard. I go to the French doors that overlook the vista and open them. I step outside.

"*Buongiorno*, Ma."

My family is gathered in the front yard below like the parishioners who cram into Saint Peter's Square on Easter Sunday to see the pope and await his blessing.

"The balcony is a nice touch." My brother shields his eyes and looks up as I lean over the railing. The front yard is neatly appointed with a pile of marble remnants of various shapes and sizes, the workmen's neatly stacked tools, and some planks of wood to be taken away for the next job.

My mother and father stand together, looking up at me. Katie wrangles Rafferty. Joe buttons Mackenzie's coat while juggling the new baby, Giuseppina, called Jo. Connie chides the girls to lower their voices as Alexa, Alicia, and Abby jump up and down hollering for me to come down. Aunt Lil's sister, Carmel, and her niece, Marina, try to help with the kids, but their overloaded fanny packs get in the way.

Angelo drives up on his turquoise scooter. He rides into the scene as he has into my life. We have work to do. The farmhouse is the beginning. I plan to open an architecture firm in Carrara, on the piazza next to the bakery, because I want a fresh *cornetto* with my coffee every morning for the rest of my life. I will continue to take work from Mauro on the mountain, but now, instead of rendering other people's ideas, I will design for clients.

I have a new enterprise with Conor. I've designed a collection of marble and granite floors that Conor will sell around the world. We will call the company Capodimonte Marble and Stone, because, after all, the stone is Italian, and so is my family name. But this time, things will be different. I won't hide my ambition or put a good man's happiness ahead of my own, because now I know what brings me joy. Is it possible that there's equality in this matter? You bet there is, and Angelo Strazza understands.

Signora Strazza joins my parents, tying a scarf over her hair and under her chin. I won't forget that she showed me the old farmhouse for the first time, revealing a dream. Angelo kisses his mother on the cheek.

"I'll be right down!" I holler. I grab my sketchbook and take the stairs down to the main room of the house. I welcome my family inside, where the blueprints are displayed on two horses. Without furniture, the fieldstone room seems big, certainly large enough to accommodate my family. They gather and look over my shoulder as I explain the redesign and renovation of the house.

Dad studies the blueprints with interest. "You drew these plans?"

"I did." I fold my arms and stand back.

"You were smart to go back to school," Dad says. "You were born to do this."

When I forgave my parents and let go of my anger about Rutgers, it made a space for me to find happiness. I might have lost one dream, but a new one arrived. In another year, I'll have my architecture degree from the University of Pisa. It was meant to be; I needed more knowledge and new skills as the commissions through the

LaFortezza quarry became more and more complex, so did my need to learn how to build.

"School is one thing, but living alone in the woods?" Mom stands at the window and looks out. "Jess, I don't know."

I point to the emerald tree line and a small slice of the gold-leafed Duomo of Sant'Andrea visible through the forest. "Have faith. I am surrounded by churches."

"I see, when in danger, you run to the church. Say it's a Tuesday when you are robbed or violated. Nobody there. That duomo gives me no comfort." Mom's eyebrows form two black triangles of doom.

"Ma, Jess is close to the piazza. She doesn't even need a car. It took us ten minutes to walk here," Connie reminds Mom.

"A lot can happen in ten minutes." Mom's voice breaks.

My father, brother, Connie, and I groan.

Mom throws up her hands. "You people don't take me seriously."

"She's hardly isolated." Connie shoots me a look of reassurance.

"You're my strangest child, Giuseppina," Mom says. "Why do you have to do everything alone?"

"Because then I know I can do it," I tell her.

"This means you're never coming back to New Jersey," Dad says softly.

Oh, Dad, I think to myself, *you tried so hard to make me happy in Lake Como. You tinkered constantly. When you weren't repairing things, you painted. You tried to make the cellar look like a real home. You installed a gas fireplace in my newlywed apartment that I never turned on. I didn't show you the Hoboken apartment because that was a dream that was never meant to come true. I never left the deposit. Some other woman will savor that view of the Manhattan skyline.*

Dad walks around the room, surveying the Montini farmhouse, floor to ceiling. "Good for you, kid."

Dad's greatest joy is to see his children happy. He sacrificed everything for us. He held us together, putting aside his own dreams, whatever they were, to give us what we needed. Now that he can see my dream on paper, and in reality, he is happy for me. Dad and I know that he was always on my side. How can I tell my father what it means to me to have him here, in Carrara, as he approves the rendering of my new dream, the one that was meant to come true, in the place I'll live for the rest of my life? I can't. I'm a Baratta and we don't share our feelings.

"I wish I was a young man, kid," Dad says. "I could help you."

"I was hoping you could paint the place."

My father smiles and claps his hands together. "You got a deal."

I will live inside the house where my grandmother was born a Montini. I felt something when I first saw Grandma Cap's childhood home in the snow, and the feeling has not left me. Somewhere along the way, in these thirty-five years, someone said to pay attention to those feelings because that is where your bliss lies. And it was true; I would think about the house no matter where I was, whether on a train, in a meeting, or right before I went off to sleep at night. I couldn't shake this house. The things you cannot live without are the only things you need. I knew somehow the house belonged to me. I was moved by its fading beauty, and even though it was falling apart, despite decades of abandonment, it was still standing, a kind of miracle, as if to say, *This is your home. I've been waiting for you.*

"I think it's a great investment. Hardly will cost you." My practical brother approves.

"The town gave it to me. I couldn't believe it. My first lucky break since Uncle Louie died."

"Louie would be so proud of you." Mom's eyes fill with tears. "He was a prince, my brother."

Diego looks at Katie, who looks at Connie, who looks at Joe; all look to my father.

"You find my process of grief funny?" Mom looks at us.

"Of course not. Let me cheer you up, Ma. The town of Carrara told me that I could name the street."

Mom looks around. "They should. You're the only house here."

"I'm calling it Via Giuseppina Capodimonte. For you-know-who."

Mom clasps her hands in the prayer position. "You honor your heritage! I have not been a total failure as a mother."

"Don't say such things!" Signora Strazza, my mom's new partner in crime, says in her defense. "You are a good mother."

"You should frame these blueprints, Jess," my sister, who's always had good taste, offers.

"Great idea," Dad agrees. "You're the artist."

"I will frame them for you." Angelo puts his arm around me.

"I thought you didn't do picture frames," Mom pipes up.

My father hits his head with the palm of his hand. "Do you people see what I live with? She forgets nothing."

"Like you have it so bad, Joseph Baratta," Mom chides him. "Laura understands me." Mom turns to Angelo's mother. "The mother is the family historian. We forget nothing in order to preserve it. We are also practical. Was it too much to hope that my child could build a home on a plot of land where she won't be eaten alive by rabid animals?"

"I won't be, Ma. I am, however, going to be eaten up."

Mom squints out the window to the woods. "Let me guess. By a wild boar?"

"Joy. Garden-variety joy." I grin.

We hear a car horn outside on the street. We go the window.

Conor and Gaetano get out of the van carrying pastry boxes tied with string from the bakery.

"Let's go, people. We have a tour on the mountain!" Marina, the travel agent who found her voice, holds up her umbrella.

"Who wants a *cornetto*?" Conor says.

The kids run outside and climb into the van.

"Do these guys get us or what?" My father nods in approval. "We are carb people."

My family, along with Signora Strazza, gathers around Conor and Gaetano as they distribute the pastries.

Inside the house, Angelo and I are alone.

"That went well. Except for the part where Mom said it's too isolated and I'll be murdered in my sleep."

"Your mother is not a very positive person."

"Not in the least, but I love her anyway." I take Angelo's hand. "I have to show you something."

We climb the stairs to the second floor.

"Kitchen here." I walk through an arch. "Bedroom there." As if I have to point out the neatly made bed with the pale blue velvet spread.

"The window placement is good. Very open," Angelo says.

"The bathroom. Didn't they do a beautiful job? Carrara marble."

"Of course." Angelo laughs. "No bathtub?"

"Do you want one?"

"Can you soak in the sink?" he jokes.

"No." I laugh.

"So, make a space. You're the architect."

When Uncle Louie was alive, I drew the designs per his orders and the customer's specifications. But I never thought about what I wanted, afraid of my own ideas somehow, or fearful that someone else might not approve of my vision. But now I can do whatever I want. The only difference between a draftsman and an architect is self-confidence.

"You're right, Angelo. A big marble bathtub, right here, under the window." I point to the open walls under the cross timbers.

"That wasn't so hard, was it?" he says, and takes me in his arms. Evidently, there is nothing more alluring to a man than a woman who can design her own house. Angelo kisses my neck, my cheek, and my lips. His soft kiss is permanent; it feels like gold gilded on the smoothest marble.

Angelo whispers in my ear. "Build what you want. What you need."

"My home needs you."

"And so, you'll have him," Angelo promises. "*E la tua vasca da bagno.*"

We hear the blast of the horn on the van. I stick my head out of the bedroom window.

"Your professor friend is going to do the tour and we can't keep her waiting." Dad looks down at his phone. "Farah Adeel?"

"She is my friend. We'll be right down."

I pull on my jacket and slip into my hiking boots. I stuff my phone into my pocket and follow Angelo down the stairs. Smokey is curled up in the sun by the window, asleep. I close the front door on the Montini farmhouse.

Angelo and I pile into the van. They make room for us. Angelo pulls Rafferty onto his lap. Mackenzie climbs onto mine. We strap in.

I want to be with my family when they see Uncle Louie's quarry for the first time. I want to show them Michelangelo's marble. After all, that's where our story began.

original farm door
Garden
Stairs
The Montini Farmhouse — Carrara, Italy

Epilogue

Dear Dr. Sharon, Raymond, Mohammed, Pamela, Rhoda, Cynthia, Albert, Elaine, Jean, Nora, Veronica, Rex, Scott, and Darlene,

This letter is to thank the team at Thera-Me for setting me on the path of enlightenment. I would never have tried therapy had it not been for all of you. But, session by session, you guided me forward. I learned to challenge my assumptions, pay attention to the world around me, react, and make changes when necessary. At first, the idea of switching therapists as I advanced through the program was daunting, but soon I was in the rhythm, and each of you brought something different to the process, which taught me to be flexible.

I have learned how to live. I sleep with the doors open, and the church bells wake me with the sun as it rises. A walk after dinner keeps me in shape better than an hour-long workout in a gym. Spaghetti doesn't make me fat and sponge cake with mascarpone cream doesn't either. Sleep is a better cure than any pill. Knowing what you want can only come from knowing yourself. Sit in an empty church on any day but Sunday and let the angels guide your prayers. Let go of everything that has ever scared you. Break the grip of fear with confidence. Happiness is not something that you can make happen; it arrives unannounced. It is not scary to get older; it's only scary to be unloved. To find love, to hold it and to grow it, be kind. First to yourself and then to every person you know. Life works out. Don't fear living or fear death; it's all part of the story. Old is good. Very old is art. What survives, sustains.

I am sure that as I go on in life, I will refer back to our exercises. You turned me into a person who understands the importance of journaling—thank you all. I don't know where you are in the world, but somehow, you managed to get through to me. The person who takes the worst that happens to her and builds upon it will be fearless. In the absence of fear is nothing but love.

For your contribution to my sanity, I am awarding you five stars over at the App Store. Thank you!

G.C.B., Carrara, Italy

Acknowledgments

The View from Lake Como is a story about a woman who decides to build a life she can live in and the house that goes with it. Jess Baratta would not have found the guts to change her life if her uncle Louie Cap had not believed in her. Throughout the process of writing this novel, I spent a lot of time reveling in memories of the moments of celebration and unity in my Italian American family from the Alps of Lombardy to Roseto, Pennsylvania, to Chisholm, Minnesota, to the Jersey shore, New York City, and to Big Stone Gap, Virginia, and back.

I dedicate this novel to the memory of my good uncles: Orlando Bonicelli of the Iron Range of Minnesota, a basketball star at Notre Dame, husband, father, and a devoted son; Michael F. Ronca was a force of nature with a heart as big as the Poconos who could have been in the Rat Pack if he hadn't been born in Pennsylvania; the Honorable Michael F. Godfrey, who was the perfect Irish uncle, a wise, pragmatic circuit court judge in Saint Louis, Missouri; and Michael R. Trigiani, whose work ethic was inspiring when he was young—he worked construction by day, and at night played saxophone in a band known as the Kingsmen. My uncles were good fathers and husbands, they might say imperfect, but I am certain their souls reside in heaven, in their Father's house, in the mansion with many rooms. They are guaranteed excellent views because they earned them.

I am lucky to be published by the spectacular team at Dutton at Penguin Random House. I thank Maya Ziv, my brilliant editor with a keen eye and a fast pencil. Maya's big heart made this creative process a joy. At the ready, Ella Kurki was always fabulous. My evermore gratitude to the A-team in publishing: Ivan Held, John Parsley, Christine Ball (now at Berkley), Amanda Walker, Stephanie Cooper, Caroline Payne, Katy Riegel, LeeAnn Pemberton, and Vi-An Nguyen. Megan Beatie is the best publicist on the planet.

At PRH: Thank you Kim Hovey, Karen Fink, and Sanyu Dillon (we started our journey working on *Rococo*; I knew she was a star back then!). At PRH Audio, I am blessed to work with my lifelong friend Amanda D'Acierno. Our producer, Nithya Rajendran, is the perfect producer, and May Wuthrich is the perfect director. Bob Eckstein, the beloved and brilliant *New Yorker* cartoonist, brought Jess Baratta's dream house alive with his beautiful illustration. I am grateful for Bob's talent and friendship.

My gratitude to the petite yet mighty Suzanne Gluck at WME and her brilliant assistant, Lane Kizziah, who works harder than ten humans. Thank you also to the tireless WME team: the magnificent Nancy Josephson (we've been together from the start), thank you and love to Ellen Sushko, Chelsea Kreps, Mary Pender, Daniel Rak, Alex Levenberg, Tracy Fisher, and Caitlin Mahony.

Over at Viking, thank you to my great editor and publisher Tamar Brazis and her team.

Andrea Rillo began her work life in books with us as an intern at the Glory of Everything Company. She has grown into her role as podcast producer and editor. Her artful eye is essential in all we do. Molly Doherty has a dazzling future; thank you for your hard work. Emily Metcalfe is a star and now a young mother; there is nothing she cannot do.

Our intern program has brought the best young talent in books, theater, and film through our doors. We thank Jack Cutajar, Sofia Lucas (thank you for the Italian translations), Frances Gray Riggs, Shay Shalem, Maeve Kelly, Phelan Halloran, Sophia Mazzella, Nora Leach, Henry Martin, Lucia Stephenson, Olivia Miller, Gia Lanteri, Amy Osella, Madeline Law, Jaden Daher, Annika Solomone, Libby Callahan, and Christina Southard.

My partnership with Book of the Month has been one of the most gratifying of my career. John Lippman loves writers and putting their books in the hands of eager readers. He is the best! Thank you, Brianna Goodman, for your glorious taste, and Anne Healy, for facilitating our events and programs.

Thank you to the team at Tre60 in Milan. I am proud to be published in Italy by Benedetta Stucchi, Chiara Ferrari, Valentina Russo, Barbara Trianni, and Francesca Motta. The great Paolo Grassi, our librarian in Schilpario, is the best.

I thank Eugenie Furniss, my fabulous agent in the UK, along with Emily MacDonald of 42 Management and Production.

At PRH UK, I am grateful to Clio Cornish, Lucy Upton, Gaby Young, Madeleine Woodfield, Deirdre O'Connell, Kate Elliott, Hannah Padgham, Louise Moore, and Maxine Hitchcock.

I am grateful to my editor, Tara Weikum, at HarperCollins Children's books.

My evermore gratitude to Suzanne Baboneau and Ian Chapman of S&S UK.

Thank you for listening to the *You Are What You Read* podcast that features the luminaries of our culture and the books that built their souls. Much gratitude to our guests, and expert producers Andrea Rillo and Lou Pellegrino. Thank you, Michael Trigiani, for composing our theme music.

Writing requires solitude, but getting the job done requires community. Thank you, Michael Patrick King, for taking the early morning call, sometimes before your first cup of tea. I am grateful to your partner in life, Craig Fissé, for his love and support.

Larry Sanitsky is a divine producer who is always in my corner. Gail Berman is the friend I call when I am most in need of wisdom. Cynthia Olson reads everything and conducts amazing research. Bill Persky is a sage, father, and pal, and performs all skills required with love and excellence. Thank you, David Baldacci, my honorary brother—you are a shining example for all writers in life and on the page. Jean and Jake Morrissey, your support, advice, and love are all any person needs. Thank you!

Italy and her culture play a central role in my work. Family history has been my north star, guiding the storytelling and suffusing it with details that can only come from being Italian. Consul General Fabrizio Di Michele and Giorgia De Parolis and their son, Riccardo, represent the country of Italy and the love of our homeland with elegance and grace. I thank them for their friendship.

I celebrate the glorious Italians and Italian Americans in my life: Anna Malafronte, Norena Barbella, Brondo Cavallo, Louisa Ermelino, Jodi Pulice Smith and Greg Smith, Frank Ferrante, Susan Ursitti Sheinberg and Jonathan Sheinberg (IBM—Italian by Marriage), Mary Pipino, Joseph Sciame, Michael Polo, Carlo Carlozzi, Joe Ciancaglini, Robin and Dan Napoli,

Mario Cantone and Jerry Dixon (IBM), Gina Casella of AT Escapes, Lisa Scottoline, Francesca Serritella, Angelo and Denise Vivolo, Aileen Sirey, John Melfi and Andrew Egan (IBM), Caroline Giovannini, Mary A. Vetri, Ed and Chris (Pipino) Muransky, Gina Vechiarelli, Beth Vechiarelli Cooper, Dominic and Carol Vechiarelli, Lora Minichillo, Theresa Guarnieri, Anna Francese Gass, Victoria Benton Frank (Peluso) (IBM), Marisa Acocella, Violetta Acocella, Susan Paolercio, and Lisa Scognamillo. I will miss Lucille "Dolly" Lomano Wright, the perfect Italian girl, mother, and grandmother.

My evermore thanks to Nigel Stoneman and Charles Fotheringham and Jann Arden, Tom Dyja, Aaron Hill and Susan Fales Hill, Mary K and John Wilson, Angelina Fiordellisi and Matt Williams, Richard and Dana Kirshenbaum, Michael and Rosemarie Filingo, Tony Krantz and Kristin Dornig, Kenny Sarfin, Sarah Jessica Parker, and Barbara Forste.

I thank the great *attriche* Mary Testa, who keeps our house key and our shared friendship of many years. Thank you Kristin Hannah, Mary Ellen Keating, Lynn Mara, Alice Hoffman, Laura Zigman, Ruth Pomerance, Elena Nachmanoff, Dianne Festa, Kay Unger, Bonnie Datt, Wendy Luck, Jasmine Guy, Jane Cline Higgins, Helene Bapis, Liz Travis, Cate Magennis Wyatt, Sharon Ewing Buchanan, Kathy McElyea, Mary Deese Hampton, Sharon Gauvin, Dori Grafft, Mary Murphy, Nelle Fortenberry, Dee Emmerson, Norma Born, Christina Avis Krauss, Eleanor Jones, Veronica Kilcullen, Mary Ellinger, Iva Lou Johnson, Betty Fleenor, Nancy Ringham Smith, Helen Rosenberg, Michelle Baldacci, Sheila Mara, Janet Leahy, Courtney Flavin, Joanna Patton, Susie Essman, Aimée Bell, Constance Marks, Rosanne Cash, Liz Welch Tirrell, Becky Browder Neustadt, Connie Shulman, Sharon Watroba Burns, Sister Karol Jackowski, Elaine Martinelli, Pamela Stallsmith, Catherine Brennan, and Lisa Ackerman (with loving memory of Lisa's bestie: the late Martha Rodriguez).

I am grateful for the Arizona Women's Board and their efforts with the Kidney Foundation in memory of the great Erma Bombeck: thank you, Candyce Williams, Margo Shein, Susan Purtill, and Robyn Lee. Kimberly Jacobsen is an angel in this world; she created a glorious event and luncheon with style, spectacle, and whimsy fueled by her generous heart.

More gratitude and love to Dr(s). Ginny (Karle) and Lou Bridges, Jerrod MacFarlane, Vic and Joyce Sharkey, Jody and Bill Geist, Willie and Christina Geist, Marolyn and Hank Senay, Tim Reid and Daphne Maxwell Reid, George Dvorsky, Anne Holton Kaine and Senator Tim Kaine, Senator Mark Warner, Emma and Tony Cowell, Hugh and Jody Friedman O'Neill, Whoopi Goldberg, Tom Leonardis, Dolores Pascarelli, Eileen, Ellen, and Patti King, Sharon Hall and Todd Kessler, Charles Randolph Wright, Judy Rutledge, Greg and Tracy Kress, Max and Robyn Westler (Max a fabulous and insightful early reader!), Tom and Barbara Sullivan, Brownie and Connie Polly, Beáta and Steven Baker, Todd Doughty and Randy Losapio, Steve and Anemone Kaplan, and Jean and Jim Enochs.

As I wrote this book, we lost some amazing human beings who knew how to live and made the world a better place.

Leonard Riggio (1941–2024) was a dear friend. It is hard for me to imagine the world without him (for consolation, I pretend he's walking the streets of Brooklyn checking out the indies instead of living in the eternal). Len was a visionary, a voracious reader who set the template for the way we put books in the hands of readers and serve them since the 1970s. He created Barnes & Noble (he and his brothers formed a supergroup to procure and sell books and designed community-based bookstores across the country, where readers would gather in a social setting and find any book from the classics to the latest hot bestseller). You might not know that aside from his business acumen and brilliance, there was no greater philanthropist in the world. He and his beloved Louise saw a problem and went to the heart of it, and worked with local folks in communities across the country and the world in order to change their circumstances to fix whatever was broken. Len built and donated homes, fostered art and artists, and tended to the most in need among us with the quiet dignity of a saint. Len would roll his eyes at that, but I observed his practical and authentic faith, love of family, and belief in the dreams of those who had given up entirely as a sign that he *was* one—okay, Len, maybe not a saint—but a mensch, the best son, husband, father, grandfather, uncle, cousin, and brother any of us ever knew. As a friend, there was no one greater. I imagine God is keeping Len very busy on the other side.

Laura Ann "Lauri" Carleton was a high-octane, beloved shopkeeper with fabulous taste who served a devoted clientele on Lake Arrowhead.

Lauri was the victim of a senseless hate crime; the loss of her to her family and the world is enormous. She was one of the good ones. Franco Harris, along with his wife, Dana, were true loves—you know him as a football legend, but I knew him as an Italian African American son of a glorious family who walked with grace, gave all he had, and quietly made his community a better place. Katie Trocheck Abel was a beautiful and bright spirit and a loving daughter, sister, mother, and wife. Her parents, Tom and Kathy (you know her as the magnificent Mary Kay Andrews), and her entire family are brokenhearted but press on with joy because that's what Katie would want.

Christophe B. Elise was a gent, a French cowboy, and Gigi's beloved.

Jerry Foley was the award-winning director of *Late Show with David Letterman*, beloved husband of Ann Marie, and father to Quinn—he gave my husband the best advice when we had our daughter. Jerry said, "Don't miss anything." Mafalda (Maj) Spolti was a beautiful cousin; when I think of Schilpario in the Italian Alps, it is Mafalda I see, welcoming us home. Doris Gluck, a sophisticated New Yorker with a heart as big as Manhattan, was my mother in the north—a loving, wise lady who could not do enough for us.

John "Jack" Cleary served with distinction in Vietnam, awarded the Bronze Star and Purple Heart. He and Marianne raised a beautiful family. Their son, First Lt. Michael Cleary, was killed in Iraq in 2005. What a family—what integrity. I take great comfort in knowing he is with Michael once more.

My fellow author, the acclaimed M. J. Rose, was a doll—funny, wise, stylish. I will never forget our lunches and the laughs. The erudite and avid reader June Harry hosted me in Florida for a book event; we remained friends for life.

Concetta "Connie" Maria Giordano Owens never missed me on book tour—her son, Robert, and wife, Karin, made sure of it. Connie loved the novel *Lucia, Lucia* because, in a sense, she had lived it. I will miss her. Florence Marchi was a champion of the Rotary Club—even though she was an Italian girl who lived in New Jersey (and raised a loving family), she looked to help wherever there was a need. The novelist Tom Robbins and the poet Nikki Giovanni are missed. I am certain they are raising hell in heaven.

My roots in Big Stone Gap, Virginia, and southwest Virginia remain deep and abiding. We lost my honorary mother, Betty Hurd Cline, who made us feel welcome and loved in her home. Johnny Wood WCYB-TV was an icon, "our" favorite anchor. The wonderful women that served their families and communities and are now in heaven include Barbara Golden Gibson; Virginia Meador; Sylvia Jo Fletcher Zirkle; the divine Phyllis Hatcher; Lola Irene (Jackson) Fletcher-Head; Linda Woodward's beloved mother, Anna Mae Goodwin Neff; Barbara Ann Horton; our beloved school secretary, Patricia "Patsy" Faye Tucker Arnold; "Mama" Sue Vaughn; Rose Timp Walleze; and Mrs. Francis "Velva" Brown of Roanoke. We mourn Garnett Gilliam, Cecil Ronald Hamblin, Estell R. Williams, Russell Wiles, Rick Gilliam, Tayloe Holton Loftus, and Bruce Robinette. Three wonderful writers from southwest Virginia left us, leaving behind an impressive canon of work: William "Bill" J. Hendrick, the editor of the *Big Stone Gap Post*; my friend Johnny Julius Teglas, a wonderful journalist and the best writer that ever came out of Powell Valley High School; and Frank Kilgore, a talented, honest writer with an original voice.

Sister Bernadette Kenny founded the Saint Mary's Health Wagon—she brought medicine, healing, and hope to the good people of Appalachia.

Proud New Yorker Donna DeMatteo, the great playwright, was my beloved mentor on the page and on the stage. She and Rosemary DeAngelis greeted me from the moment I landed in New York City and were there whenever this once-young writer needed them. Joe LaRosa, the brilliant ad man and sage, was extended Italian family through Bill Persky. Alisyn Camerota's beloved husband, Tim Lewis, was a force for good in a weary world. Our family at Convent of the Sacred Heart included the irreplaceable and irrepressible Sister Angela Bayo. As a mother, I joined a circle of friends at Sacred Heart that included Catharine Abate, who was an extraordinary woman, creative and loving, who lit up any room she entered. When it comes to hearts, Catharine's was the most sacred of all.

Sylvia Macioci Cicetti was a beauty, a voracious reader, and an early champion of my work. Sylvia spread the word through her book groups in New Jersey.

In our Italian family, we take the word *cousin* seriously—it carries honor, history, and connection. We mourn Michael F. Godfrey Jr. of

Saint Louis. We lost Ralph Stampone, the dazzling interior designer; Barbara Trigiani; Theresa "Terri" Ballanti Trigiani, Isidore "Iggy" Farino (now reunited with his beloved Dolly); and Philomena "Mamie" Ciliberti, whose ties to our family go back to the old country—her life was an example of true Christian values. Cousin Peter J. Matthews (IBM via Monica Spadoni) was an exemplary husband and father, a veteran who knew his way around a roll of wallpaper and then some! Diana (Cantrella) Palermo, Nicky's beloved wife and Nicole and Marianna's magnificent mother, was the original Jersey girl: chic, fun, and beautiful. Whenever I toured through, she and Nicky were there.

Patricia Parks Plucinski was my beloved aunt by marriage. She was a gem and we miss her.

From the garden of Roseto, Pennsylvania, we mourn the gifted artist and author Anna Marie Ruggiero, the adorable Christopher Checho, Sandee Turtzo Woolley, journalist Maria Cascario, honorary cousin Phillip Michael DeFranco, and with memories of Our Lady of Mount Carmel School, Mary G. Vietro and Rose Marie Vietro.

From our extended Saint Mary's family, we lost Chet Maccio, Peter Cannon, Christine O'Connell-McAleer, Barbara Koch-Santoro, Frank Oelerich, Joan Shaughnessy, and Mary Catherine "MC" Shaughnessy. David Weber, a gifted set designer and my stage craft professor, taught us wisely and well. Marguerite Quinn Zappa was the perfect Saint Mary's woman, wife, and mother.

The Origin Project has served over 25,000 students in grades 1 through 12 since 2014 in my home state of Virginia. The program's Appalachian roots have grown a garden of talented young debut writers, their work published in our annual anthology and anniversary cookbook.

The in-school writing program would not exist without our late, great executive director and cofounder Nancy Bolmeier Fisher's vision and tireless work. Thank you, Ian Fisher and Ryan Fisher, for sharing Nancy with us all these years. Nancy was a champion of all students and recognized the writing talent of Zahra Wakilzada immediately. Zahra is our new codirector and a graduate of the Origin Project. Nancy would be thrilled. Nancy also established relationships with Virginia's finest—including the late Doris "Jill" Carson, a glorious public servant who, from her beginnings with Head Start, became an elected official and, with her beloved husband, Ron, founded the Appalachian African American Cultural Center in Pennington Gap, creating a legacy that will last forever.

Our participating teachers, K through 12, facilitate the program with knowledge, energy, and love. This program would not thrive without our teachers, current and retired, who work with the students to craft their writing skills and creativity. The Library of Virginia hosts us and shares their programs, space, and staff to facilitate the students; thank you, Scott Dodson and Elaine McFadden! Monica Hoel of Emory & Henry University makes a home for us. The divine Linda Woodward organizes the year-round in-school programming, edits the anthology, hosts the guest artists, and keeps us in line. Rhonda Carper took us into the digital sphere and connects the students, teachers, and guest artists online.

We are grateful to the wonderful folks who support the publication of the anthology, including the distinguished Gupta Foundation led by Shashi and Margaret Gupta. Our designer is the gifted Carmen Baumann. Our programming is supported by the Slemp Foundation, whose mission is to invest in and serve the people of southwest Virginia with grants that make a difference in their lives. The foundation is stupendous—and their forebear, the visionary C. Bascom Slemp, a Virginia statesman, would be proud of his family. Thank you, Nancey Edmonds Smith, James Campbell Smith, Kelly Smith, Melissa Jensen, Pamela Orcutt, Mary Anna Edmonds, Melissa Smith Swatzyna, and Virginia E. "Libby" Sircy.

Thank you to my family, my sisters and brothers and in-laws, and especially Tim, who built our home, and Lucia, who filled it with love and adopted our rescues, Smokey and Lola. Smokey has gone to be with Saint Francis, and we miss her. However, her spirit lives on in the story on these pages.

Thank you, dear readers, for sticking with me for twenty-five years. *Big Stone Gap* made its debut in 2000; without your support there would not have been another. Let's keep this conversation going with the tools at the ready that create community, including book events, book clubs, and listening to our podcast. As the daughter of a librarian, I learned very early that to share a book is to share the world. Thank you for sharing your world of reading with me.

About the Author

Adriana Trigiani is the *New York Times* bestselling author of twenty-one books of fiction and nonfiction. Her writing has been published in thirty-eight languages around the world. An award-winning playwright, television writer/producer, and filmmaker, Trigiani wrote and directed the major motion picture of her debut novel, *Big Stone Gap*, adapted her novel *Very Valentine* for television, and directed the documentary *Queens of the Big Time*, among others. In 2023, President Sergio Mattarella of Italy awarded Trigiani the Cavaliere dell'Ordine della Stella d'Italia. The Library of Virginia bestowed their highest honor, the Patron of Letters degree, to Trigiani in 2024. She received the 2025 Ellis Island Medal of Honor for her significant contributions to literature, culture, and community. Trigiani grew up in Appalachia, in the mountains of Virginia, where she cofounded the Origin Project, a year-round, in-school writing program that has served more than twenty-five thousand students since its inception in 2014. Trigiani is proud to serve on the New York State Council on the Arts. She lives in Greenwich Village with her family.